BUDDY COOPER

FINDS A WAY

—A Novel—

Neil O'Boyle Connelly

Simon & Schuster

NEW YORK • LONDON • TORONTO • SYDNEY

SIMON & SCHUSTER
Rockefeller Center
1230 Avenue of the Americas
New York, NY 10020

SIMON & SCHUSTER and colophon are registered trademarks
of Simon & Schuster, Inc.

For information regarding special discounts for bulk purchases,
please contact Simon & Schuster Special Sales:
1-800-456-6798 or business@simonandschuster.com.

Manufactured in the United States of America

1   3   5   7   9   10   8   6   4   2

Library of Congress Cataloging-in-Publication Data
Connelly, Neil O.
Buddy Cooper finds a way / Neil Connelly.
p.   cm.
1. Wrestlers—Fiction. 2. Wrestling—Fiction. 3. Violence—Fiction. I. Title.
PS3603.O546B83 2004
813'.6—dc22   2004045282

ISBN: 978-0-7432-7415-6

For Beth,
who brought back joy.

Acknowledgments

I wish to acknowledge the boundless love of my parents and the rest of my overgrown family, the support of my friends and colleagues, and the inspiration of writers, published and otherwise. All of you enrich my world.

I feel particularly indebted to Warren Frazier, Adam Johnson, George Clark, Michael Horner, Tim Gautreaux, and Chris Naddeo.

I'd also like to thank the almost innumerable wrestlers who drove my face into the mat all those years ago. If I were any good at wrestling, I doubt I would have tried writing. I appreciate the clarity.

BUDDY COOPER FINDS A WAY

CHAPTER THE FIRST

*In Which Our Hero Attempts to Return Home. Trophies and
Medals. A Perfect Record. The Therapeutic Value of Giving Up.
Churches Without Roofs. Wishing for a Script.*

J ust as I'm nearing the turn that will lead to safety, the second
moon appears before me, hung low over the Cape Fear River
at the end of Market Street. I pretend I don't see it, look left,
and steer my Ford into the alley. Up ahead I can make out the yellow light on my deck, and I'm almost bold enough to hope for the
impossible: Today's plan might work. A crackling a.m. voice from
WAOK reports that the evening will be clear, mild temperatures, no
rain—news I instantly take as omen. This will end up as just one
more fine day in a life that's fine. On the seat next to me sits a box of
Domino's pizza and two rented videos: *The Green Berets* and *True
Grit*. From here on out, the plan is simple: get up off the street, bolt
the door, unplug the phone, forget the moon, and spend the night
in a world where things make sense. It won't be like last year.

I pull to the side of the alley, kill the headlights, and turn the key,
bringing silence and calm. I loop the strap of my gym bag over my
shoulder and grab the pizza and flicks. From the floor I pick up the
final element for tonight's mission—a two-liter bottle of ginger ale,
which doesn't remind me at all of champagne or the tink of forks
off glasses. This morning I dumped a six-pack of Bud Light into my

kitchen sink, transforming my apartment into the alcohol-free zone it's supposed to be these days.

Taking the steps that lead up to my apartment's deck one at a time, I envision the comfort of the brown couch, the security of the remote control in my hand. As I climb, I'm aware of the urge to turn and face downtown, peek at the second moon haunting the sky. Of course it's not the second moon that bothers me, it's what I can't help picturing in its shadow: Alix, taking risks she doesn't need to for money she already has.

So I focus my eyes down at the faded wood of the steps that lift to the faded wood of my deck. The yellow lightbulb illuminates the Map-of-the-World welcome mat I apparently ordered from QVC in a drunken haze. $29.95 plus shipping and handling. I step up to my door, one foot in the Atlantic and one crushing China. On top of the world.

Hugging the soda inside one arm, balancing the pizza and tapes, I dig for my keys in my pocket. Five seconds from the vault, I sense movement to my right and turn. The fact that it's just Dr. Winston in my hammock barely registers before my eyes leap to his feet and the golden, knee-high sneakers. I drop the pizza box, which flips once and splats. John Wayne clatters to the ground.

Dr. Winston swings free of the dirty white netting and steps into the yellow light. "Dr. Cooper," he says. "We'd almost given you up for dead." He shakes my hand, a practice he insists on every time we meet. His shaggy black hair, knotted with dirt, drapes his bearded face as he checks out the upside-down pizza box. I'm staring down too, but my eyes lock on the boot-length gold sneakers I haven't seen in four years. On the sides are tiny black horns I painted myself, though now they look like little dark wings.

"I don't believe it," I say.

"Indeed. The generosity of my fellow citizens gives me great hope." His teeth, though straight, are the color of mustard.

"Goodwill?" I ask.

"Second Chances," Dr. Winston corrects me, naming the homeless shelter four blocks east. They accept donations from the public, recycle them to needy folks like Dr. Winston. I picture Trevor, climbing into the attic on Asgard Lane, ripping open the dozen cardboard boxes I double-sealed with packing tape. But this doesn't bother me. I have the life I want.

"Is that pepperoni?" comes down from above, and I look up into the grinning face of Dr. Gladstone, on all fours leaning over the rain gutter. He's wearing the battered baseball cap Alix gave me when Brook was born that reads WORLD'S #1 DAD.

"Pepperoni and sausage," I tell him.

Gladstone drops off the roof and studies the upside-down box, then flips it over. Melted cheese stretches from the cardboard lid. "This is completely salvageable," he decides.

Dr. Winston lifts his chin. "Dr. Cooper, we need your help to join the information age."

"We're gonna watch TV," Dr. Gladstone beams, peeling free a limp slice. "Remember *Welcome Back, Kotter? Happy Days?*"

I step back a few feet, scan the roof for the third member of the Brain Trust. Dr. Bacchus's rounded form leans onto my chimney, one hand gripping the 1950s-era antenna bolted to the brick. He looks like the Pillsbury Doughboy silhouetted against the deep cobalt blue of the June sky. "There's no way this will bring in the premium porno channels," Dr. Bacchus reports.

Gladstone giggles nervously. All this time I'm concentrating on ignoring Winston's boots. I focus on where I am and say, "You need more than an antenna to get a clear picture." My logic sounds like bad Bob Dylan.

"Already taken care of," Winston announces, bending into the darkness beneath the hammock. He stands up holding the black-and-white twelve-inch Sony that Alix and I bought when she was working on her master's thesis at UNCW. I take it from him, hold it in my hands like a sacred artifact. In the mornings before she left for class, while I spooned Brook breakfast, Alix would turn on *Cardiac-Attack* and kickbox aerobically. Or aerobically kickbox. I never could figure. Like the boots, like the baseball cap, this TV belongs enshrined in an attic uptown. Some nights, with Brook barely asleep in the bedroom crib, with Letterman smiling at us from this very screen, Alix and I would make love on the couch.

"Ancient history," I say. "It can't still work."

"Believe it," Winston says. "The altar's got juice. We discovered a live outlet in Jesus's feet."

Overhead, Gladstone nods. "It's a miracle. Like on *Touched by an Angel.*"

I glance across the alley at the Salvation Station of the Holy Redeemer, formerly Most Precious Suffering of Christ the Genuine. The city's been threatening demolition since Hurricane Fran collapsed the roof and the near wall. But the other three walls survive, and the rickety steeple still stands, stretching for heaven. Above the steeple now, the true moon rolls on its back. I cannot see its false twin from here, blocked by trees and downtown buildings, but I'm angry at myself for being tempted.

I turn back to Winston, hand him the TV before it explodes in my hands. He says, "We'd hoped you might consider donating your antenna."

"Our cause is just," Dr. Bacchus shouts, still at the chimney. "Plus it's tax-deductible."

"Take it," I tell them. "I got cable." Forty-four dollars a month for soap operas and late-night anesthesia. "There was a cape with those boots," I say to Winston. "A golden cape."

"Sure thing," Dr. Bacchus says, now at the roof's edge. "Had a black cow on it."

"It was a bull," I explain.

With a full mouth, Dr. Gladstone mumbles, "One of the Princess Street crew got it."

"How did you know about the cape?" Winston wants to know. But I don't answer. For a moment my mind gets away from me, and I imagine driving to Second Chances, finding the table where volunteers have set out the relics of my former life alongside broken blenders and board games with missing pieces. I shake these images from my head. My life is a fine one.

When Dr. Bacchus jumps down onto the deck, the whole thing rattles. His hair is combed, his face clean. He may shower at the shelter. Bacchus hunches over with Gladstone for a sloppy slice. "Flippin' bolts are rusted shut. And that steel is old school—the real deal." He stands with the droopy piece of pizza and chucks my shoulder. "So you got a hacksaw or what?"

Head down, I'm trying not to picture Trevor digging through the boxes I left behind, turning the worn pages of the Bull Invinso scrapbook. And then it occurs to me that like Alix, Trevor is probably working tonight. Out of the house. I raise my face. "I got a better plan."

After I make the left onto Oleander and take my place in the evening traffic, I look over my shoulder at the boys, huddled around the pizza like a campfire. They insisted on staying together in the bed of the Ford. On WAOK, *The Family Man* is trying to sort out Frank from Jacksonville's problem. He wants to know if he should buy his daughter the breast implants she's demanding for her sixteenth birthday. I'd change, but my radio's jammed, locked into this one station. A Volkswagen Bug putters ahead of me with a license plate that reads C841KME. I'm convinced it's one of those vanity plates, but I can't decipher its clever message, so I pass fast in the right lane.

Distractions like license plates and *The Family Man* have been part of my battle plan all day, staying in the here and now of my fine life. This morning I ran Greenfield Lake. Then I changed the oil in the Ford. Had lunch at Whitey's. I limited myself to one hour of afternoon soaps—*Waves Will Crash*—and went to the gym for a late workout with Hardy. Before I hit Video Galaxy, I drove over to Wrightsville Beach and took a few laps in the Atlantic. Today, I've been working hard to keep my mind where it needs to be.

But as I near the light at 16th, I glance into oncoming traffic and boom—here comes our limo. It rumbles past me like a ghost ship, and in the tinted windows I catch a flash of my reflection. This should be no surprise. It's almost nine o'clock after all, and it's time we were on our way downtown, heading for O'Leary's, a club that's been out of business now for five years.

"Red means stop!" Bacchus shouts through the window.

I stomp on the brakes and feel the weight of the truck hunching up on me. Bacchus gives me a dirty look in the rearview mirror. Behind him, I can see our limo trailing cans and I turn away, face the red light.

Across the street a Quicky Chicken spins its orange bucket, and I consider scrapping the new plan, hitting the drive-thru instead and picking up some extra greasy and then a case of Bud Light, sharing it with the boys back in the collapsed sanctuary they call home. Making the right I have in mind will send me down the memory gauntlet of 16th. I'll have to pass Shipyard. But after all these years, there's not a street in Wilmington that isn't lined with flashbacks, perched like rooftop snipers. If I make a left here, I'll pass the Dairy Queen where I used to buy Blizzards for Alix when she was pregnant as well as the intersection at Market where the Subaru died. If I go straight, I'll encounter the Planet Foodville from which I've recently been banned.

When the light goes green, I make the right, barely clipping the curb. We pass the looming lights of New Hanover Hospital, where they brought Snake the night his truck found that phone pole and where Brook spent a week when she was eight for what the doctors would only call "observation." My face is known by the staff up on seven.

A quarter mile later, gravestones rise from the grounds of St. James Cemetery. In the back, beneath a sycamore tree I can't see in this dark, are the side-by-side plots Alix bought one rainy afternoon from a telemarketer. Typical Alix, always overplanning. I've wondered some nights, if Trevor gets my grave now too.

Closing in on the crossroads at Shipyard I brace myself for the strip mall. It's got a Wendy's and a florist and a beauty salon called Skin Deep. Once upon a time it was home to Tae-Kwon-Do for Tots—give Alix credit for the snappy name. She had more for the little groups we formed: Ninja Niners, Assassin Eighters. As I pass, I can't keep my eyes from roaming over, expecting somehow to see Alix through the huge glass front, leading the kids through their piercing side kicks and double thunder punches. Instead I see the painted puffy white clouds that are supposed to be popcorn. Our old space was rented out to people who sell gourmet varieties. Bolstered by a six-pack buzz, I went in there one night. They have the display case I built loaded with exotic flavors: cherry, cinnamon, jalapeño. Once we kept our trophies there. Our trophies and our medals.

But those were the days before Trevor and ReelWorld came to town, the days when things felt certain. Between bouncing at O'Leary's and the spot work as Bull Invinso, I was bringing in decent money. Alix got a part in the community playhouse's *Camelot*. At just seven, Brook was set to test for her green belt. Martial arts were hot, and Alix was talking franchise. We bought the house on Asgard and everything was perfect.

My life is perfect now too. I wouldn't change a thing. It's just a different kind of perfect, that's all. Since the split with Alix I've lived a pressureless, failure-free existence. No stress, no doubt. Because I'm not Bull Invinso anymore. Nowadays I'm the Enigma Warrior from the Isle of Wykoki. I'm Agent 17 and AKA Rat. I am the Grave Digger and the Widow Maker and Ivan Sputniski and Deadbeat Dad. Some nights my face is too hideous to show in public, an acid burn or a bear attack, even radiation from Chernobyl. I've been wanted by Israeli counterintelligence, in the witness protection program, believed to be dead by high-ranking members of the United Nations, and on the run from a wife who's sworn to shoot me for withholding child support. In the ring, under the mask, I just follow the script, and I can do no wrong.

The strip malls and fast food joints behind me, I slide across the four lanes of College Avenue, invading no-man's-land—suburbia central. If the Ford had a stealth mode, I'd engage it. Officially, I have no business in this quiet development, making this left onto Valhalla, this right onto Asgard, except every other Saturday when I get Brook for an overnight. That's when I pull up to the curb—not the driveway!—and honk just once. Twice is making a big deal out of it, according to Alix. But tonight, as I slow to a stop, there's no need to honk. I'm not here as part of some court-appointed visitation.

I shut off the engine and the Brain Trust piles out. Gladstone wipes pizza grease onto his tattered jeans. Winston kneels to tighten the high laces of the golden sneakers, eyes up the dark Colonial. "How many bathrooms?"

"Two and a half," I answer.

He nods his approval. I have no emotional reaction to seeing the house. It's just another address. I point to the living room window, partly obscured by azaleas that Trevor hasn't kept trimmed. "Here's the deal. Inside that room is a forty-two-inch Trinitron. You'll have to hop the fence and come in through the sliding back door. The lock's been busted forever. Go through the kitchen, then head for the stairs. The Trinitron's on your right, can't miss it."

Gladstone adjusts my baseball cap on his head and smiles. "*Mork and Mindy,* na-nu, na-nu."

"Breaking and entering," Bacchus states for the record.

I make hard eye contact. "That TV is mine. We're not stealing anything. This is a rescue mission."

"If it's yours, you save it," Bacchus says.

The food in his stomach, or the ride in the open air, has sobered him up some. He has a good point. But it's been four years since I walked out of that house. "If you want the big screen, get it. Otherwise, we go hacksaw hunting."

The three of them huddle. When they break, Winston flashes his mustard smile. "We choose to accept the challenge."

Bacchus steps into me, pokes a chubby finger into my thick chest. "We'll still be wanting that antenna."

"Fine with me," I say, and the three of them shuffle across the lawn. They climb onto the air conditioner and clamber over the wooden fence. I get back into the truck, knowing that in a neighborhood like this, suspicious characters bring cops in a hurry. And these days, I absolutely qualify.

I tilt my wrist, see that it's nine-fifteen. At this moment, downtown, we're crashing through the doors at O'Leary's. They've queued the jukebox to play "Celebration." Our guests—my fellow workers at the bar, Alix's grad school pals, some friends we had from the Y—stand up and applaud like we're movie stars. Champagne waits on the tables. Alix's hand feels warm and fragile.

A car horn blares and the bar disappears. I look up into the headlights of an Aerostar, rolling slowly toward me. It pulls alongside, driver's side to driver's side. With an electronic hum the window eases down, and I recognize the familiar face of my former neighbor. "Buddy," she says. "How you doing?"

"Every day my life gets better and better."

Marlene raises her eyebrows. "You know you shouldn't be here. I'm not sure I should let Brook out."

On the far side of the Aerostar the door rolls back, and a moment later the lanky form of my daughter rounds the rear of the van, my old gym bag slung over her shoulder. Long auburn hair, the same shade as her mother's, is bunched up behind her head. She leans into the open window of my passenger side. "Hey, Poppa-San. It's not Saturday."

"Hey, Bird. You get a good workout tonight?"

"Jhondu helped me get my half tuck," she says. "It's bullet sweet."

I smile, as if I understand. Brook likes dancing, but she confided in me during one of our Saturday night dinners at T.G.I. Friday's that she misses kicking people.

"Seriously, Buddy," Marlene says. "I really think you should be somewhere else. You're in enough trouble."

"We're missing *Buffy*, Mom." This comes from the depths of the Aerostar.

"Tell you what, Mar," I finally offer. "You take care of your family, I'll take care of mine." At a Fourth of July neighborhood picnic back in the day, Marlene slid up behind me while I was making a pitcher of margaritas and nibbled on my ear, then told me her laundry room was empty. In the here and now, she huffs once, then pulls away.

Brook squeaks open my cranky door, climbs in. "She's, like, such a pit worm."

I have no idea what this phrase means. "Don't use language like that."

"How's the Kentucky Horror?" she asks.

"Terror," I correct her. "And great. Got crushed in Greenville on Monday night. I'm at the Civic Center on Friday."

"Against Hardy," she says. "I saw the commercial."

"Your mother doesn't want you watching SWC."

"Just a commercial. Besides, Mom doesn't want a lot of things. Anyway. Good luck Friday. Hope you win."

We both laugh, this one of our favorite running jokes. The truth, as everybody knows, is that about twelve minutes into the match on Friday, Hardy Appleseed, the All-American Dream, will flatten me out so the ref can beat the mat three times. The Dream will live on, retain the Supreme Victory Belt of the Southeastern Wrestling Confederacy, and my record will go unstained by success. In the four years since I traded the gold cape for a mask, I have a perfect record, 0–186.

When Brook was little, Alix would bring her to my matches. They'd sit ringside, Brook's tiny voice screaming "Go Bull! Go Bull!" as I sprang from the top rope. Back at home after we got Brook to sleep, Alix would massage my shoulders and share her professional observations, theories from her graduate courses in drama—what the crowd liked, ideas for the next match. Even then, she had a talent for choreographing chaos. Sometimes her fingernails would bite into my muscles, but I never told her to stop. Nowadays Brook is barred from my matches because during the divorce proceedings

Alix insisted that as a minor Brook be protected from "the inherently violence-fostering atmosphere of professional wrestling." What didn't come up in court was that on the Monday night I left the house, the alpha of all this omega, Alix smashed a commemorative *Star Trek* plate over my head and stabbed me in the ass with a shard.

I realize we've fallen into a silence and I ask Brook one of my standard I'm-a-really-good-father questions: "When are you dancing again?"

"That benefit," she says. "Day after mañana? I left it on your machine."

"Right," I say. "Absolutely." It's some deal arranged by a group Trevor belongs to. Generally, I avoid these competitions.

Again, we're quiet for a few moments. Brook angles her face at her feet and takes a long breath. "I was, like, going to call you when I got in tonight."

I ask her why.

She shrugs. "Just wanted to know how you were doing with the day. I've got a calendar too, you know."

For thirteen, there really isn't much you can get past her.

"I'm doing fine," I tell her. "Really." And this is the absolute truth. Since first donning a mask my life makes more sense. Giving up that Rocky Balboa crap was a one hundred percent therapeutic decision. When you embrace defeat as a way of life, it's hard not be successful. "Bird," I say. "Everything's cool. My life's good."

She wipes away the auburn bangs from her eyes. "Then how come you're here, Dad?"

I'm stumped for a moment, honestly just wondering this myself. Then the front door bangs open and Drs. Winston and Gladstone stumble onto the steps, struggling to keep the giant Trinitron from falling.

Brook sees them and looks back at me.

"That TV is mine," I explain, both hands up. "Ask your mother."

"She'll call Kowalski. You know she will."

"Let her," I say. "I've been hoping for a chance to renegotiate the terms of my surrender." These words escape without editing, and I regret them. Brook's put up with too much already. I inhale, exhale, and tell her I'm sorry for what I said.

She nods and says, "I'll tell them the TV was gone when I got home. I'll tell them I saw a green van."

"No. I don't want you lying to your mother. Or Trevor. It's important to always tell the truth."

"Whatever," she says as she turns away.

I climb out and meet the boys as they reach the truck. I hoist the TV from them, lift it over the sidewall, and set it down gently in the bed.

"Show off," Winston says. Gladstone folds in half, sucking air. At 280, I weigh about as much as both of them combined.

I'm about to ask where Bacchus is when I hear his voice at the house. He's talking to Brook on the steps. She disappears inside but doesn't close the door. Bacchus ambles down the lawn, and as he comes closer I see he's carrying one of Trevor's Wild Turkeys, expensive bourbon in bird-shaped bottles.

"There was a whole flock of them in there. And this." He pulls a dinner plate–sized satellite dish from behind his back. "It was on the roof of the toolshed. It's a sign. God wants us to have the porno channels." Looped in the same hand is a long coil of dirty cable, ripped free of the earth.

"Put those back," I say.

"You did designate this as a rescue mission," Winston argues.

Frozen in a standoff, nobody moves. Behind them, two houses down, I see a dark figure in Marlene's kitchen window. She's looking this way. Alix and Trevor both own cell phones, and I'm calculating the odds of a call when Brook reappears, hopping down the steps and crossing the lawn. Without comment, she hands Bacchus the remote control and a cable guide with Mel Gibson on the cover. Half his face is blue.

"I appreciate this," Bacchus says.

She looks at me and shrugs. "No sweat."

Together, we all watch her march back inside, close the door. Dr. Winston says, "She handled all that with remarkable dignity and aplomb."

Gladstone simply says, "Neat kid."

Dr. Winston wasn't joking about the power behind the altar. The second we plug the Trinitron into the outlet in Jesus's feet, static bursts to life on its screen, casting a strobey static glow onto the weeds growing down the center aisle. Sitting in the first moss-covered pew, Dr. Bacchus struggles to read from the cable guide in the haze of the screen's snowstorm. "Nine o'clock . . . *Angela's Ass*: an Irish girl . . . arrives in New York . . . with only her wits to survive."

Over the altar, I say, "You sure it says wits?"

Next to his pal, Dr. Gladstone giggles and takes a drink from the beheaded turkey. Then he asks, "Are we gonna get Nickelodeon and Comedy Central?"

"Man," Bacchus says, "we're gonna get it all."

Dr. Winston has disappeared into the steeple, trailing the cable along with him. He's decided to mount the dish in the bell tower for better reception. I offered to help but he explained that his Ph.D. in physics best qualified him for the installation of a satellite dish. I found it hard to argue.

I wish Brook knew the truth about how well I'm doing today. Like right now. Standing behind the altar, looking out over this fallen church, I'm not thinking about that other church and the ceremony at all. I'm not thinking about how Alix winked at me from beneath her veil. I'm not thinking about how when Father Callahan gave us the all-clear to kiss, Alix simply hugged me, a desperate squeeze that seemed designed to crush us into one body.

I turn to my apartment, beyond the pews, past the rubbled remnants of the wall that Hurricane Fran collapsed. Above the alley, the yellow light shines. The church wall to my right still stands, housing weary stained glass windows shattered by rocks from the neighbor-hood hooligans. During the day, they shine like Technicolor shark teeth. Behind me, the spire rises into a sky darted with stars. All churches, I decide, should be open to the heavens.

A shadow shimmers on the outside of the steeple, what looks to me at first like a giant dark spider. But then I see the spider has golden feet. "Winston!" I yell.

Bacchus and Gladstone stand. Bacchus pulls a DayGlo green cell phone from his back pocket and says, "Should I summon the fire department?"

"Where'd you get that?" Gladstone asks.

Bacchus smiles. "It got rescued too, man."

I sigh, but a clatter turns our attention skyward just in time to see a slate spin from the darkness and crash to the marble floor. Winston clings to the side of the steeple.

"Don't move!" I shout up—good advice in any crisis. I sprint into the sacristy, duck through a crooked doorway. Charging blindly up the twisting steps, I bounce off dark walls. Something skitters past my feet and disappears below. At the top of the steps I find an empty room with wind, maybe bats, snapping in the open cone over my head. There is no bell. A two-by-six is absent from a huge boarded-up window, and through this opening a slim rectangle of moonlight shines on a pile of ashes and what could be tiny bones. I jam my head outside, look down, see no body, and yell, "Dr. Winston!"

"Here," he answers, as if this were roll call. His voice comes from around the side of the steeple.

I snap two more boards free so I can fit through, then step out onto the thin ledge, keeping my eyes away from the ground. Win-ston's hand is off to the left, about ten feet up. Embracing the steeple myself, like some prodigal son filled with joy at returning to the church, I shuffle around until I'm beneath Winston. On his foot hangs the satellite dish.

"I thought we could reach the cross," Winston explains. "But I ran out of cable."

"Shimmy down," I say.

"If I move, I'll drop the dish."

From below us, Bacchus shouts, "One hundred seventeen channels. Five HBOs and Sexcitement Plus. Do not—drop—the dish."

"I'll catch it," I say.

"Promise?"

"Absolutely." Here's one thing I'm sure of: You can always apologize later for broken vows.

I lay my hands out, a wide receiver ready for a touchdown pass, a father waiting to be handed his baby daughter. Winston lifts his foot, and the dish skitters down the slate. It kicks out away and cartwheels into the air, but I reach for it, snatch it from disaster, and only then realize I'm teetering on the brink, sixty feet up. Below me, the blue glow of the TV makes a pond I could high-dive into. I find my balance, pull back in, and lay my face into the slate. Its coolness feels good as I hug the sides. Scant cheering breaks out from the two-man congregation. Winston scrambles down and scoots along the ledge, back to the safety of the bad mojo room. I pass him the satellite dish and he says, "Maybe we'll just set it up inside." But before I step in, my head turns on its own and my eyes take in the full view of downtown. And there it is, that undeniable second moon, staring at me from just over the Cape Fear and pulling at me with a gravity all its own.

Winston and I emerge from the sacristy to find Bacchus and Gladstone bathed in the Trinitron's aura. "Good job," Bacchus says, "but bad news." He points to the screen, where a CNN correspondent is explaining that amateur astronomers in Borneo are reporting what could be a rogue asteroid on the distant fringes of our solar system. We are shown a grainy star field with a menacing circle around a gray dot.

"I've been telling you guys," Gladstone says. "The sky is falling."

"Please, people," Bacchus huffs. "Consider the source. This is Borneo."

But Winston is unconsoled. Gazing into the constellations, he shakes his head. "I suspect that NASA has known for some time. Those arrogant fools would never listen to me."

When the story ends, the screen fades to black for a moment and then fills with a blond woman with too much mascara.

"Jackpot," Bacchus says.

The blond bats her eyes, pouty with invitation. She says, "The tree of life is rich with possibility when you call Carolina's own, Psychic Sidekicks."

A gypsy appears, hands floating over a crystal ball. "Yes, Brenda, I can see that you're pregnant. You're going to have a healthy son, and he's going to be a writer!" A smiling black woman lays cards on a table. "It's a happy day, Charlie. Those tech stocks are going to rebound." A man with blue sunglasses says, "She still loves you, Estevan. Go to her." Here's one thing I'm sure of: Reliable prophecy is rarely all good news.

The number on the screen, 1-800-ILL-KNOW, doesn't make any sense until you realize the apostrophe is missing.

Another mystic appears on the screen. This one's a redhead, but her face is covered with a black veil. All you can see are her eyes, and they are green and penetrating. "My mother had a vision of Reagan being shot. My sister knew about Bhopal. The one true gift flows in my veins. I know your future's truth."

"Change it," I say. The truth is not something I need to be reminded of.

But the commercial is clearly coming to a close, and Winston lets the redhead deliver her final pitch. "I'll be waiting for you. Decide now what one question you would want answered."

"Will the asteroid end life as we know it?" Winston says.

Gladstone asks, "Did my father mean what he said?"

Bacchus grumbles, "Which channel is porn?"

They turn to me in my silence, wanting to hear, I suppose, the question at the center of my heart. I picture two moons. "I need to go," I say. "Good night."

Dr. Winston shakes my hand. "Your contribution will not be forgotten."

"Sure thing," Bacchus says. "Thanks."

Gladstone runs a ragged sleeve under his nose. "That pizza tasted really good."

I walk to the rubbled wall. Before climbing over, I pause by the holy water repository and consider blessing myself. But after a second I just walk away. It's only rain, after all. I look up at the yellow light and consider the safety my apartment offers, but I move no closer to the stairs.

It's just after eleven. Soon, we'll be leaving our own reception early, eager to be alone. The Hilton. Room 341. We'll eat hot wings left over from O'Leary's. Any minute now, somewhere in the beautiful yesterday, Alix and I will be making love, so excited that we rush things and end up, by accident, creating the best part of our lives: Brook.

Somehow I find myself wandering down the alley, though I don't recall making this decision. When I step onto Market, I turn and face the Cape Fear and bang—the big perfect moon is right where I left it, out over the river. Head down, hands in pockets, I walk west, passing Keenan Plaza without looking at the stone turtles squirting water in the fountain. Once I cross 3rd, I can see the crowd's a mix of UNCW students up too late and the usual downtown groupies, corralled by a few local cops and ReelWorld security. As I move closer, past the support trucks and the rumbling generators, I get a good look at the crane atop the Jacobi Warehouse that's holding the false moon in the sky like a silver medal.

When ReelWorld first came to town it was a blessing. The cash Alix made as an extra kept Tae-Kwon-Do for Tots afloat and helped us keep the house on Asgard. Then one fateful day she improvised in midtake during a catfight in *High School Hellions*, and the director—he couldn't believe her skills. He had her rechoreograph a few action scenes. One thing led to another, and a few months later the studio hired her on as an assistant stunt coordinator. Alix was a quick study, and it wasn't long before my wife was spending her days slamming motorcycles into parked cars, being set on fire, charging from buildings seconds ahead of the bomb's detonation.

Of course, like any good husband I worried about her, despite the hours of calculations, the precautions she always took. "Buddy," she told me one night in bed, "there's a huge difference between danger and risk." Her eyes were sad when she saw I didn't understand. This was toward the end.

A couple of the crew wear T-shirts that read THE CREATURE FROM BEYOND TOMORROW, so I figure he's the reason we're all gathered here. I step into the back of the crowd, and somebody yells "Quiet on the set," and then a moment later "Action." I freeze. Three stories above us, along the rim of the Jacobi Warehouse, my wife leaps onto the ledge and starts running. My ex-wife. She's wearing a blond wig, but I know it's Al. Her feet lift and plant so cleanly along the edge of disaster.

What looks like an eight-foot-tall cockroach has appeared in Alix's path. For the camera, it turns and looks down, pumps all four of its twitching arms in the air to appear menacing. Instead of running away, Alix charges, delivers a vicious spinning side kick to the critter's head. This maneuver sends them tumbling out of vision, back onto the roof, and I feel the old tug. I have a good life. But I want to be up there. This is a fight I want to be in. I start shouldering through the crowd.

When the creature reappears, he's carrying Alix in his arms, like a bride about to be brought across the threshold. Silhouetted by the false moon, the creature steps up onto the ledge. With a heave, he hoists her limp body over his head. My eyes drop to the sidewalk ahead of me. There is no air bag.

I wish I had a copy of the script. To know for sure if this is part of Alix's plan.

The creature roars, and it's a sound that terrifies me, something wounded and hopelessly lost. It seems impossible that a human being, let alone an actor in a cockroach suit, could make such a noise. That demon might be the real thing.

My fears are confirmed a moment later, when the creature heaves Alix into the open air. Legs pump me forward, and I charge through the crowd of statues. These people are petrified by fear of catastrophe, by the awesome feeling that everything has gone terribly wrong. I'm accustomed to this. Alix's wig trails behind her as she plummets. Her body spins end over end, like the satellite dish I plucked from the sky. A security guard's eyes widen as I approach, and he lifts one hand like a crossing guard. I plow past, spilling him sideways, then burst out into the lights, and it's just like in O'Leary's basement thirteen years ago. I can feel her fragile hand in mine. My bride is falling from the heavens, but this is a catch I know I'll make. This is why the moon pulled me here. We're about to step back into our lives together. And they'll have it all on film. Alix will look at it for years to come, and Brook too. The night Dad saved Mom.

It's a power cable, or a curb, or fate, that catches my foot and drives my jaw down into concrete. My tumbling wife is stolen from my sight and pain flashes white in my mind. One heartbeat later, I wince at the dull thud not five feet away. I would've made it. I wait for the screams. But instead, people start laughing. Someone, maybe Trevor, yells, "Cut." Someone asks, "Who the hell is that?"

I lift my head and force my eyes to my wife's corpse. The rubbery face yells at me, ruby red lips painted in an expression of horror, like it's still falling. The dummy is undamaged, and reminds me of the Tony Tough Guy figure Alix and I used to practice karate on at the Y. I roll over, flipping onto my back like the appointed time has come for me to be pinned once again. Above me, the false moon rises over the top of the Jacobi Warehouse, and next to it, Alix and the Creature from Beyond Tomorrow lean over the ledge.

When I get to my feet, for some reason the people stop laughing. No one tries to stop me. Quite the opposite really, they back out of my path, press into each other to be clear of me, so I walk off the set without incident and head up the hill, back to my apartment. Thirteen years ago, at this moment, we were lying arm in arm, spent. Alix fell asleep first, I remember, but I stayed awake for a long time that night, listening to her breathing, planning the beautiful life ahead of us.

CHAPTER THE SECOND

*In Which Our Hero Prepares for Combat and Disobeys
Doctor's Orders. The Trouble with Lumberjacks.
Noah's True Origin Revealed.*

I
f anybody here needs to be praying it's probably me, but Hardy
Appleseed's the one who kneels in the far corner of the practice
ring, putting in another express call to God. As I lean into the
tight ropes of my own corner, something in me I can't quite control
paints a bull's-eye on the back of Hardy's prayerful head, and I find
myself wondering what it would feel like to drive a knee into the
base of that square skull. I shake off this impulse. Hardy is my
friend, I am not a violent man, and—most importantly—it's not
part of our approved script.

The Mad Maestro, who's been stretching old muscles at ringside,
sticks his head under the bottom rope. "I say, old chap, must he be
so utterly absorbed in his character?" His handlebar mustache rolls
to the edges of his face.

"Look who's talking," I say quietly. Maestro's from Jersey. He
gives me a knowing look and says, "No shit," then steps away and
climbs onto the XO Byke 3500. Maestro's the longtime centerpiece
of a crew of baddie wrestlers managed by Snake Handler. At
Greenville, after the Maestro got disqualified for gouging Hardy's
eyes, Snake taunted Hardy from ringside, "Sssleep well, Appleseed.

Ssssoon we will have your ssssoul." The "we" is Snake and Lucifer, an albino python he keeps looped around his neck. Recently, Lucifer has taken to whispering evil instructions to Snake, an act that sends Hardy into genuine panic. The fans love it.

The digital voice of the XO Byke squeaks out, "Five more miles. Feel the burn," and Maestro pedals faster. The computerized weight machines scattered around the floor are Quinn's babies, part of his transformation of the old gym into this, the SWC Training Facility. Despite months of sweat, it still smells like fresh paint. On the new track that loops overhead, NinJa Z, who raps about gangsta life and spins nunchuks, jogs smoothly beneath the massive air conditioner's hum. On the floor behind Maestro, the Native American Spirit Warrior—formerly Tommy Hawk, He-Who-Scalps-by-the-Midnight-Moon—strains inside the Squatmaster G2000, which urges him on, "Don't be such a loser."

"Amen," Hardy shouts, and I turn as he finally stands, rising up to his full six and a half feet. "You all set, Mr. Cooper?"

I miss the old gym. Rusted weights. Concrete walls and cold showers. Back in those days, Mrs. Q paid us in cash. I lift my face toward Hardy's good ear and shout out, "Affirmative."

To begin, we circle one another just like we've done ten times in the last hour. Then Hardy lunges in, bear-hugs my chest inside hay-bale-hoisting arms, squeezes a sigh from my tired lungs. His head tucked tight to my aching ribs, Hardy asks, "You OK, sir?"

"I'm perfect," I say. "Couldn't imagine being a whole lot better."

"Go easy on him, Hardy," the Warrior yells behind me. "These old guys ain't so sturdy."

I stay focused on Hardy. My pathetic double karate chop into his neck would disgust Alix. Still, Hardy drops me, stumbles back in feigned agony. I duck down and charge into him, but Hardy leapfrogs over me and spins fast, so when I ricochet off the ropes, Hardy's cocked elbow clips me under the chin and my head snaps back. I don't go down. When I look over at the Mad Maestro, I see five of him riding five exercise bikes. I'm leaning over the ropes.

— 21 —

Hardy puts a hand on my shoulder. "I forgot about your face, sir. I'm awful sorry."

A tender bruise fogs my chin from last night's sidewalk kiss.

"Hardy," I say, "how about we skip to the finale and call it a day?"

"That'd be fine, sir." He nods his head like a loyal cartoon dog. His hair is the color of rich wheat and wet with fine sweat. I take in another breath, hands posted on my hips.

Overhead, NinJa Z shouts down, "Hey, Cooper. Maybe you should start thinking about the senior tour."

"Be careful," the Warrior adds. "I hear they drug test for Ben-Gay."

His Squatmaster squeaks, "C'mon, Fatty! Didn't your mother have any sons?"

Like most of the punks around here, the Spirit Warrior and NinJa Z joined after I folded up Bull Invinso's gold cape. They don't understand that I'm a loser by choice.

"Don't pay them no mind, sir," Hardy tells me. Moving to the center of the ring, he settles back into the linebacker stance he perfected during two scholarship seasons at NC State. Only the NCAA's stringent academic regulations—and an inability to fathom basic math—prevented Hardy from becoming a real All-American. I collect myself, rock back deep into the ropes, bounce toward Hardy with a clothesline arm extended to the side. But Hardy shifts into me, catches my arm and spins, flipping me flat-backed onto the mat. Then he scrambles up over me, locking my head and arm together and planting his weight solid on my chest. At this point in the match on Friday, Barney the ref will slide to my side and slap the mat three times. I'll be pinned. The All-American Dream will be victorious once again. The fans will scream. All will be right in the world. What could go wrong?

"Cooper!" a voice shouts. From the mat, I turn my face. Under the bottom rope I see Cro-Magnum Man, a young up-and-comer from D.C. He's wearing a prehistoric toga and carrying both a caveman club and an AK-47. "Quinn boss man want see friend Cooper.

Quinn boss man want see friend Hardy. Before bright ball fall from sky." The rookie's a bit overzealous.

"Roger-dodger!" Hardy shouts. After getting off my chest, he tugs me to my feet. We climb out of the ring and squirt bottled water into our mouths. Cro-Magnum and Maestro step into the ring and start circling one another. "Cro-Mag smash!" the caveman shouts, stomping both feet onto the canvas and sending a *ba-wang* reverberating through the gym. Maestro gives me a look, shakes his head. He's old school. Above us, NinJa Z starts rapping. *Can't you feel that I'm keepin' it real? C'mon! Can't you feel that I'm keepin' it real?*

Hardy reaches into his gym bag and pulls out his Miracle Ear, then fixes it into place. "I don't figure a caveman for understanding how to use a gun," he says, mostly to himself. He lost hearing in that ear during the sailing accident that claimed his father. This was when he was just a kid. Eight or so.

When Brook was eight, after she was finally released from New Hanover, we put a trip to Disney on our new Visa. Alix was mad because the Pirates of the Caribbean were out of commission. And then there was that business with Paul Bunyan. Alix swore I was imagining things, but when a lumberjack puts his arm around your wife, there's only so much room for interpretation. Luckily for me, that axe was only a prop.

"You did good, sir," Hardy says, flashing me a smile. For a moment I think he's approving how I handled Bunyan. "We're gonna be great on Friday."

"The best," I tell him.

The Spirit Warrior steps over and asks Hardy if he wants to work through a few moves. "Now that you're done warming up and all."

I give him the finger. "Kiss my ass, Tonto."

Hardy tells the Warrior he'd be happy to work out some, and they head for flat practice mats in the far corner. With a towel around my neck, I weave through the graveyard of weight machines. Just as I reach the hallway, the Abdominator 2600 squeaks out, "Hey, Tubby, don't give up now."

Waiting for the elevator, I consider the worst-case scenario: I'm fired. In the last few months, The Salty Dog walked the plank for the final time and The Mental Maniac was forced to hang up his strait-jacket. As it's gotten more lucrative, even regional pro wrestling has become a young man's game. Nobody's said anything to me, but I've lost a few steps—I'm not quite the loser I was in my prime. And with all that Quinn's got going on, the magazine, the pay-per-view action, the interactive website, I'm kind of a dinosaur around here.

Of course it could just be that he wants to chat about my next incarnation. After I lose Friday's high-profile match, it'll be time for a new identity. Just a few weeks ago Quinn told me he wanted something fresh for a marquee event at the Civic Center. I'd been watching late-night reruns of *Mysteries of the Unknown Universe*, a show that has improved my understanding of the spontaneous combustion of humans, the Tunguska blast of 1908, and the Old Testament evidence for extraterrestrial life. Noah, it appears, may well have been a Martian. What makes the program unnerving is that despite all the evidence and theories their experts come up with, nobody ever proves a damn thing. So, with no better idea for a new identity that day, I offered Quinn, "The Unknown Mystery."

"Strikes me as a tad redundant," he said. "Besides, who's afraid of mystery?"

"How about the Unknown Horror? That's scary."

"Very much so. If you're four years old and your name is Sally. It conjures an image of a black-and-white low-budget. I'm picturing Vincent Price on a creepy island."

I had to concede the point. "Terror?" I tried. "The Unknown Ter-ror."

"Better, better. But abstract. It lacks something specific for the fans to latch onto."

When he brought up Kentucky I was against it. Too often, this business relies on stereotypes and clichés, the easy shorthand of the middle class mind. Besides, I couldn't do that country twang, and I was worried that the fans wouldn't buy my accent.

"Buddy," Quinn said. "Nobody's paying you to be Meryl Streep here. As for the fans—they don't want to believe. They want to pretend to believe."

And that's the absolute one true origin of the Unknown Kentucky Terror.

On the fourth floor, the door to Quinn's office at the end of the hallway is open. As I approach, I hear his voice—only I can't understand what he's saying because he's not speaking English. Could be Chinese, I guess, or Japanese maybe. Inside, he's leaning back in the leather chair, one thumb sliding inside his suspenders, feet propped up on his sleek black desk, a cut piece of granite. Fitted to Quinn's head is one of those walkie-talkie headsets the management uses at McDonald's, but it's real cutting-edge, James Bond issue. Quinn's eyes meet mine and he sits up, waves me in. Along the wall lies the tanning bed he had installed a few months back. A thin glow escapes along the cracked lid, and I imagine the box to be some kind of sunlight-filled coffin. When I draw closer to Quinn, I can see the pie charts and graphs spread across the massive desk, an altar to the gods of big business. He covers his tiny microphone with a fist and says, "I need one minute here, B. C. Things are unfolding in Jakarta. Relax."

I can't read any of the charts on his desk because the room is windowless and the lighting is low. Most of the illumination comes from the wall behind Quinn—a tic-tac-toe board of nine TVs—like you see in Sears or JCPenney. The volume is off. Each one has a different man at a different desk. But, strangely, they all seem to be wearing the same blue suit. Beneath each analyst runs a continuous stream of letters and numbers, teeming symbols I can't interpret. I wonder if these guys know what those astronomers in Borneo see coming our way.

What I hear Quinn say into the headset is, "Cheek jo. Fun Bobby. Ken shee noho Cooper jay. Sign in horror." Then he fingers a button on his desk and slides the James Bond headset off, folding it with one hand into the pocket of his white shirt. He sees me eyeing the screens and shows me his business school smile. "Ever dabble in the stock market?"

I've got ninety-seven dollars in my checking account. "Not lately."

From his desk, he pulls out a Palm Pilot and uses the pen to tap in something important. "Where the little brains see just a jumble of random numbers, those with the eye detect heartbeats, pulses, patterns that can guide you. Do you follow me?"

"One hundred percent."

Quinn throws a hand at a cushioned chair across from him and I sit. In the dim light, his deep tan seems even darker. I wonder if, in addition to the tanning bed, he's using chemicals. I also suspect the wisps of gray in his iron black hair to be artificially maintained.

"How'd things go in Greenville?" he asks.

Saturday night at the Greenville Armory was my fourth appearance as the Unknown Kentucky Terror. Jambalaya, the Creole King, knocked me out with his Mardi Gras Mauler twenty minutes into the match. He scattered corn on my unconscious body for his rooster mascot Gumbo, whose enthusiastic pecking led me to believe he hadn't been fed all day.

"Greenville went perfectly," I say. "I got beat up."

Quinn forces a laugh and says, "Well, there's the story of life." Leaning forward in his big leather throne, he opens a desk drawer and pulls out a box of Triscuits. He waves the box at me but I decline. He steps over to the birds, two parrots side by side in their hanging cage, the only evidence that Mrs. Q ever ran the SWC. Only guilt made Quinn keep the parrots, though he's developed an unnatural attachment to them over the last year, calling them his "babies," pretending they call him "Daddy." Only someone who isn't a father would throw around terms like these.

Offering a Triscuit up, he starts coaxing them. "Who wants a Triscuit? Would Shirley share a Triscuit? Wouldn't Laverne love a Triscuit?"

In grade school we made fun of kids like Quinn. In the Army we did worse.

"Triscuits make a tasty treat!"

Listening to Quinn's voice, I start calculating just how many folding wooden chairs I've taken across my back for him and his family. That entitles a man to something. I find myself contemplating the scenario in which he tells me he'll have to let me go after the match Friday and in a red flash Quinn's body lies crumbled beneath the wall of TVs, his nose pounded to hamburger and one ear hanging on by a meaty thread of flesh. I've stuffed Laverne down the hatch, and I've got Shirley by the throat. And then the red flash is gone. It's just a flash is all. Dr. Collins is exaggerating when he calls them "episodes." Planet Foodville was a fluke.

"Should I set you free?" Quinn asks the birds. "Would you like to fly around Daddy's office?"

The birds are safe from me.

"Wouldn't Laverne love to leave her little cage?"

Because I don't get angry.

"Surely Shirley wouldn't leave Daddy, would she?"

I took my pink pill this morning like a good boy.

"You know Daddy loves you."

"Mr. Quinn," I say, "is there something we needed to talk about?"

And one of the parrots finally lets loose. "You betcha!" it squawks. "You betcha!"

Quinn beams at the new trick, then comes over and slides one cheek onto the edge of his desk, a bona fide business school move. Up close, I can see the cartoon characters parading down his suspenders. Bugs. Tweety. Foghorn Leghorn. He says, "We're contemplating a significant change in your match with Hardy."

"Change?" I repeat. "What kind of change?" Here's one thing I'm sure of: A fundamental component of change is the potential for disaster.

Quinn reaches for a gold-framed picture he keeps of Mrs. Q on his desk. "You know, Ga-ga was a model grandmother, and a shrewd business lady. Nobody disputes that. But since I've taken over we've increased revenues by twenty-two percent. Just this week, seven more stations have made *SWC Fury!!!* available pay-per-view. Current coverage is eighty-six percent in North Carolina and fifty-three percent in South Carolina. The Caribbean market is ours for the taking. But certain demographic anomalies disturb me. Frankly, I foresee the potential for audience stagnation."

I nod and say, "Anomalies." Quinn used this word expecting me not to know its meaning. He hasn't read my file. Unlike Hardy, my GPA had nothing to do with why I didn't finish college.

Quinn goes on, "Men with vision like us have to anticipate market forces. Conceive and execute strategic action plans. This situation demands a bold stroke. Wouldn't you agree?"

"Absolutely," I say. "A bold stroke."

"I'm glad we're in agreement on this, B. C. It brings me back to the adjustment we're making for Friday's match. We've decided to have you win."

For two beats the world stops spinning. All nine TV analysts smile at me in unison.

Quinn says, "You'll beat Hardy."

I try to read the streaming symbols and strange fractions. BGV is down twelve-fifteenths.

"Snake will interrupt your match. The light show will let you know he's en route," Quinn explains. "Hardy will stare at him and Lucifer, become agitated the way he does. That's when you ambush him. Once the crowd gets worked up, pin him. But nothing too extravagant. We'll need it to look bad."

"Bad?"

"More fake than usual fake. Fraudulent, in fact, as if Hardy were taking a dive. That's how this has to appear—constructed. I'll arrange for some plants in the audience to chant 'Fix! Fix!' Or 'Appleseed sold out.' Something. We've got a couple days to iron out the details. Bottom line is that we need to have Hardy run out of the ring disgraced, a moral man corrupted—that's the Cliffs Notes version here. At that point, B. C., you walk away with the belt."

"Buy buy buy!" one bird squawks.

"I'm making you champion," Quinn says.

The other cracks out, "Sell sell sell!"

I stand up. "No thanks."

"No thanks?" Quinn repeats. "Explain these words to me." He's standing now too.

I realize I've knocked my chair over. "This isn't for me."

He rakes a hand through the iron black hair. "Listen, B. C. We're not connecting. This isn't something I'm asking you to do. This is the plan. This is the script."

"Not my script," I say. "Winning's not in my contract."

"Don't be rash. We both know your contract's a finely polished piece of shit."

"Watch your mouth!" one of the parrots scowls. Mrs. Q hated cursing.

"Look, Mr. Quinn, I don't understand why you'd want to bring Hardy down. The fans seem to—"

"Understanding is not something I require from you. Now I didn't anticipate your reluctance to this project. If I have to send in somebody else with the mask on, so be it. Hardy works well with you. Everybody knows he looks up to you, and I thought your participation in this would help him through. But if you want to file for conscientious objector status, I'm sure I can find someone in the corral who wants a shot. Someone who appreciates the importance of being a team player."

I rub my chest, still dotted with scabs from Gumbo's pecking. I tell Quinn, "I am a team player. I just need to think this over is all."

"Fine, B. C. You think it over. If you decide it's not something you're able to do, I'll understand completely. No hard feelings. If we have to go separate ways, so be it. Unemployment's only at four percent, and Wal-Mart's always hiring smiling faces."

He whips that erector-set phone out and steps back around to his chair, thus ending our interview. I head for the hallway, thinking about a quick shower and my Ford and driving. Behind me I hear Quinn's voice say, "Get me H. A. Expedite." And it occurs to me that Hardy doesn't know about the change in plans yet. He doesn't know that he's now scheduled to lose. And I'm kind of glad that he was praying before, though I don't think this is what the kid had in mind.

After I pull in behind the strip mall that houses Dance! Dance! Dance!, I park by my Dumpster and lean back into the shadows. Alix always drives in from the other direction, down by the Donut Hole. At this distance—about fifty yards from the door—I can usually hear Brook's laughter and see Alix's smile. Tonight though, I've come here for more than just recon.

It's only a little after eight-thirty, so the parking lot is just starting to fill up with Aerostars and Caravans. On the message board is a reminder about the dance show tomorrow night. The one Trevor is helping to sponsor. I promised Brook I'd try to make it.

I reach into the CVS bag on the seat and pull free my third Bud Light. Dr. Collins specifically warned me of the "negative interactive potentialities" but I'm feeling in a negative mood. After leaving the SWC Training Facility, I circled Greenfield Lake for an hour, listened to WAOK, considered my options, then hit CVS. After a quick pit stop at the Salvation Station, I came here.

A logical question I suppose is why I would mind Quinn's offer, why it would bother me to wear the championship belt for a couple days. In the course of my last two beers, I've decided that Quinn must have some ulterior motive. I've been wondering too if Snake might not have some reliable intelligence on all this, since he's clearly involved. For a while I considered driving down to Carolina Beach to Snake's recently reopened, no-longer-topless bar. But since the night of his wreck, Snake and I have history, so I came here instead.

One thing I'm sure is not behind my decision is a fear of success.

Dr. Collins claims that my "habitual hyper-aggressive behavior suggests an aversion to accomplishing tasks and achieving preset goals." But my discharge from the Army was caused by a C.O. with a glass jaw. And later on, I didn't leave NC State by choice. I didn't quit the wrestling team. So Collins can stuff his "self-sabotage" theory. Here's one thing I'm sure of: I never quit anything in my life.

The beer tastes warm but still feels fine going down. I'm not catching anything like a buzz, but when you're my size it usually takes more than a couple. I wonder if the pink pills will prevent me from getting drunk. That would be negative.

Hoping for clear words of encouragement, I reach for the radio. I click on WAOK and hear, ". . . Which is why you should always keep a sterile spoon in your first aid kit." I click it off. Since leaving the gym I've been trolling for signs, even though I don't really believe in them. During my wrestling days at NC State, I took this English class about heroes. Alix sent me and a bunch of other jocks into it, telling us it was an easy C and had a lot of violence. "Great Legends of Literature" dealt with Gilgamesh. Beowulf. King Arthur. Those kinds of guys. But these heroes were always receiving omens—everywhere in the stories were these deeply symbolic messages. So when I tilt the rearview mirror and check the bruise on my chin, part of me is hoping it might resemble Excalibur or a fist or something. What it looks like though is a bruise. I tilt the mirror back.

When Alix pulls in tonight, I'll do what I've never done before. I'll get out of the Ford and cross the parking lot. I'll smile when she sees me and raise one hand. We'll go sit on the steps behind the pizza joint and I'll apologize for the Trinitron and tell her I'll replace Trevor's Wild Turkey and I'll hand her back the green cell phone, which I retrieved earlier from Dr. Bacchus for just this reason. She'll tell me Trevor shouldn't have donated my things to Second Chances. She'll kick at the ground before looking at the bruise on my chin and saying, "Coop. It was you last night, wasn't it?"

At this point, I feel quite certain that we may embrace.

Then I'll tell her about Quinn's offer, how the championship we always dreamed of is mine for the asking, but how it doesn't feel right. Alix will listen and understand. She'll help me decide what it is I should do.

I'm just reaching for my fifth beer when Trevor's Lincoln Towner rolls into the parking lot, docks right next to the minivan fleet. In the dark behind the wheel, I see Trevor's head—bald on top with a crown of aging blond. Alix gets out the passenger's side, Trevor unfolds from the driver's side. I sink an inch farther into my seat, into the darkness. As Trevor takes the steps two at a time on those long crane legs, Alix seems to look in my general direction. If she has any idea I'm here, she doesn't show it. She moves up the steps and through the door being held by Trevor, who follows my wife inside to get my daughter, bring her home from the dance lessons he writes checks for.

There are nights I'm not proud of. Nights when I dream about Trevor. I could lie and say it was the booze that causes it, but even when I've gone dry the dreams still come. They go like this: I'm getting into my truck or driving along in it when I hear scuffling sounds from an alley or a dark warehouse. Sometimes I'm in a crazy place I can't figure, like the set from *People's Court.* When I investigate the sounds I see Trevor hurting Alix or Brook. Some nights he's pulling Alix's hair and slapping her, coming at her with a baseball bat. Other nights he's shoving Brook up against a brick wall and . . . he's doing the kind of things that mark him as more than just bad. And suddenly I have every God-given right in the book because he is clearly evil and I am clearly good. The one constant in all the dreams is that I always use the tire iron. The rusted one I keep under the Ford's front seat.

The doors of Dance! Dance! Dance! split open and out they come. Trevor's face is not smashed in. He extends a long arm at the Lincoln and beeps the locks, then opens both passenger side doors like a gentleman before loping around and getting behind the wheel. They all talk for a minute. Their heads rock with laughter. Then the Towner's engine rumbles up and Trevor backs out slowly, leaving the lot in the opposite direction. Probably heading for Dairy Queen. The whole time Alix never once looks my way. I could tail them, wait for a chance to get Alix by herself for a minute, but I'm starting to feel like a stalker, so I let them go.

I polish off the rest of my beer watching the other families pull out one by one, until I'm alone. The lights go off in the building, and as I finish my sixth beer a strip mall security guard rolls toward me in a golf cart. I'm hoping that he stops. The action would be good and quick. But he doesn't even notice me.

I pick up the green cell phone and consider calling Alix, telling her that I need her advice. But since I've got her phone, I can't call her. My fingers start moving on their own, and I realize the clever words they are spelling out. Once again, I am unnerved by the absent punctuation. I lift the phone to my ear just in time to hear, "Welcome to Carolina's own, Psychic Sidekicks. If you're calling because of financial trouble, press one. If you're calling because of love problems, press two. If you're calling because of trouble with your job, press three. If you're calling because of other concerns or general anxiety, press four."

Playing it safe, I go with four. After a recorded message explains the billing options, a live female voice comes on the line. "Say your name, three times. Slowly."

"If you're psychic, why don't you know my name?"

"Look, the meter's running, pal. I need your name or I can't get a psychic fix on you."

This seems reasonable. "Seamus," I say.

She insists I say it three times slowly, so she can get a psychic fix on me. And though I'm sure it's just a scam to keep clocking time, I follow her instructions. "Seamus, Seamus, Seamus."

"Alright, Seamus, my name's Tina T. I sense you are deeply troubled."

"No. I'm not," I say.

"Well, you're going to be, Seamus. Sometime real soon. This is not a guess."

"Which one are you?" I ask. "The blond with the crystal ball?"

"You can't talk to her. She's not even a real psychic. Look, I can transfer you across the hall to the adult chat line if you want, but I'm not about to start getting tingly and breathing heavy."

I recognize the grit in her voice. "Your mother knew about Reagan," I say. "You're the carrot top. The one true gift flows in your veins."

"Listen, Seamus, this is not how we do things. You call. I tell you your future."

"I know my future," I say.

There is a long pause, maybe fifteen seconds, and Tina sighs. "Hey, I can tell you're in a not good place. I can sympathize, you know. But my boss monitors these calls sometimes. If I'm not predicting the future, it's my ass. And I need this job."

"Why?" I ask. "What's wrong? Tell me your problems."

"I can't do that. And listen, I'm not kidding about trouble in your future. Sometimes I see things. For real. I'm getting a weird vibe off you. Trust me. I know about bad streaks."

Something in her voice disturbs me. Despite all the evidence I have, despite what I know, I'm suddenly certain that she's the real thing. I cradle the cell phone to my face. "Please," I whisper. "Tell me what you see."

She inhales deeply, and I imagine those green eyes gently closing. "Something is chasing you through dark woods. I see you struggling with yourself, confused. I see a dance floor. Strange disco lights. A man with no tongue. Thunder cracks. Blood pools at your feet. It pumps from a still heart on the ground. No wait, that's not a heart. Sweet Jesus, the heart has eyes and a mouth and there's a kid who—"

I snap the cell phone shut and drop it to my lap where I hold it very still. Twenty feet to my left, the mall security guard's golf cart sits in shadow. A cigarette glows red. Slowly, I reach for the key and crank the Ford to life. I maneuver around the mall, past the Donut Hole, to the light on College. Considering that I came to the mall

seeking answers, I have to consider this mission an unqualified failure. I should retreat to the safety of my apartment. Maybe it's the
strange buzz, or maybe it's the temptation of prophecy. But when
the light turns green, I aim the Ford at Carolina Beach and head for
Snake's Pit. His bar has got a dance floor and funky lights. Not that
I really believe in these things. But if I'm destined to be part of
something ugly, I don't want to be late.

CHAPTER THE THIRD

In Which Our Hero Seeks Further Advice. The Memory of
Reptiles. Oliver Stone's E-mail. An Advantageous Wrong Turn.
Monday Night Football. An Old Friend Returns.

*T*ake *care of Lucy,* the napkin read.

That's what I'm thinking about as I step up to the double doors of Snake's bar. I haven't been in this building in almost a year, not since the Baptists shut down Heaven's Gate and Snake took that drive down River Road. The old neon sign—complete with clouds and harp-playing sexy angels—has been replaced by a piece of plywood nailed above the entrance with the words SNAKE'S PIT painted across it. This is the first of many changes I'm expecting. But when I open the doors and walk into the smoky dimness, right in front of me is the same runway where Moniqua danced naked with her python, where Sally did lasso tricks in nothing but a white cowboy hat. And the gold poles Glori once whirled around still stretch into the ceiling, now useless and lonely. Lining the edges of the raised stage, a brotherhood of a half dozen guys man the bar stools waiting for the return of their goddess. The somber men bow their heads over their beer mugs as Johnny Cash preaches fire from the jukebox.

A bar girl comes toward me in black high heels and a leopard miniskirt and at first she seems completely topless. But as she nears I make out the tassels swinging from the pasties on her breasts. This must be the legal compromise worked out between the Baptists and Snake's lawyer. She smiles at me and says, "You're allowed to come inside, y'know."

The tassels tumbling from her breasts are red and green. Stop and go, I think.

"I'm here to see Snake," I tell her, and she cocks her head toward the booths back by a pool table, where two players stand side by side, consulting on a shot. The taller one's missing an arm. Heading toward them, I pass Lucifer's glass cage, a giant aquarium built into the wall. You really can't blame Hardy for his phobia of this thing, though the fans think he's acting when he waves his arms and hollers. The albino python's face settles against the glass in sleep, and she seems possessed of some secret knowledge. The slim smile on her face makes me wonder if she's dreaming of wounded baby goats. Though for all I know she may be missing the old days with Moniqua, replaying nights in the spotlight. I don't know how much memory reptiles have. Or how much regret they are capable of.

Closing in on Snake's booth, I realize it's the same one we drank in that last night, after the shutdown. The night his truck cracked that phone pole on River Road. Alix scolded me for letting a friend drive drunk, said I was a bad example for Brook. When I step up to his table, Snake keeps looking at the blueprints unrolled before him and says, "No more autographsss tonight. Pissss off."

"Relax, Paul," I say. "The civilians are busy drinking your swill."

Snake raises his angular face, sunken cheeks folding into a sharp chin capped by a black goatee. Through the thin cigarette fog, he grins. "Ladies and gentlemen, the Unknown Kentucky Terrier."

"Woof woof," I say. "You're funny."

The windshield scars on his forehead never completely healed, so fine pink lines crisscross his skin. When he's Snake Handler, the white makeup covers them. He lifts one of his scarecrow arms and shouts, "Hey, Sweetcheeks, a pitcher and two mugs. Got a man dehydrating over here." I slide into the cone of light spreading over the booth, where I consider the advisability of having more beer.

My head feels light and my fingertips tingle. But I'm feeling fine really—I knew Collins was putting me on. Snake rolls up the blueprints. "Christ, I thought you were one of the Dark Disciples come to worship."

"I got better ways to waste my life."

His thin lips tug on his Marlboro, release smoke. "One of those nutjobs left a dead rabbit on the hearse last night."

I shake my head. "You're the one calling for lost souls and sacrifices. What do you expect?"

"Yeah, but I just had the damn thing waxed for Friday."

Friday. The reason I came. Snake's eyes meet mine, like he somehow knows why I'm here. I shrug my shoulders, turn away and face the bar, which really hasn't changed much at all, except there are no naked ladies and almost no customers. "I like the extensive remodeling."

"I've got plans," he says, nodding at the tube of blueprints. One bony hand lifts an accordion folder from the seat next to him. "Plus I've got an appeal that's gonna make those Baptists pray overtime. Meanwhile, I'm looking into the legality of hosting a little female mud wrestling. The way I see it, if a bra comes off in the middle of a sporting event—oops!—that's just fucking providence, you know?"

"Absolutely," I say. "Providence."

One of the bar crew wanders to the jukebox, which is now crooning Sinatra's "My Way." The one-armed pool player misses a bank shot and shouts, "Sumbitch!"

Back in the day, even on weeknights we were standing room only, bikers and business suits forced to mingle in the only all-nude club between Myrtle Beach and the Golden Triangle. Snake knew me from the SWC and hired me on as muscle to enforce one rule: Don't touch the ladies.

The bar girl drops off the pitcher and fills both our mugs. I lift mine and say, "Well, to the good old days."

Snake's face sours. "Good old days my shriveled ass. I'm tomorrow's number one fan. The future's so bright I gotta wear shades.

Don't look back 'cause something might be catching up to you. Face it, Buddy, nostalgia is for suckers. What was so great about the good old days? The protests? The fines? The raid?"

We both take a long drink in silence. The thing that's upsetting Snake the most, the thing he'll never mention, is how Moniqua skipped bail for Vegas, left him with a bond note and her python. I think again of the napkin I found in my pocket and decide to steer the conversation in a safer direction. "Ever hear from Tony?"

He exhales, calming some. "Not after he headed for the good life in Montana."

"Fat sonuvabitch tended a mean bar."

Snake nods. "I'll always drink to Tony."

"Remember the night those frat boys came back with the .38?"

"Jesus," Snake says. "Alpha Beta Dipshits."

I can tell Snake has questions about my sudden return, but he's playing cool like always. He never asked why I didn't stop by New Hanover after what happened on River Road, or why I didn't attend the grand reopening of the bar. But with no dancers to protect, there wasn't much use in hiring me back. As for wrestling events, we did our jobs professionally, but pretty much skipped the socializing. After all, we had that napkin between us.

Any lingering awkwardness we feel now gets drowned by the beer, and we set to work draining the pitcher while trading war stories about Heaven's Gate. How he spent Hurricane Fran out here with some of the dancers who lived in trailer homes. The night some drunk claimed to be Alec Baldwin and we quizzed him on his movies. Story by story, drink by drink, I'm renewing my affection for alcohol. That pleasant buzz in the top of your head, the fog that rolls in over your problems. A few beers later, Snake's finishing a story about his failed attempt to convince ReelWorld to finance a low-budget porno on the premises, and I'm having a hard time recalling all the important things I came here to discuss. But I don't care. I'm laughing and the beer's going down smooth.

Only the empty pitcher snaps us from the past. Snake hoists it up and yells, "Sunshine! How about earning those big bucks I pay you?"

Sunshine nods from the bar, and Snake says, "So, Buddy. Quinn gave me a ring. He said you might be calling."

"Oh did he?" I ask. "Did he tell you what I was supposed to say?"

"That you've got concerns about Friday."

"No way Hardy goes for this deal. For openers, he's got a serious aversion to Lucifer."

Snake leans back in the booth, pulling his triangular face into darkness. After a pause he sends smoke into the light. "Hardy's a good kid. He'll get over his fear and do whatever we tell him. And at last hisss sssoul will be mine."

I can't tell if I'm imagining the hissing or not.

"You need to trust Q, Buddy. The man's a certified genius."

"I'd like to know who did the certifying."

"Hey, when Q came up with the idea of having Lucy 'talk' to me, I figured he was whacked. Since then my fan mail has tripled. That dead bunny was nothing. The kids either love to love me or love to hate me. Last week I got a death threat—a real live cut-up-newspaper-headline death threat!"

"I don't think we should define this as positive feedback."

Sunshine shows up with a fresh pitcher.

Snake says, "Thanks, Sugar Pie." He tops off my beer. That buzzing in my head starts to whine like a weed whacker and I'm beginning to think the alcohol was maybe not an award-winning idea, but it tastes too good to stop now.

"Q's not like you and me. We're talking about a guy who golfs with senators. He's got Oliver Stone's e-mail address. I don't think you realize how big this thing could get."

"Paul," I say. "It's already big." I think of Alix on the roof last night. I try to remember exactly why I came here. I lift my beer, which I swore Snake just filled. Now there's barely a swallow left.

Snake snaps a match to life and lights a new cigarette. "Things are happening, Buddy. Big changes are coming. If Q's long-term plans go through we could be sitting in a meeting with Ted Turner eighteen months from now."

"Ted Turner?" I say. "You're delirious."

Snake jabs that cigarette at me. "Enough. You want to keep playing Mister Martyr, that's fine. But don't muck it up for the rest of us. Q's got big plans for the future—you know, that thing after tomorrow? And if you were smart you'd be cashing in. With a few grand in my pocket, I could be all nude again in no time. Hire some Raleigh lawyers, get those bogus charges against Moniqua dropped, build a new stage for her, hire a primo dj, add on a kitchen, pick up a karaoke machine, run shuttles to downtown, have dollar drafts, ten-cent wings, free popcorn. We'll have college night, bachelor night, ladies night, couples night, sports night, senior citizens night, veterans night, disco night, Hawaiian night. Dwarf-tossing. They'll come from miles and she'll know I had the right idea. I'm talking about fucking vindication here. A chance to prove that all that happened didn't happen for nothing."

Snake sucks hard on his cigarette, blows smoke over the empty pitcher, then stares down into the ashtray.

The night Moniqua skipped town, he asked me to meet him here and we drank alone with Lucifer prowling the sticky floor. Snake seemed supernaturally calm. He said everything made sense, which made no sense to me. All night, he kept telling me everything was going to be fine. Here's one thing I've learned: When someone in crisis says everything is fine, it's time to break the glass and sound the alarm.

The next morning I found the napkin in the pocket of my jean jacket with shaky handwriting: *Take care of Lucy.* This confused me until I got the phone call: Snake swerved to miss a deer on River Road and took out a phone pole. That was the official story. I burned the note. It's a night we've pretended never happened.

That's how thin the line is. That's how much you can risk.

I stare at Snake. All his posturing gone. The scars seem brighter on his forehead as he struggles for something else to say. With one thin finger, he traces a tight circle over and over again in his goatee. The wall behind him shimmers like it's an illusion. My eyes feel loose. Looking down into the last inch of beer, I wonder if Brook is finishing an ice cream cone right now. I picture the three of them sitting on the fender in the Dairy Queen parking lot, Trevor pointing out the Big Dipper to Brook, explaining things to her about how the world works. I stand suddenly, lightness rushes to the top of my head. I stumble, catch myself on the edge of the table, and straighten.

I drop a ten next to my empty mug.

"For Christ's sake, Buddy, c'mon. Don't leave like this."

I walk away. The dance runway I once protected lies before me, and I move toward the faded gold shine of the poles. I'm looking at them when I bump hard into something. "Sumbitch!" I hear and turn to the pool player.

On the table, the cue ball rolls into the far right pocket.

"M'sorry," I offer.

"Sorry don't give me my six ball back."

Snake steps up. "Next game's on the house."

The kid is in my face. I've got eighty pounds on him, easy, but I'm still about to clock him when my eyes fix on his empty sleeve, folded neatly and safety-pinned to his shoulder. Was he born without the arm? Did he lose it somehow? While I'm staring, he raises the only hand he's got. I look up just in time to see the fat end of the pool stick descending. I drop hard, ass then head, and find myself staring at the unlit disco ball hanging from the ceiling. My hand finds a little blood on my forehead, though I'd hardly call it "pooling." This is the kind of inferior prophecy you get for 99 cents a minute. The one-armed pool player steps into view over me, fisting his stick like a warrior. "Mutashoo," he says. I swear. "Mutashoo! Mutashoo!"

I brush away the helping hands and climb to one knee, stagger toward the door. Snake's holding my shoulder, and he's saying something about a taxi. "Lawsuit," I hear. "Full liability." But I shove him out of my way. He's still shouting as I push through the double doors, but his words make no sense.

The air outside clears my head a little, though I still don't understand what's happening around me. The gravel parking lot rises and falls like a waterbed. The beer is full inside me, and I look around for a place to relieve myself. Out back I come across Snake's hearse, a big black monster from the '70s he drives to all the matches so he can haul away the dead bodies of his wrestlers' opponents. Leaning on the shiny black surface, I work my way to the sideways back door. The license plate reads, SSSNAKE 1. My hands fumble with my zipper as I envision a hot stream spraying Snake's plate. But a few seconds later my toes are growing warm and I realize my marksmanship skills have grown rusty.

I should sober up and go back inside, pound teeth from the punk with one arm. But I'm old now, too tired for anything but my brown couch and the sure comfort of late-night TV.

Driving is not easy. Every set of headlights I figure for a cop. This was a stupid, bad idea. The worst of all plans. I lock up the brakes at a green light by accident and almost get rear-ended by a pizza delivery boy. The bleeding on my forehead stops. WAOK's broadcasting an hour of New Age music. All clicks and whistles. I shut it off to concentrate on the road, but my mind is so fixed on staying between the lines it forgets where we're supposed to be going. Old instincts take over. I make a right instead of a left, go straight at the light where I'm supposed to turn, and suddenly I find myself back in the old neighborhood, cruising down Asgard Lane.

I pull to the curb five blocks away from the house, shut off the engine. I roll from my Ford and stumble into the gully, a ten-foot-wide ditch the city owns that runs through the middle of the development. Everybody's backyard has got a fence up to block the sight of the thing since the city doesn't do much in the way of maintenance. So I'm sloshing through six inches of still water, stirring mosquitoes up into the humid June air. I keep quiet and hope if anybody hears me they'll figure me for a possum. Twice I stop because I hear voices whispering in the pine branches over my head, but it's only the chatter of insects.

I come up to the eight-foot fence I installed myself and climb the little incline to it, stick my face up against a knothole like a boy without a ticket for the big baseball game. Best-case scenario is Alix is in the kitchen, or alone upstairs by a window. But all the lights are out. I figure it for about 22:00, way too early for everybody to be in bed already, but late for them to still be out on that ice cream run. I try to jimmy the lock but splinter it away from the wood, then slip through, into the backyard I used to mow once a week from May to September. Trevor's letting the crabgrass take over. Bald spots from mole crickets.

Up close there are still no signs of life in the house, so I step up onto the deck. Trevor's bought himself a new grill, the GasMaster 5200. A nice model: side burner, dual beer holders. For spite I crank the gas nozzle closed, wondering how long it will take Mr. Director to figure that one out. I cup my eyes and lean into the sliding glass door. Inside I detect no movement. No sound. Recon complete—negative occupancy. I try the door and it gives, so I slide into the air-conditioned cool. I think about wiping my feet but then figure what the hell and track a little mud onto the carpet we paid an extra hundred bucks to have StainGuarded.

In the darkness I do the blindman shuffle toward the kitchen, knocking over a chair that's not supposed to be there. I flip the light. Magneted to the fridge are pictures of Brook in costumes from her different dance routines. Here she's a baseball player, here a soldier in fatigues. In one my daughter is dressed as Elvis. In another she is dressed in bright scarves, a harem girl or something, and Trevor is standing beside her, grinning.

Next to these pictures is a photocopy that reads: "Jhondu's Five Steps to Being a Better Dancer and Finding Inner Peace." Number four reads, "Eliminate the source of all negative rhooshies."

In the back of my head, some still-sober voice is telling me I'm nuts. If I get caught in here there'll be real trouble. Court-ordered quarterly chats with Dr. Collins and pink pills won't be enough to keep them from taking away my Saturdays with Brook. But it's clear I'm in the middle of something and the current is pulling me along now. Habit has me crack open the fridge, and I scan some old salad and a Saran-wrapped pyramid of barbecued chicken. The twelve-pack of Heineken draws my interest, and I decide Trevor won't notice one missing beer.

With the opened Heineken in my hand I start toward the stairs. Suddenly I want to see my old bedroom and the pillow where Trevor puts his head. I want to go through Alix's drawers and find fading pictures of me, of us together. But then I see blue light glowing from the living room. The television's on—a clear impossibility since the Trinitron is downtown in the Salvation Station. Stranger still, it sounds like football but there can't be football on in June. I poke my head around the corner and sure enough there's Frank Gifford on the big screen talking to Al Davis about the Raiders moving back to Oakland, which is screwed up because they moved back years ago.

The couch is empty, but I see somebody's legs extended out on my La-Z-Boy. I can't tell if it's Alix or Trevor but I'm pissed now. That old chair was about the only thing I asked for in the divorce and she swore—under oath!—that she gave it to Second Chances. I step in front of the Trinitron to confront the chair stealer and everything—the whole wide world—makes no sense at all. 'Cause it's me in the chair. Buddy Cooper.

"Hey," he says, "where'd you get the Heineken?" He holds a can of Bud Light.

After ten seconds of silence, I say, "The fridge."

He asks, "You want to trade?"

"No."

He points at my face. "You're a mess. Between the chin and that goose egg on your forehead, you're not about to win any beauty prizes." When I don't say anything, he goes on. "Take a load off," he says. "You're kind of late."

I settle down onto the couch and stare at my younger face. It's smooth. And my crew cut is thicker. Young Buddy is watching the game. He lifts his beer and I catch the glint of gold on his finger. That ring is in a shoe box in the back of my closet downtown.

"What the hell's going on here?" I ask.

"Nothing good," he says. "Jackson's running all over Seattle."

And then of course the wave of déjà vu crashes. This is the Monday night Alix comes home and we cross the line. The night she kicks me out. But somehow I've been given another chance.

"Buddy," I say quickly. "Do you recognize me?"

"Sure," he says. "You're Buddy Cooper."

"Great. That's great. You've got to listen to me. Bad things are going to happen tonight."

"I'll say," he says. "I've got twenty bucks on the Seahawks and they're gonna lose thirty-seven to fourteen."

"You don't understand. This is the night our life falls apart."

Buddy giggles at the screen and I look. It's the "Where's the Beef?" commercial. "That one kills me," he says.

"But we have a chance to save it," I say, trying not to get angry. "A chance to save our life."

He looks at me. His face is warm. "Buddy," he says. "You shouldn't have stopped reading good books after you left college. You're looking at this from a strictly Hollywood viewpoint and that's just a flawed perspective. This ain't *It's a Wonderful Life*. Hell, it's not even *Back to the—*"

"Shut up," I say. "You don't understand. We have to stop this from happening again. You don't know how terrible—"

"You whine a lot," he says. "And you're not a very good listener. You should try watching Oprah instead of those soap operas. Oprah knows how to listen."

I stop. Calm. I say, "We—have—to—stop—this."

"No we don't," he says. "We can't. *This* already happened. You think I don't know what's coming? Five minutes from now Alix comes in mad from Harris Teeter. The Raiders are driving. You offer to help but she knows it's token. She tells you to enjoy the game. A bag of groceries rips. Bo Jackson plows over Brian Bosworth on the two yard line and sends his career spiraling toward bad movies. The jar of Ragú shatters and splashes spaghetti sauce. Alix curses. You can't find the paper towels. Brook locks herself in the bathroom. Before long we get the Spock plate in the ass. We're out of the emergency room by midnight and in the Motel 6 by one a.m. That's tonight's script, Buddy. We can't change it. You can't change it."

I rise up, step between this joker and the NFL. I gather his shirt front in one fist and yank him out of my La-Z-Boy, spin him hard, and jack him up against a wall. I say, "You're gonna tell me who you are or I'm gonna beat hell out of you right here before the national television audience."

"Who I am is a complicated question," he says, not at all worried that I might smash his face to pulp, which is absolutely my plan. And suddenly I feel the weight of the tire iron in my hand, cocked up behind my shoulder like a hatchet. I squeeze to be sure it's no illusion, and the grip is certain. It's real. I don't remember getting it from under the front seat of the truck. I don't remember carrying it inside.

"Oops," says Buddy. "And who'd we bring that in here for?"

The answer hangs in my head. "This isn't happening," I say.

"That's one possibility. Or this could be one reason Dr. Collins told you not to drink while you were taking the brain candy."

I lower the tire iron, let go of Buddy. Behind me I hear the crowd cheer and turn to see Brian Bosworth flattened in the end zone. Bo Jackson, always a gentleman, hands the football to the referee. I reach for my beer and down it in two gulps.

Young Buddy straightens his shirt. "That's not gonna help," he says. He looks at his watch, a Timex that Alix gave me for our fifth anniversary. "Hey, I've lost track of time here. Look, we were supposed to cover a lot of ground but I'd better cut to the chase. You know Brook's dancing tomorrow night, right? Eight o'clock."

"Tomorrow tomorrow?" I ask. "Or four years ago tomorrow?"

"Tomorrow tomorrow. Trevor's benefit deal. You have to be there. Brook wants you to come and it's important to her."

I look him in the eye. "But what about the match Friday?" I ask. "What should I do about Hardy Appleseed?"

"Believe me. It's important you go see Brook dance tomorrow."

"If you're really me," I say, "you're the last person in the world I want to believe."

He shakes his head. "I came a long way for this. You try to beat me up and drink premium beer in front of me. Geesh, exactly when did I turn into such an asshole?"

"We were always an asshole," I say. "I'm just the one who figured it out."

He shakes his head, turns to the TV. Standing side by side we watch the point-after attempt. It's good.

I say, "Listen, I'm sorry. This is all just weird, you know?"

"No blood, no foul." He offers me his hand and I shake it.

Young Buddy sits back in the La-Z-Boy. Feeling guilty I head for the kitchen, planning on handing over one of Trevor's Heinekens before trying to figure out any more of this. But from the hallway I hear a car pull up out front. I go back to the living room for a view of the driveway and the TV table is empty, a dusty field with a clean square. My La-Z-Boy is gone. A corner curio cabinet displays a tight flock of Wild Turkeys, one clearly missing from formation. I'm alone in the house. Alone with my tire iron. Outside a car door slams, and I hear voices and the jingle of keys. I don't know if that's Alix and Brook and Trevor coming in late from Dairy Queen or Alix and Brook loaded with groceries four years ago. But either way, I decide I don't want to be here when that door opens. I haul ass through the kitchen, through the sliding glass door, through the backyard and the fence I installed. And in no time at all I'm back in the gully sloshing through stagnant water, stumbling through the hot darkness with a rusted tire iron and no plan at all.

CHAPTER THE FOURTH

A Rude Awakening. Evaluating Crucial Evidence.
Taking a Spin at the Big Wheel. Watching Waves Crash.
Our Hero Tries to Explain.

I dream of explosions, being pursued as I weave across a field of burning bodies and smoldering craters. Overhead, bombers float low, drop their load, and coast away in the orange bloom. From the forest behind me, the enemy lobs shells. When I sit straight up in my bed, it takes a moment for me to realize that the source of the *crashbangs* is not bombs or mortar fire but someone pounding the glass of my bedroom window, twenty-five feet above the ground. I flip back the sheets, stumble across the room in my boxers, and tug the cord that raises the miniblinds. Dr. Bacchus perches in the branches of an elm tree and looks like a well-fed but eager squirrel. "Open up," he hollers through the pane. "This is your wake-up call."

I rub my eyes and wish for bombs. My head feels heavy.

Palms in, I hoist the window and Bacchus barrels through. "Have you seen Dr. Winston?"

I pull on a pair of jeans that reek of bar smoke. The cuffs are still damp. "Should I have seen Dr. Winston?"

"Crap crap crap." Immediately he starts poking around my bedroom, as if Winston might be hiding in my closet or beneath my bed. When he spins around to me, his eyes take in the goose egg on my forehead and the bruise on my chin. "That shade really works for you."

"Matches my life," I say. We stare at each other. I scratch the back of my head. "So, is there a reason you're here?"

"That's the sixty-four-thousand-dollar question of life, now isn't it?" With this, he scoots into the living room and zigzags, confirming that nothing is under the brown couch or behind the TV. Then I follow him into the bathroom where—with dramatic flair—he yanks back the shower curtain. Except for the grimy tiles, it's empty. "A little Formula 409 could go a long way here."

At the bottom of my toilet, two dozen pink pills nestle like tiny eggs. I reach for the handle and flush. Without comment, Bacchus watches them get sucked down the vortex. I grab some Tylenol from the medicine cabinet, and when I close it, Bacchus is unzipping his pants. "You wouldn't begrudge a man a little hospitality?"

"Aim for the middle," I ask.

On my kitchen counter a note waits for me. In my own handwriting it reads: *Brook's Dance. 8:00 Tonight. Be There.* I have no memory of writing this, but I doubt it's a reminder composed by Phantom Buddy. Here's one thing I'm sure of: Doctors' precautions about the interactions of drugs and alcohol should be taken very seriously. So I'm not regretting last night's decision about the pills, however hazy it may be now. As of today, I'm off my medication.

I open the fridge and drink from a carton of orange juice, wash down the Tylenol that I'm hoping will loosen the clamps on my skull.

The toilet flushes and Bacchus reappears. "Nothing like two-ply," he says as he walks past me toward the door. With all that's going on in my head, I'm grateful that he's leaving. But when he opens the door, Gladstone stands in the entrance, WORLD'S #1 DAD hat still on his head. Apparently Gladstone reads the failed expression on Bacchus's face. "I told you he wouldn't be here."

"Nobody likes a know-it-all." Dr. Bacchus comes back into the room and opens a cupboard, pulls down a mug, and goes to the sink.

Gladstone steps up to me. His eyes are soft and desperate. "Dr. Cooper. They've got Winston."

I fold my note into my pocket. "Hold up. Who's got Winston?"

"Where do you keep your coffee?" Dr. Bacchus wants to know.

"No coffee 'til I know what's going on."

"That could take a while."

"The ones he warned us about," Gladstone says. "We should have listened. We should have believed."

I look over at Bacchus, who has found my Folgers crystals and is stirring them into cold tap water. "No chance for a little sugar, huh?"

Gladstone pushes his face into his hands. "Go ahead and don't believe me. But I have evidence. I'm the one with proof."

Bacchus and I glance at each other and shrug. It's hard to argue with evidence.

Moments later, Gladstone leads us onto my porch, where the brightness of the Carolina sky brings my hand up to shield my eyes. Even so, tiny splinters work into my brain. A mockingbird twitters at us as we descend the stairs. Admittedly, last night's darkness seems distant. Then we pass the Ford, and I see the tire iron in the bed of the truck. I turn away. It was the pills last night that made me see what I saw and do what I did. The pills.

"Coffee's a bit crunchy," Bacchus complains.

We cross the alley and step up onto holy ground, pass the fading city signs posted on wooden stakes: NO TRESPASSING. THIS PROPERTY CONDEMNED.

Following the boys, I climb the collapsed rubble wall, and when I get to the top I see Bob Barker on the altar. He's got his arm around a blue-haired woman. "Which do you think is less expensive," he asks, "the fabric softener or the smile brightener?"

Bacchus votes for the fabric softener.

"Mock me all you want," Gladstone says. "Winston is in terrible danger."

He leads us into the church, which seems somehow more tragic in the light of day. Sunlight illuminates the few stained glass shards—red and blue still clinging to the windows, but their broken fragments litter the ground. Everywhere are muddied pieces of colored glass, puzzle pieces with bizarre half images, a saintly finger, the gold curve of a halo, one letter orphaned from a sacred inscription.

"Here," Gladstone shouts, pointing to the ground behind some rotted pews. Bacchus and I huddle on either side of him and look down—there's a clearing of weeds and dirt, an immaculately clean space in the shape of a perfect circle. Inside the sphere, the bright cobblestone shines. Just outside the perfect circle are the shattered pieces of Trevor's Wild Turkey.

"He was holding the bourbon when they beamed him up," Gladstone explains.

Bacchus lifts the mug. "This is the good part."

"Their ship was shaped like a croissant," Gladstone says, dreamy-eyed.

"Maybe the alien abductors are French."

"Maybe if you weren't passed out, we could have saved him!"

"Guys," I say. "This sounds like a situation. Let's not start pointing fingers."

"You don't get it, do you?" Gladstone shouts, storming up the aisle, snatching the baseball cap from his head and clutching his hair. He stops in front of the altar, and while a leggy blond fondles a Salad Shooter, Gladstone screams into the wide sky, "They took Dr. Winston! And surely, he was the best among us!"

Bacchus leans in to me. "He's been like this all morning. We checked Second Chances. We checked the shelter. You were our last hope."

Gladstone starts weeping softly, a strange sound beneath so blue a sky. A mockingbird, maybe the same one, maybe a new one, flies into the church and lands on a pew. It nags me until my feet start moving. I walk up to Gladstone and lay a hand on his shaking shoulder. "The ship," I say. "I saw it."

"What?"

"Last night in the sky when I was coming home. It passed out over the ocean."

"You believe me?"

"Absolutely. I'll contact the authorities. Maybe the airport radar picked up something. We'll call WAOK, the FBI, whoever we have to."

"Not NASA!" he urges.

"No way. They're clearly not the ones to get involved with this. Maybe we could get the Air Force to investigate."

"They have fighter planes. They have rockets."

"Right," I say. "Heat seekers."

When Gladstone hugs me I almost feel guilty. But I'm convinced that by nightfall, Winston will have returned. Bacchus walks past us while we're hugging and gives me a look. He chases the mocking-bird away to witness the Showcase Showdown, where an elderly man with Coke-bottle glasses steps up to the big wheel, ready for his chance to spin.

Coming up my steps, I hear my phone ringing so I charge through the kitchen and into the living room, yank the receiver up quick and say hello.

"Metricius?"

"What?"

"Let me talk to Metricius."

"Wrong number."

"I know he's there. You put him on."

"Pal, you misdialed."

"Fine. That's how we play this then."

"Fine."

"You just tell Metricius I know what's what."

"I'll do that."

"You tell him I'm coming, and you know who's coming with me."

"Absolutely," I say. "We'll all be waiting." After I hang up, I regret not asking the guy if he'd seen Dr. Winston. Suddenly, anything seems possible.

I notice the red light on my answering machine blinking away and figure this moron actually left a message for Metricius while I was outside. Then it occurs to me with the way my head feels like a bowling ball that I could've slept through a whole telethon of phone calls this morning. I push the button and Quinn's voice pipes up. "B. C.? We need to expedite Plan X. If I have to activate a contingency, I need to know that. But because I still value your input and feel confident you can bring a unique contribution to the project, I'm prepared to discuss additional incentives and compensation. Respond."

Erasing that one's a pleasure. I don't know what to tell him. But I sure as hell don't want to do that match tomorrow night.

I push the button for a second message. "Hello? Mr. Cooper, sir? Are you there? It's me, sir. I was hopin' we could maybe talk. Are you there?" After ten seconds of silence, Hardy hangs up.

I push the button for the third message. "It's me," Alix says, then the beep. Today is Thursday, the day she runs errands when she's not on a shoot. Her call means she'll be over.

I get into the shower and the hot water feels fine on the back of my neck. I splurge with a new razor so my shave is tight and neat. After I get dressed I move on to the apartment. I squirt blue liquid in the toilet so it smells nice, stuff the laundry into the closet and close the door, check the sheets before making the bed. While I'm straightening the living room I click on *Waves Will Crash,* just to see what's going on. But I get sucked in and find myself taking a break from cleaning detail. The brown couch welcomes me again. At Mercy Hospital, Lauren Gales emerges from her three-episode-long coma only to discover that amnesia has stolen her memory. So when Stack and Longley Worthmore both show up claiming to be her true love, she doesn't know which brother to believe. The truth of course is that Longley sabotaged the elevator in the first place, after Lauren told him she had to follow her heart and leave him for Stack. I was glad when she made this decision. All Longley ever wanted was her money.

Matters are further complicated after a hemorrhoid commercial, during which I run the vacuum. Mercy's top doctor announces that Lauren is pregnant. Both Worthmores immediately claimed to be the daddy, but the doctor explains that because they are brothers, the standard paternity test would be useless. I recognize this for the clumsy plotting that it is, but still maintain my disbelief. As Stack and Longley look on, Lauren lays her bandaged hands on her stomach and starts crying. The credits roll.

I click off the tube and get back to work. But as I'm finishing the vacuuming, I decide Lauren's looking at this amnesia thing the wrong way. It's a free ticket. This could be a chance to start life again with a clean slate. Imagine the liberty that not having a past could grant somebody.

I give the kitchen floor a quick sweep, then check the dishes in the sink for significant food deposits as I stow them in the dishwasher. I make a mental note that Bacchus still has my coffee mug. All the while I'm working I never think about Alix being here. I don't care if she shows up or not. The place needs a cleaning anyway.

I'm almost through the stack of dishes when gravel crunches outside. Then comes a car door and Alix's footsteps clacking up the stairs. She's wearing those black, knee-high boots.

I slam-dunk the last few plates in the Maytag and snap it on, knowing that I'm forgetting the detergent but not wanting Alix to catch me fixing the place up. I'm standing just inside the door but I make her knock. Casually, I open it. She asks, "You not taking calls today?"

I tell her I was at Whitey's for breakfast.

"Hhmph," she says. As she strides past me, I look down at her auburn hair, cropped short these days, and I see the darker brown fur along the back of her neck.

"I saw the Trinitron from your porch. That's a precious touch, Coop. Please tell me those bums weren't in the house with Brook. Just tell me that much."

"Hey. Trevor shouldn't have given my stuff away."

"Trevor carried the boxes. I drove the car." She marches through the living room, and I follow. Even from behind her, I can tell her hands are working the buttons on her white blouse. "I told you six times to make a pickup. Your choice to ignore me. By the way, we'll be contacting the insurance company about the other night, and to do that we need to fill out a police report. Fair warning."

I ignore the implications and wonder if she looked through the boxes before she gave them to Second Chances. Did she see the WORLD'S #1 DAD hat and think back? "What's the rush anyway?" I ask her. "You planning on finishing the attic all of a sudden?"

In my bedroom doorway, she pauses and turns to me. The top buttons of her blouse are undone. Her bra is white lace. I lift my eyes to her face, and it is still. "We're putting the house on the market, Coop. I thought Brook would tell you."

I shake my head. "That didn't come up."

Alix shrugs. "Any leads on a green cell phone?"

I head back to the kitchen and my jacket, hoping it's in the pocket. I'm picturing the house on Asgard with a FOR SALE sign staked into the front lawn, and I find myself calculating how I could purchase it myself.

When I return to the bedroom, she's flared her shirt free of her jeans. Her abs are four tight boxes, the result of a stuntwoman workout program that involves two hundred crunches a day. I hand her the cell and she nods. "Thanks. You make any long distance calls?"

I think of Tina T at Carolina Psychic Sidekicks. "None worth mentioning." Alix slips her blouse off and folds it neatly on a chair, sets the cell phone on top, dead center. Her hands reach for her belt.

Still standing in the doorway, I say, "Hey. I heard that they're shooting downtown. *The Creature from Behind Tomorrow*. Is that one of yours?"

She studies my face, trying to decide why I'm asking what I already know. *"Beyond,"* she says. "And yeah, I'm in it. Another damsel in distress. They've got no interest in backing strong female roles." She hasn't mentioned the bump crowning my forehead or the bruise on my chin. Clearly, she knows I was the one who tried to save her dummy self. Maybe she just doesn't want to embarrass me.

"Look, Coop, I've got a long list today. Can we get to it or what?"

I step closer to her, crossing the threshold into my own bedroom. "Sure, Al," I say. "Of course. I was thinking before we did, we just might talk for a minute."

Alix's belt is undone, but not out. The two ends hang between her thighs. "What exactly do we need to talk about?"

I want to tell her about Quinn's offer. I want to ask her what she thinks I should do. I want to tell her that last night I met myself in our home and I don't know what it means. "Brook," I say. "We should talk about Brook."

Alix backs away and lowers down onto the edge of my bed, bends over and starts loosening the laces of her long black boots. "Brook is fine. You had last Saturday and you know she's fine. Are you saying she's not fine?"

"No no," I say. I'm standing at the foot of the bed.

"Because she is," Alix says. "Brook is great."

I remember a tidbit from our last T.G.I. Friday's. "She told me there's some new instructor at dance, some guy you're not crazy about."

Alix shakes her head. "Jhondu's a New Age nutjob. Has them meditate before practice. Brook told me last night she's reading a book he gave her about being a vegan."

"A who?"

"Vegan," Alix says. "According to Trevor, it's all the rage in L.A. It's like being vegetarian but worse."

"What's eating meat got to do with dance?" I ask.

"That's my position. I don't trust anyone who won't eat a hamburger. And Brook seems kind of charmed by this whacko. But don't sweat it. I've got everything under control."

"So do I need a ticket for this thing tonight?"

From the bed, she looks at me. "You can buy one there. I didn't know you were planning on making an appearance."

"Sure. You know, for Brook. Are you going?"

"I always go, Coop. Remember?"

"Right," I say. But then I can't think of a line to keep the conversation going, so we stare at each other for a few seconds in silence. Alix tilts her wrist, eyes up her watch. Then she scoots along the mattress, reaches out and starts working my belt. She says, "C'mon, Coop."

I'm picturing the Thursday list she wrote up this morning. Beneath *Get gas* and *Buy broccoli*, did she actually write it down? *Hump Buddy.*

"I have an opportunity," I say. "With work."

Her fingers freeze. She doesn't look up. "That's great, Cooper. In what city?"

I wonder what answer she wants.

"Here," I tell her. "Right here. Quinn wants me to be champion. Can you believe it?"

Alix looks up at me and is smiling. Smiling at me for me. I had completely forgotten. "See what a little ambition and initiative will get you?"

We look at each other. Between our eyes hang lifetimes, entire planets of could-have-beens, wasn'ts, and almosts. She says, "Really, this is great news. Just terrific."

Ten seconds in the future, one of us will begin a sentence with "Do you ever wonder if," and we'll both regret it. Alix will tell me how bad Trevor really is and why she comes here some Thursdays and she'll say how much she thinks of all the good times we had together. I'm waiting for her tender words and she looks at me and says, "Let's celebrate" and yanks down my fly.

"Wait," I say. My hand touches her hand to still it. This is the first flesh-to-flesh contact between us.

"Fine," Alix says, head still down.

She releases my zipper. "Fine. Fine. Fine."

She hops down the mattress, jams her feet into her boots, then stands and snaps her white shirt from the chair. The cell phone clatters to the floor. "Just fine."

"Al. I'm sorry," I say. "I just wanted to talk to you about—"

"You want to talk?" She punches her arms into her shirt and bends for the green cell. "You got my number."

She storms through the living room and I trail her into the kitchen. She doesn't look back as she closes the door, which I expected her to slam. I stand there with my fly undone listening to my wife's boot steps clacking down my stairs, a sound that quickly gets swallowed in the *chunk-a-chunk* of the Maytag.

CHAPTER THE FIFTH

In Which Our Hero Watches from the Shadows
Before Taking Action. One of the Problems with Words.
Facts They Leave out of Textbooks. Symbolic Implications.
Insights from Lewis and Clark.

The moment I step into the basement auditorium of the Cape Fear Community Arts Center, a sense of déjà vu settles over me. Heads turn at the light that comes in through the door, so I close it quickly, slide into the darkness along the back wall. Onstage, twin girls with flowing black hair leap and spin to Aretha Franklin and Annie Lennox singing "Sisters Are Doin' It for Themselves." It's like they're swimming up there, the way they sway and slide in unison, alive and in sync. Behind them hangs a white bedsheet with a painted message: UNITED DANCERS OF WILMINGTON R-ALL-4 BATTERED WOMEN! Fifty rows of dance moms spread between me and the stage, every one with a head crowded with dreams of success for her daughter. Prom queen. Miss Wilmington. Miss America. Miss Intergalactica.

I can't shake the feeling that I've been here before.

Next to me in the shadows, standing in the back of the center aisle, is a guy bent into a video camera on a tripod. Under his breath he's singing backup for Aretha and Annie, "So we're comin' out of the kitchen, 'cause there's something we forgot to say to you!" I figure him for an assistant coach.

Somewhere in the audience are Alix and probably Trevor—I came across the Towner while I was frantically circling the parking lot looking for a spot. Almost an hour ago I showed up right on time, but at the wrong community center. Across town—at the Wilmington Arts Center—a cancer-survivor group is putting on a production of something called *Return to Oz.*

As Aretha and Annie finish up, the dancers spin off stage and everyone claps politely. Five rows down a skinny mother stands up screaming and waving her hands like she just opened the door and Ed McMahon had a mattress-sized check with her name on it. Sooner or later everybody wins. That's what these people believe. Here's one thing I'm sure of: Trust what the fine print says—making a purchase does not increase your odds of winning.

There's some trouble getting the next song cued up and in the interim I scan the crowd. I'm not really looking for Alix. And I'm also not searching for clues as to why I'm here. The Phantom Buddy that my drug-soaked mind concocted told me to attend, but that doesn't mean anything. My déjà vu won't scatter, and I'm deciding we may have brought some of the Tae-Kwon-Do for Tots kids down here to a tournament. Or maybe Alix competed here. Something.

Not everyone in the audience is a dance mom. One group off to the side seems different. Their heads aren't turning like everyone else, their bodies are perfectly still. Their faces angle down. These are residents of the domestic abuse shelter, sitting just across the aisle from the dreaming mothers.

A cymbal crashes through the speakers and the audience jumps. While the opening of "Walk Like an Egyptian" pumps out, a tribe of veiled, bare-bellied girls bounce on stage with gold anklets rattling above their naked feet. Their eye makeup is Cleopatra-black. Some have bright plastic jewels shining from their belly buttons. I can't tell if the tall one in the back is Brook or not, but from the way she's gyrating her hips I'm sure I don't want it to be.

Midway through the second verse a boy comes out, some kid dressed in a turban. He's pretending to round the women up. He seems familiar.

The tall one spins toward the front of the stage and I catch Brook's smile, confirming my fears. Her auburn hair is bundled on top of her head. I don't know when her legs got so long. She's beautiful up there, and happy it seems, twirling and grinning ear to ear surrounded by the other dancers. They're in a bubble all their own, separate from all the crap in the world, and that's worth more than I can say. I just wish they'd wear more clothes.

Suddenly the little turban kid unsheathes a scimitar from his belt and that washes my déjà vu. Five, six years ago, at the height of my career as Bull Invinso, I wrestled in this basement auditorium. Back then this place was a Moose Lodge or some Sacred Brotherhood of the Holy Elk deal. My opponent was the Arab Assassin, a guy named Eric Whatever from New Jersey. This was during Desert Storm, of course. Americans were actually patriotic for a couple months. That night we sang "The Star-Spangled Banner" together, me and the crowd, all of us gazing with hope and belief at the flag. And when the Arab Assassin came out, I thought they'd riot. They were shouting "Raghead!" and "Baby-killer!" and by the time he got to me in the ring I was ready to kill him myself. Ten minutes into the match I hit the Assassin with my signature move, the Bull from Heaven, where I climbed the turnbuckle, jumped onto a taut side rope, and sprang high into the air before crashing on my opponent. Long ago, I lost the strength or balance for such a maneuver. But that night I was in the zone, ten, twelve feet high easy. And OK I may have come down a bit hard, making Eric take most of my weight. And yes I could've pinned him then—that was the plan— but the fans wanted to see more. So I propped his limp body up on all fours, positioned his head between my knees, lifted his feet up to my shoulders, and drove his skull into the canvas, the Patriot Piledriver. He yelped like a dog and the fans roared. The ref called the match, swung his hands over his head, and stepped in between us. But I pushed him out of the way and grabbed the Assassin, body-slammed his camel-loving ass just on principle. After they carried Eric out on a stretcher, the fans rose and applauded and I stood in the middle of it all and sucked up their adoration like some kind of war hero. Looking back, I guess they may have thought the stretcher was part of the act.

As the Egyptian song comes to a close, the harem shuffles off stage and everyone starts clapping. I push away from the wall I've been leaning against and clap too, hoping perhaps that Brook might see me back here in the shadows being a good father. The camera guy in the aisle, still bent and gazing through his viewfinder, says, "Oh yeah, that was a keeper" and suddenly I have the urge to ask for ID. I mean, I'd like to know where the copies of these tapes are going exactly.

A woman in a yellow dress walks out as the lights come up a little; she's got on a thick silver necklace and her hair was done at a shop. Mrs. Somebody Rich and Important. A member of the board with Trevor. She cold-stares a few persistent clapping mothers into silence, politely thanks the dancers, and says, "For our final number tonight I'd like to introduce a very special guest who has agreed to perform for us. Rhonda came to us at Sanctuary House three months ago. After years of abusive interactions she found the strength to break the cycle of terror. Because of the generous financial support of people like you, she's proud to be on the road to reclaiming her selfhood. Ladies and gentlemen, Rhonda."

The stage lights dim and I think, *First names only*, which was always the deal at AA.

The lights come back up again on a gigantic pile of laundry center stage. A flute—a real one, not a recording—sounds a couple notes somewhere up front, and the heap shimmers. A long thin arm stretches from the clothes. The fingers unfold from the end, reaching into the air and grasping an invisible rope. Rhonda's head and chest rise from the laundry grave and suddenly she's unfurling, like a flower or something, and her body twists and she keeps rising, and somehow she's gone from being curled up on the floor to standing straight up. This Rhonda is tall, six feet and change. Stray pieces of clothing cling to her white leotard—a black sock hangs off her arm, a grimy T-shirt drapes her shoulder. Her hair is hidden, wrapped inside a kerchief as if she were doing housework in the '60s. The symbolic implications are clear.

The flute puts together a few notes, enough that I recognize "Proud Mary." But the opening is soft and slow, the way Tina and Ike did it, not CCR. It's hard not to think of the "abusive interactions" Ike shared with Tina. Sometimes when Alix and me would spar—when we'd trade choke holds and armlocks—she'd make jokes about how she'd kick my ass if we ever really went at it.

Rhonda plucks the laundry from her body and flings pieces into the audience. What could be underwear scatters a small crowd of dance moms, one of whom actually shrieks. They didn't come here expecting Rhonda.

She sweeps a pointed foot and flips the rest of the laundry off the stage, until the hardwood is bare, and as the flute gets to the faster part where the horns take over, Rhonda flutters across the floor, exploring it for the first time. Her arms trail behind her as she rushes around in circles. Even from the back row I see her smile, and it makes me smile too. Then she skitters up to the corner of the stage and everything shifts. Her legs lock at a sudden stop, and she pretends to see something, somebody. One arm flashes up to protect her face and she's backing away. But whatever she's retreating from is gaining on her, so she flips over backward, her long arms stretching out to find the floor just before her head hits. Once, twice, three times she tumbles backward heels over head, crossing the stage diagonally. Tentative applause crackle across the audience. Then Rhonda reaches down and grips the end of one foot. She lifts and eases the leg up until it's almost straight over her head. There's more clapping.

But the leg she's standing on is trembling. Even through the leotard I can see the muscle spasm. And her smile has changed. It's the cheerleader smile, the fake one the little kids wear when they want to cry and run off stage.

We're almost at the end of the song now, and Rhonda lets her leg down. She's in the far back corner of the stage, and she takes this deep Mary Lou Retton breath and three stomping steps then launches forward into the air, her hands shooting out to her sides, her legs scissoring over her head. The kerchief brushes the floor halfway through the forward flip, but her legs come down too fast, and one heel kicks the hardwood like a hammer shot. Rhonda crashes to the floor. The flute stops.

Nobody moves and nobody says anything. These moments happen in the ring, when even the fans can tell something's gone wrong. Off the stage, nobody knows what to do. Rhonda is turned away from the audience and the way her back is moving she's either breathing heavy or crying softly.

After fifteen seconds of silence, Mrs. Somebody Rich and Important appears at the edge of the stage and raises one finger. "Perhaps a brief intermission—"

But Rhonda's got other plans. Slowly, she rises and limps—literally limps—back to the far corner, ignoring the flustered master of ceremonies. "Again, Sarah," the dancer says, nodding toward the flute. This I do not believe. Pockets of women shake their heads. But Rhonda's got no time for nonbelievers, she's got a script to follow. Sarah tries a few notes from the flute, but Rhonda's not waiting. She yanks the kerchief from her head, pouring apple-red hair onto her shoulders, and her voice sounds instantly in my mind: *The one true gift flows in my veins.* This is my green-eyed prophetess, my Carolina Psychic Sidekick. Before I can process meaning, Rhonda bolts forward, launches again into the air, legs spinning, red hair tumbling. This time she lands squarely on her back. The boom rocks the room like a body slam.

People can't watch this kind of thing. A lady gets up on the stage and moves toward her, but Rhonda snaps, "Get back, Sarah. I just need a minute." This woman, she'll kill herself. But part of me, I know, admires this. I'm probably the only one in here who wants to see her get up and try again.

Everything is quiet except for some stifled weeping and then I hear from next to me, "Geez Louise, lady. Stay down." It's the video guy. He's got one eye shoved up against the viewfinder, probably zooming in.

"Turn that thing off," I say.

He pretends not to hear me.

I step in and say louder, "Hey, Jackson. Turn that thing off."

A couple people close by look at us. The cameraman straightens up and looks me over. "I'm staff," he says, puffing out his chest with a name badge clipped to the pocket of his shirt: CHAS. Chas says, "I'm doing my job." Then he bends again and sticks his face back up against the machine, recording Rhonda crippled on the floor. And I realize she's right back where she started, crumbled dead center in the middle of the stage.

I open my right hand and smack Chas in the back of the head, driving his face into the camera and spilling them both down the center aisle. From the ground he looks up at me, shocked that his name badge didn't protect him. For some reason he grabs one of the legs of the tripod. Chas's eyes get pretty big when I lift my boot up over his face, but my target shifts and I crash my heel down on the recorder, sending plastic shrapnel exploding everywhere.

I turn to the crowd, give it a hard scan. On the stage Mrs. Somebody Rich and Important holds a hand to her mouth. Rhonda stares over her shoulder, squinting into the darkness I'm on the edge of. The rest of the audience is looking my way, and I can feel the weight of Alix's eyes. I spin, hoping nobody got a good look at my face, and bolt. My open hands ram the door, my feet hit every third step going up, and the ticket geek stands up when I brush past him. Out in the parking lot I weave through the maze of cars, sliding around fenders and even across one hood, all the while imagining the perfect getaway. But just as I reach the Ford, I hear the sound of the arts center door opening behind me and hop for cover into the bed of my truck. My ass bounces on metal. Risking just my eyes, I peer out at the nine-dollar-an-hour security guard sweeping the lot with a flashlight. He's between me and the only exit. These guys are worse than the real thing, desperate to prove those police academy entrance exams all wrong by shooting some poor bastard like me in the back of the head. I feel around the bed, hoping for a tarp I can hide beneath. But there's nothing here except an empty pizza box and the tire iron.

I huddle up against the near wall and stay low, thinking about making a break for the forest beyond the perimeter of the parking lot. But then my truck would be stuck here, and they'd figure out who I was. I can already hear Dr. Collins with his same old "habitual hyper-aggressive tendency" shtick. I'd lose my Saturdays with Brook. I let one hand find metal, curl around its coolness. Then I wait.

The dome of the night sky is clear. High above I can see the blinking lights of a plane moving across the field of stars. I wonder if Dr. Winston is back with the Brain Trust, if the croissant-shaped ship has returned my friend home. I worry about Hardy too. I never called him back.

When I hear the first ignition it sounds like a chain saw, but then I recognize it for good news. Peeking again over the lip of the bed, I see people streaming slowly into the lot. The rent-a-cop closes in on them, his arms out like a shepherd's, like he's protecting them from a vicious wolf he's got cornered. But they refuse to be herded back inside, scatter instead for their cars, and he turns again to the lot. Once a few cars get moving, I'll be golden.

Headlights spin over the top of the truck as all the friendly dance moms try to kill each other to get home. It's just like the parking lot after leaving church in the old days.

A small group walks by, and I wait ten heartbeats then roll over the passenger side, away from the community center. Casually, trailing one hand along the bed, I walk around to the driver side. I keep my head down to avoid eye contact and I'm almost at the door when the flashlight shines on it. "Hold it just a minute."

The voice is twenty years old. I can picture Sparky, Model Security Guard, with one hand on the gun he's never fired at a human being. I hear him stepping closer. My hand slides from the lip of the bed down inside and finds the sure grip of the tire iron. If the kid talks again I can get a fix on his height, maybe just graze him, a love tap him across the forehead. Though tapping someone with a tire iron is a tricky proposition at best.

"Don't make any sudden movements." He is still too far back.

I crank out the appropriate line: "What's the problem, officer?"

"Turn around real slow. Show me the palms of your hands."

I lift the tire iron off the metal.

"Mr. Cooper! There you are." Alix's voice startles me.

The kid says, "Stay back, ma'am. Official community arts center business."

"And I'm glad to see you conducting yourself so well. My husband here is on the board of directors."

Over my shoulder I see the kid, five feet back, holding the flashlight and a nightstick. There's no gun. Sparky's looking at Alix and Trevor, who is wearing a tux. Trevor says, "You're doing a heck of a job tonight, son. Top-notch."

Far behind them, along the curb of the center, is a police cruiser. A real one. I set the tire iron down gently.

Sparky examines some ID Trevor is flashing from his wallet. Then he aims the flashlight in my face. "Do you know this individual?"

"He's the father of one of our dancers here tonight," Alix answers.

Trevor waves at me. "Hi, Buddy." To Sparky he says, "Buddy and I play golf twice a week. I'll vouch for his moral character but not his short game."

The kid doesn't smile, but he buys the lie. I don't like Trevor vouching for me.

Alix says, "Mr. Cooper, Brook's gathering her things and said she'll be right out. I'll tell her you're waiting."

"Just a second, ma'am. We've got a 617: Hostile Intruder, and I need—"

"You need to listen," Alix says. "This man is not your 617. He was sitting next to my husband and me when the incident took place. I suggest—"

"Now, Alix," Trevor says. "This young man's just doing his duty." He slides a gawky arm around Sparky's shoulder. "You've got quite a presence, young man, has anyone ever told you that?"

Sparky turns the flashlight from my face to Trevor's. The light shines on Trevor's bald top, crowned by that maturing blond hair.

"Strong jaw," Trevor says. "High cheekbones. Decisive eyes. Have you ever had a screen test?" His directing style must be all flattery.

"No, sir. I mean, not professionally."

Trevor magic-tricks a card from his palm, hands it to the guard, whose eyes brighten. "The thing is," Trevor says, "we're looking for some advisors and a few extras for a series pilot we're putting together, *Under the Gun*. It's a great concept—authentic re-creations of violent crimes. Very exciting. I think we could use someone with your charisma."

Trevor and Sparky wander off, and I'm left alone with Alix. I'm about to ask her if she remembers the Arab Assassin when she shakes her head and says, "Brook doesn't deserve this, Coop."

"You didn't have to leave today."

"She's got a lot invested. You need to think about your daughter's best interests."

"We could have talked it out. Isn't that what you always wanted? Me to talk about my feelings? Don't you want to know how I'm feeling now?"

She dips her head and pushes her fingers into her forehead. "I know how you're feeling, Coop. And I'm sorry for it. But those real cops are gonna come out here and start asking questions soon."

"Maybe they could arrest me for stealing my own TV."

"Hey," Alix says. "Somebody just pulled your ass from a sling."

"Right. Somebody and her husband."

She shakes her head. "Trevor's the one who saw you and came over. He did it for Brook and for me. And because he's a good man."

"A good man who doesn't know about Thursday afternoons." It's a line I instantly regret. But one of the problems with words is they can't be pulled back.

Alix is silent while a dancer and her mom walk past. The mom is gesturing with her hands. The dancer wears a Walkman. Once they're gone, Alix steps into my chest. "Cooper, there are days when I wonder why we split up. That's the honest truth. And then there are days when I wonder why we got married."

She turns and walks away. I almost yell after her *Aren't I giving Brook a ride home?* But then of course I realize that this too was just part of her lie.

When I climb the steps to my apartment, I see the TV light over in the Salvation Station. Its blue glow shines down on a handful of homeless. I pick out the doughboy form of Bacchus, and Gladstone—still wearing my baseball cap—but the others are unfamiliar. Some might be from down by the bridge. I scan the group for Dr. Winston but can't find his thick mat of hair. I'd go check in, but I'm eager to be off the streets and indoors. And I have a thirst for beer.

After I lock my door behind me, I stand in front of my open fridge. Finally I push aside the ginger ale and open a Bud Light, then head for the security of the brown couch. I hit the play button on my flashing answering machine—another call from Hardy, two more from the guy looking for Metricius. I consider turning the ringer off, not wanting to be disturbed by the outside world for a little while, but leave it on in case Alix calls. With the phone in my hand, I consider Rhonda/Tina T at Carolina Psychic Sidekicks. But there's no way she could be working tonight, not after the beating she took up on that stage.

So I open my beer and click on the TV to distract myself, flip back and forth from the *Hogan's Heroes* where Hogan finds Schultz a girlfriend to a Dirty Harry movie I have somehow never seen before. Every now and then I linger on a PBS documentary about Lewis and Clark. After the mission, after leading such a good life and being a hero to millions, Clark went crazy. Shot himself in the head because he couldn't cope with the real world. That's not the kind of fact they include in textbooks.

With each empty beer I crack a fresh one, a habit Dr. Collins calls "chain-drinking." It sounds like a magic act, like sword swallowing.

CNN is replaying highlights from a NASA press conference held this afternoon. At the bottom of the screen is a yellow box with the words *Asteroid Alert!* Four scientists sit at a table, besieged by questions from a frenzied press corps about the reports of that asteroid heading our way. While the bald one on the end sits silently, the other three scientists take turns delivering strange answers:

"It is quite likely that this body will pass us harmlessly."

"Its movement is not what we would necessarily expect. We'd expect something different."

"The object is the size of an office building. Maybe a parking garage. A small one."

"Well, the worst-case scenario would be no scenario at all. Is that clear? Tunguska would be a rain shower."

"I don't think our religious beliefs are relevant to this matter."

"Naddeo's new theory makes the Torino scale obsolete."

Finally the bald one stands up. "Listen to me. We shouldn't even be out here talking to you people. These kinds of half-truths, this pseudo-information, it can only cause widespread panic. Without further data we're guessing at what might happen. At present we are only certain of one thing: We are not completely certain of anything."

This is the moment when my phone chooses to ring, a decision which makes my heart rocket to the top of my head, clang the bell, and thump back down to its place. I scoop up the receiver, but then say nothing.

After a brief silence comes "Poppa-San?"

"Hey, Bird," I say, "it's late." I put down my beer, shut off the news conference.

"I know," she says.

I can't think of what to say.

"So like, that was you, wasn't it?" Brook asks. Would Alix want me to pretend I wasn't there? But I never lie to my daughter. "Yeah," I say. "That was me."

"I figured," she says. "You know, nobody likes that Charlie guy. He's so much a dildo."

I almost tell Brook not to use that word. But then she might ask me what it means. Instead I ask if the cameraman is OK.

"He's fine," she says. "But . . . look, he made like this big deal about the whole thing to some cops. They came into the back and asked all the dancers if we could describe the attacker."

"Attacker?" I say.

"Charlie says you had a knife. Don't worry though, I don't think anybody believes him."

"I did not have a knife," I say.

"Yeah, that's what that Rhonda lady said. She told the cops she got a good look at you from the stage, then said you were tall and skinny with long hair and a beard."

I'm silent. I go 6'1". On a good day, 280. Black hair in a crew cut since the Army. And I shave every morning. My psychic lied for me.

"Hey, Poppa-San," Brook says. "How come she said that?"

"I don't know, kiddo," I tell her. "You'd have to ask Rhonda, I guess."

"Well, I figure you're in the clear. Jhondu talked to Charlie about perpetuating negative rhooshies, so I don't think he ended up pressing charges."

I almost tell her to thank Jhondu for me, but I'm not sure what rhooshies are and I'm afraid to ask, so I say nothing. Again, it's Brook who breaks the silence. "I should go. I just wanted to make sure you were OK and everything."

"I'm fine. Just catching up on a little TV. Did you know Lewis and Clark were guided by an Indian?"

"Yeah, Dad," she says. "Sacajawea."

Our conversation sounds like something from a sitcom. There's a funny joke about that name that'll take us to the commercial.

"Dad, are you, like, sure you're alright? You sound weird."

"I'm great, Bird," I say. "But look, I have a couple projects I have to finish up tonight. Your dad loves you."

She says, "Your little girl loves you."

I wait for the click, and it comes fast.

This is the way we've always said good night on the phone, since the separation. The first night I called from the Motel 6, Brook sobbed so hard I could barely understand when she asked me when I'd be home. I started crying too and told her a week, maybe two. A hundred phone calls later, nobody's crying.

After I get a fresh beer I return to PBS and Lewis and Clark, who have just reached the Rockies. The image is a sprawling shot of the entire range, jagged peaks rising to the ceiling of the sky. As they neared the top of that first mountain, they expected to see the Pacific and began to celebrate. The explorers thought they had to cross only one mountain, but they learned their error at the summit, when they saw the awesome truth laid out before them. The narrator says, "Imagine their disappointment and terror knowing the long winter was almost upon them."

I want that phone to ring again. I'll pick it up and it'll be Rhonda calling me. She talked to some of the dancers and somebody somehow knew the secret identity of that white knight in the back of the hall. And Rhonda isn't calling to make a pass at me and we're not going to talk all night and then meet and make love and then have French toast at the start of a whole new wonderful life together. She's just calling to tell me that after I ran out of the auditorium she stood up on the stage and started applauding, and all the people stood up and started clapping too.

I hear the phone ring and snatch it up. "Hello?" I say.

But there's only the dial tone.

I'm not disappointed. I can still hear the crowd. Everybody understood why I did what I did. And Rhonda lied for me later, because she believed.

With the phone still in my hand I dial Quinn's office. His

machine answers and I hear his voice in English, then a language that sounds like Klingon. When the beep finally comes I say, "I'm doing the match. See you in the morning."

I put down the phone and click off the TV for the night. Some fresh air is what I want, so I wander out into the yellow light of my porch with what I promise myself will be my last beer. After all, I'll need to put in a full day with Hardy tomorrow. I hear noises down below, and I see more bums I don't recognize stumbling over the bricks into the Salvation Station. There are a lot of them, probably from the shelter. It's a congress of the homeless, and they're holding a service of some kind for Dr. Winston.

I face the east end of town, where Brook is reading Jhondu's book about the benefits of a meat-free diet. Trevor is down the hall brushing his teeth so when he makes love to my wife his breath will be minty. Alix is lying in bed with the script for *The Creature from Beyond Tomorrow*, calculating the physics of her next stunt. And in one of the back rooms at Sanctuary House, green-eyed Rhonda lies curled in her bed. She's running her hands slowly over the bruises on her legs, wishing the pain away, and remembering the sound of my voice and the crash of that video recorder. In her memory she peers into the darkness and tries again to see my face, and she strains to use the one true power flowing through her veins to discover the name of the man who saved her.

CHAPTER THE SIXTH

An Encounter with Potential Investors. Insights into the Master Plan. Hardy Prepares Our Hero. Our Hero Prepares Hardy.

After the rising stops, the elevator doors split onto a slim hallway. At the far end a stiff, thick man sports an extra-large tuxedo and mirrored sunglasses. His shoes reflect the shine of the lights. When I start toward him, he lifts one wrist to his mouth, and almost immediately the double doors behind him open and his clone—same size, same fashion sense—emerges. They stand side by side, legs split, arms behind their backs. Up close, I hear voices beyond the doors. The guy who came from inside the Deluxe Skybox raises one hand and says, "Pardon me, sir, this is an invitation-only affair."

"I'm with the band," I say. "Tell Quinn the main event is here."

They glance at each other, then the first one lifts his wrist again and speaks into his cuff link. For thirty seconds I stare at myself in the designer sunglasses, study the bruises from the sidewalk/pool stick combo. Tonight, I'll be glad for the mask.

Despite the Hollywood tough-guy eyewear, I get a professional vibe off these guys. They've been brought in from outside the city, probably outside the state. Under those custom-made jackets they've got holsters with loaded .38s. The safeties are off. Here's one thing I'm sure of: People only pay to protect two things—money and secrets.

A whirring sound above the door draws my attention to a flash-light-sized camera. The lens narrows on me, so I grin. Ten seconds later, one of the goons touches his ear and nods. He reaches for the doorknob and says, "Good evening, Mr. Cooper."

Inside the Deluxe Skybox, three dozen top-bracket taxpayers entertain themselves. About half of them crowd against the far wall—tilted glass that looks down on the arena where soon I'll be crowned champion. Closing the door reveals a middle-aged man with chronic acne and a pinky ring sipping a martini. "Save your time," he offers. "This party sucks."

I follow the buffet line, attracting some attention in my sweats and sneakers. A man with Middle East–olive skin and a white cowboy hat picks at a three-foot-tall shrimp tree. A woman holding a Siamese cat feeds it caviar with her fingers. Standing over what looks like sushi, a punk in a Yankees cap wears patched blue jeans, so blatantly casual he has to be the richest prick in the room.

Past the catered spread, Quinn stands by a wide-screen TV with three slender black women, each holding a glass of wine. Even though the real thing is taking place just outside, they're watching the pay-per-view simulcast. On the screen, NinJa Z is applying a submission hold on the Native American Indian Spirit Warrior. Quinn catches my eye and waves, then touches one of the women on the shoulder and whispers to her before starting my way. He cuts past two girls on a leather couch sniffing cocaine from a glass coffee table. His headset wraps over his iron black hair, freshly streaked with fake gray. In the dim lights, I can't be sure, but the patterns spiraling up his suspenders look like DNA. "What a completely unanticipated pleasure," Quinn says. "Don't you have pending concerns in the arena?"

"Where have you been all day?" I ask.

His eyes come into mine. "Say again?"

"I've been trying to find you. I've got some demands."

The woman with the Siamese looks our way, and Quinn smiles at her. "Let's dialogue constructively somewhere not in the middle of the room." He leads us to the far corner of the glass wall, where we can see the five thousand fans surrounding the ring below. On the Civic Center's billboard-sized video monitor, the Spirit Warrior folds his arms into his side and pumps them like wings. Quinn says, "Demands? Somehow I've become involved in hostage negotiations. Explain."

"I only want what I'm entitled to."

"Tonight, you're entitled to eight hundred and fifty dollars."

I look past his shoulder. The nearest group of partygoers is ten feet away. Christopher Walken stands at their center. I'm sixty percent certain of the i.d.

"Demand one," I tell Quinn. "Quit yanking my chain. These people are buyers. You're selling the Confederacy and I want a guarantee that I'll be part of the buyout package. I want assurances that—"

"Hold the phone, B. C. I'm not sure when you got this assertiveness training, but allow me to clarify our current situation. These people are my guests. Think of them as potential investors. With the expansion I've got planned, we'll need what we in the business call venture capital. I'm not confusing you yet, am I? I maxed out all my credit tonight to impress these yahoos. But when the overnight ratings come in, we'll be flooded with cash. This initiative will benefit everyone, including you. Rising waters lift all boats."

I don't know whether to believe him or not, but he sounds pretty convincing. I turn to the ring, where NinJa Z is now riding on the back of the Spirit Warrior, on all fours pawing the canvas. Barney the referee has had it, and waves his hands over his head, ending the match. The bell rings. Booing rolls from the audience, especially from the pockets of Dark Disciples. The Spirit Warrior, dazed, is helped to his feet and staggers from the ring. NinJa Z grabs a mike and announces, "The man will never let a brother have power. He's afraid of my skills and what I might do. And he should be!" With that, he leaps down next to the operations table, spikes a smoke bomb, and disappears through a trapdoor.

"Hardy told me you promised him he'd be champion again," I tell Quinn. This happened this afternoon, when we were rearranging tonight's match.

Quinn holds a finger up, then says into the microphone suspended before his mouth, "Negative. Standby." When he comes back to me, he smiles and says, "H. A. required some incentive. You've seen him. Losing doesn't come naturally to him like it does for you. How's he doing, by the way?"

I tell Quinn that Hardy's fine. I left him down in the locker room, getting ready for his ritual prematch shower. "You didn't need to lie to him," I say. "I don't like being part of a lie."

"Yeah, but you'll do it for eight hundred and fifty bucks."

I wish I were the kind of man who wouldn't.

"Relax. I was telling Appleseed the total truth. Tonight he falls victim to dark forces, outraging the faithful. Which is why, next week, when he breaks Snake's spell live at the beach, the ratings will exceed all projections. Think of it like New Coke. People want the same old thing. Once Hardy's his old self, I assure you we'll arrange a good shit-kicking for you. Then everything will be just like you want it again. You really think I don't have a master plan?"

"You could've just come clean with me up front."

"Life's a PR game, B. C. It's all information management, image control. I contain leaks. I release misinformation. Now I don't tell you how to lose; you don't tell me how to run the business. Watch and learn." With this, he taps his headset and says, "Victor. Let's roll the interview segment now. Prompt J. F. to lead in."

Quinn looks over the arena. The giant video screen shows huge action photos of Cro-Magnum Man and the Mad Maestro, the next wrestlers. But in a flash they disappear, and there I am, standing across from Hardy with Big John Franko between us. My blue-masked face is twelve feet tall.

"Now then," Quinn says. "As long as you're up here, let's exploit the opportunity. Amplify your enthusiasm. These three are live ones."

I follow him back to the wide-screen TV, where the trio of black women still stand, now watching the interview.

"You missed it," one says. "That ninja got disqualified for using mind control."

"There's the story of life," Quinn says. "Never trust a ninja. Ladies, I wanted to introduce you to one of our living legends, Buddy Cooper. Buddy, meet the three Graces: Charlotte, Charlene, and Chantrelle."

In unison, they raise their wine to me. Charlotte says, "So you're a wrestler."

"That's what I put on my income tax form."

"See for yourself," Quinn says, lifting his artificially tanned face to the TV.

We all turn to the wide screen, where Big John stuffs the mike in my blue mask and says, "Terror, as a relative unknown, do you really think you have a legitimate chance of besting the All-American Dream?"

"Dreams are great for kiddies!" I shout. "For punks who still want Mommy reading them bedtime stories. Yeah, Big John, I may be unknown, but that's what makes me dangerous." Here, I jab a finger into Hardy's thick chest. "Ask yourself, Hayseed: How can you hope to defeat something you can't understand?"

"Nice line," Charlene says approvingly. Quinn grins.

Hardy's concentrating so hard on his lines that he looks intense. This afternoon, it took us ten takes just to get this usable stuff. He says, "I know you talk an awful lot and don't say nothing worth hearing."

Charlotte nods. "He's got the hick thing nailed."

Charlene asks me if the mask itches when I wear it. I shake my head. Clearly, she's checking out my wounds.

Big John turns to Hardy. "Mr. Appleseed, are you aware of the allegations that Snake Handler has bribed you to alter the outcome of tonight's match?"

"I don't like allegations. Who said that?"

"Sources close to SWC."

"Sticks and stones can break my bones," Hardy recites. "But words can only hurt me."

"How about these words," I shout on the screen. "Punk! Pretender! Fake!"

"I'll shut you up good tonight," Hardy promises, "or my name's not Appleseed. And my name is Appleseed."

The interview stops after that last bit of improv, and we cut back to Big John Franko, live at the operations table ringside. All around him are digital displays and control panels. The technician to his right is wearing a headset just like Quinn's. Big John says, "That championship bout coming up shortly, fans. But now an update on the Spirit Warrior. He's receiving the best medical treatment available and is apparently no longer under the impression that he is a chicken."

"I thought he was a horse," Chantrelle says.

"A horse with wings?" Charlotte snipes.

"Ladies, let's not quibble," Quinn says. "You'll have to excuse Buddy. He needs to expedite."

Charlene dips her chin and smiles. "Certainly a pleasure, Mr. Cooper. Any predictions before your match?"

"Absolutely," I say. "Expect the unexpected." This line takes me completely by surprise.

On the TV, Cro-Magnum Man enters the arena. He looks like a cross between Rambo and Fred Flintstone, wearing camouflage pants and a furry vest that according to Big John Franko came "from the very last saber-tooth tiger." Strapped across his back is an AK-47. One hand shakes a caveman club at the crowd, the other trails behind him, gripping a headful of tangled blond hair. The cavewoman, dressed in a prehistoric two-piece, doesn't protest as she's dragged down the aisle, perhaps because she's lying on a skateboard. She chews on a piece of raw meat and snarls at the audience.

The Grace sisters nod approvingly, calculating dividends. Something about Cro-Magnum's hand in that woman's hair disturbs me.

Downstairs, when I push through the locker-room door, Hardy's still showering. Steam billows out of the showers like smoke from a burning building. He endures these long, stinging showers just before every match, claiming it helps him get focused. Sounds like something a crazy high school football coach beat into his soft brain.

NinJa Z and the Spirit Warrior are peeling off their sweaty costumes. "Good crowd, Pops," NinJa tells me. "Try not to disappoint them." The Spirit Warrior gives me the peace sign.

Behind them, a small TV hangs in the corner. Cro-Magnum Man bashes the canvas with his caveman club. "Cro-Mag smash funny Music Man. Crush! Stomp! Kill!" The cavewoman stands on the ring apron, pretending to pick bugs from her hair and eat them.

I open my locker and see the blue, body-length latex suit hanging there. The mask droops from a separate hook. I lift a roll of white tape off the top shelf.

From the shower, I think I hear weeping above the rush of water, but I can't be sure. It could just be me. The Spirit Warrior and NinJa Z don't seem to notice. Hardy did OK this morning while we reworked our match. But in between practice bouts his prayers got longer and longer.

At one point he asked me if I ever felt bad about losing on purpose.

"No, Hardy," I told him. "Losing's just a different way to win."

I strip to my jock and start taping my ankles, turning to watch the TV. They pulled out all the stops for this Civic Center. There's talk of Wilmington attracting a WNBA expansion franchise, maybe a semi-pro ice hockey team. We're a growing community with bold plans for the new millennium.

On the simulcast, the Mad Maestro strolls into the ring, strutting in his neon purple tails, swooshing the air with his baton, pretending to conduct his theme song, "Ride of the Valkyrie." The cavewoman lobs a handful of uncooked meat at him. Since Snake manages the Maestro, typically he'd be out there now, working the Disciples into a frenzy. But tonight, we're saving Snake.

I wrap white tape around my wrists, tight enough to make the skin go a bit purple. I have no idea what purpose this serves, I only know that I've always done it. When I finish I open and close my fist and see the blood rising around the tape. The bell rings and the new match gets under way.

The Spirit Warrior and NinJa Z enter the shower, and Hardy emerges from the steam naked and frightening. His shoulders mountain up to his neck, thick as an oak stump. Even in my prime back in the Army I never had a body like Hardy's. He nods at me. "Howdy, Mr. Cooper." I get the feeling he was hoping I wouldn't come back.

But seeing Hardy calms me. I feel more centered. He and I, we have a script to follow. Between us, we have a clear understanding about the future.

"Howdy, Hardy," I say. "What's the mission status?"

He turns and looks at me, lifts his chin.

More loudly, I repeat myself, "What's the mission status?"

He gives me a wobbly thumbs-up. "We have a go code." Still naked, he digs through the pants in his locker and fishes out his Miracle Ear, works it into place.

On the closed circuit, the Maestro has Cro-Magnum up against the ropes. He doubles him over with a knee to the gut, then executes the Thunder Symphony, a series of rapid elbow blows to the back of Cro-Mag's skull. The caveman goes down.

"How's your face feeling?" Hardy asks.

"I'm fine, pal," I say.

"I'll try not to whack it too much."

Hardy shines a towel across his back, then bunches it up and rubs his armpits, his crotch. I wrap both my knees with Ace bandages while he slides on his jock, then his red, white, and blue shorts, pulls on his white pro boots and the red cape he'll wear into the ring. The fans roar and we turn to the set, standing side by side.

"T-minus fifteen minutes," I tell Hardy, who now looks a bit like Captain America really. Nervously, he smiles.

I'm glad that it's me Hardy is going to lose to. I'll be gentle about it. Help him along like a father helping his son.

Handing Hardy an Ace bandage, I ask him to do my shoulder. He's wrapped it before and does a better job than the hack trainer that Quinn hired.

I sit on the bench facing the TV and Hardy starts his wrap job. Under one armpit, up over the far shoulder, looping across my chest and under the arm again.

From the top rope, Cro-Mag attempts a move Big John calls a Jurassic Bomb, plummeting knees first toward Maestro on the mat. But Maestro rolls left, and Cro-Mag's knees crack canvas. The cavewoman covers her eyes and howls at ringside.

Pulling the Ace tight on one shoulder, Hardy says, "Mr. Cooper, sir, do you ever get scared?"

"How do you mean, Hardy?"

"Like a little kid scared. Like being afraid of thunder or what's under the bed, that kind of scared."

"I hated the dark when I was little," I tell him. "Couldn't stand going into my room at night without my mom or dad."

"My dad brought me out in his boat," Hardy says. "I cried and cried 'cause I was so afraid of the ocean. I could hardly swim. But my dad taught me how, and then I took to swimming real good."

Maestro has scrambled up and rolled Cro-Mag onto his stomach for a submission hold. He's kneeling on his spine, one hand cupping his chin, the other grabbing a knee. He pulls them together. The Beethoven Backbreaker. Snake's Dark Disciples scream, "Bravo!"

Hardy's hands have stopped. "Do you ever get scared like that still?"

I think this over before answering. "I suppose so, Hardy. Everybody does." He is silent behind me, so I prompt him, "Are you scared now, Hardy?"

"No, sir. It's just I had a funny dream last night. That's all. Kind of woke me up."

"Do you want to tell me about it?" This is the line Alix would use with Brook when she crawled beneath our sheets crying.

Hardy takes a deep breath. "It was a terrible dream. I was in the ring and snakes were coming out from underneath it like that was their home down there. And when I tried to run, the floor was all covered with them sliming around. Like in the movie when Han Solo has a whip and is going after the Ark of the Covenant."

"That's a good one," I say. Hardy's hands tremble as he unrolls the wrap across my chest. On the screen above us the Mad Maestro twists Cro-Magnum's arms around the top rope. While Barney the ref is distracted by the crowd, Maestro grabs the caveman's club from the corner and begins beating Cro-Mag in the gut. The cavewoman tugs her hair in protest.

Hardy finishes the wrap job, pats my back. I roll my shoulder twice to test it. "That's a good job, Hardy."

"Thank you, sir," he says. "We learnt about the Ark of the Covenant back in Sunday school. It ain't the same as Noah's ark."

"Is that a fact?"

"Yes, sir. The little Ark is more important on account of it's like a box. And in the box is, you know what?"

Brook and I have watched *Raiders of the Lost Ark* three times, but I shake my head so Hardy will go on. He says, "The Ten Commandments that God gave to Moses."

His eyes brighten with belief. "Now all among the Israelites did witness the thunderings, the lightning flashes, the sound of the trumpet, and the mountain smoking; and when the people saw him and that he held before him the truth of God, they trembled and stood afar off."

He waits for me to say something. "Well, I guess people are like that."

"One time Moses turned his staff into a snake, but it was a good one. It didn't bite nobody."

I get up, step to my locker. I lift out the familiar blue suit and say, "I remember hearing about that, Hardy."

"Most snakes are bad, you know?"

"I know, Hardy. I know."

I step into the skin of the Unknown Kentucky Terror. The body-suit covers me, stretching from my ankles to my wrists. It zips up the back and I have to ask Hardy for help.

On the simulcast Maestro flattens Cro-Magnum on the mat. The cavewoman leaps onto his back and claws at his face, but he doesn't let up. Barney slaps the canvas three times, and it's over. Cro-Magnum hops up and wails, "Bad Music Man cheat Cro-Mag. Cro-Mag mad. Mad!" He threatens to go for the AK-47, but calmer heads prevail.

From behind me, Hardy tugs the zipper snug up by my neck. When it's tight, his fingers stay where they are. Then one hand settles on my shoulder. I turn.

"Mr. Cooper, sir," he says. "I got a awful bad feeling about tonight." His eyes are red and puffy.

I reach up, cup one hand over his on my shoulder and pat it. "Hardy," I say. "Everything's gonna be just fine. We'll do it just like we practiced and everything will be fine. You'll see."

I feel bad for the kid. I'm trying to comfort him. This is, after all, his first time.

Still, if he thinks he's going to change the plan at this point, he's completely out-of-his-mind bonkers. I am committed to this course of action now, and I mean to see it through. Tomorrow, I will show the championship belt to Alix.

Hardy sniffles. I look away so he won't be embarrassed, and my eyes roll back to the screen, where the victor is being interviewed. "Mr. Maestro," Big John Franko asks, "shouldn't your use of the club have disqualified you?"

Maestro smooths his handlebar mustache and works his British accent. "Are you suggesting that I needed to resort to unsporting tactics to conquer such a troglodyte buffoon? Snake constantly reminds me what simpletons you Americans are, and I fear he is not exaggerating. What comfort it must give you to see me as plainly bad and see others as plainly good. But all childish comforts end."

There's a pause. Hardy tenses. Maestro looks directly into the camera. "On one point I can enlighten you—sometimes good apples turn rotten. Especially when big checks get written." Looping his hand through the air, he makes an S with his baton. This brings howls of delight from the Dark Disciples, and boos of disbelief from the good people, who also let loose a barrage of crushed Coke cups. "Mark my words," Maestro says as he strokes his baton. "Hardy Appleseed is soon to sing a new tune."

Big John nods at the ringside operations table and "Ride of the Valkyrie" again blasts over the loudspeakers. Maestro storms off through the crowd. As he passes, scattered Dark Disciples shout "Bravo! Bravo! Encore!"

Hardy can't even watch. He's turned his back on the Maestro and me. "Mr. Cooper, sir," Hardy whispers, "I need you to pray with me."

I haven't prayed since Brook was admitted to New Hanover, when the doctors couldn't explain. And even then I did more threatening than anything else. But Hardy is close to bailing out. I don't want to lose him now.

"Of course I'll pray with you, Hardy."

He turns and we genuflect together, each with a knee down, and Hardy takes one of my hands in his and says, "Oh Lord God, please watch over your servants tonight. I do not understand why you want me to get beat but it is not my station to question your divine wisdom. If it be your will, let this cup passeth over me. But if not, I will accepteth it. Even though I do not understand how this can be part of your mysterious plan, like Abraham I will obey."

Hardy pauses and I get the feeling I'm supposed to interject something of my own. So I say, "Please Lord, don't let either of us get hurt tonight." For good measure, to reassure the kid, I throw in, "Let me learn like Hardy to accept the wisdom in your plan."

Hardy smiles and says, "We humbly ask these things in the name of Jesus Christ. Amen."

"Amen," I say.

We stand up. The door kicks open and some staffer steps through. "Showtime, gentlemen."

I turn to Hardy. He seems content. But I feel guilty for saying what I did, for pretending to believe in his prayer. "Hardy," I say, "are we doing God's work tonight? Is that why you're doing this?"

He smiles. "Everything that happens is part of God's plan, Mr. Cooper. And besides, Mr. Quinn told me a secret." He looks around the empty room, then leans in close and whispers, "He told me a angel came and visited him and told him everything was alright."

I nod.

Beaming, Hardy says, "This plan is a angel's plan. It's all God's idea."

With that the doors crash open and the Maestro and Cro-Magnum barge through. The caveman drags his AK-47 in one hand, his club in the other. As he passes, he grunts, "Cro-Mag need Tylenol with codeine. Double recommended dosage."

Hardy studies my expression and asks, "Don't you think God's got a plan?"

"Sure I do, Hardy. Absolutely. Of course he does."

"If he don't," Hardy says, "what would be the point?"

"That's right, Hardy. But he does have a plan." I push my face into the blue mask of the Terror and tuck it tight, ready for the arena.

"I mean, if he didn't, that'd just be, well horrible," Hardy says. "That'd just be awful terrible."

CHAPTER THE SEVENTH

Featuring the Terror vs. the Dream,
Metal vs. Flesh, and Maybe Some Glossolalia.

The slow opening of "Dueling Banjos" brings boos from the crowd, and a strange fear settles in me: When I step into the arena, I'll find Alix and Brook leading the jeers. To escape this vision, I yank back the black curtain and storm into the aisle just ahead of schedule, before the fans have a chance to come to full boil. The moment they see me, misguided kids lean over the rails and throw their hands out for high fives. I slap them away and charge toward the ring. "Out of the way, little pukes!" I shout. "You can't make friends with the unknown." Someone shakes a cardboard sign in my path that reads APPLESEED IS AWESOME! so I snatch it away and rip it in half, frisbee the pieces over their screaming heads. This is the kind of thing I'm supposed to do, but I'll admit that tonight, I find it more satisfying. When I reach the ring, I take two big steps to the apron, then duck between the ropes. Barney the ref nods hello and says under his breath, "Welcome to the nuthouse."

I shake both fists to show how upset I am by the fans' unfriendly reception. I face the camera platform, mounted ten rows back, and yell, "Boo all you want to, if it'll make you feel better about your crappy lives. Just don't forget tomorrow it's back to work. Say it with me: Do you want fries with that, sir?"

A Dark Disciple in the front row, one of many with their faces painted white, raises a finger and carves an S in the air, planting Snake Handler's sigil on me. "You must submit to the will of the master!" he shouts.

"Yeah sure," I holler back. "And you must be home by ten or Daddy's gonna ground you."

Above the camera, in the Deluxe Skybox window high above, three tall dark figures look down on me. I spin and face the crowd behind me, where we've stacked plenty of folks with signs for the camera's benefit. I WANT HARDY'S SEED one reads. Another claims A GOOD MAN TO FIND IS HARDY! I grab my masked head, showing how these messages enrage me, and turn into the ropes to my right. Before me, three college boys are passed out in the aisle, empty plastic cups piled at their feet. I point and shout, "Hayseed's family made it in from the countryside. Too much moonshine." Sitting close by, a man wears an oxygen mask, one hand resting on the nozzle of a green tank on wheels at his side. His free hand raises slowly and he unfolds a shriveled middle finger. Arena-wide laughter erupts. Above him, the giant video screen shows a sideways view of his obscene gesture. Next, something hard cracks my back. I turn just in time to see the barrage of two dozen apples raining down on me like artillery. I cover my face. They crash into my arms, splatter against my legs, and the crowd roars. Once the volley has subsided, I scan the canvas, pick up half an apple, and yell into the crowd, "This is the crap you want to believe in?" I climb the turnbuckle and offer the apple over my head. "This the dream you want?" With this, I take a huge bite from it, chew fast and then spit, showering the first couple rows with my apple cud.

I freeze though when I realize who I've just spit on. A freckled teenage girl, not much older than Brook, sits crooked in a wheelchair. Rhinestones spell out M-A-R-N-A across her shirt. Black straps crisscross her legs. Her arms twist in on themselves and end in clenched hands. Her eyes roll and she smiles absently. Bits of chewed apple hang in her curly black hair.

Though I know it would be horribly out of character, I'm about to climb out of the ring to clean her off when Big John Franko's voice booms through the loudspeakers. "Ladies and gentlemen, would you please rise?" I glance over and see him nod at the techie, who reaches over a field of controls and snaps a switch. Immediately, Kate Smith belts out, "Oh say can you see?" and everyone goes nuts, leaping to their feet and snatching off their hats—not out of respect for our fine and noble country but because this music means Hardy Appleseed is coming to town. Even the wheelchair girl cranes her head, and I look over the crowd, to see what she cannot. With his red cape flapping behind him like Old Glory herself, Hardy strides down the aisle, slapping high fives left and right. Two young Disciples—dressed in black, faces painted white—jump the railing and lob rubber snakes at Hardy, who bats them away frantically. The fans think his fear is part of the act.

A gray-haired lady charges forward with a sign that reads KISS ME—I'M ALL-AMERICAN. Hardy wraps his arms around her and plants one on her cheek. A grandma kiss. The investors have got to be drooling. An innocence like Hardy's can't be faked. He's the absolute real thing.

As he nears ringside, fans stretch their hands to touch the SWC Victory Belt circling his waist. In the middle of the dinner plate–sized gold buckle, two Greek Olympians grapple. Wrestling is the world's oldest profession, despite what the hookers and the pimps would like to believe. When he reaches the ring, Hardy skips the steps, leaping instead straight up onto the apron. He grips the upper rope with two hands, leans back, and vaults over the top. His feet land with a thud that shakes the canvas. Our eyes meet for a second and I try to send him a telepathic smile. Hardy spins his cape off, then unhooks the Victory Belt and loops it over the post behind his turnbuckle. Facing the fans on the camera side of the arena, Hardy stands at strict attention and snaps the sharp salute that I helped him perfect. Thousands snap back. Then he heel-spins to the Skybox and does the same thing, though now I am behind him, mocking his salute with a sloppy one of my own. Hardy ignores me. And the fans don't care about me either. From north, south, east, and west, Hardy's followers fire back their responses. When he turns, I see his grin, wide and pure. For the moment, he's forgotten that tonight he's not walking away a winner.

The bell sounds twice, the call for us to settle into our corners. I lean back into my turnbuckle. Big John Franko enters the ring with a mike, stands centered in the cone of light, and begins. "Wrestling fans, our main event for the evening. A no-time-limit match for the Heavyweight Category Class AAA Southeastern Wrestling Confederacy Championship." Mild applause. No one really expects a change.

Big John points at me. "First the challenger, a man who defies introduction. He must keep his face covered whenever in public as part of a confidential agreement with the governor of Kentucky. From the wild hills of the Southland, I give you—the Unknown Kentucky Terror!"

Boos. I scoop up apple guts from the canvas and heave a handful into the crowd.

Big John turns away from me. "And in this corner, the undefeated, undisputed champion of the SWC, the Cream of the Crop, the All-American Dream, Hardy Appleseed!"

His fans go berserk. Five, six thousand hopping on their feet like Winnebago winners on *The Price Is Right*. Even Marna pumps her crooked hands as the chanting begins, "Apple-seed! Apple-seed! Apple-seed!" I slam my feet into the canvas and cover my ears, infuriated by their adoration for my opponent. Eight rows back a group of girls, maybe eighteen years old, wear white T-shirts that together spell out H-A-R-D-Y. They bounce and jiggle like the ones at the Stones concerts used to before stripping off their tops.

I turn to Hardy, who has stepped to center ring with his sculpted arms outstretched, bathing in the hero worship. It's not like with most winners in this league though, because Hardy's eyes glow with love for these people. He reads the signs that say WE LOVE YOU, HARDY!, sees the Magic Marker hearts, and he believes them. The fans pick up on that I think, and this feeds their faith in him. And together they all live in this magic little bubble that's got nothing to do with reality. I know about bubbles like that.

Big John Franko returns to the operations table and the techie with the headset hands him a note. I wonder if it's from Quinn. Hardy returns to his corner, kneels down to say a quick prayer. Out of respect, the rumbling auditorium falls almost silent. A handful of Snake's Dark Disciples hiss. Hardy's prayer is more than an act, but for Pete's sake—we prayed ten minutes ago. How good does the guy have to be? Even worse, I know in my heart Hardy's probably asking God to guide and protect us both.

The bell clangs once, and before Hardy can get up or face me, I bolt across the ring and drive a knee into the back of his head. He slumps forward into the ropes, groping at them and barely staggering to his feet. From behind Hardy, I wrap my arms around his waist and lift him, hoisting his body up and over, tumbling us backward. His shoulders hit first and make a good strong whack on the mat, but I let him go and we roll apart.

We get to our feet and Hardy smiles. That was my best suplex in three years. And he's wondering if I didn't go a bit heavy on the knee smash. I did. Can you see it in my eyes, Hardy? Tonight I'm taking it all back.

We circle now and just as planned I come in high and Hardy goes low, scooping his arms around my midsection and bear-hugging me off the ground. Hardy's not even squeezing, but I twitch like a cockroach. My double karate chop into Hardy's neck would make Alix proud. He drops me, grabbing his neck with those huge paws and doubling over.

While Hardy is momentarily stunned by my expert kung fu, I bounce into the ropes, recoil, and rocket at him, launching one boot up into his midsection. But Hardy catches it on cue. He straightens with my foot wrapped in his hands. I hop on one leg, trying to keep my balance. Hardy can do anything to me from here; I'm helpless. As part of the act I start shaking my hands, pretending to be all afraid at what Hardy might do to me. I lock my fingers together in mock prayer, begging for mercy, and I say under my breath, "C'mon, Hardy. Just like we practiced."

Without his Miracle Ear in, I know Hardy can't hear my low voice, but I give him hard eye contact and he understands just fine.

Hardy nods his head and gingerly sets my foot down, even bending over slightly to do it. This shows what an all-around swell guy he truly is. Some fans clap at this display of good sportsmanship. But as soon as that foot is down I plant it and kick hard with the other, clipping Hardy just below the chin. His head snaps back, no act here, and he collapses. I leap in the air, both legs rising out in front of me, aiming an elbow at Hardy's stomach as I fall. But just before impact Hardy rolls out of the way and my elbow drives into canvas. I sit up and grab the elbow, which burns with real, honest-to-God pain. Hardy spins behind me, kneels pressing into my back.

His arms loop around my neck and head in a sleeper hold. Barney the ref immediately slides out in front of me to see if I'm still conscious. With his mouth right next to my ear, tucked in tight where no fan could see him speak, Hardy says, "Mr. Cooper, sir, you're doing awful good tonight."

He is completely sincere. I don't get angry.

Hardy releases the sleeper and stands me up. I'm doing the groggy thing in the middle of the ring, barely able to stand up straight. Hardy takes two ropes to pick up speed and clotheslines me, forearms my neck so hard it spins my feet over my head. My skull smacks the mat. Hardy steps to the near corner, climbs up and mounts the turnbuckle with his back to me. The fans scream. They anticipate the Flying American, Hardy's signature move, a variation on the Bull of Heaven that we developed together. From five feet up, still facing the crowd, Hardy crouches, rides down and up with the bounce of the ropes, springs high into the air as he back-flips in a beautiful arch aimed at me. His body comes around and his chest crashes dead center on mine. Even with Hardy throwing his hands out to absorb some of the weight, this maneuver knocks the wind clean out of me. Barney the ref spins around on the mat, raising one hand to begin the three count. He slaps the mat once.

On cue, the lights in the arena drop and we are cast into total darkness—midnight black. Hardy makes a little noise like a kid who wants to pull the covers over his head. He's remembered the script. In his good ear, I whisper, "Here we go, big guy. What's the mission status?"

There's no answer.

From the operations table, I hear a series of clicks. The strobe lights ignite, pulsing white and altering the perception of time, stealing every other second. Over the loudspeakers comes, "Do you senssse my presenccce, oh sweet children of darknesss?" From the flashing arena come a few tentative boos, but they are swallowed by the rumble of applause and excited screams.

Quinn's plants start chanting "Fix! Fix! Fix!"

"Hardy," I whisper. "I need a mission status. I need the go code."

I can hear him breathing above me. His weight is crushing me.

From the darkness at ringside somebody shouts, "Appleseed's a cheat!"

"We have come for the sssoul of He-who-walksss-with-the-sun."

I punch the sunwalker in the ribs. "Give me the damn go code, Hardy."

"Fix! Fix! It's rigged!!"

"Co gode," Hardy says. "Yessir. Co gode."

A spotlight opens on one of the arena doorways. Hardy and I both turn our heads to see Snake Handler in the steady circle of light, Lucifer draped around his neck. With his scarecrow frame, it always surprises me that he can support her. As always, Snake's dressed all in black—black pants, black shirt, black tie, black jacket. The white face paint is broken by his black goatee and shiny black lipstick. Lifting his skull-capped cane in the air, he draws an S with the tip, and every one of the Dark Disciples responds with the same sign. He starts slinking down the aisle, one bony hand on the cane and the other gently holding Lucifer's pale ivory head. He pokes her face at fans who come too close.

"No nakes," Hardy says. "I told Mr. Quinn no nakes."

We may have to skip a few pages in the script. Appleseed is not going to make it.

As Snake approaches ringside more switches snap at the operations table. The strobes cut off and a red-tinged light shines over us in the ring. It's like we're in a heat lamp, a crimson cone.

The fans remain in the dark.

Snake clacks up the steps with his cane and stands outside the ropes. With his withered hand, he casts an evil gesture toward Hardy, still draped across my chest, and says, "You will sssubmit to my will." Snake is miked, so his voice echoes through the arena. Most fans boo. But I hear clapping too. Quite a bit. More than just the Disciples could muster. Maybe Quinn is right about what these people want.

Hardy lumbers off me and stands frozen. I gulp air. Hardy's staring at Lucifer, six feet away on Snake's shoulders. He shouts "No away."

His fans cheer. They heard "No way."

I get to my feet and work my way into the corner in front of Hardy, climb the ropes so now I'm the one standing on top of the turnbuckle. I've skipped ahead to our finishing move. The plan now is I slam Hardy from up here, flatten him out. Barney slaps the mat three times. End of story.

Snake unwraps Lucifer from his neck and sets her down on the apron, despite Barney's vehement protests. "Sssay hello," Snake tells Hardy, "to your new massster." The albino python's pink eyes shine.

Half the crowd begins chanting "Apple-seed! Apple-seed!" and half start chopping out "Snake-Snake-Snake!" Hardy might hear this, he might not. He certainly has no idea that I'm about to level him. His eyes are stuck on Lucifer, coiling on the canvas. Part of me is sorry I have to catch the big guy by surprise, but part of me is thinking I'm fifteen seconds away from my championship. I leap in the air, angling my body sideways so I'll slam Hardy chest on chest, all 280 of me knocking him on his All-American ass. But when I hit Hardy nothing happens. Time freezes. He doesn't fall and I don't drop.

The son of a bitch caught me. This is not at all in the script. Stupid big dumb bastard.

I squirm to free myself, but Hardy's too strong. Barney asks, "You OK, kid?" but Hardy doesn't answer. One hand gripping a leg and one on my throat, Hardy hoists me over his head. He squeezes my windpipe.

"Look out, Cooper!" a female voice from the audience yells. Not Brook. Not Alix.

"No more kidding around," Barney says to Hardy. "Put him down!"

"Sssubmit!" Snake commands.

"Nilla sha ulla kuku!" Hardy shouts beneath me, and with a heave I'm weightless, tumbling backward through the air. I sail over the top rope and slam into Snake and we both crash off the apron, down onto the operations table of Big John Franko. The table snaps in two and the black boxes of equipment collapse on top of us. A circuit board gets dumped on my lap and wires spill out. There are sparks and smoke and suddenly the strobe lights come on again. It's like a disco in here, but the red heat lamp light stays on. Disco Inferno. Big John and the techie are up and staring down at us. Snake is beneath me. His thin arms are still and there's something dark all over his forehead that I'm taking for blood. The fans applaud, most rising to their feet.

"Get up, Cooper!" the female voice yells. I kick free of the equipment and get to my feet, face the crowd and stare into the disco strobes. There. A dozen rows back. Red hair and waving. It's Rhonda, my beautiful wounded psychic dancer, come to see me crowned champion.

Snake moans behind me, so I reach in and pull him free of the wreck, but we hit something that again starts up "The Star-Spangled Banner." For the second time in ten minutes, Kate Smith asks, "Oh say can you see?" and the audience explodes with more applause. My mind flashes to Quinn, who's right now no doubt lying through his teeth to the investors, pretending this is all part of his master plan. Here and there I hear Quinn's plants still stupidly yelling "Fix! Fix! Fix!"

I step around to the edge of the ring, peek into the strobing red light just in time to see Hardy backhand Barney, knocking him unconscious to the canvas in front of Lucifer, whose tongue flicks the red air. Hardy looms over both of them like Frankenstein's monster. In a photo shot of strobe, I see Hardy's stoned expression. He's gone.

The fans chant "Apple-seed! Apple-seed!"

Kate sings, *at the twi-light's last glea-ming!*

I look behind me, thinking of Rhonda, vaguely recalling her prophecy. I scoot under the bottom rope, back into the ring, and my hands ache for the sure grip of the tire iron.

I circle around Hardy, who doesn't much seem to notice me. He's watching Lucifer wrap herself around Barney's chest. I'm six feet from the Dream when I shout, "Hardy! Everything's OK. Why don't we sit down for a minute?"

He stares straight through me, then looks back at Lucifer and points. "Nalla sha ulla?"

I had to try.

And the rock-et's red glare . . .

Behind Hardy, I reach over his turnbuckle for the SWC Supreme Victory Belt. I'm afraid for a second that I won't be able to lift it, like all those sad knights trying to free the sword in the stone. But it rises easily in my hand and I know it's mine. I hold it and feel its weight, a good twenty pounds of solid metal. It'll do.

Kate works toward the finale like only she can. *Oh say does that star-spangled ba-a-nner yet wa-ave?* and I cock the belt back like a Louisville slugger and through the red strobes I fix my eyes on the base of Hardy's skull.

For the la-a-nd of the freeee, and the hooome

I go.

of the—

I brain Hardy. A home run shot to center. Nobody hears the last word.

Appleseed drops like an oak, falling onto Barney and Lucifer.

Now the wrestlers—NinJa Z, Mad Maestro, the Spirit Warrior, even Cro-Magnum Man, stream down the aisle. They've raced up from the locker rooms to save the day. But everything's under control now. The day has been saved. By me. I'm the hero. And Rhonda witnessed my victory. A whole new life is—

"Ouchie!" Hardy shouts from below. He springs up in front of me and yanks the Victory Belt from my hands. In one strobe flash I see him lift it and in the next black blink something collides with the side of my face and I'm down hard, my head dizzy and light. The edges of my vision go dark and the canvas rolls beneath me. A few feet away, Hardy kneels beside Barney, like he's going to pray again. Lucifer's white coils now swallow Barney's chest, her head resting on the mat. The red strobes make it like watching a cartoon with missing frames. One frame Hardy holds the belt over his head with two hands. In the next it's sunk in Lucifer's skull. Something wet hits my face. My fingers have gone numb. Hardy pumps the belt now, smashing the snake's skull into mush frame by frame. And all the while he's explaining, "Nabble. Nabble. Nabble."

"Lucy!" comes from the side. Snake's head pokes over the apron. His goatee soaked in blood. White face paint smeared with black lipstick. "You son of a bitch!" he shouts at Hardy, then rolls up into the ring. His voice is no longer transmitting to the arena speakers— his mike must be busted. I'm the only one who hears Snake now.

The pool of Lucifer's blood puddles on my hands and is sticky. The wrestlers have reached ringside, but none of them know what to do.

Standing over his decapitated pet, Snake shouts down at Hardy, "You'll pay for this. You hear me, you miserable fuck?" I'm finding it hard to stay awake. Hardy may have given me a concussion.

Snake's eyes shift up to behind Hardy. He shouts, "And who the fuck are you?" Then there's one loud *pop* and a red splash explodes from Snake's leg.

An adrenaline burst sends me sprawling for the nearest cover, which happens to be Barney the ref. Groggy, I crouch behind his limp body, wrapped in dead Lucifer. A few feet away Snake lies slumped in the corner, shiny blood oozing from his thigh. Screaming fans stampede for the exits in the strobing light, sweeping the wrestlers away. Hardy hasn't moved and is still kneeling just on the other side of Barney. But he's in the open. In a red snap of light I see past Hardy, to the far apron, where a dark figure holds a gun. "Snake Handler," he says. "You have failed our unholy master." The youthful voice doesn't go with the large body, and the next strobe shows his face to be bright and boyish. Our attacker is a man-child. The teen is dressed in a preacher suit, tie and all, very proper, but he's sporting long rebel hair that looks gray in the red strobes. "Lucifer demands retribution for this desecration of his earthly host." The gun flashes again and Snake's body jerks with the impact.

I see the new wound on Snake's chest, but then the thumping in my head diminishes, and time itself slows, almost stops, and I understand. I feel remarkably alert, enlightened. I was a fool for thinking that things could change. That I could be part of a plan that worked. This will be much better. This feels so much more right. Even better than SWC Champion. The absolute best kind of hero. Blaze of glory. Alix weeping at my grave. Brook crying at school as she reads her essay about her daddy. Rhonda remembering my last brave act as I defied destiny. My notion sweeps away the last of the grogginess, and I stand up and step over Barney, passing Hardy, heading right for the kid.

"Infidel!" he shouts and fires—sledgehammer shot shocks my shoulder and spins my feet into the air. Above me the red hot sun. A pile of coals burns my arm. My heartbeat pounds behind my eyes. The man-child assassin leans over the ropes and his long gray hair drapes his face. Looking down at me, he aims the gun so I'm staring into the barrel. Behind it, his eyes are vacant.

"Nabble! Nabble!" comes from my other side. Dear sweet Hardy stands in the pulsing red light, one hand up like a crossing guard stopping traffic. In the other he holds out the bloodied Victory Belt like some kind of badge.

The kid shifts his aim to Hardy. "Fools!" he shouts. "How can you defeat that which you don't understand?" But Hardy's simply not in right now. He takes a slow, deliberate step and the kid pulls the trigger. I wince at the report but nothing happens to Hardy. He's not hit. Behind him Barney's body spasms. Hardy takes another slow step and the man-child fires again. A spark flashes off the Victory Belt, spinning it from Hardy's hands, but he keeps coming. "In the name of Lucifer!" the kid shouts and fires again as Hardy steps over my body. Still nothing. Now Hardy stands at point-blank range. I close my eyes, plant my face into the canvas. Another shot cracks loud and sharp. But when I look up, Hardy's still standing there. He grabs the kid by the jacket collar and yanks him clean over the top rope, then starts shaking him like a rag doll. "Nabble," he explains. "Nabble, nabble."

The gun drops free and I reach for it. My hand likes the weight.

Hardy hoists the kid up over his head and slams him down onto the mat. The heaviness has returned to my head, and my vision is now nothing more than a long tunnel with a tiny bit of light at the end. So it takes everything I've got, but I drag myself on top of the man-child. I push the muzzle up under his smooth chin, cock the hammer. He is defenseless. Our eyes come together and he says, "This is but a mortal vessel. Destroying it will not stop me."

I say, "Like I give a shit," and pull the trigger. The hammer clicks. Cock pull click. Cock pull click. Cock pull click. The gun is empty. Typical. How else could my story go?

With that the real lights come up. On cue. Bright white everywhere that hurts my eyes. Beneath me the boy—whose hair really is gray—begins laughing. I wish for the energy to beat him with the gun, but even my head feels too heavy to lift. Down the long tunnel of my vision, I see Marna just outside the ring. She smiles at me, waves with a perfectly healthy hand. Behind her, a few fans peek out over the chairs they were using for cover. Dr. Winston, returned by benevolent aliens, sits grinning with Rhonda. And behind them, Alix and Brook. Even Dr. Collins has come. All my great friends and loved ones assembled. Their smiling faces blur and the arena spins into blackness and from above me I hear Hardy say quite clearly, "Mr. Cooper, sir? It looks like somebody shot you."

CHAPTER THE EIGHTH

The Power of Subliminal Suggestion. Presuming the Unknown Hostile. Altering the Power Dynamic. Looking at Amnesia the Wrong Way. Plus, Our Hero Faces the Scrutiny of Squirrels.

I wake alone into darkness, on my back in either a small cave or a big coffin. My head's under heavy gravity, twice its size and full of crushed rocks. During the course of what could be a minute or an hour, my vision focuses on something above me; over my body hang two red stars, tiny bright blurs that shimmer with heat. I blink and squint hard, sharpen the hazy blurs into what they really are: eyes. Red eyes watching me in silence. They shine with an anger I know. Just beneath them, what could be a metallic kind of gray smile. Waking up was clearly a bad idea, but I can't go back to sleep now.

A yellowish burning glows behind me, barely enough to register as light. It's so faint I can't make out the face or the body that the red eyes belong to. They stare through me, gaze as hard as Uncle Sam in that I WANT YOU! poster I fell for in the Army recruiting office. And the impression I'm getting is that the message of these eyes is pretty much the same. Seems I'm always wanted, just never in the right sense.

These eyes aren't making any moves, so I pull a quick recon. For all I know, I could be surrounded. I'm in a bed with metal guardrails, hospital stiff sheets. My entire left arm is encased in some kind of sling Velcroed to my body. My forearm crosses my stomach, and when I try to move it, pain bites my shoulder. Dipping my chin, I see a white square taped high on my chest, stretched over the shoulder. A tube runs from my right arm up to a hanging IV. This arm, I note, is not handcuffed or strapped to the bed frame. If I'm at New Hanover at least I'm not on seven.

I look up again and it's no real surprise that the demon eyes have vanished. I scan the black air hanging over my bed but it's empty. I decide they were some remnant of a nightmare that didn't want to die. I file the demon eyes away and return to the situation at hand. Something's on my face, and my free fingers find soft gauze covering my head like a burn victim's. I must look like the Invisible Man. Through cutout holes I touch my eyebrows, feel my lips. No scarring. I try to recall a fire but it's hard to concentrate. I don't think there was a fire. The central image I'm getting is an oversized boy in a preacher suit aiming a gun at me.

I try to lean up, thinking about getting a look at my chart down at the foot of the bed. But the effort of lifting my head exhausts me. Besides, they probably only do that on *M*A*S*H*. As my eyes adjust to the lack of light, I can make out the outline of a chair to my right. Beyond that is what might be a window with the shades pulled shut. The edges of the room still hide in shadow.

Suddenly the air conditioner hums on. Cool air shivers down from vents in the ceiling. But with the coolness comes a sound over me, a twinkling of light, and the sensation of movement. Something is up there. When under surveillance by an unknown entity, standard procedure is to presume the unknown hostile. I try again to rise but can't. My bandaged head anchored in the pillow, I look straight over the bed, and the goddamn red eyes have returned.

"Just who the hell are you?" My voice sounds whiskeyed. The eyes make no response.

"What do you want with me?"

The eyes bob. Could be nodding.

"Can you understand me?"

The eyes rise and fall slowly. A definite yes.

"Have you come for me?"

Rise and fall. Barely noticeable. Somber. Stern. Like my visitor expects me to be upset. Part of me wants to ask "Who sent you?" but I'm probably better off not knowing.

The eyes hover closer now, descending, just on the edge of the thin yellow glow around me. I wait for them. My whole life will flash before me any second now, and I want to be ready. After four years of rewinding the episodes myself, I'll be interested in seeing the edited highlights. But when I close my eyes all I picture is Brook dancing, her toes aimed down into hard wood, her arms perfectly arched over her smiling face.

A soft touch settles on my stomach, and when I look the red eyes are right there in front of me. Only now I can see the round edges of the shiny, one-dimensional face, which indeed has not only a gigantic smile but a purple nose and a message printed along the bottom: QUIT CLOWNIN' AROUND! GET WELL SOON!

The crinkly clown balloon hovers lightly on my chest, and I capture it inside my right arm. I tug on its string, causing a bouncing bubble sound behind me. I peer up over my forehead, where maybe two dozen balloons watch over me like guardian angels. Similar sounds call my eyes down to the end of the bed and there are little sparkles of light there too, and it's like somebody wanted to see if they could make my bed float. Who the hell would buy me balloons? Using the string, I pull down one bunch, fumble one-handed for a card that I can't at all read in the half light. I release the healthy balloons, let them rise back to the end of their leash. The Evil Clown, low on helium, stays with me, and here we sit, two has-beens. Could-have-beens. Should-have-beens. Might-have-beens. Weren'ts.

If I'm not officially dead I'd like to know how close I am, so I reach off the side of the bed, my hand groping for the *Jeopardy*-style button used to summon nurses. Up on seven I had to yell for one to come in and scratch my nose once. God, I was about to go crazy. Finally I find the nurse alert, but when I thumb the ignition a TV hung in the corner sparks to life, damn near scares the shit out of me. Still, my eyes are drawn to the gray picture coming into focus; a man in a sports jacket holds things up to the camera. Along the edges of the screen run a series of boxes loaded with numbers. It's QVC.

Desperately I click the button to change the channel, but nothing happens. No matter how hard I pound on the remote, the screen remains unchanged. All I need is for one of those *Star Trek* specials to come on with Sulu or Scotty. They sell those plates.

QVC drains the soul, and as such is one of the things it is very important to avoid late at night when you're tired or weak. Like the *Christ Is King Redeemer Global Satellite Crusade*, a channel I simply erased from my menu. Such things may seem silly and harmless at first, but late at night, when your mind is thin and vulnerable, they start to make sense. And suddenly you can't help wondering about the possibility of being reborn, or it seems obvious that a clock that makes different birdcalls to welcome every hour really might lift your spirits. At three, four o'clock in the morning, QVC preaches wind chimes and Rollerblades. The forever-smiling man's enthusiasm for better living through EZ Pay never fades.

Some sound mumbles beneath my pillow, and when I reach back I find a wire attached to an earplug, which is spitting out the rapid-fire spiel. Picturing Hardy and his Miracle Ear, I jam the plug in and face the screen, where the forever-smiling man has begun hawking a series of limited edition Beanie Babies. "Now you all know the story behind Nip the Cat. The day after he was retired an entire shipment was destroyed in a mysterious warehouse fire in Newark. This had a profound influence on the global Beanie Baby economy. If you find Nip anywhere for less than a hundred dollars, I suggest you buy him. Immediately. But I'm selling this little cutie for only sixty-nine dollars. I know it's crazy. They may lock me up. Don't ask me how Harvey got his hands on these for this price. It may not even be legal."

Off camera, someone forces a laugh.

Nip the Cat looks like three dirty socks stapled together. I literally cannot tell his head from his ass.

"Now if you're smart, you won't just buy one. You'll think about your future and invest today. The Beanie Baby market is running, folks. According to what our experts tell us, Beanie Baby prices are rising at a rate superior to NASDAQ and the S&P 500. So you can stake your retirement on precious metals if you really want to. Just don't forget what happened to the tin market in the seventies. Think about your future."

The camera zooms in for a closeup of Nip the Cat, and beneath his saggy body a counter starts spinning off quantity sold. In less than a minute the counter rattles past one hundred. I've watched these counters before and I used to find myself wondering who the hell else was awake at four in the morning. But little by little I came to envision a whole nation of half-drunks and insomniacs, single moms with kids who won't sleep and divorced salesmen wide awake on the edge of motel beds, all of us bathed in the blue light that binds us together. Now from my hospital bed, I imagine the Brain Trust in their collapsed sanctuary, enjoying a hundred channels, and again I hope that Winston has returned.

"Please make your calls now, as we'll need to switch to a new item in just a minute," the forever-smiling man says from off camera. But then his voice changes. "This next one's a real treat. Oh yeah." The tone sounds oddly familiar. "A one-of-a-kind special we won't be able to offer ever again: *the future of Buddy Cooper*."

The camera pulls back and I'm on TV. Only it's the younger version of me. I'm in a sports jacket and I'm standing behind Nip the Cat.

"People, think this over," the TV Buddy says. He grabs Nip, shakes him like a wet dishrag. "I mean geesh. These are beanbags. Total material cost might be twelve cents."

I find myself hugging the clown-face balloon, which looks at me and smiles again, GET WELL SOON!

"Crazy what people get excited about, isn't it?" he asks.

I nod. "What are you doing on QVC?"

"Things have gotten a bit more complicated since we parted ways," the TV me says. "So I figured I'd better check in with you."

I look up at the joy juice in the IV, but the TV me says, "C'mon, Buddy, let's not play that game again. Don't insult me by thinking I'm drug induced."

"A man can hope, can't he?"

He sighs, plops Nip back on the stand. "Here's the breakdown: I'm here to help you out of the jam you're in. I am absolutely your best friend in the whole entire world. And I'm not in the mood for attitude."

My head's starting to feel heavy again, soggy almost. I think to myself, *Why did it have to be QVC?* and even though I don't say it out loud, my younger self on the screen smiles instantly. "You're the only one who's actually seeing me right now. Well, you and a handful of the gifted who just happened to be tuned in. Some tall glass of redhead recognizes me—she's cute. Tell me, do you own many Beanie Babies?"

"Rhonda's watching? Was she at the match?"

"If you do, I'd unload them. In a couple days a first-grader in Paducah is going to rip one open and choke to death on the beans during her little brother's baptism. Poor kid goes down right on the altar. And worse, the whole thing gets caught on video. The bottom's going to fall out of the market. Death does that."

Suddenly the Beanie Baby counter stops cold, frozen at 252 sold. "Oops," TV Buddy says. "You forget the power of subliminal suggestion. Anyway, we've got important matters to discuss. So what's your next move?"

"Move?" I ask.

"Yeah. We need to get a game plan together. A mission profile."

I struggle for a reason not to answer him and can't think of any. "Well," I finally say, "first off I'd like to talk to a doctor about my condition, I guess."

"You're going to be fine. Hardy brained you pretty good with that belt, but that thick nugget's been concussed before. As for being shot, the left wing will be bitch sore for a while. Snake and Barney are worse off. Especially the ref. He caught a stray bullet. And then of course, there's the kid."

A flush of blame rises in my face. "I figure I'm in all kinds of shit from what I tried to do. Is he alright?"

"Oh sure. He's fine. Up on seven actually and doing quite well."

My eyes flash to my wrists, which are still not strapped to anything. But the thought occurs to me that I should probably be in handcuffs. If the cops saw what I tried to do. They could be waiting outside the room for all I know. Being charged with attempted homicide will almost certainly muck up my visitation rights with Brook.

TV Buddy knows my thoughts. He reaches off screen like Bugs Bunny and pulls back a copy of the *Wilmington Star-News*, the front page. The headline reads, "Champion and Masked Wrestler Stop Maniac, Save Crowd."

TV Buddy rattles the paper around and clears his throat. "When the gunman began shooting indiscriminately into the helpless audience, which included women and children, Mr. Appleseed and the as-yet-unidentified masked wrestler teamed up to thwart the deadly youth. Regrettably, Paul 'Snake Handler' Hillwigger and Barney Henderson were seriously wounded in the fighting. The would-be assassin is undergoing psychiatric evaluation as he recuperates but remains closely guarded by police."

"But that's not the way it happened," I say. "That's not the truth."

"It is now. The story's been printed."

I wonder how the story came out with that kind of spin, and TV Buddy says, "That Quinn—give him lemons and he makes lemonade, huh? Still, it's a good thing that kid only brought a six-shooter or you'd have ventilated his skull for sure."

"I'm sorry about that. Listen, you understand that I didn't start off with the intention of actually hurting—"

"I know who you were actually intending to hurt, Buddy, but

confession's a whole different division. That kind of thing concerns the past, an important realm for you to consider. As for me, I'm here to talk market future."

With that he tosses Nip the Cat and reaches off camera again. This time his hand comes back with a Beanie Baby Unknown Kentucky Terror. It's got a little blue suit on and a blue mask and everything. TV Buddy grins my grin and says, "Our market research shows real potential for this model. Though of course, new versions automatically come with a certain risk."

I don't like the way that sounds. "What do you want from me?" I ask him.

"What do you want for yourself?"

My body feels suddenly weary. I aim the remote at the TV and try the off button.

"Cut that shit out!" he snaps. "This is serious. Now what do you want for yourself?"

I close my eyes. Breathe slowly and calmly. "I just want to get out of this mess. I want my life to be like it was a week ago."

"A week? Buddy, you forget who you're talking to. I was here when we wore the golden boots, when total victory wasn't an *if* but a *when*."

Maybe it's the weight of this craziness or the joy juice in the IV, but I feel like I'm about to slide into a coma. Everything's moving slow and heavy. I mumble, "So why don't you tell me what I want if you're such a fortune-teller?"

"Geesh. You're getting hostile again and I'm just trying to help you out. All I'm saying is this: You're clearly in the middle of something here—I mean, you'll agree with me that this certainly qualifies as a situation, right? Now getting completely out of it might not be too hard. But then where would you be? Back on the brown couch at three a.m.? I know what you want, Buddy, and I'm here to tell you: All the scripts are shot to hell now. It's time to take control and improvise."

Take control of what? I'm confused and drowsy. And I'm slightly hurt by the fact that according to the counter on the screen, not a single Unknown Kentucky Terror has sold. My Evil Clown balloon has lost almost all its air.

The room darkens.

"Don't try the frontal assault here. Trust me. Covert action has never been more called for. And Buddy, keep your head down. We're in this thing together."

The screen seems to be growing fuzzy. The voice plugged in my ear is fading away. "I'll try to rendezvous with you somewhere down the line but I can't guarantee anything." The last words I hear him say are, "And one more thing, about that carrot top Rhonda . . ." but then my head goes light and I'm out cold.

Some time later (an hour? a day?) I awaken to squeaking sneakers in the hallway, the predawn shuffle of hospitals. The second sensation I am aware of is my bladder, full and impatient. With my attention focused on that zone, I also realize I've been cathetered. I have tape in places no man would want to find adhesives. Groggy, I find the nurse's call button and consider sending up a flare, getting detached from the plumbing and inquiring about my official prognosis. I'd like to know who's been running what tests. But I hold off, caught by the strange suspicion that information is the key to my dilemma; something about all this seems horribly wrong, phony. Right now the only edge I've got is that everybody figures me for Captain Vegetable. So I decide to follow TV Buddy's advice, stay covert until I gather some reliable intelligence. Having formed a tentative action plan, I release a stream of urine, though it's hard to overcome the sense that I'm wetting the bed. Also, it is unsettling that I cannot shake.

After all the excitement, I spend time watching the sun slowly color the thin curtains. With the gradual illumination, my surroundings come into focus. Just past the foot of the bed, a wall of flowers blooms—a whole garden of reds, yellows, and greens.

Brook is the only person who ever gave me flowers, and it's been years, literally. Recalling the balloons, I reach behind me and tug down a bunch. I split a tiny card and read, "We love you, Terror. We're all praying for you."

Two cushioned chairs—one green, one pink—sit next to the bed. My shoulder feels cold. The gauze is stained with dark matter leaking from my wound. Beneath the bandages encircling my head, my cheeks tingle.

Footsteps at my door cue me to close my eyes. They move to one of the chairs, and its wooden legs scrape along the floor and then there is quiet breathing and the rattle of what sounds like cheap jewelry. The whispering that comes is so low it barely even sounds like breath is escaping. I take the chance and crack open one eye. It's a woman—her head bowed, her eager fingers working a rosary. She is dressed in black, but wears no habit. This woman is clearly a nun of some kind, though why she is here I haven't a clue. Imagine her surprise and joy if I came out right now. If I were to sit bolt upright and scream, "I see the light!" I could make her whole life make sense.

I settle back into the darkness, tiring again, and consider silently saying the rosary with Sister X. Ten Hail Marys, an Our Father, ten Hail Marys. Or is it the other way around? My weary mind falls to old habits, boyhood ways, and I end up praying the way my father taught me when I went to bed at night. Thank you for Brook. Thank you for the doctors. Thank you for Hardy. Please help Snake. Please help Barney. Please help Dr. Winston. Please help Rhonda. When I get to Alix, I'm not sure what to say—thank you or please, so I just stay quiet and settle into the dark listening to the whispering nun.

My next awakening is quick and sharp, snapping me from a dream in which everyone I knew was a Beanie Baby. A voice, in the dream at first, but then here in the real world, speaks. "Smile, B. C."

My eyes almost open at the shock, but Quinn's the last one I want to know the score. The way he played Hardy off me, telling him we were part of a divine plan. And then there's the newspaper deal. Leave it to Quinn to score PR points from a shooting. Those investors are either drooling with envy over Quinn's scavenger skills or they're offended by the actions of a sick brain. I'd hope for offended, but my money's on drooling.

Quinn's steps circle the bed. There's a *chik-chik. Whir. Chik-chik.*

A man's voice from the hallway says, "Sir? Could I ask what exactly you're doing?"

"My standing policy is to always invite open dialogue. Feel free to make any constructive suggestions." *Chik-chik. Whir. Chik-chik.* It's a camera.

"Please, sir, if you'd just explain what exactly you're doing. I don't want to have to contact security."

"No one wants to contact security, son. It alters the power dynamic in frightening and unpredictable ways." *Chik-chik.*

"Sir?"

The clicking stops. "I have a significant financial investment in this patient's well-being. Furthermore, I write checks to his insurance company, which writes checks for this hospital, which writes checks to you so you can write checks to your landlady. So the moral of the story is: Piss off."

The man huffs once, says, "Asshole," and leaves.

There are more camera snaps and clicks. I can hear Quinn breathing and imagine him beaming that perfect smile from that always tanned face. Whatever his purpose is for pictures of the Broken Buddy, all I can do is lie here and listen to him go through half a roll before new footsteps enter the scene. The door closes. The three of us are alone.

"Lowell, this is my job, and my job is important—to me and to my family."

"Can you pull those curtains open a little, J. K.?" Quinn asks. "Some heavenly light falling behind him will really create a nice effect."

"Lowell, I'm dying here. An intern tells me somebody's taking pictures and I figure it's the damn cops. My irritable bowel's a total mess. It's burning my insides." A shooshing sound brings a brighter glow through my eyelids.

Chik-chik. "You've got access to medication. I have complete faith in your abilities. What I need now is an accurate assessment of the current situation. You said he would regain consciousness by morning. It's after lunch, and this is not conscious."

"After this deal we're even, OK, Quinn? No more Exit 351's."

They are on either side of me, and their silence hangs over my bed. Finally, it's Quinn who speaks. "Let's discuss the future of our relationship as we walk. I need to secure some shots of Snake, and you can play doctor. Proceed."

As they step into the hallway I hear the doctor say, "Lowell, this is my job, and my job is important—to me and to my family." Clearly, he prepared this line in advance and hoped it would have a significant impact.

After they're gone, I roll around the idea of what Quinn's got going on with this doctor. My list includes: drug trafficking, under-age abortions, the black market sale of babies, and plastic surgery on individuals needing deep cover. This last thought makes me reach for the gauze wrapped around my face, and I wonder why my skin tingles and what's waiting beneath these bandages.

With the curtains open, I can see the tree outside my window. The June air sends its leaves waving and twisting, and I wish I could be at Wrightsville Beach or Greenfield Lake, feel a breeze on my stale skin. Squirrels tightrope by on a telephone wire, and after a while I get the feeling it's not many squirrels but just one, getting offstage of the window frame and then turning around again. Just as this idea occurs to me the squirrel pauses. He stares at me, as if studying my mind, a notion I don't care for at all.

But I'm distracted from these important considerations by the familiar piano music that floats in from the hallway. Somebody in the room next to mine, or maybe somebody at the nurses' station, has the TV tuned in to *Waves Will Crash*. Once the action starts, I can recognize the voices but not what they're saying. As I strain to make sense of the dialogue, I'm dying to grab that remote and get the TV running. I'm somehow convinced that this might be the episode Lauren finally remembers if Stack or Longley is the father of the child in her womb. For her sake, I hope it's Stack. Back before she had amnesia, Lauren believed Longley only hit her because she deserved it but it's really because he's a sick bastard who needs to be pistol-whipped. I close my eyes and focus on tuning in the words more clearly but it's no use. I feel myself sliding back into sleep and I start inventing my own version of the story, making Lauren strong and confident, putting a butcher knife in her hand one night after Longley comes home from the bar and hits her, after he passes out in his favorite chair.

I don't remember falling asleep, but when I come to, Alix is holding my hand. Don't ask me how I know it's her, I simply do. She has it lifted just slightly, and her hand rests beneath it. Almost like I am holding hers. That's what she used to like. She didn't just want to have our hands together. She wanted me to grip hers, like she was always afraid I might let go. Thinking of the apple perfume she used to wear, I inhale, but I only get a lungful of hospital anti-septic. I wonder how long she's been here. When she talked to the doctor, how did she introduce herself? "Please, doctor, you have to tell me, I'm his—"

It's hard not to squeeze Alix's hand when I've wanted to for so long. Hard to just lie here like a dead fish. But I always hate the movies when they zoom in on the patient's hand, held loosely by the caring blond nurse or the son named Billy, and the patient twitches a bit then gently folds his fingers around the loved one's hand. I want my return to be original. Any second now Alix will bend over and whisper into my ear, "Coop, I don't know if you can hear this or not, but don't leave me. Hang on. We need you." And I'll open my eyes and blink back tears and whisper, "I'll never leave you."

I know that's been done before too, but I like the way it plays.

I hear pages being turned and become aware of weight against my leg. Alix is reading something heavy and hard. She must have a Bible propped open on the bed. She's come to pray over me, upset because of the way our last meeting went in the parking lot the night of the dance benefit. She can't stand the notion of that being our final scene together. When she heard I was hurt she must have been terrified that she'd lose me before she had a chance to set things right between us. She slides her hand out from under mine and the weight on my leg disappears. The cushions of her chair squeak and sigh. Right now, she's begging God not to take me away, searching the scripture for the words that will help her through this dark period. This could be a real opportunity for me. If she begins to read something out loud, I could take advantage of that. Or maybe she'll say something like, "Oh Lord, please give me a sign."

If she asks for a sign of any kind I am definitely taking it as a cue for decisive action.

Another set of footsteps enter. "Ally, has Lowell stopped in? He never showed up in the cafeteria." This is the voice of Trevor, the man who married my wife.

Alix says, "Haven't seen him. How's Snake?"

Trevor says, "Fine. A little confused, kind of giddy really. The thing is, he just keeps yapping about some crazy dream he had."

"Yeah. They've got him on Vicodin. Stuff can make you loopy."

"Bottom line is he signed. Very exciting. So we'll be good to go once, uh . . . How's Buddy?"

"No change," Alix says. "Do you trust Karmichael? He seems nervous for a doctor."

"Everybody's nervous, Ally, just not everybody hides it."

Trevor is screwing up the works. How can Alix concentrate on spiritual matters with his interruption?

Alix asks, "What's an eight-letter word for a character's new understanding? Starts with E-P."

The shock opens my eyes but I lock them down again quick. In the flash though I see the title of the book Alix is holding: *1,001 Hol-*

— 115 —

lywood Crosswords. It's one of the phone book–sized jobs like the one she worked start to finish during Brook's hospital stay.

"I don't know," Trevor says. "Epidemic?"

"How is that a new understanding?"

She's doing crossword puzzles.

Trevor says, "Check the back for the answers."

"C'mon. Starts with an E-P. I had *epilogue* but that's not right. I know this word."

"Epidermis?" comes from the hallway. It's that doctor coming back.

Quinn is with him. He says to Trevor, "T. W.? Is my Palm Pilot wrong or did we have a meet in the cafeteria?"

"You were late," Trevor says. "I came up here to find you."

"Episode?" prompts the doctor.

"Eight letters," Alix snaps.

Quinn insists he wasn't late. Trevor tells him it doesn't matter, then delivers the good news. "Snake gave up his Herbie Hancock. Didn't even read the small print."

Quinn says, "Spectacular. Did you hear Hardy won't leave his bedside? Slept on the floor last night. They told me that when Snake woke up Hardy cried. I'd give stock options for video of that. Think there's any chance we could get Hardy to do it again for us?"

"In my business," Trevor says, "anything's possible."

"Excellent," Quinn says, and for a second I think that's his guess for Alix's crossword.

"Everything's set then. All our ducks are in a row except . . ."

In the long silence that follows I feel the stares falling on my gauzed-over face. Trevor. Alix. Quinn. The doctor. I'm a piece of somebody else's plan.

Trevor breaks the quiet. "I hate to be the one to suggest this, but our hot window is closing. At what point do we suggest casting an extra?"

Trevor wants to replace me. I'm about to be cut out of whatever puzzle is coming together. He adds, "After all, he was wearing a mask. How about it?"

"Epidural?" the doctor offers.

"Epiphany," comes from under my pillow. The TV earplug. "The answer is *epiphany*."

It's the voice of the TV Buddy, whispering a word I immediately recall from that legend class at NC State. And I think of the headline Buddy showed me, how somehow the official story is that I'm a hero.

More piano music from the hallway, the closing-credits theme of *Waves Will Crash*. I picture poor lost Lauren and remember thinking that she was looking at amnesia the wrong way, that I'd pay cash to have the last four years of my life burned from my brain.

Cradling this thought, I take a deep breath, and open my eyes.

Alix shouts, "Cooper!" and squeezes my hand. But she doesn't hug me. Not with Trevor looming above her.

Quinn quickdraws his NASA headset cell phone from a pocket and unfolds it onto his head as he steps into the hallway. Over his shoulder he hollers, "Welcome back, B. C."

Dr. Karmichael, a little overweight and wearing glasses, shoves through to my bedside. He aims a penlight in my eyes and blasts them, then asks how I feel.

"I'm hungry," I say. Which is the truth. None of them suspect.

He smiles. "The hunger's a very good sign."

I say, "Thanks. Could I ask where exactly I am?"

Alix pats my hand. "You're in New Hanover, Coop."

I look at all their happy faces and the perfect line comes to me: "Is Brook alright?"

Alix considers my question, then says, "Sure. Brook's fine."

"The seizures stopped?"

The doctor asks, "Who's Brook?"

Trevor laughs nervously, scratches at the blond hair along the side of his balding head.

Alix's eyes come into mine. She understands something is

wrong. I feel caught up in something, like we're performing a play. The balloons floating over my bed, the flowers along the wall, all these are props arranged by stagehands.

"Cooper, you know what the doctors figured out. You know Brook was OK all along."

I look her straight in the eye. "Why'd you cut off all your hair?"

The doctor asks, "What's the last thing you remember?"

"A wrestling match," I say. "Were you there?"

"Me?" the doctor says. "No."

Everybody exchanges looks. Hard looks. When their eyes come back to me, it's my cue to ask sincerely, "Who are all you people?"

Alix says calmly, "Buddy. You know me."

"Of course I do, Al." Grins all around. "You're my wife."

This is where the camera would zoom in on my innocent face, then cut to Alix's shocked expression before fading to a commercial. But here in the real world, her face freezes, then drops down into her open hands. I say, "Aren't you?"

I have to say these things. I am committed to this plan of action.

Trevor calls into the hallway, "Lowell. Lowell! You'll want to hear this."

Dr. Karmichael summons his professional smile, digs a pinky into his ear.

Quinn walks back in and closes the door, cutting off the last of the soap opera theme music. Trevor whispers the news of my amnesia to Quinn, who thumbs his suspenders and says, "Unexpected developments. New stratagems are required."

Alix begins weeping. I feel filthy. I feel great.

The doctor brings his cheeky face in close. "Can you tell me your name?"

I think hard, scrunching my forehead. "Buddy Cooper."

"Who's president?"

Intentionally, I rub my chin. Actually, the gauze covering my chin. "Gerald Ford? No. George Bush." Quinn winces, shakes his head.

Trevor's hands settle on Alix's shoulders. He says, "Ally, we should let Dr. Karmichael do his work."

"I'm not leaving," Alix says.

Dr. Karmichael asks me if I know what state we're in.

"Yes," I say, and they all smile again, hopeful. Until I say what I must. "Kentucky. We are in Kentucky."

"Oh God," Alix says. "Please tell me he did not just say that."

"That's where you pretended to be from," Quinn explains. "When you wrestled. You were the Unknown Kentucky Terror."

"Terror?" I say. "No. That's not right. I'm Bull Invinso, the Invincible Man. I'm certain of that much. That, and this is my wife. Those are the two things I'm absolutely sure of. Al, why are you crying? Everything's going to be alright. I'm back now."

Quinn's headset starts beeping but he doesn't reach up to click in. Dr. Karmichael looks down at his shoes. Trevor pulls out a white handkerchief and offers it to Alix, who lets it hang in the air. From their faces I can read the horrible truth, and it settles on me like a nightmare—they believe me.

CHAPTER THE NINTH

A Standard Interrogation. The Significance of Twizzlers.
Unreliable Testimony. The Search for Truth.

Breakfast brings bad food and news of impending planetary doom. I lift the plastic lid to reveal an unmarked purple carton, a hard puck of meat, untoasted white bread with charred stripes, and steamy scrambled eggs. On TV, CNN's *Asteroid Alert* reports that the asteroid's size has been upgraded from a parking garage to a professional football stadium. Its trajectory and speed are erratic, behavior that causes one scientist to express "deepening concern." An expert with a French accent thinks the asteroid will likely strike the moon, scattering lunar matter into the earth's atmosphere. Another argues its mere proximity to our planet will affect the tides. She predicts coastal flooding. Shifts in global weather patterns. The realigning of tectonic plates.

Yesterday, after everybody was cleared out, Dr. Karmichael returned alone and briefed me on my condition. Apparently I've been out for a couple days as a result of severe blunt force trauma to the head. Hardy's Victory Belt blow is also being blamed for what Karmichael is vaguely calling "some type of mental displacement." As for my body, the bullet clipped my collarbone, ripped a chunk from my deltoid on its way out. The arm needs to be in the Velcro "immobilizer" for a week or so, and I should expect throbbing pain, followed by thumping, perhaps thudding. At present, the wound is giving off the smell of milk past its prime, something that does little for my breakfast enthusiasm.

When I asked why my face was wrapped up, he avoided eye contact and explained that he was concerned about an infection spreading from a wound on my chin. He hadn't wanted to risk what he termed "an outbreak," he said, so he had treated my skin with light rays and administered a heavy dosage of antibiotics. Sensing my suspicion, he told me I needed to get some rest, and left me alone. Thanks in large part to the drugs, I slept most of the night.

I'm watching TV now, not to stay on top of the developing threat to the planet, but in hopes of catching another look at a segment CNN put in rotation early this morning concerning the "Wrestling Riot" in North Carolina. In exclusive footage—who knows what Quinn charged for that—the gray-haired man-child stands on the ring apron in the strobing red light. He raises his arm and there is a white burst from his hand. Snake crumbles. Then the view rolls and for fifteen seconds we see flashes of the girders that line the ceiling of the Civic Center. The audio consists of screaming fans, more gunshots. Apparently, all the cameramen abandoned their posts when the shooting started. There is no evidence of what happened after that.

I stick with CNN long enough to view the segment three times, but finally I grow weary of news. I spend the next couple hours fading in and out of a *Columbo* marathon on A&E. It's always been my favorite mystery show because they always tell you the murderer right away. Just after Peter Falk locks up Johnny Cash, Alix appears in my doorway. My wife is holding a pack of Twizzlers, this the only vending machine selection I ever made during the long days and nights we spent here keeping vigil over Brook before we learned the truth. In silence, my wife approaches me cautiously and offers me the candy, beginning the ritual we developed. Still without speaking, I accept the package, open it, peel off the first piece of licorice, and hold it out to her. At this moment she starts crying.

The tears are not part of our tradition. For a few seconds she holds her hands over her face. Then she reaches for the box of Kleenex on my nightstand, blows her nose, sniffles, and says, "I'm not at all sure I can do this."

"Do what?" I ask her.

Alix shakes her head. "All this." She wads up a blue tissue and banks it off the wall into a plastic pail, then sits in the pink chair. "I hate women who cry." Perhaps it is my altered perception, but despite her auburn hair being shorter, despite the wrinkles spreading from the corners of her eyes, Alix seems younger too. Maybe it's just that she's weeping, something I haven't witnessed in years.

"Dr. Karmichael says I'm out of danger," I tell her.

"That's a good place to be." She stares out the window. The squirrel is watching.

I say, "So I guess we've got a lot to talk about."

She laughs, an anxious weepy chuckle. But after this fades, we slide again into a silence. I consider the full weight of what I'm pretending, that this woman sitting here is still my wife, that her mind still finds peace in my presence, that I am her husband and protector and lover. That our life together has not yet fractured. The magnitude of my deception fills the room like leaking gas, and I have the clear impression that any spark or movement might ignite an explosion.

Alix reaches into her purse and pulls out a wallet-sized photo of Brook, the same one I've got jammed into the corner of my dresser mirror downtown. She passes it to me.

"Wow," I say. "She looks just like you."

"She looks like us, Coop."

From this safe first step we venture further out. I move us through a series of soft questions. "How is Brook doing in school?" "Does she have a boyfriend?" "So has she started driving?" "Has she tested for her black belt yet?" Alix falls into an easy rhythm on this familiar territory, teaching me the history I already know as we work our way through the Twizzlers. She retells the story of Brook's disastrous first driving experience (mall parking lot—Caravan vs. Dumpster), of her rocky first semester at high school ("Does not live up to academic potential"), of her summer job lifeguarding at the Y (no rescues, lots of water-winged brats). Alix carefully edits our daughter's past, leaving out her two runaway attempts after the divorce, her crank calls to the suicide hotline.

"I'd love to see her," I say.

"Dr. Karmichael told me soon. It'll be traumatic, you know?"

I nod my head, though I'm not certain if she means traumatic for me or traumatic for Brook. "I'll be out in a day or two. Once I'm free, I want to go to Greenfield Lake, OK? Just the three of us?"

Alix reaches for the Kleenex. Fully in character now, it seems perfectly natural to me that the three of us would visit Greenfield Lake and take out the paddleboats. Afterward we'll drive back to Asgard Lane, Brook will ride her ten-speed, leaving Alix and me alone for what we always jokingly called "afternoon delight."

"These days Brook's really excited about a new dance instructor, Jhondu," Alix says, deliberately changing the subject.

"Is that his first name or his last?" This is something I've honestly wondered.

"I'm not sure. The girls and the dance moms all buy into this philosophy of his, the *Arrow's Path Complete Life System*. Something like that."

"Doesn't sound too dangerous."

"Last night Brook was chanting. This morning she told me drinking coffee multiplies my negative rhooshies and will lead to chaos in my mind."

At this, we both laugh. The sight of my wife's smile makes me bold. "Al," I say. "What about the two of us? How are we getting along these days?"

Her laughter cuts off. The Twizzler knots in her hand.

"Brook and me. We're still close and everything, right?"

"You and Brook? Oh, you're still peas in a pod, Coop. She loves her Poppa-San."

We chat for a while longer, though only about Brook. It's like we're defusing a bomb, picking our way from safe topic to safe topic, careful to avoid anything that involves us directly. Between us we sense our joint mission. We know that sooner or later we'll have to choose the red wire or the green one, and we have no way of knowing for sure which one will kill the countdown and which one will trigger detonation. After half an hour, we just stop, exhausted. Alix stands up suddenly and says she has to go. "I'm still working with the studio. You remember ReelWorld, right?"

I nod, then ask, "Promise me something?"

She hesitates before she answers, but finally says, "Anything, Coop."

"When you come back tomorrow," I say, "bring more Twizzlers."

I smile and find myself leaning forward, pushing my bandaged face out in the invitation that comes naturally when man and wife part. Caught off guard, Alix freezes for a moment, but then she steps in, lowers her face and slips her lips into the opening, pressing them softly against mine. In the last six months, we have had sex on a dozen Thursday afternoons. No moment compares with this.

Not long after Alix leaves, a nurse named Arthur arrives for my afternoon wound-dressing. He talks nonstop, telling me about his mother, who's gambling away his inheritance across the border in South Carolina, and his sister, who runs a volunteer group that guards sea turtle hatcheries against ecotourists. When he finally leaves, I scan the channels looking for TV Buddy, hoping for a chance to report in or something. I want to see if I'm on the right track or not. But from QVC to VH1 to ESPN2, he's nowhere to be found. Where am I when I need me?

Finally I stop my surfing and settled in for today's *Waves Will Crash*. Lauren's been released from the hospital in the hopes that returning her to familiar surroundings might resurrect dead memories. I wonder if perhaps they will try this therapy with me. Longley leads her from room to room, elaborating shamelessly about the happy times they'd had in each one. He even shows her their wedding album, but none of it helps; she still doesn't feel close to him. The dramatic conclusion finds her standing at the bathroom mirror, staring at her own forgotten face. From second one, I know that mirror is doomed, and sure enough, Lauren smashes the glass with a silver-handled hairbrush. She looks down at the shards in the sink and two dozen jagged faces stare back at her.

At this crucial moment a black man dressed in a sports jacket walks into my room. He looks at me, then back at the television. I click the TV off and say, "Can I help you?"

"That," he replies, "is exactly what I'm hoping."

He introduces himself as Lieutenant Tyrelli and informs me that he's working the case. Those are his exact words: working the case. Immediately I distrust Tyrelli because he likely has access to files from my former life. He stands at the window—no sign of my squirrel—and says into the open air, "I thought we might go over Friday." He has no notepad, another detail that concerns me, in the same way I'm unnerved by waiters in fancy restaurants who memorize elaborate orders.

"The thing is," I explain, "I don't remember the incident at all."

"Do you recall forgetting it?"

"I remember being Bull Invinso. If I hadn't seen CNN I would hardly believe what the doctors are telling me."

"Ah yes," he says. "CNN. Can you think of anyone who might wish to harm Mr. Hillwigger?"

I think for a moment before coming up with, "The Baptists. They're opposed to his strip club."

Tyrelli frowns. "That affair was apparently settled some time ago."

"Baptists have long memories," I say. "Cover your bases."

"I appreciate the advice. Can you think of anyone who might have had a grudge against Mr. Henderson?"

My heart pumps once. "What do you mean *might have had*?"

Tyrelli pauses, takes two steps toward me, then looks back over his shoulder at the window. "My condolences," he says. "He passed early this morning. I was under the impression you'd been informed."

"No. I didn't know." Barney and I were never close, but we'd had a few beers. After his wife got sick, we made a lot of plans to watch the Series together, that kind of thing. But I can't get emotional. Because in my new reality, I never met this man who's now dead.

"This is the reason why I'm asking these questions," Tyrelli explains. "What we're dealing with now is a Cobra 6 homicide. I'm the department's specialist."

I ask him what exactly he specializes in.

"My tactical training covers anti-terrorist, anti-cult, and anti-gang activity."

I picture the gray-haired man-child. "Which one is this?"

"We're not sure yet." Tyrelli props one foot up on the pink chair. His jacket splits open, revealing the metal in his shoulder holster. I can't be sure, but it looks like a modified 9mm. "So your recollections fail to—"

"Look," I say, "don't you guys have this kid in custody? Isn't he strapped down up on seven? Can't you just show a jury the CNN videotape and call it a day?" The confidence in my voice is vintage Buddy.

Frustrated, Tyrelli crosses his arms. "Thanks to your intervention we do indeed have a suspect in custody. Unfortunately his oars aren't all in the water. Fact is, he doesn't really seem to have oars, if you want to know the real truth. He rants constantly, something about serving the master. Before I come to any conclusions about who else might be involved, I'd like to develop an accurate account of exactly what happened."

"How about the five thousand eyewitnesses?"

Tyrelli informs me that stampeding fans and strobing light tend to combine for unreliable testimony. Everyone saw something different. When I ask about Snake and Hardy, the lieutenant tells me, "Mr. Hillwigger's and Mr. Appleseed's version of events are similar, but somewhat dubious."

"Dubious how?" I ask.

"Trust me when I say dubious. So we could really use some further corroboration."

"I can't supply corroboration. Read my chart. I've got amnesia."

"I understand that. Trauma-induced partial amnesia. That's part of the official record. Do you know how rare actual cases of amnesia are?"

"If I did know, I've forgotten."

"You're being clever. I appreciate cleverness. Let me ask you this, Mr. Cooper, do you believe in the search for the truth?"

"Absolutely," I snap out.

"Then you'd be willing to work with a hypnotist?"

Behind Tyrelli, the squirrel has reappeared. He is sitting on the line, holding a nut, as if he were watching a matinee. I say, "I thought you were with the police."

"Hal's my brother-in-law. He's licensed. The very best in the business."

I don't believe in hypnosis, licensed or otherwise, but I can just imagine if this guy happens to be for real. After all, if Rhonda can see into the future, it only makes sense that Hal could unveil the past. "No," I say. "Hypnosis is not an option."

"Hal helped a witness crack that coed murder in Chapel Hill last year. He's amazing when it comes to past-life regressions. Maybe you saw him on *North Carolina Now!* He was on *Montel* last fall."

Montel is a semi-reliable reference in my world, but I shake my head no.

The detective asks, "Why not?"

"Hypnosis is against my religious principles."

"Really?" Tyrelli says. "Might I ask what religion you are?"

I look him straight in the eyes. "I'm with the Church of Buddy Cooper."

He stands there for a moment, trying to get a read on my face through the bandages. But before he can come to any determination, Quinn storms in—suspenders, tie, briefcase. "Welcome to the end of this meeting," he says.

Tyrelli turns to him.

"I'm Lowell Quinn, acting as legal counselor for Mr. Cooper. Dr. Karmichael, his physician, is prepared to sign an affidavit to the effect that Mr. Cooper's condition prevents him from assisting you. This questioning is invasive and potentially detrimental. Desist."

Tyrelli raises one pink palm. "No one's under suspicion here, Mr. Quinn. I'm simply gathering information." He offers Quinn his hand, and the two of them shake, uneasily.

I'm feeling left out and decide to reinsert myself. "Excuse me," I say to Quinn. "But I don't believe we've met. I'm Buddy Cooper."

Tyrelli and Quinn share eye contact. The detective heads for the door and says, "I'll leave you two alone to get acquainted. I need to check in up on seven. I'm sure we'll all be in contact."

As soon as Tyrelli leaves, Quinn turns to me. "I'm Lowell Quinn, your boss and best friend."

We look hard at each other, neither of us completely convinced by the other. It's like a staring contest between two bluffing poker players. I have a distinct advantage because the bandages cover most of my face. Finally Quinn starts pacing back and forth beneath the TV and says, "You do recollect being employed by me, right?"

"I work for Mrs. Q."

Quinn winces, then explains that after his grandmother died, he inherited the SWC. "And your contract along with it. But that's irrelevant in the big picture because we're friends, B. C. It's crucial that you fully comprehend the closeness of our relationship. You and I have a code that goes beyond contractual obligations."

Quinn's lie makes me want to leap from the bed and beat him with my bedpan. But I have to stay undercover. None of these folks knows it, but I'm the one in control. I say, "I'm sorry about your grandmother. She was a beautiful lady. I'm glad you and I are friends."

Fueled by false confidence, Quinn continues. "Prior to the incident, you and I were collaborating on a project of some import. Recollect?"

I tell him I'm drawing a blank.

He dismisses my amnesia with a wave of his hand. "Your plan called for the current champion—Hardy Appleseed—to lose his crown under somewhat dubious circumstances, then regain it in a subsequent match, restoring his honor and increasing our ratings. Kind of like what the Coke people did. That was your plan."

"Well, I've seen CNN. So much for my plan."

"That's the story of life, B. C. Plan A goes awry. You formulate Plan B. That's what I'm here to discuss with you. The contingency I'm initiating would benefit greatly from your participation."

"I'd love to help," I say. "But I'm not exactly one hundred percent." Beneath the immobilizer, the fresh gauze has begun once again to bloom with blood and pus.

"It's not so much your body that I need," Quinn says.

I'm eyeing him up, trying to get a read on what he's got in mind, when a candy striper shows up with dinner. She whips the lid off to reveal a cube of lasagna, a heel of garlic bread, a bowl of green Jell-O, and two Percocet in a plastic cup the size of a shot glass. "Care to join me?" I ask.

Quinn smiles, pulls out his Palm Pilot. "I've got a meeting with the head of hospital security. Apparently Hardy refused to leave Snake's bedside last night. You do know who I'm talking about, right?"

"I heard about the Hardy guy on CNN," I say. "And I bounce at Snake's bar."

"Of course. I forget how long you two have shared an association. We'll discuss specifics at the appropriate time, B. C., but to highlight the central points of our dialogue: One, Lowell Quinn is your friend. Two, he's got a plan."

"Plan B," I say.

"That's right. But consider it from a positive perspective. After all, you've got to agree: Plan B is better than no plan at all." With that, he's gone.

Quinn's last line makes me think about what will come of all this. My fingers touch the gauze wrapped around my chin and I can't help conjuring the soap opera scene waiting on the next page. Alix will be holding the hand mirror as the doctor unwinds the gauze. And part of me believes that when the bandages are gone, my face will indeed be four years younger, that somehow this amnesia fantasy I've concocted may transform into prophecy. That I'll actually be the man I'm pretending I am.

CHAPTER THE TENTH

Midnight Visitor. The Healing Power of Crystals.
An Unveiling. The State of Our Union.

My light snaps on in the middle of the night, pulling me from a dreamy green field thick with wildflowers. A nurse stands with her hands posted on her hips at the end of my bed. I don't recognize her. "What's with the ruckus?" she demands, like I'm the one who just intruded on *her* quality REM.

"What ruckus?" I ask.

"We've got recuperating people around here. Sick people who need to sleep. We simply can't tolerate ruckuses."

I scan the room for evidence of some disturbance. Chairs. Balloons. Flowers. "Sorry," I say and shrug my free shoulder. "No ruckus here."

She flips off the light and swings my door closed as if I'm a child being banished to the darkness. I settle my head back into my pillow, but not two seconds later a sound escapes beneath my bed. "Psst. Psst."

I try to convince myself it's my imagination, or something from the pipes, but then I hear it again, more insistent. "Pssssst. Pssssst."

Best-case scenario is that it's Buddy, come to deliver more guidance. Clicking on the tiny yellow light behind me, I gain the courage to ask, "Who's in here?"

There's a sliding sound, and out from under the bed my daughter emerges. Brook smiles and whispers, "That nurse is an A-1 mega-bitch."

Quietly, I tell her, "Don't say *mega-bitch.*"

We both grin, and then she gently lays her chest onto mine, careful not to put too much weight on my immobilized arm. With my free one, I hug her into me. Chins on shoulders, we exchange "Baby Bird" and "Hey, Poppa-San."

"How'd you get here?"

"My bike," she says, "and the steps. I told the emergency room my sister was giving birth. Then I just worked my way up. Mom said I wasn't allowed to see you yet, but I was, y'know, worried."

"I'm glad you came."

She tilts her head, taking in my mummy look. "I wasn't even sure it was you under there until I heard your voice."

"The bandages come off in the morning."

We stare at each other in the thin light for long moments before she says, "So you remember me and all, right?"

My amnesia had completely slipped my mind. I nod my head. "Absolutely. How could I forget my baby?"

"I knew Mom was just jazzing me. She said you'd been hit on the head so hard you thought it was the past. That I was like nine again and we were all still living together." Though she knows this to be a fantasy, she can't keep from smiling a little bit. She says, "So like, what's up? How come Mom told me that?"

I don't want to lie to my daughter. "Baby," I say. "This is a lot more complicated than it looks."

"Complicated how? It's the truth or it's not."

"It's not the truth. But your mom didn't lie."

"Cool." She nods her head, processing. "So you understand the way things really are?"

"Of course," I say. "What do you mean?"

"Well, like with Trevor and all. You know about him."

"I know Mom married him."

— 132 —

"I never call him Dad, even when you're not around. Just Trevor. But he's cool with that. He knows enough not to push his luck."

I want to tell Brook that I'm glad she gets along well with Trevor. I take a deep breath and say, "I'm glad you get along with Trevor."

"Whatever." She shrugs her shoulders. "I brought you something."

From her pocket, she pulls out four blue stones on a string. "I made the vsaji myself. Jhondu says the crystals redirect positive energies. They'll help you heal."

She shows me the necklace and I notice letters scratched into the surface of the rocks. They spell out W-W-J-D. I've seen this before and I read, "What Would Jesus Do?"

"They can mean that if you want. Jhondu's clean with Jesus. He says all religions contain great truths, but not all great truths are contained by religion."

"This Jhondu guy says an awful lot."

"Yeah. He's bullet smart. He sounds like Yoda."

I can think of no reply. I do wonder, though, which *Star Wars* character my daughter would compare me to.

Brook asks, "Did you know the website says you're like, in a coma?"

"Website," I repeat.

"SWC.com. They've got pictures of you in here, but the Mad Maestro's personal page claims it's all being faked. Of course, in the fan chat room there's a rumor that you're dead."

"Well, I have felt better."

"Yeah, it just got me nervous, reading that stuff. But now I know you're OK and all, I should cruise. Mom'll blitz if she comes in to wake me up and I'm not in that bed. I'll give the vsaji to her to give to you. Then nobody'll ask questions."

Awkwardly, we hug again, and then Brook moves to the door.

"Be careful," I say quietly, another stock father statement.

She waves, peeks her head out into the hallway, then disappears.

Almost immediately I begin worrying about her. The curtains are still dark, so I imagine my daughter pedaling home along unlit roads, the thin wheels of her ten-speed hugging the cracked edges of the asphalt. I try to calculate exactly when she turns onto 17th Street, try to picture her safely passing St. James Cemetery, safely crossing the intersection at Shipyard, maybe glancing over at the popcorn store where once her tiny fists split boards.

After twenty minutes, I start itching to phone Alix's and make sure Brook arrived safely. Of course, according to my cover story, that particular phone number won't exist for another two years. But the not knowing is driving me nuts, and only after a long while does sleep settle over me. Even here though, I am not safe from my mind. In my dreams I follow my daughter's journey. I am flying behind her as she pedals past the Baptist church. The camera angle I have makes me think I'm a balloon she's towing, or some bird cruising along in easy pursuit. She stops at the light on College, and I hang behind her, hovering. When she gets the green we move again, down into the familiar streets of our development. She should be safe now, but still I stay with her. She turns down Asgard Lane and right up ahead is our house. A van comes toward her and I tense, but it rolls by without stopping. Brook pedals up the driveway and walks the bike around to the side of the house. She's ten seconds away from being in the house and safe, and that's when the dark figure roars from the azaleas. He tackles her to the ground and she screams just once before he covers her mouth with a filthy paw. The floating sensation vanishes and I fall, the ground rising toward me as I drop onto the attacker. It's like I just came off the top rope, the Bull from Heaven. I yank him off Brook, and we tumble to one side. When we stop rolling, I'm on top of him and I see his face clearly: Trevor.

The front door opens and Alix stands there in a wedding dress and Brook runs into her arms. "Stay back!" I shout as I reach for one of the bricks lining the front bed. But what my fingers fold around is the thin certainty of the tire iron. Kneeling on Trevor's shoulders,

I bring the metal down onto his widening eyes. His body jerks beneath me.

Twin screams freeze my pumping arms, and I see Brook nestled into the white folds of Alix's gown, both of them staring at me in shock and horror. They don't recognize me. Suddenly, I'm aware of the latex covering my face—the blue mask of the Terror. I reach up to pry my fingers beneath its skin, but I can't find the bottom. The latex has melted into my flesh.

I stand and walk toward them, but they back away like I'm Frankenstein on the march. Desperate, I claw my fingers into the eyeholes of the mask and tug. The material stretches but won't give. Alix pushes Brook behind her and holds up her hands, gloved in white lace. "Get away!"

Fingers hooked inside the eyeholes, I pull as hard as I can, elbows up, like a man bending prison bars. One hand rips away a shred, and cooler air covers that cheek. I tear away at the mask as if it were a second skin I needed to shed.

Finally I'm free of it, my true face exposed, and I stand there panting before my wife and daughter. In a moment of recognition they rush toward me. Alix pulls back her white veil and kisses me, then they each slide inside my arms and help me through the open front door of our home.

A voice says, "What's wrong with this picture?"

I awaken, eyes blinking back the morning brightness. A puzzled Dr. Karmichael is standing next to me, holding up a pair of scissors and a mirror. My free hand is a fist, tightly clutching tufts of gauze. Shredded pieces litter my chest, lay scattered across the bed.

"Got a little anxious to see my handiwork, huh?" Karmichael asks.

"There was an itch," I say. "A terrible itch in a dream I was having."

He stares at me through his glasses. "Well, you may as well have a look."

With this, he hands me the mirror, and I hold it up to my new face, framed in shredded gauze. My skin looks puffy and a little raw, but the sidewalk bruise on my chin and the egg the pool player raised on my forehead are both somehow gone. I am healed.

Lowering the mirror, I say in my clearest Bull Invinso voice, "I'm ready to go home now." I picture Asgard. "Let's call my wife."

Karmichael digs his pinky into his ear and twists. "Home," he repeats. "Listen. Mr. Quinn asked me to bring you up to date on a few things. There have been some changes." He sits on the edge of my bed and sighs, then begins.

The day passes: *All-New Family Feud.* Turkey noodle soup. Restless napping. *Waves Will Crash.* When Alix finally appears, I'm halfway through an above-average *Jerry Springer.* Today's smile is the same as yesterday's, so I'm guessing she wasn't intercepted by Karmichael. Alix has no idea I've been debriefed about the state of our union.

"Hi," I say.

Her eyes take in my unveiled face. "You're looking more yourself." She glances at the TV, where twins Cindy and Sally have got each other by the hair. They're twirling in that spin common to catfights. "What's with them?"

I explain what I've learned, that both women claim to be Sally, wife of Frank, now seated center stage. Both Sallys make the same claim: Cindy wants my car, my job, and my man, so she's pretending to be me and sleeping with my husband. Frank, who has obviously slept with each woman on many occasions, can't tell the difference. At least that's the story he's sticking with.

"Screwed-up world," Alix says as she pulls a giant bag of Twizzlers from her purse. We do our usual routine and she smiles, settles into the pink chair.

I aim the remote control at the TV and bring the sound down, but leave the set on—the local news has promised an update on the Chaos at the Civic Center. Alix hands me a bright red gift bag. "Brook sent this."

I reach into Brook's bag and pull out the vsaji. Playing my part, I ask, "What is it?"

"Some kind of New Age necklace. That's what she told me at least."

"When did the Old Age end?" I ask.

"They're into it at the dance studio these days. That Jhondu guy I told you about."

"Right. Sounds creepy. Like black magic." I slip Brook's necklace over my head. "Maybe when I get out I could talk to her about it."

"This thing's just a phase. I'm sure I'm overreacting. I doubt she really believes any of this stuff, it's just pretend."

"Yeah," I say. "Pretend." I reach over for Alix's hand and she puts it in mine. I feel the great altering power of what I'm about to do. Part of me wants to go on forever just living in this hospital room and watching TV, getting daily visits and sharing Twizzlers with my wife. But with my release, this bubble is about to burst, so now my top priority has to be damage control. "Al," I say, "they told me about us."

The words are a live wire, and she twitches her hand free and stands straight up. She turns her back to me and says, "Aw hell. Aw hell. I'm sorry, Coop. Aw, Coop."

"It's OK. Sit down."

"I should've told you myself. I should've. Aw, Coop."

"It wasn't a surprise," I say. "I knew something was different." I don't need to see her like this. I don't want to see her like this. I should feel guilty.

"I should've told you myself."

"Don't beat yourself up. This must be really weird for you."

"You have no idea. There is so much you don't know, Coop. Even before you got shot there were things I should've told you."

"What kind of things?"

She turns and puts her hand back in mine. "They don't matter now. Let's just forget I said that."

I nod.

"Can we please promise to forget that I said that?"

"OK," I say, "forgetting is my specialty."

"'Cause we're still friends. We stayed friends for Brook, y'know? That's important. You need to understand that."

"I understand. You're still my friend."

"That's right. That's what we both wanted. Friends."

We linger in the silence. On the TV the twin sisters are embracing now, apparently reconciled. Frank sits off to the side, elbows to knees, face in hands.

"Just tell me one thing," I say. I wish I could stop myself. "Was it me? Did I cheat on you or something?"

"No. Nothing like that. It just got to be too much, you understand? Too much."

"Too much what?"

"Too much not knowing."

Though this is a mysterious answer, it is the clearest one I have ever got. Back in the days when things started to sour, long arguing nights and fights that rattled pictures from walls never brought about this insight, and I am desperate, crazy to know more about what she means. But in the here and now Alix is not going to give me any more.

There's a knock on the door and before I can say anything Alix lets go of my hand. She swipes her eyes and in seconds flat seems composed. She shouts out, "C'mon."

Quinn strides in. "How's the world's toughest hero?"

"Good," Alix says. "He's great."

"Just heard the news. Tomorrow you're a free man."

"That's the word," I say.

Alix snatches her purse from the chair. "I need to go."

"Why the sudden egress?" Quinn asks. "I thought we might update Buddy on the specifics of the studio project."

"Later," she says. At the door she pauses, looks back at me. Our eyes hold each other's. She says nothing and steps into the hallway, leaving us in a vacuum of awkward silence. This lasts until Quinn notices the muted *Springer Show* and says, "Hey, twins. Does the volume work?"

I click up the sound and Quinn takes a seat. Both sisters now claim to be Cindy. Neither wants to live with Frank. This is because Frank has confessed to sleeping with Cindy when he thought she was Sally and Sally when he thought she was Cindy.

"He wanted it all and ended up with nothing," Quinn says. "There you have it: the story of life." He turns to me. "In the morning, I'll be here to pick you up. I have to be at a burial service across the river around noon but I can drop you off on the way."

I picture poor dead Barney the ref. I'd figured he was already buried, but I suppose they had to do an autopsy or something. I'd like to pay my respects.

"If it's at all possible," I say, "I'd like to go."

Quinn grins, does some strange reconfiguring in his head and says he'll have Alix get a suit from my apartment for me.

"Thanks," I say. "Now tell me about these other projects. I figure it's that wrestling match you talked about before."

"The Beach Bash is small potatoes. I've entered negotiations with a vice president at ReelWorld. Any problem working with Trevor?"

"No problem," I say.

Quinn hesitates. "Uh, you understand that he's, uh, he's—"

"I understand everything. Tell me about the project."

Relieved, Quinn goes on. "Trevor's directing a pilot show— *Under the Gun: True Crime Mysteries.* Everyone's very enthusiastic about a segment based on what happened at the Civic Center. A dramatic re-creation. But before they'll commit, they want to guarantee the authenticity of the product—they want you. We'll utilize a stuntman for most of the actual wrestling on account of your injuries, of course. We've already signed up Snake and Hardy. There'll be money, real money, for all of us."

I picture the three sisters Grace and the other potential investors. Quinn's fattening the chicken before he offers it up. He asks, "So B. C., can I count on you?"

I think hard about what it will be like playing myself on film. For a moment, my bed tilts and rolls.

"Alix is helping coordinate the stunt work."

"Absolutely," I say. "I'll help any way I can." Quinn shows his teeth. His right ear is a different tone than the rest of his skin. It could be his tanning bed is malfunctioning.

The thrill-a-minute music for the five o'clock news turns both our heads. To the rapid shot of quickening drums, a montage flashes past of exciting Wilmington places: the beach, the river, the courthouse. From behind her news desk, Mandy Fielding greets everyone with the same sunny smile she shines every day at this time. A graphic box appears over her shoulder. A giant rock hangs in space, trailing a whooshing tail. The rock is aimed at Earth, a fragile blue marble in the corner. "Our top story," Mandy says. "Scientists at NASA have issued an official Asteroid Watch, claiming that Asteroid X may indeed pose a threat to the planet depending on its progress in the next seventy-two hours."

Quinn's pocket makes a beeping noise and he whips out his headset. "Quinn here. Go."

Mandy's eyes hardly move as she reads from the teleprompter. "NASA officials stress that this is not as serious as an Asteroid Warning, which indicates the potential for an actual impact, or an Asteroid Alert, which indicates a high probability of impact."

"Achtung!" Quinn shouts into his headset. "Nine-nine." He continues in German, but my *Hogan's Heroes* only gets me so far.

Mandy says, "For those of you tracking Asteroid X with the KPBC Quicky Chicken Doomsday Asteroid Tracking Chart, the most recent coordinates are 07X by 63 by 87.4. Speed is estimated at 5,000 miles per hour. You can pick up your own chart free with any Quicky Bucket at all participating Quicky Chickens or here at KPBC."

Quinn rips the headset off and says, "Gaps in intelligence are what turn whole wars."

On the screen behind Quinn, the graphic with the asteroid disappears and a picture of the gray-haired man-child takes its place. Quinn says, "I got to go. Some Wrightsville Beach commissioner is claiming we need another permit for Saturday."

I point at Mandy. "Don't you want to hear the update?"

"I'll stay current. Expect me in the morning. Recuperate."

I nod my head and Quinn leaves, folding his hi-tech phone into his pocket as he steps out into the hallway.

Mandy leads in to a taped interview with Lieutenant Tyrelli. He says, "Recent discoveries seem to contradict our initial theory. We are no longer advancing the notion that this individual acted alone. We have indications in fact that this person may have been acting in collusion with another figure or figures. We have not at this time ruled out the possibility of cult activity."

They cut back to Mandy, who polishes off the report by saying that the suspect is expected to be moved to a more secure facility sometime soon as his condition has stabilized. "Coming up next," Mandy says with a look of deep fake sadness, "tragic death in Paducah. And the Beanie Babies are responsible."

I click to QVC. They're selling green face creams. No Buddy. I shut the TV off.

I stare at the ceiling and try to take in all that's happening. I wish I had a commanding officer to report to. Or someone else was in the field with me here. I've gathered a lot of good intelligence; I just have no idea how to begin to decipher it.

Following a dinner of baked ham and mashed potatoes, I settle in for my last night of TV viewing here in the hospital. Clicking often to QVC in search of my AWOL alter ego, I watch the national network news, which ends with an interview with a science-fiction author who is an expert apparently on Killer Asteroids, having written three novels with them as main characters. Behind the closing credits they run an impressive series of computer graphics illustrating the effects of a direct strike. These include mile-high tidal waves, planet-wide earthquakes, and an ashen "death pall" which will cut off all living things from the sun. As the computer-simulated world is laid waste, the author states ominously, "What we human beings face now is nothing less than the end of life as we know it. The meteor doesn't care if it passes by or blasts us all to oblivion or worse. I'm talking about chaos here. Anarchy. Cannibalism. And now it's just a matter of chance." The last computer image, of the pyramids being vaporized, fades to black, and from the darkness fades in the bright spinning rainbow of *Wheel of Fortune*, which is broadcasting this week, according to the cheery voice, "Live from Las Vegas!"

I'm distracted from Pat and Vanna's introductory banter by a sound at my door. It opens but no one enters.

I lean forward in the bed. "Hello?"

A low voice whispers, "Sir? Is that you, Mr. Cooper?"

"That's affirmative, soldier."

Hardy barrels around the corner like a St. Bernard and lunges into me, wraps his arms around my head. He pins me deep into the mattress, igniting my shoulder. With my one good arm I pat him on the back. "It's good to see you, Hardy."

He pulls up and looks ready to cry. "Sir, I thought you was dead. I been having terrible dreams all week that you got shot and died and nobody told me on account of they were mad at me."

"I'm not dead, Hardy."

"I know. That's great." He smiles at me and pulls a card from his back pocket. "I was worried awful. I bought this for you."

He hands me the card, on the cover of which is a pastel drawing of a simple church. I split the card open and read the printed message: "The Sisters of Saint Guadalupe De La Riviera will remember you in their prayers this week. May God see you through this time of crisis."

Hardy beams. "It didn't cost but fifty dollars."

I recall the foggy memory of the nun at my bedside. Hardy paid for her, bought me heavenly blessings with cash. "Thanks, Hardy. That's very thoughtful."

"They were selling novenas too, but I didn't want one of them 'cause it sounds too much like hyenas, you know?"

"It sure does."

"Mr. Quinn told me I could come and see you finally. When they were telling me I couldn't see you I was afraid you was dead."

"I know, Hardy, but I'm not dead. Tomorrow I'm going home."

"Mr. Quinn told me you might not recognize me, but I knew you would."

As with Brook, my amnesia had slipped my mind. Innocence and deception just don't go together.

"How could I forget you, Hardy? You're my good friend."

"Yessir. I missed you awful. It's been a bad week. Mr. Snake's hurt real bad. Mr. Barney is dead."

"I know, Hardy. We're all going to his funeral tomorrow."

Hardy frowns. "I was just at his funeral today. Is he gonna have another one?"

Before I can answer, Hardy asks, "Can I have some Twizzlers?"

I nod and he reaches for the bag on the table, peels off a couple. Hardy must have been at Barney's wake today, and doesn't know yet there's a second part.

"Hardy," I say. "Has anybody talked to you about what happened in the ring?"

"Yessir. Everybody. Sometimes I'm supposed to say *No comment*, and sometimes I tell them the story Mr. Quinn helped me remember."

"Helped you remember. But what do *you* remember? You can tell me. I'm your good friend."

"Well, bits and pieces." Hardy chews his licorice contentedly.

"Hardy," I say, "tell me the story."

Hardy nods, swallows. "Well, Mr. Snake's mean snake got away from him, and that crazy boy come in the ring and started shooting out into the crowd. Mr. Snake tried to stop him but got shot. So me and you teamed up on him. Like we was tag-team partners. Did Mr. Quinn tell you he's gonna have us be tag-team partners?"

"No, Hardy, he didn't."

"So anyway, we attacked the crazy boy and he tried to shoot me only he couldn't. He just missed me and missed me. That was the spirit of the Lord. Those bullets passed right through me. Like a miracle." I remember burying my face in the canvas when the kid aimed that gun at Hardy at point-blank range.

Hardy chuckles, "But those bullets didn't pass through you though, that's for sure." He laughs and nods at my left arm, still strapped in the immobilizer. I'm not laughing. He goes on with his story. "So we saved everybody and now we get to be on TV."

"Hardy, did you tell everybody about the miracle?"

"You bet. I told them about that crazy boy standing right in front of me with his gun. I remember him pointing it right at me and a loud, loud bang. I thought I was gonna be killed. But I was saved."

"And you told people this?"

"Yessir. I told Mr. Quinn and the nice black policeman and the pretty lady reporter. But she didn't say nothing about it on the TV. And the newspaper guy too. None of them did. That got me mad at first, but then I figured it out."

"Tell me what you figured out."

"Well, the miracle's not for everybody to believe. Just for some folks. That's part of God's plan."

"I understand."

"You remember God's plan? We was in the locker room and you didn't believe it, I could tell. But I knew there was a reason God wanted us to be in that ring together. We had to save all those people. Mr. Cooper, I been waiting to say 'I told you so.'"

"You told me, Hardy. You told me."

Both our heads turn to the hallway, which is suddenly alive with the rapid clatter of footsteps, people running hard in heavy boots. The door explodes inward and two cops leap in. The young one lands in a kneeling position and the older guy slides to a halt with legs spread for stability. Both have their guns drawn and aimed at us. Hardy throws himself on me, covering me like a blanket just as they yell, "Police, freeze!"

A gun backfires and I tense, but feel only Hardy's weight.

"Hold your fire!" I yell at the same time the older cop yells, "Jessie! Jesus!"

Jessie says, "I thought he was attacking him."

"We're clear! We're clear!" the older cop shouts into the hallway. "All clear! False alarm."

"It looked like he was attacking him."

"Hardy," I say, "you can get up."

He climbs off me and scowls at the cops, "What'd you try to shoot us for?"

"Honest mistake," Jessie explains. "We thought the patient in this room might be in a danger zone. And what are you doing in here, sir? It's after posted visiting hours."

"Jessie," the older partner says, then shakes his head.

I turn to my headboard, which has a spiderweb splintered into it. At the center is a tiny bullet hole, not six inches from my head.

The older cop forces a grin. "Good thing my partner's a lousy shot, heh?"

"Good thing," I say.

"I don't like you," Hardy tells Jessie.

The older cop's walkie-talkie crackles and he picks it up. "Room 215 secure."

"Roger," comes back. "Maintain perimeter. Unknown hostile still at large."

"Look," I say. "What's going on? Is that a fair question?"

The older cop answers, "That kid made an escape. The crazy one you two put down."

"A locked room on the seventh floor," Jessie says. "Two guards outside the door. They didn't see a thing. He's just gone. Disappeared."

"We'll be in the hallway," the older cop says to me. When Jessie doesn't immediately follow him, he adds, "Both of us."

Hardy turns back to me. He looks at the bullet hole. I think about where Jessie was, kneeling not five feet away from the edge of the bed. And how Hardy was doubled over me, a bull's-eye big as a barn. I reach up with my finger and probe the hole. It is real and still warm. Hardy can see the calculations I'm making about trajectories. From the hallway I hear the old cop whisper, "Goddamn, Jessie. What the hell were you thinking? It's a miracle you didn't kill them both!"

Hardy grins wide and sly. His eyes light up like a Christmas tree and he mouths, "I told you so."

CHAPTER THE ELEVENTH

The Afterlife According to Snake. Bad Feelings About Penguins. Beloved Champ. Three Moose. An Unexpected Mourner.

Quinn shows up ten minutes into *The Price Is Right*, hands me the suit Alix picked out and a pair of oversized sunglasses that he hopes will disguise my identity, though from whom I'm not exactly sure. While he takes care of the release paperwork, I struggle into costume. I've had the wounded wing free of the immobilizer a few times, but it costs me five minutes of distilled agony to slip into the white dress shirt. The Percocet does little to dull the throbbing in my shoulder, and I decide to opt for comfort over style, securing the arm back in the Velcro sling before slipping the jacket on, leaving the left sleeve empty. Standing before my bathroom's tiny mirror, I try on the sunglasses. I look like a one-armed, blind private eye, like someone who's been searching for clues in all the wrong places.

I lift Brook's vsaji from the nightstand drawer, the only memento I need to keep of my time in 215. When I slide the healing necklace into my jacket pocket, I find a slip of paper. Unfolding it reveals Alix's handwriting: *In Raleigh tomorrow—Dance. Greenfield Lake, Sunday around 12:00? I could bring Brook.*

When Quinn returns, he looks at me in my Stevie Wonder shades, says, "Hey, where'd B. C. go?" and laughs. I leave my hospital room without a good-bye or a backward glance, and Quinn leads me to a gray service elevator that lowers us into the basement. We weave our way through the back of the cafeteria, workers turning to stare as we pass. The muscles in my legs are stiff, but the movement feels good. Finally we cut down a concrete corridor and Quinn opens a door. I step into the cloudy gray day and draw my first breath of nonrecycled air.

"Our chariot awaits," Quinn says, pointing. Parked amid the ambulances is the same vehicle I pissed on last week—Snake's hearse, big and black, engine rattling like a getaway car's.

As we approach I see Hardy's thick form hunched behind the wheel. Even with the overcast sky, his wheat-colored hair shines. He manages half a smile and a wave. I follow Quinn around back, where he pulls open the long door above the bumper, the one you'd slide the coffin through. He tilts his head and says, "All aboard."

Peering into the darkness, I see skinny bent legs and a cane. Snake sits in shadow toward the front on a sideways padded seat. I recognize it as one of the red booth cushions from Heaven's Gate. A thin hand holding a cigarette floats into the slanted light. "Come join me."

I crawl in and settle down across from Snake. Quinn swings the door shut and drops us into darkness. A few seconds later we rumble off. Daylight leaks around the black curtains masking the windows, so as my eyes adjust I can make out Snake's hand lifting and falling from his mouth. I can hear him puffing, but I smell no cigarette smoke. Sitting sideways in the darkness but traveling forward is disorienting, the sensation of movement without progress.

Snake's trembling hand extends toward me. "My name is Paul, Paul Hillwigger. We were friends before the accident. I owe you my life, and I—I deeply appreciate you coming today."

Snake's feeble handshake is a dead fish, and when he leans into me I glimpse one of his eyes clouded with red blood. "I remember you fine, Snake, just from what they tell me is a long time ago. It's all pretty screwed up."

"Call me Paul."

The hearse hits the drilling hum of the Cape Fear Memorial Bridge and then the smooth whine of the highway out of town. We're heading west and south on 74.

Snake's odd request makes me strain to see more of his face, but I can't. "Sure," I say. "How are you feeling?"

"Much better than I was." His thin hand again stretches across the darkness, and I open my palm to receive what he's giving me. It's a paper clip. "That's how close the bullet came," Snake says. "The surgeon told me it missed my heart by the length of a paper clip. I'm keeping one in my pocket to remind me of that, forever. I made a vow."

I think of Brook's vsaji. "We both got lucky."

"Let's note the distinction, friend, between being lucky and being fucking blessed." Snake lifts his cigarette to his lips. I hear him inhale, blow into the air, but still I smell no smoke. His hand lingers on his sharp chin, and he scratches at his goatee.

I hand back his paper clip. "I take it you're counting yourself among the fucking blessed."

"Bet your ass. I'm a new man, Buddy. Even if you hadn't gotten smacked in the head, you wouldn't recognize the man I am today. That ring was my grave and my womb. You know what heaven sounds like, Buddy? Patsy Cline. Believe it."

An eighteen-wheeler rumbles behind me, close enough to make me jump. "I completely believe you, Paul. I'm just not clear on what you're talking about."

"The paramedics told me I flatlined in the ring. My physical body perished. But I was saved. Redeemed. Resurrected. You follow me?"

"Absolutely."

"One minute I'm on the mat, bleeding all over, feeling ragged and beat, then boom, I'm looking up at Patsy, onstage in this classy bar. She winks at me and smiles and a waitress brings me draft beer that's on the house. I don't recognize the other folks in the audience, but everyone's cheery and laughing, all real glad to see me. We're all singing along to 'Back in Baby's Arms' and this cute old couple start dancing. Everything's beautiful and light. Then Patsy just stops midsong and looks to her left. That's when the penguin comes waddling out."

"Did you say 'penguin'?" I ask.

Snake nods. "The crowd gets all somber, and the penguin aims a flipper at me. 'He's the one,' he says. So all the customers, all these good people I've been drinking and having a ball with, they grab hold of me and drag me down a hallway. They kick open the bathroom door and heave me in, only when I fall I land in swirling water, dark and crappy, like I'm in a giant toilet that just got flushed. Everything's pitch-black now, and I'm spinning and dizzy in the cold water. Something slimy keeps licking at my legs. It has ahold of me, Buddy, do you understand? I'm going down."

Not sure of how to respond, I say, "Yeah, I had a bad feeling about that penguin."

The hearse slows and pulls to the left, loops down what must be an off-ramp. Snake moves his hand to his mouth and away again. "I slip under the surface of the murky whirlpool, gulp pure filth and gag. But then I hear the voice. *Take hold of my hand.*"

"Patsy?" I ask.

"No, no. Hardy. His arm plunges into the whirlpool and grabs me, pulls me against the vacuum trying to suck me down forever. Then *blam*! I wake up in the hospital with Hardy at my side, holding my hand."

"Appleseed went nuts in the ring," I say. "He's the one who smashed your python." I hear myself and realize I've just blown my amnesia cover, but Snake doesn't seem to notice.

"Hardy fulfilled his role. By killing poor Lucy—rest her soul—he liberated me from a dangerous life. In the hospital, Hardy told me I was part of a glorious plan, that God wanted me to live for a reason. Is that such a terrible thought, Buddy? Is that so unthinkable?"

I find myself contemplating the plans in which I've become

involved. Their author seems a mystery to me, it's true. We are both quiet for a while then, listening to the hum of the tires. The hearse clacks over railroad tracks, makes a left, slows to a stop.

When the back door swings open, the whiteness shocks my eyes. I don't hear Patsy Cline. I duck out and Hardy stands before me. "Hello, Mr. Cooper."

"Hi, Hardy." Though it's overcast, I put on my blindman sunglasses.

Hardy stares at my empty sleeve and asks, "Are you all better now?"

The pulse of blood in my shoulder is regular and even, though not painful. Fortunately, the draining and the accompanying odor have subsided. "I will be, Hardy. How about yourself?"

"I'm sad today."

He leans in to help Snake from the hearse. In the light I see a purple bruise spread down his sunken cheek and disappear into his goatee. Blood stains the white of his left eye. It looks like a special effect. Snake lifts the cigarette to his mouth, but then I see it's no cigarette at all, but white plastic. He notices me staring and explains, "Nicotaint. The body's a goddamn sacred temple. From now on, I'm respecting mine. Like I said, I made a vow." With this, he inhales and then flares his nostrils, blowing invisible smoke into the air.

Quinn appears at the side of the hearse and says, "Gentlemen, shall we proceed?"

As the four of us move across the parking lot, Snake leans heavily on his skull-capped cane—no longer just a prop—and Hardy's strong arm.

The cemetery is the size of a small racetrack, clear-cut from a forest of pine trees a long time ago. We're heading up a gentle rise topped by the chapel, a whitewashed cinder-block cube with a tiny steeple holding high the cross. Some kind of colorful mural brightens the side, but from this angle I can't make it out. The grass is wet from an early morning rain and the sky is gray overcast, fine weather for a funeral. To our right, a serious black tent covers folding chairs.

This I suppose is where we'll lay Barney to rest. At the sight, Snake turns away. I'm curious about who will give the eulogy.

Alongside me, Quinn says, "I'm hesitant to discuss business on such a somber occasion, but I think it best that we plan on gathering tomorrow around noon. It's imperative that we all share the same creative vision for the Bash. Coordinate."

"Are you gonna go to the beach, Mr. Cooper?"

"You bet, Hardy."

"Mr. Q," Snake says, peering over his shoulder with the bloody eye, "I'm not sure I'll be up for a public appearance. Not the day after."

"Don't underestimate the therapeutic value of work, P. H. View it as an integral component of the healing process. Plus, our investment at this stage is sizable."

"I'll do what I can," Snake offers.

Closer to the chapel, the paved path cuts through a section of what I fear must be the graves of children. The small markers crowd each other. BELOVED LILLY: 1983–1990. Seven years old. IN SACRED MEMORY OF LITTLE MAX: 1986–1994. Eight years old.

"That there is Saint Francis of A-sissy," Hardy says. I look up at the chapel mural, which indeed depicts a robed man surrounded by happy animals. In addition to the usual dogs and horses, there's a panda and a moose. I tip my sunglasses to confirm what I'm seeing. The moose sports enormous antlers. Thankfully for Snake, no penguin is present.

I tell Hardy, "You're exactly right."

"Saint Francis loved animals. Whatsoever you do to the least of my creatures, so too you do unto me."

Snake reaches into his pocket and pulls out a white handkerchief, brings it to his face. He sniffles and leans into Hardy.

A patch of fresh yellow flowers on one of the graves draws my eye. Someone put them here today, stood over this grave and prayed. A second color shines behind the yellow flowers, and I tilt my head down to see what else was left at the foot of the tombstone. A red dog dish.

The epitaph reads, CHAMP. A LONG, GOOD LIFE: 1980–1994.

The tombstone next to it reads, SUNSHINE. YOU WERE MY EVERY-THING.

And behind that, SCHULTZIE. ÜBER DACHSHUND.

My eyes jump to the chapel, now just ahead. Hardy holds the door as Snake and Quinn step inside. Over them arches a carved sign that reads ST. FRANCIS'S PERPETUAL CARE BELOVED ANIMAL CEMETERY.

I'm so jarred by the realization that I'm standing over the graves of dead dogs and cats that I actually let out a laugh. Hardy scolds me from the top of the steps and I stifle my reaction, bow my head, and start toward the open door, not knowing what to expect.

What I see from the back are about a dozen mourners scattered across the pews, alone and in little groups. A calico cat wearing a rainbow-colored collar greets us in the lobby. It figure-eights Hardy's legs then prances toward a simple wooden altar. Before it, positioned in the center aisle, is a seven-foot-long shiny black box, one foot wide.

Snake's skeleton legs fold, and Hardy grabs him by the arm. "C'mon, sir, I'll help you. You'll be alright."

From rafters overhead hang four different chandeliers which illuminate the murals decorating the cinder-block walls: to the right a Technicolor-bright Noah's Ark, and to the left a rendering of Adam naming the animals before Eve showed up. Both cartoony drawings feature moose prominently, and it occurs to me that I've never seen one in the Garden of Eden before.

The four of us follow the calico up the aisle. We pass three blonds huddled together in a pew on the left, out of place and nervous. They're waitresses from Snake's Pit, ex–exotic dancers come to pay their last respects to their boss's dead pet. One waves at Snake, who raises a weary hand like the Pope casting a blessing as he shuffles by.

On our right sits a group of wrestlers, huge shoulders bulging in jackets. Cro-Magnum Man nods sympathetically. The Native American Spirit Warrior kneels in prayer. The Mad Maestro, dressed in his purple neon tails, rolls his handlebar mustache between two fingers. At the end of the pew sits Jambalaya, the Creole King. On his lap he holds Gumbo, his rooster mascot, who flaps his wings when he sees me. My right hand slides up to cover my chest, and I smile in tentative recognition at my colleagues.

A Doberman wearing a rainbow collar—red, green, yellow—trots across our path, ignoring us. Snake lays one thin hand on the coffin, then we move on to the front pew. I slide in behind Snake and Hardy, who both kneel. Quinn sits on the other side of me and asks under his breath, "Funeral expenditures related to business would qualify for tax exemption, don't you think?"

I look left at Quinn to shush him, and across the aisle, Rhonda's green eyes sparkle. She's kneeling alone in the opposite front pew, red hair wrapped beneath a black shawl. Our eyes come together, and she smiles.

"Excuse me," I say, sliding past Quinn.

"Where are you going?" he wants to know, but I ignore him. I scoot past the coffin in the aisle and slide in next to her. Since Rhonda's kneeling, I get down too. She says quietly, "Hi, Seamus, Seamus, Seamus."

"How did you find me? What are you doing here?"

"The one true gift flows through my veins, remember? Besides, I thought we had a date at the drive-in."

"Lady, I have zero idea what you're talking about."

Her smile thins. "Listen, no kidding around," she says. "I need to talk to you about my future."

From the back of the church, a booming female voice calls out, "All please rise and lift your voices to make a joyful noise unto the Lord. Turn to page seventeen of your hymnal for 'All God's Children.' "

Rhonda and I turn to the minister, dressed in a huge flowing robe that's rainbow-striped like the collars of the Doberman and the calico. She reminds me of Mama Cass. We stand, and Rhonda flips a few pages of the hymnal, finds the right page, and holds the hymnal in front of me the way Alix used to when we'd bring Brook to mass. In the here and now, the minister proceeds up the aisle, belting out lyrics a cappella,

> *It's a gift to have feathers,*
> *It's a gift to take wing.*
> *It's a gift from God*
> *To hear the humpbacks sing.*

Next to me, Rhonda sings too, raising her eyebrows in mock anger until I start mumbling the words.

At the end of the song I whisper, "I'm having enough trouble with my own future." But Rhonda brings a finger to her pursed lips, bows her head. The high animal priestess stands solemnly behind the wooden table. She unfolds her hands and raises her arms. "Sisters and Brothers, I am the Reverend Evangeline and I bid you great welcome. Please be seated."

We sit, and Rhonda places the hymnal back in its holder. She wears no rings. Rhonda catches me studying her hand but doesn't seem to mind.

"We weep this day for Brother Hillwigger," Reverend Evangeline tells us, "who has lost a beloved friend and now must put her to rest. Though it be clothed not in skin but by plumes or scales, all life reveals the beauty of the Lord's creation."

Snake sniffles, and Hardy pats him on the back.

Rhonda leans into me. "Say, that creep with the suspenders, does he always have that aura?" Quinn, clearly unnerved that I'm with an unknown, is staring at us. I shrug, a gesture intended to address both of their concerns. Two mallards swoop down from the wooden rafters and circle the chandeliers. One lands on the altar, eyes up the congregation like guests past their welcome.

"I can't see auras," I whisper to Rhonda.

Reverend Evangeline ignores the duck. "Brother Hillwigger and I prayed together on the phone last evening and he shared memories of the dearly departed. He told me how Lucy loved to come up into his bed when she knew she wasn't allowed there. How she craved the spotlight and was always fidgety before a big performance. How she knew when he was low in spirit and would comfort him simply by her presence. And now, he must wonder, as we all must when death and disappointment visit us, why has God stripped the joy from my life?"

This question strikes me, and for a moment I'm back in the Motel 6, where I waited three days for Alix to call before opening the classifieds for an APT. FURN.

The calico leaps up onto the coffin and begins to sniff. She claws at the top and makes a chalkboard *skritch*. The Reverend Evangeline snaps out, "Ecclesiastes! Shush now," and the cat scampers away. To Rhonda's left, the Doberman trots down a side aisle. She says, "I put it all together after I saw you on QVC. Look, Seamus, I need your help."

The smile on her face makes me feel certain she knows I was the one who defended her when her dance failed. I don't want to disappoint her by letting her know the truth, that whatever she saw on QVC wasn't really me, that I have no special powers of perception.

The Reverend goes on. "When our lives sour, when the world around us seems ruled by chaos and anarchy, where do we turn? From where do we seek consolation and understanding? To what do we cling when madness rules our lives?"

This question turns Rhonda's face away from me. She seems to tense, and I wish I knew what she was thinking.

"Amen!" one of the wrestlers shouts, though I'm not sure which one.

"The righteous man surrenders not to the darkness. Though his face be streaked with tears of anger and regret, still he turns to God and declares *I will do better*. Brother Hillwigger is just such a man. Starting Monday, he will be closing the drinking establishment he has misguidedly operated in the past. After a brief renovation period, he will reopen as a nonprofit animal shelter." The Reverend raises her huge hands. "Praise God!" she shouts, and the duck flutters off the altar and back into the rafters. From somewhere behind us the Doberman barks twice, as if he too agrees this animal shelter idea is a winner.

One of Snake's employees shouts out, "That's just great, Paulie." Faced suddenly with unemployment, she excuses herself past her co-waitresses, sidles to the end of the pew, then clacks in high heels down the aisle toward the door. Ecclesiastes the cat pads silently behind her. But when the blond reaches the exit, she stops abruptly. A dark silhouette blocks the doorway. "This heresy must end." The intruder steps into the light and is dressed as Snake Handler: black pants, black shirt, black tie, black jacket. Top hat. White face paint, black lipstick. Cane. The blond says, "Oh Jesus. Another freak. Just what we need." The man lifts his cane and smacks her across the neck. She goes down.

Reverend Evangeline cries out, covers her mouth, and everyone stands. But immediately he freezes us again by raising his other hand and showing us what else he's holding: a grenade.

Cro-Magnum says in a loud, clear voice, "Remain calm. Let's just see what he wants."

Next to me Rhonda says, "This is far from good" and reaches into her purse. When her hand comes out, she's holding her keys, attached to which is a tiny yellow can. The intruder leads four young punks into the church. Each wears a white T-shirt and a black beret. One stays at the door, holding what I think is a baseball bat. The other three follow the leader to the coffin, where he stops and announces, "We have been sent to claim the body of Lucifer, as he has been betrayed by his First."

Snake, the real Snake, says, "Please don't do this—"

"Silence," snaps the leader. "You have lost your right to speak for our Master. You would stand side by side with his murderer!" He aims his cane at Hardy. "We know the full truth of what happened. You will pay for your transgressions."

Hardy yells, "I don't like transgressions" and steps toward the leader. Suddenly Hardy clasps one hand to the side of his head and looks straight up, then around. "Hello?" he shouts. "Who said that? What? Oh. Yessir. Yessir, I understand."

The leader is as confused as the rest of us. Hardy takes up a defensive posture in front of Snake and says, "Jesus don't want you to hurt Mr. Hillwigger."

The leader offers the grenade and says, "All who oppose us will face the wrath of the true Disciples."

"Just let them take the goddamn thing," one of the blonds suggests.

Rhonda pushes into the small of my back and quietly says: "Like Mace."

I reach behind me and she presses the tiny canister into my hand.

"Let us be gone!" the leader shouts. But when two of the punks position themselves to lift the coffin, the Reverend Evangeline charges around the altar and hugs one end, anchoring it with her considerable weight. "I will not allow this holy vessel to fall into the hands of the vile."

One of the kids snaps, "Let go of the damn box, you hippie bitch."

The leader offers the grenade. "You don't think I'll do it? You don't think we're all ready to die for what we believe?" He drops the cane and grabs the pin.

"I believe you," I say, and the leader spins to me. "I know you're ready to die for what you believe."

Grim with resolution, he nods his head certainly and I step toward him, ready to raise Rhonda's Mace, when Reverend Evangeline shouts, "Leviticus, Vitken! Vitken!"

The Doberman explodes from behind her robes, jaws snapping. He latches onto the leader's wrist and the grenade tumbles into the air. The leader screams, drops to the floor with the dog writhing on his arm. The two Disciples release the coffin, sending Reverend Evangeline flailing backward with a huff. The coffin clatters to the ground, dumping the desiccated body of Lucifer into the aisle. Snake wails.

"Grenade!" Cro-Magnum Man yells and Rhonda tackles me, pinning me down behind the pew and flaring pain through my shoulder. There's a loud pop, but no explosion. I open my eyes to Rhonda's red hair in my face and pink smoke in the air above us. Over the growling of Leviticus and the leader screaming, "Get it off me!" I hear scuffling. Hardy shouts out, "I don't like you," and a few pews back there's a loud crash. Above us, the ducks circle, quacking madly.

"C'mon," I tell Rhonda, who gets off me and helps me up. In the soft pink haze floating from the grenade, Hardy bear-hugs one of the young thugs. Cro-Magnum's working his arms into a choke hold around the neck of the second, and Jambalaya and the Spirit Warrior corner the third against the mural of Noah. In front of the altar, Evangeline grabs hold of Leviticus's collar, and the leader tucks his bloody arm into his body. Rhonda says, "This I did not see coming."

"We should evacuate ASAP," Cro-Magnum announces. "Certain additives in the coloring agent can be harmful if inhaled in sufficient quantities."

I'm wondering just how he knows this when the Disciple with the bat emerges from the pink fog, heading for his wounded leader and Evangeline. Behind him, for just a moment, I swear I see a dark figure standing in the doorway, the man-child from the Civic Center. But with the Disciple bearing down on me, I have no time for a second look. I block his path, raise the Mace straight-armed to his face, and say, "Don't be a martyr, son. This shit really stings."

He looks at my empty sleeve and says, "Out of my way, gimp."

I'm not in the mood for games, so I pump the button, but it's my eyes that explode, my head that shocks away from the burning pain, my legs that go instant rubber. And just like that I'm back on the floor, cursing and rubbing at my eyes locked down tight. "That only makes it worse," Rhonda says, her face down close to mine. "Try to breathe slowly."

"Swift," I hear the punk say.

The jingle of keys and a misty hiss.

"Bitch!" the punk shouts, followed by the distinct sound of a bat clattering to the ground. Rhonda's arm slides inside my good one and she says, "Let's get you out of here."

She leads me shuffling down the aisle, and around us is growling, sniffling, someone coughing with the fumes, cursing from the beaten Disciples. I keep my eyes closed tight against the pain.

"This stuff can't be legal," I say.

"My ex-fiancé isn't respecting the restraining order," Rhonda explains. "Three steps here."

Suddenly the air cools and breathing is easier. My hair is wet. We take the steps together and she guides me to one side. With my right arm around her shoulder, Rhonda lowers me onto what feels like a stone bench and says, "Opening your eyes would be good. This rain will help, but you have to open your eyes. Just look up."

I nod my head, then lift my face to the sky and force my eyes wide, blinking back the tears and letting the pure rain rinse the poison. The world is a gray haze. "I can't see anything," I tell her.

"I know," Rhonda says. "But this is a condition that will pass." Gently, she squeezes my hand and we sit together outside the chapel, waiting for the healing she has promised.

CHAPTER THE TWELFTH

*Your First Time. Convergences. Our Hero Learns the
Distinction Between Weeds and Wildflowers.*

As my vision clears, the first image that comes into focus is the chapel's steeple, aimed at heaven. Smoke drifts from its point and floats off into the thin rain. Some of the smoky cloud coalesces into hard shapes that break away in flight, a phenomenon that makes no sense until I recall those ducks inside the church. They are fleeing, driven from their sanctuary by the mad actions of true believers. The air shifts around me, and the raindrops hitting my face become larger and more frequent. Rhonda says, "Storm's just getting started, Seamus. What do you see?"

When I turn to her voice, all I can make out is an outline, a tall silhouette. Even more upsetting, her red hair is black, her face a dull gray. The world is an out-of-focus black-and-white film. "My colors are gone," I announce.

"Don't panic," Rhonda tells me. "This is a documented side effect. Everybody's gathering under a tent."

"What about the bad guys?"

"They've had enough with that Doberman. They're sitting on the ground."

I ask her to bring me over, and we weave through a few tombstones on our way to the burial tent. Finally, we step out of the rain.

"Mr. Cooper, sir, your eyes are all red. Did you hear Jesus in the church?"

I raise my good hand and say, "Everything's going to be OK, Hardy."

Snake says, "Buddy, please, the Reverend went back inside to check on Lucy. I've got just a terrible feeling." I hear him blow air and hope the Nicotaint is steadying his nerves.

Quinn's voice surprises me. "I'd advise against disturbing a crime scene. When the authorities arrive we want to provide full cooperation. I'm certain they can ascertain how these little miscreants learned about our private ceremony."

A snicker rises from the ground, where several blobs crouch together. The young leader speaks. "We were guided here by dark forces beyond your comprehension. Our master is truly omnivorous."

"Good thing education is a state priority," Mad Maestro adds.

One of the perky blonds says, "I'm being fired because a snake died."

I aim my face at the gray blob that spoke with Quinn's voice and say, "You mentioned authorities."

"I called the cops as soon as we cleared the building."

Rhonda squeezes the muscles in my good arm, settles her chin on that shoulder. "He's lying."

I turn to her gray featureless face, wish for the return of her green eyes.

"I am not firing you," Snake says. "You'll be retrained as an animal caregiver."

"Outstanding," the blond says. "Think of the tips."

"Those goats are getting away," Hardy says.

"I haven't got any goats." Evangeline's voice comes from behind us. Her large gray form comes in from the rain, and everyone looks into the field.

Hardy says, "Oh. Maybe they're wild goats."

Evangeline runs a hand over her head and says, "I don't understand this, Brother Paul, but brace yourself. I bear dreadful news."

"It can't be," Paul says, his voice hardly a whisper.

"Your loved one's body. It's not inside."

"Our master is triumphant!" one of the punks shouts. Leviticus barks twice and shuts him up.

Paul collapses into Evangeline's arms and sobs. Coming to the tent was a bad idea. I turn to Rhonda and ask, "You got a car?"

"I sure didn't walk out here, Seamus."

"His name ain't Seamus," Hardy says.

I face my friend. "She knows, Hardy. Everything's OK."

The Quinn-shaped blob puts a hand on my shoulder. "B. C., considering your current condition, I would be remiss in my obligation as your legal counsel and your friend if I failed to advise you to remain here and assist law enforcement. Besides, members of the media should be on-site any minute."

"How do they know what happened?" Mad Maestro wants to know.

There's a long silence, then Quinn offers, "Police scanners. They monitor all frequencies."

Again, Rhonda gently squeezes my arm. She doesn't believe him. "Quinn," I say. "I'll talk to the cops later. My eyes."

"This man needs medical attention," Rhonda says. "I'll drive him to the hospital."

"Just a moment, miss. Could I ask exactly who are you?"

"She's with me," I tell Quinn.

"Nevertheless, I'm sure we'd all feel better if we saw some ID. Preferably something with a photo."

"Show me your badge," Rhonda says, "and I'll show you my ID."

"I vouch for her," I say. "She's a friend."

"How can you vouch for her," Quinn asks, "if you've got amnesia? Clarify."

"Don't push it, Lowell. Remember, I'm not the man you think I am. I'll see you tomorrow." I take Rhonda's hand and turn, take a step and plant my foot squarely into what I figure at first for a water-filled ditch dug for pipe or cable. When Snake wails I realize

I've just desecrated the open grave of his beloved pet. I wonder now if they'll fill it in empty.

After she's buckled me in and we've left St. Francis's behind, Rhonda accelerates through the pine forest at unsafe speeds. The tall dark shapes of the trees whiz by, and I hear the gears shifting rapidly. Oncoming traffic—a series of black and gray blocks—shushes past in the wet of the rain. The radio plays chaotic jazz, New Wave stuff with no beat or rhythm I can detect. I run my blindman's hand along the dashboard and announce, "Ford Escort. '95." If I had to guess at the color, I'd say white.

"Honda Civic," she says. "No notion what year. Listen, we could go find a hospital, yeah, but the stinging will wear off on its own."

I'm not sure how she wants me to respond to this. "Did you see that kid with gray hair?" I ask. "Back in the church?"

"Can't say I did."

"In the doorway, just standing there."

"I'm no help." She shakes her head. "So where do you want me to take you?"

"I don't care," I say. "Wilmington. Anywhere. I don't care."

She swings wide left to avoid what looks to me like a centaur walking on the shoulder. "Look, Seamus. I've got an offer for you: I'll bring you to my special place and in return you agree to help me."

Instead of contemplating what help she might need, I find myself imagining Rhonda's special place, a secret garden to which I've been invited. But I'm distracted by the whine of sirens, growing louder. In the oncoming lane, bright white lights sparkle and flash from a black block that races back in the direction from which we came. "SWAT team," Rhonda reports. "Side of the van had a picture of some kind of killer pig."

"I'm glad we took off."

"Me too. Those friends of yours are nutjobs." The sirens fade behind us. Rhonda says, "You seemed pretty rattled when you saw me. I apologize if I spooked you. Really, I thought you'd be expecting me, you know? I thought you'd maybe have foreseen it."

"Things have been a bit hectic lately," I say. "I haven't been foreseeing all that much." I reach up and rub at my shoulder.

"This is not on my list of wrongdoings. I hate to say I told you so, but . . ."

"I'm not blaming anybody. I hung up on you. I acknowledge that."

"Good. I was afraid you'd be mad and maybe wouldn't help me. But you didn't seem mad at the dance benefit, so I was kind of hoping."

This tiny admission, that she has connected my phone call with my actions at the benefit, makes me feel strong and fine. Then we curve up an entrance ramp and blood slides into my wound. Rhonda merges us into eastbound traffic and we drive listening to the jazz and the windshield wipers. The gray billboards we pass seem like giant square balloons. I loosen the seat belt to improve the blood flow in my immobilized arm. Rhonda says, "The thing you did that night, that was an act of genuine kindness."

"It was no big deal. I don't even know why I did it."

"You did it because you are a fundamentally good person, Seamus. This to me is clear. I can see it in your aura."

I want Rhonda to describe my aura. I want to know what brilliant colors radiate from my body. Even more, I want to see hers. "What you said about the restraining order," I ask. "Your ex-fiancé, that was legit?"

"The truth is all I speak," Rhonda says.

I think of where Rhonda lives now, Sanctuary House, and I wonder at the size of the man who could physically abuse such a strong woman. I'd like to ask her, but these issues, it seems to me, are out of bounds for now.

"So tell me the truth," I say. "What exactly do you want from me?"

My question causes her to accelerate and we pass a block so large it must be an eighteen-wheeler. Finally she says, "I told you. I want you to tell me my future."

"Why not ask one of your psychic sidekicks?"

"Look, the best of them couldn't predict the seasons. But what you did on QVC, calling that kid in Paducah, that was proof enough for me. Don't you see, Seamus? Everything's connecting, you know?"

For this observation, I have no response, and we cruise along in silence. She takes a long swooping exit off the highway and turns us south, I think. Traffic isn't heavy on this road. Even in the emptiness I take for fields around us, I see no house shapes. "Not far now," Rhonda promises.

I'm afraid to tell her the truth, that I cannot forecast her future. I worry that this is my only asset to her. So I remain silent as she drives, listening to a ten-minute saxophone solo and trying to come up with a convincing story. Maybe I could say the planets aren't in the right alignment, or perhaps I might argue that my pain medication is interfering with my psychic powers. But before I can fully craft my lie, the sax song ends and the Honda slowly turns onto what sounds like gravel. We pass a small gray cabin and then she stops the car. Tiny rain beats on the roof. "Can you see it?" she asks.

Peering through the windshield, all I can make out is a large white block at the end of a dark field.

"I can't imagine who built out here in the middle of nowhere. Must've been somebody's dream." She opens her door and says, "Let's go."

I unbuckle my seat belt and step out into the drizzling rain. Again, the coolness soothes my eyes. Rhonda takes my hand and we start walking toward the huge white rectangle. I wonder if I hadn't maced myself if our palms would be pressed together like this. The ground beneath us undulates, rising and falling in mounds like low moguls. Our legs drag through thick weeds, two feet tall.

"I had my first vision at the Star-Lite Drive-In. Schwenksville,

Pennsylvania," Rhonda says. "This was the night I lost my virginity with Nelson Lee. Later, my mother explained that sex generates a lot of raw psychic energy. How about you, Seamus? When was your first time?"

"If you seriously want to know your future," I say, "why not just look yourself? After all, you've got the one true gift."

"You of all people should understand,"she says. "We've got the same problem—can't see the path in front of us. At least, I presume that's why you called me in the first place."

I nod my head. Her explanation makes a kind of sense, I guess. I want to come clean about the night I called her, tell her of the two moons and the masks I wear and the pink pills I no longer take and the daughter I love and the other Buddy.

"That night was the starting point, Seamus. Don't you understand? There's no such thing as coincidence, only convergence. Your phone call. The dance benefit. The match. The vision I had of you in that pet cemetery. Yesterday afternoon in a trance, I saw you here, standing right in this spot."

"But you brought me here," I say.

"Only because you got in my car."

I give my crooked shrug and let go of her hand. We've stopped walking. As Rhonda predicted, my vision is clearing up some. In the giant white screen before us, I can see black squares from where sections have fallen away like rotten teeth or pieces missing from a puzzle. I ask her, "So what exactly do you want to know? If you'll get back with your ex-fiancé or not?"

"Ronnie's out of my life," she says, and this makes me smile though I try to hide it. "That much I'm sure of. But the vision of you getting shot unsettled me. This is important for you to understand. The night of your match, without clear intention, I went to the Civic Center. Only when I was there did I realize I'd come to break my mother's golden rule—I was going to alter the future."

Something rumbles to our north, maybe thunder, maybe trucks. My jacket is soaked now, and the immobilizer, which I was instructed to keep dry, is taking on water. Beneath my shirt, the gauze bandage that covers my wound feels soggy.

"So you really knew I was going to get shot?"

"From my seat, I could sense everything that was about to happen, but I couldn't do anything. I was forced to witness it all unfold. I was completely helpless."

Rhonda's head hangs, and she sniffles once. I see the hazy shape of her hands rise up to cover her face. I reach out for her shoulder and say, "Welcome to the planet."

I hear soft weeping and Rhonda rubs at her eyes. "That's just it. That night got me thinking. We're all at the mercy of fate. Like with this asteroid. It could hit us, you know. This is exactly what I'm talking about. What good is seeing the future if you can't do anything about it?" And now she turns full into me and plants her face in my unwounded shoulder.

I wrap my right arm around her, tug her into me. Her wet hair chills my cheek. I shake my head. "I don't know what I can say. I don't know what I can do."

"Can't you just look?" she pleads. "All of this can't be for nothing. It must mean something. You must have a vision for me. Look, it's not like I want stock tips. I don't want to know if I'll find true love or become famous. I just want to know that I haven't screwed everything up. I want to know I'm going to be OK. That's all. I just want to know if I'm going to be OK."

She sobs inside my arm, and I feel tears threatening to rise behind my eyes. What she's asking for seems so familiar, so small, and I truly wish I could grant her this tiny boon. *But I'm only Buddy Cooper,* I want to explain, *I have no gift of prophecy. I'm not the man you think I am.* Yet even thinking this triggers something in me, and suddenly I remember my amnesia. In the wind I hear the flapping of my gold cape. I remember being invincible. I raise my eyes to the giant movie screen and, when finally I speak, my voice is certain as stone. "Rhonda, you never made a decision you knew was wrong. You always did your best. You are standing right now exactly where you are supposed to be standing, doing exactly what you are intended to be doing. And you are not alone."

My hand slides inside her wet hair to the back of her neck and I guide her head out of my shoulder, turn her face to meet mine. "Believe me," I say, and our rain-cooled lips come together. Kissing, we drop to our knees in the tall weeds and Rhonda eases me onto my back into a muddy puddle, then climbs on top of me. My shoulder feels no pain. My eyes burn no more. The features of her face are clearer to me, though everything's still black and white. When she sees my immobilized hand stretching for my own belt, she undoes it quickly herself and tugs down my pants. My excitement is hard to miss. "This sling?" she asks. "Should we take it off?"

"I'm fine," I say, between quick breaths. The wound will not be pretty.

Dress slacks and underwear tucked to my knees, still wearing my tie, I almost laugh at the absurdity of the image. But when Rhonda slips her panties out from beneath her dress and settles on top of me, her knees squeeze my hips and I shiver at the crazed rightness of this moment. She rocks gently above me, guides my one good hand to her breasts, and I knead the flesh beneath her wet black dress. My fingers trail to the taunt dancer muscles of her belly. Above her, vague gray shapes float past in the sky, birds perhaps. Even with my impaired vision, I can see her smiling down on me, and this makes me smile. I'm aware of a rock beneath my plate-scarred ass cheek and the fact that she is pressing me down into the mud, but this fails to distract me.

Little by little, our urgency increases, and we buck into each other and she folds over me and her hands grab at the weeds on either side of my head. Her elbows dig into my chest. Rhonda hums, that beautiful song of contentment that only a lover can bless you with, and I squeeze my eyes tight as I feel my release bearing down on me. My mouth opens and I sigh, "Alix."

When Rhonda freezes on top of me, I realize what I've said. I open my eyes and am shocked by the green fire of her irises, the red shine of her hair restored. "Oops," she says, trying to force a smile, turning to the blank movie screen.

"Shit," I say.

She slides off me and sits in the mud. She cradles her knees. With my full vision returned, I look at the crushed grass around us and see the plants that have claimed this abandoned lot are not just weeds, but wildflowers as well. Yellow, blue, and purple buds cap the tall stalks.

"I'm sorry," I say. Still on my back, I stare into the thickening rain. "It's been so long since—"

Rhonda's curled into herself, rocking gently. "Don't explain," she says. "I understand."

"I wasn't even thinking of her." This is the truth, and I hope she can sense it.

She turns to me, presses her lips tight together, and nods. "Look, Seamus, I said that I understand. I'd like it if we could maybe just sit here for a few minutes. That would be good I think, OK?"

With my silence, I agree, and Rhonda and I look up into the gray sky. The thickening rain falls on us. Beneath a cloudy heaven that could be hiding an asteroid heading our way, we wait in the wild-flower weeds, together.

CHAPTER THE THIRTEENTH

Big Questions and the Price of Curiosity. Kissing Fish.
Two Readings from the Chronicle Wall.
A Discussion of Svobodian Society.

When Rhonda pulls her Honda—which really is white after all—to the curb in front of my building, we both sit listening to the engine run. On the drive back, we haven't said much. I told her I could see colors again and she said it was good. Later, she pointed out an egret spearing a fish. But mostly, we both kept thinking about what we weren't talking about, the same thing we're not talking about now. Rhonda's hands fidget on the steering wheel. I reach across my wounded arm and unbuckle my seat belt. She looks out the opposite window. The dull sun sits low in the cloudy gray sky, but there is no rain. Apparently the summer storm we outran together hasn't hit here just yet.

"Thanks for the lift," I finally say. "Thanks for everything."

"No problem," she says. "Look. What you told me back there, beforehand. Those were good things for me to hear. Really."

I nod my head, glad that my fake prophecy provided her with some comfort. "I don't know what to say about the other thing. Me and Alix, we're divorced."

"Yeah."

"Four years. That's a long time."

"Yeah."

"It was really just—"

She holds up a hand. "It happened. It was a not-good moment. But it happened. So listen, am I going to see you again or what?"

For a moment I think she's asking for another prophecy, but then I realize it's a simple question, the kind normal human beings ask each other every day. "I guess that's kind of up to us."

Rhonda faces me and smiles at my response, the single best line of dialogue I've come up with in recent memory. She says, "This is a good thing to keep in mind."

I climb out but linger inside the open door, leaning into the Honda. I want to stay in this moment, retain the fragile feeling of rightness that eye contact with Rhonda creates. I know I'll head around back and up my steps, make some tricky phone calls to Quinn about tomorrow and Alix about Sunday before crashing on the brown couch. But for now I just want to stand here, savor the sensation, and try to imprint it on my brain. Oddly, I'm not worrying about the future consequences of my actions or the symbolic meaning of how Rhonda is supposed to fit in the big picture of what I'm caught up in now. I'm just here and feeling fine.

"You know my number, Seamus," Rhonda says, looking over the steering wheel.

The moment I close her door she pulls away. I watch her turn down Market, and even after she's gone I stand in the darkening street. Finally I walk over to my mailbox, stuffed with a week's worth of free offers and bills, slip them inside the immobilizer, and head up the side walkway. Around back, I'm surprised but happy to find my pickup parked beneath my deck. Alix, I decide.

Across the alley a sharp crack, what could easily be mistaken for a gunshot, echoes off the three remaining walls of the Salvation Station. It's followed by a second, then a third. Piled high outside the collapsed wall is a mound of bulging Hefty bags. A splotchy mutt scrounges through them. While I'm watching, a bag arcs over the crumbled wall as if catapulted and drops onto the pile. A grim

notion takes hold of me: The city is finally making good on its demolition warning. Judgment day has come while I was gone.

I cross the alley and step for the second time today onto holy
ground, scowling at the faded THIS PROPERTY CONDEMNED notices stapled to half-rotted wooden stakes. With my good arm out for balance, I carefully pick my way up the collapsed wall. Just as I reach
the top, another tossed Hefty bag nearly beans me. I dodge left and
turn to confront what I'm sure will be a careless city worker. But
instead I'm faced with a black man wearing raggedy painter's pants
and a red bandana. He's raking debris into the mouth of a garbage
bag being held open by another man, this one's shirtless white back
peeling with sunburn. Behind them, another homeless man holds
up the arms of a red wheelbarrow. Clear across the church, a thin
woman carefully pries stained glass shards from a window like a
dentist removing teeth. In the corner, a pale man with a black wool
cap drives a pickax into a pile of bricks. There must be two dozen
homeless, all working away like content dwarves waiting for someone to start whistling. The marble altar, a week ago buried thick in
muck, now rises up immaculate, sharp and bright. The Trinitron on
top beams Martha Stewart, who's hanging a white valance over pink
curtains.

"You're late!" the man with the red wheelbarrow complains. I
tell him I'm sorry and cautiously descend into the church. The other
homeless ignore me and I wander uninvited along the aisle, past
pews that have been freed from ivy and crud. The wood of the first
few rows glows with the dullest of shines, and I pause when I see
why. Down one row, a ruddy-faced man kneels over a green bucket.
He's scrubbing the pew with a rag. "Hi," he says. "I have a lot of
work to do."

"I see that," I say back, then ask, "What's going on here?"

"Big question," he says. "Could you be more specific?"

"What are you doing?"

"I'm cleaning off these damn benches. I deserve a raise."

Next to me, the red-wheelbarrow worker wheels his load over to the baptismal and dumps dirt and rocks into an area a pear-shaped woman just swept clean. I turn back to the man at my feet and ask him, "Who's in charge here?"

He dunks his rag in the bucket of dark water. "I thought you were in charge."

"No. I'm not in charge."

He returns to his scrubbing and says, "We're in real trouble then. Somebody has to be in charge. Right?"

"Well, who told you to do this?"

"It needs to be done," he says, talking over his shoulder. "Who told you to interrogate me? Just do what you're told. Curiosity killed the cats."

"The cat," I correct him. "Curiosity killed the cat."

Disappointed, he shakes his head and says, "Son, you just haven't been around long enough."

Laughter comes from behind the altar, where Martha Stewart now holds a box and stands by a refrigerator. I ascend the steps, close enough to hear her say, "Don't make the mistake of throwing away freezer-burned ice cream." In the doorway of the sacristy stands a bald man wearing khakis and a white shirt. He's talking to someone inside, swinging his hands and throwing his head back as he chuckles madly. I take him for some kind of city planner or an outreach activist, come to clean up our neighborhood, a community project he can put in italics on his résumé—and he's figured out a way to draft some cheap help. He's probably conned them into a day's work for a few bucks or the promise of a warm bed. Later he'll take a group Polaroid to prove what a swell guy he is. Meanwhile, I still haven't seen any of the Brain Trust, which means he probably chased them off. Busted wing and muddy funeral clothes or not—for this, I will not stand.

I stride toward the stranger, lift my chin, and say, "You in charge here?"

When he turns, his eyes come directly into mine and he shouts, "At last—Dr. Cooper!" He charges into me with his arms outstretched, and before I know it he's got both arms wrapped around me and he's squeezing me tightly, reigniting my shoulder.

From the sacristy, Dr. Gladstone steps out, wearing my WORLD'S #1 DAD baseball cap. And only then do I register the voice of the clean-cut stranger. Dr. Winston. Still embracing me, he says, "It has been so long. I drew comfort from the thought of you so often." He pulls back and beams, radiant with joy. The last time I saw him, his shoulder-length dirty hair blended into his scraggly black beard. Now his head is shaved Mr. Clean–tight, and gray and white pepper his neatly trimmed beard. His mustard teeth have been cleaned. Beneath brand-new khakis slip the gold of Bull Invinso's boots.

"Winston," I say. "You look different."

"Oh, Buddy," he sighs, "I *am* different. I'm so much more than I was. I knew you'd see it. You were always gifted with such quick insight."

Dr. Gladstone asks me, "Where the heck have you been?"

"I was sick," I say, glancing at my immobilizer as proof. "In the hospital."

"I was completely right," Gladstone informs me. He turns to Winston. "Did you tell him I was completely right?"

Winston looks straight up at the steeple and nods reverently. "The proof of your faith is evident for all to see, Brother Gladstone."

Gladstone bows his head away from the tower, as if he's afraid to glimpse the face of God.

"Hey," I say. "Where's Dr. Bacchus?"

Gladstone and Winston trade glances, but avoid my eyes. "He's moved on," Winston says. "He didn't believe in the work we had to get done here." His arms spread out toward the workers in the church. "As you can see, we are rebuilding the temple."

"The temple looks just great. But where's Bacchus?"

"He expressed concerns that the government had kidnapped you," Winston explains. "He mentioned Washington, Quantico, and a secret base in the Dakotas for political prisoners."

I picture Dr. Bacchus hitchhiking across America in search of me.

Sounds like an ABC TV series from the '70s. Along the way he'll help the oppressed. Of course, it's more likely that he's simply boozed up under the bridge or behind the Greyhound station.

"Wherever he is," Winston says, as if reading my thoughts, "he is no longer our concern. Each soul falls as it should."

Head bowed again, Gladstone parrots Winston's tone. "Each soul falls as it should."

"So what happened to you?" I ask.

Winston lifts his face again to the steeple. "I have been to a place few can conceive." The faith in his voice reminds me of Snake and his encounter with Patsy Cline in the afterlife. But a near-death experience wouldn't explain where Winston got the khakis from.

"Show me," I say.

With his arm around my good shoulder, Winston escorts me past Gladstone, who keeps looking at the ground. In the sacristy we pause at the vault that once held chalices and Eucharists. Winston lifts a kerosene lamp from a shelf stocked with buckets of yellow paint. After lighting the lamp, he opens the door that leads up to the haunted room where we mounted Trevor's satellite dish. "Choose now to follow me," he says, "and nothing will be as it was." He and the bubble of shifting firelight drift up the stairway. I start up the creaky steps.

As we climb, a flapping sound above grows louder. It makes me imagine a flag snapping in the wind. Winston starts mumbling under his breath, some kind of chant or incantation. Stepping into the room, I see a sheet of thick, clear plastic nailed over the window through which we both once climbed. The wooden slats have all been removed and the wind rattles one corner of the plastic sheet. Early evening light leaks through it, but not enough that we don't need the kerosene lamp, which sends swinging glows sliding up the steeple, bouncing into the vast empty cone over our heads. The floor has been swept free of ash and bone, and the satellite dish sits exactly where I last saw it. Fresh yellow paint, ripe in my nose, dries on three walls. But graffiti covers the fourth wall, the one across from the window. Only when I move closer, I realize I'm looking not at graffiti, but at handwriting, tight black scrawls in rows like newspaper type.

Standing behind me, Winston stops chanting and lifts the lamp. "It took me almost twenty straight hours, starting on my first night back. My fingers cramped up. You can tell where I switched to my left hand. See how it slants suddenly? There was so much I wanted to get down, it was like my brain burned with the words. Have you ever felt like that, Buddy, where the truth felt like something alive in your skull trying to claw its way free?"

I consider this for a moment, then say, "No, Winston, but it sounds terrible."

He sighs. "Quite the opposite, my friend. It is ecstasy."

I lean in close and try to read the ecstatic truth. But I can't understand the symbols, which look like the hieroglyphics Indiana Jones is always trying to decipher inside pyramids and on the sides of sacred artifacts.

"The Chronicle Wall details what happened to me," Winston explains. "What I learned while I was away."

Across one line I see an upside-down triangle, an eye inside a box, and what looks like two fish kissing.

Winston steps between me and the wall, raising the kerosene glow. He aims a finger at the symbols I was studying and begins to speak slowly. *"While the probing pained me deeply I do not blame the Svobodians for that pain because it helped me focus. Just as intense fire burns but purifies. They did not realize the probing was uncomfortable for me. The pain of the probing, I believe, was strictly unintentional."*

He pauses and looks at me over one shoulder. My face remains blank. His hand floats across the scribbled wall and settles on a passage toward the end of the final column. "Ahh, yes," he says. "I think I got this part just right: *When they informed me that I was to be returned I wept bitterly, and seeing me weep they hummed to me in their way the songs that soothed. For they cannot stand the sight of discomfort in any sentient. Once I was calmed they revealed to me the truth of why I had to be sent back, and my mission was clear to me, and I stopped all my weeping, for weeping is for those lost and without hope."*

The wind picks up and the plastic rattles hard, snapping like it's about to give way. Winston turns to it. Without looking at me, he says, "You think I'm crazy. Don't you?"

"Crazy isn't a word I would use," I say.

"It's OK. People thought Wilhelm Hoade was insane. *The opinions of others do not molest the truth.* That's the third of the Seven Sacred Svobodian Tenets."

I point at the strange symbols. "So this is Svobodian."

"As close as the untrained human mind can comprehend it."

"And you learned all this in the last seven days?"

"No, no. It took me about three months. Their language is very complicated. Conjugating is a nightmare, worse than Latin. But that has to do with the Svobodian concept of time. They don't make the same kinds of hard-core distinctions we do between past, present, and future. *Now* and *forever* mean almost the exact same thing. Recall the seminal work of the French mathematician-philosopher LaPlace. He claimed that if given enough mathematical data he could reasonably calculate where you'd be for dinner and what you'd eat on any given day five years from now. Très Svobodian. They have no translation for words like *might* or *maybe*. No conditionals, do you understand?"

"So these Svobodians have no use for free will, is that what you're telling me?"

"You're free to make any choice you want. But that choice isn't random."

"Winston," I say. "You have not been gone three months."

He takes a deep breath and says, "Dr. Cooper, with God as my witness, I have been gone for almost two years. Inside the homeship dimension, time flows differently."

I feel tired and heavy. Still, I can't take my eyes off the symbols. I find the kissing fish in a few places, and I also notice a recurring symbol that looks like a four-fingered hand. Behind me, the plastic rattles with the wind.

"Once the Svobodians realized that they were right about me, a series of operations were performed. When my neural pathways were clear of debris, when I had the capacity to comprehend the vast amounts of poetic mathematical understanding with which they wanted to bless me, I was plugged into a huge living machine for three days and nights. On the third day I awakened and I understood. I achieved perfect clarity. I saw."

I turn from the Svobodian words and see his eyes reflecting the kerosene flame, flickering and clear. I think of Hardy when he told me he was saved by a miracle, of Rhonda when she said there had to be a reason, of Snake in the back of the hearse, convinced he'd come back from the dead, even of Alix, when she told me she'd love me forever with all her heart. And I think of myself when I told Rhonda she was not alone, when I claimed to see her future as a thing rich with hope. The sensation of rightness that came in the field and out front in the car. But those moments were fleeting, and based on my pretending to be someone I no longer am, a man with gold boots and a sure dream.

I find Winston's eyes and I whisper, "Tell me what you saw. Please."

"What's coming is nothing less than a planet-wide transfiguration of man. We'll shake off these shabby skins and metamorphosize into beings of pure light, like the Svobodians."

He lifts a hand to the plastic covering the window and snaps it away, like a man revealing a curtained painting. The wind tears inside and sends the lantern flame twisting and ducking. Staring over the city, Winston says, "Look at us."

Eagerly, I leave the wall and go to his side. The wind rips at our faces but we stand and look together at the entire city spread out before us. The dull brick barracks of Simplicity Gardens, its windows blocked with plywood. The long corridor of Castle Street, where even the cops won't go alone. The strip malls lining Market Street. The condos crammed in behind the MegaWal-Mart. The new franchise gentlemen's club that was too powerful for even the Baptists. The five-mile run of chain stores along College. The giant bucket rotating on the roof of the Quicky Chicken.

Winston opens his hands, palms up, as if he's displaying Wilmington for me. He says, "I've stood here for days and studied them, Buddy. I've mapped the straight lines they race in, driving from work to home to the bar to church to the shopping mall to home to work to the bar to church, scattering desperately past each other like rats in a maze, certain the way out was the way they came. All of them afraid to slow down for fear someone might speak the terrible truth: *There's no way out—this is just the way it is.* And like those same dumb rats, so few of them with the sense to be calm and stop running and turn to one another for more than the diversion of biting or humping. It's so terrible, Buddy, how can you stand it? How can any of us stand it?"

I want my remote in my hand, Alix beside me in bed, the mask tucked tight over my face, a beer and a pink pill, to be on my knees.

Winston, his voice cracking with tears, goes on. "All this. This filth and pain and regret. This is not how we were intended to live. We were meant for paradise. This has all been a big mistake. But the Svobodians understand and want to help us realize our destiny. Their world is a utopia, a place with no hunger, no disease. Since everything is as it was meant to be, there are no questions, no blame, no guilt, and no doubt."

The thought of such a place washes over me like warm rain, and I say as a joke, "When do we go?" But when I hear my own voice I'm frightened by its conviction.

He pats my shoulder. "That's the best part. I know now what NASA knows. What Donald Trump and the WTO have known for a long time, I suspect. We don't have to go at all. It's coming to us. Though the Svobodians are beings of pure light, they still require a physical host. Their homeship is the asteroid, Buddy. They live at the heart of its hollow core. They're coming right at us."

CHAPTER THE FOURTEENTH

*An Assault on the Beach. What People Used to Think
the World Was Like. Columbus's Men. Prayers and Such.
The Healing Properties of Salt Water.*

Where Quinn got his hands on an amphibious assault vehicle I'll never know. But this doesn't seem to concern Hardy or Snake, both of whom are occupied in their own worlds as we skip across the waves along Wrightsville Beach. As for myself, I'm having a hard time staying in the here and now, can't keep from replaying scenes from the dozen D-day flicks I've watched alone on late-night TV. I keep picturing all those movie-soldier faces set hard with determination, ready to stare down destiny like real Americans. How the men in open boats just like these josh each other as they storm toward Normandy Beach, laughing about killing Krauts, dreaming about all the long-legged ladies waiting in Paris to be saved. There's always a single nervous one, some kid from Nebraska on the verge of almost thinking about crying even. But a salty veteran, John Wayne or Robert Mitchum, calms him down by passing on his lucky rabbit's foot, pressing it into the kid's palm with a hearty male handshake. "You give this back to me on the beach, Jimmy." At this point, you know the salty vet's a dead man. He's just signed his death warrant. Here's one thing I'm sure of: As a rule in movies about D-day, or invasion films of any kind, never give away your lucky rabbit's foot. And even if you need to believe that you'll live through the special-effects explosions waiting in your future, never predict it.

I find myself reaching for my own lucky charm, the vsaji Brook gave me, but the space on my chest is empty, and only when I feel that nothing do I remember removing the necklace back at the SWC Training Facility, when I was getting suited up. Quinn had to order a fresh Terror costume since the original is currently bloodstained and bulleted, probably in an evidence box in police lockup. Though the throbbing in my shoulder has dulled and the drainage has all but stopped, I still had to work the arm slowly into place. I offered to go without the immobilizer, but Quinn wanted me to wear it. "The sympathy factor combined with the air of dramatic realism," he explained. This is the same rationale he used when asking Snake to cover his bloody eye with a black pirate patch. If it's possible, my new suit's even hotter than the old one, and though I've been trying to stay in the shade, this boat is basically a deep tin box with a motor, so my body's getting cooked out here inside the spandex. I look down at the mask on my lap. It seems empty, deflated, like my guardian angel/demon balloon back at New Hanover.

Across from me in the boat sits Quinn, whose artificial tan only seems more odd in direct sunlight. He's on a bench fiddling with a Pentium PowerBook connected to a toy-sized satellite dish. His NASA headset-phone is wired into the computer. But on the monitor, only a static blizzard rages. He twists a knob on the side of the headset and says, "Victor, let's not point fingers at solar flares for everything. Demonstrate some initiative. And expedite. Our time constraints are nonnegotiable."

A few moments later, the static clears on Quinn's monitor. I step over, shield my eyes, and lean in to check the reception. But instead of the Beach Bash wrestlers I expect to see, ballet dancers skip across a stage. For a second I think of Brook, then of Rhonda. But these dancers are genuine professionals, dressed in light pinks and dark blues, hitting their marks sharp and tight. A monster, what looks like a Chinese dragon, chases a blond ballerina. Quinn sees me watching and says, "PBS has this kind of broadcast power and still they demand federal funding. Absurd."

The boat pitches with a wave. Overhead a plane flies by trailing a message, but from this angle I think it reads T-SHIRTS SAVE YOUR LIVER. Leaving Quinn alone with his hi-tech gadgets, I balance my way to the rear, where Snake sits bent over a stack of index cards. The black pirate patch hangs crooked over his bloodied left eye. Sweat has lined little streaks down the white makeup on his gaunt cheeks, so his bruise is starting to show, and his black goatee seems wet with milk. With trembling fingers, he plucks the Nicotaint from his black-lipsticked lips and recites, "Everyone is entitled to a second chance. It's never too late to begin again. Today can be a fresh start for you too." He glances down at his notes, then back at me. "Honestly, Buddy, doesn't this sound a little too preachy?"

"It sounds good, Snake," I say, and his face sours. At this morning's meeting, he reminded us all to call him Paul. I apologize and go on. "Paul, the fans'll eat it up. You and Quinn should be proud."

He nods toward the front of the boat and says, "This is just so important. I don't want to let him down."

The him in question is Hardy Appleseed, standing on a metal box in the bow, looking over the side, pressing his face into the wind. His All-American cape streams behind him like the flag of certain victory. The Victory Belt is secured around his waist. When we were getting changed at the Training Facility, he made a point of showing me the dent on the belt, from that bullet's impact. I pushed my finger into the tiny crater.

"Just be yourself," I tell Snake. "You'll be fine." I pat his shoulder, trying to ignore the Kevlar vest I feel under his shirt, this a precaution insisted on by Lieutenant Tyrelli. Paul nods and puffs on his Nicotaint, turns back to his notes. Balancing myself against the rocking of the boat, I sidle up to Hardy on the metal box and look with him over the edge, across the ocean. His face is turned to the horizon.

"This is nice," he says. "My pap had a sailing boat."

"I remember you telling me that," I say.

"When I was real little I used to be afraid," Hardy tells me. "I used to cry if we got too far from the beach."

To our left, the shore is maybe two miles in. I can see the bright patchwork of beach towels. "The beach is right there, Hardy. We're safe."

"Full stop, Antonio!" I hear Quinn shout into his headset, and the engine shifts into a lower pitch. The boat slows to an idle. Quinn says, "Victor, in two minutes I'm either seeing what I want on this screen or placing an advertisement for your current position. 'Help Wanted,' it will read, 'Incompetents Need Not Apply.'"

The triangle top of a circus tent rises from the beach about a half mile down. Back at the Facility, when we were reviewing the day's plan, Quinn told us that overnight the pay-per-view orders doubled, spiking right after the five o'clock news, when word of the attack at the cemetery started spreading. He's hired extra security for our protection. All afternoon the other wrestlers have been pairing off. We're the grand finale.

Hardy says, "Mr. Cooper, I ain't afraid no more. I like to go swimming. I always been a real good swimmer. Pap even taught me to do the backstroke."

I tell Hardy I can't do the backstroke, but I'm not sure he's listening to me. His eyes remain fixed on the horizon. He points. "That's what used to scare me."

I scan the smooth blue water, thinking a shark fin might be slicing along or something like that. But there's nothing.

Speaking apparently to the waves, Hardy goes on. "The map was in a big book in the room where Pap slept. It had shiny pages. It was a old kind of map, a painted picture of what people used to think the world was like. There wasn't any America yet and Africa was all skinny. Along the edges in some places there was pictures of sea monsters coming in and out of the water with scary faces. But that ain't what made me afraid because even when I was a little kid I knew there was no such thing as monsters."

He pauses and looks at me for a second, as if he's asking for confirmation on the nonexistence of monsters. I nod and he turns back to the water to continue. "What I always snuck in there to look at was the boat falling off the end of the map. It was tilting over the edge of this giant waterfall that just went right off the page. There wasn't any bottom to it. Them people thought the planet was flat as a pancake."

He points to the horizon. "They thought that was the end of the world."

Together, we study the flat line where the sea meets the sky. I say, "But they were wrong, Hardy. The world doesn't have an end."

"I know, I know. It's round like a basketball. That's what Christopher Columbus proved. He had three ships. The *Nina*, the *Pinta*, and the *Santa Maria*."

"That's right," I say. "1492."

"I'll bet those sailors were awful afraid," Hardy says. "I'll bet they prayed a lot."

"Absolutely." I know none of those ancient sailors thought the earth was actually flat by that point in history, but they had no real idea what they were sailing into. I think of the stories they'd heard, of the friends who'd sailed out and disappeared. Out there in the middle of the unknown Atlantic, rocking on the waves of the same ocean I'm rocking on now, past where the mapmakers had charted, Columbus's crew had only the rolling, open sea and the shifting stars in front of them, only their faith and the word of their good captain.

"Maintain that frequency, Victor," Quinn shouts. "Target reception optimum."

Hardy and I turn from the water. Paul is hunched over our fearless leader at the monitor, Nicotaint pinched between his black lips. We head back to see what's being tuned in. On the screen the Mad Maestro stands center ring beneath the tent, gripping the microphone. Quinn punches a key and the volume booms from the PowerBook. ". . . The hour is almost at hand. And where is your champion? Licking false wounds! Quaking in fear at the fury of the inevitable Thunder Symphony!" He pinches one side of his handle-bar mustache and rolls it, trying to look sinister.

This brings some applause from the crowd, but they are drowned out by booing and catcalls. Somebody yells out, "Take your classical crap back to Australia!" The camera scans the audience, rolls over a lot of bare flesh—smooth round shoulders and flat tan bellies. Tank tops and two-pieces. Several pockets of black clothing suggest groups of Dark Disciples, but I can't be certain. The screen is too small.

Quinn touches the control on the side of his headset. "Antonio, slow and steady on final approach. Initiate."

Instantly the engine whines and we start forward. On the screen, Maestro launches into a speech about his plans to restore calm to the SWC. "Order must be established in the wake of this chaos. And only a strong and noble leader can accomplish such a feat. Is Appleseed such a man? Who among you has seen him here? Will he show his face? No! Because he fears the consequences. That boyish whelp would rather forfeit the championship than face me."

Quinn says, "Rev it up, Antonio."

We lurch ahead, and the front end rises slightly.

Quinn stands, walks to a small gray box attached to the bow. It looks like a tiny cannon. He hollers, "They'll talk about this for years."

Maestro continues his rant. "I stand before you to reveal the unfettered truth. Hardy Appleseed and his co-conspirator the Terror are fraudulent."

The crowd boos loudly and I feel strangely validated. It's like they're sticking up for me. Like they're protecting my good name. Somebody lobs a plastic yellow bucket into the ring, the kind Brook once used to make sand castles. It bounces past Maestro, who punts it through the ropes and over the audience, a nice improv.

"If this is not so, then where is the All-American Blunder? He has abandoned you. Rather than face the music he has shown his true colors as an unmitigated coward."

Grinning, Quinn presses a button on the gray box. Three firecracker shots launch three streaks arching into the late-afternoon sky ahead of us. The three flares, roaring side by side toward the beach, trail three smoky tails colored red, white, and blue. On the monitor, the Maestro turns toward the ocean and says, "Egads!"

Quinn touches his headgear and says, "Victor, if you please" into his mike and a moment later I hear it through the monitor, blasting over the speakers under the tent: Kate Smith's full-bellied voice asking, *Oh say can you see?*

"It cannot be!" Maestro shouts into his mike.

The crowd goes berserk, burying Kate's deep bass.

"Full throttle now, Antonio. Hardy, prepare for disembarkation, we're approaching implementation of phase two."

Hardy turns to me and I translate, "Get ready for the go code."

We start crashing through the breakers, rising and falling with each smashing wave. Quinn puts a hand on my shoulder and I turn. He offers me the sagging mask of the Terror and shouts, "Don't forget your face."

I lift the mask with my good hand, take a breath, like I'm about to go underwater, and duck my head into the tight fabric.

Wash and spray from the ocean splashes over the rim and we get dowsed pretty good. Then the boat slows. Over the metal walls, I can hear fans yelling. We slide to a sandy halt and everything is still. Lots of yelling now. Someone barks directions to the crowd through a bullhorn. Overhead a gray seagull circles us.

"Clean and tight," Quinn shouts, and Hardy nods his head sternly to all of us before leaping over the side of the wall. Paul and I crowd around Quinn's monitor and see Hardy charging up the beach through a corridor of red-shirted security guards. The fans scream wildly, whipping their beach towels over their heads. The national anthem's conclusion blares at full strength. Hardy jumps up onto the ring and vaults the top rope, lands with a thud on the canvas. Maestro backs away and lifts the mike. "Just a moment now, old chap. Marquis of Queensberry rules." Hardy locks his huge hands on either side of Maestro's head and lifts him onto his tiptoes. A female voice screams, "Crush his skull!" But Hardy merely slams Maestro to the canvas, where he slides under the bottom rope and bolts off in the opposite direction, down a roped-off path through the audience.

Hardy, following the plan, searches the canvas for the microphone. Holding it with one hand, he snaps the other to his forehead and salutes the crowd. The camera shows them roaring their approval, saluting him back. One young lady, above the crowd on somebody's shoulders, is naked from the waist up. The camera cuts away.

"I. Have. Returned," Hardy says solemnly, and they scream, applauding as if he had risen from the grave. He lets them go for a minute, then lifts his hand to calm them so he can continue. "You all know I ain't so good at speech making, but I sure do appreciate all them cards and prayers and such while I was in the hospital. As for what the Mad Mushroomhead just said about me being a coward, *don't believe it*. He is a liar and liars can't be trusted. I ain't no quitter. I will always be your champion."

The chant rises quickly. "Apple-seed, Apple-seed, Apple-seed." He lets it build, takes a long slow walk around the ring with his arms outstretched, as if he's absorbing their faith in him, like their adoration is healthy radiation. Again he quiets the crowd. "I know you might be surprised by who come with me today. We wasn't always friends. But we must put the past behind us for the sake of the future." Hardy hesitates, remembers. "Of the great future ahead of us."

I swear I hear someone yell "Amen!" The camera shows the security guards circling the ring, arms locked together, straining to keep the fans back. Quinn taps me. "Stay focused on our objectives and execute the action plan. I have complete confidence in both of you."

I help Paul to the front of the boat. He's leaning on the cane with one hand and me with the other. His thin body is shaking inside the long black coat. He reaches up and pulls the Nicotaint from his black lips and tosses it onto the metal floor of the assault vehicle, crushes it with his foot as if extinguishing a real cigarette. He reaches into the pocket of his black pants and opens his palm to me. Sitting dead center is a single paper clip. Paul looks at me with his one eye and says, "For luck," then folds it away. Amazed at myself, I respond, "See you on the beach."

We hear Hardy now over the loudspeakers ahead of us. "Because when the chips were down these boys showed me what they was really made of."

Like the drawbridge of a castle, the front end of the assault vehicle slowly lowers. At first I see a blue split of sky, then the red-and-white top of the circus tent's peak, then the heads of the crowd, then the whole scene before us, the security corridor holding back the fans, the clear tunnel leading up the beach, and Hardy standing in the ring looking in our direction, waiting for us.

Hardy booms into the mike, "Please welcome my new tag-team partner, the man that saved my life, the Unknown Kentucky Terror! And this here is gonna be our manager, the man formerly known as Snake Handler!"

As he announces us we step off onto the sand, out into the open, and the crowd is stunned into a strange silence. Good and evil can't join forces. Moving slowly for Paul, we shuffle through the sand up the security tunnel, and the fans stare in disbelief. One kid sticks his face out and points at his forehead, where a cobra tattoo curls from his hair. "A hundred and twenty bucks!" he shouts. "And this don't come off!" Security shoves him back into the masses. Another one, a Disciple complete with black overcoat, cries out as we pass, "You think this is a game? You think this is just my hobby?" And then just when we reach the ring, a girl slips through and throws herself at his feet. "Please," she begs, "we'll be all alone." A guard carries her away.

I help Paul up the steps into the ring, and Hardy splits the ropes for him to climb through. I follow, and Paul and I stand on either side of Hardy, who takes our hands and raises our arms. Though the Disciples bury their faces, the audience at large erupts in a spasm of excitement. Everybody likes happy endings.

As we turn to give all the fans—and each of the three pay-per-view cameras—a good look, I can see over the heads of the crowd, out past the rolled-up walls of the tent. The beach beyond is practically deserted. Everyone is here, or on their way toward us. But down by our amphibious assault vehicle, away from everyone else, is someone just sitting there, a girl I think. I can't see her face, but she's sitting on a bike or something right along the water's edge, not even looking to see what all the excitement is about. Maybe she's fishing.

We finish a full rotation and Hardy passes me the mike. I start in on my speech, "Standing here, beside a great American hero like Hardy Appleseed, is the finest privilege of my life. And because I was injured fighting side by side with this man, I wear this wound as a badge of honor. From this day forward, I pledge myself to him and the ideals which he embodies."

The fans applaud and I feel their love, the quick acceptance they'll grant me now that I've converted to the good side of the Force. I look at the cameras and hope some of these pictures make it to the website where Brook can download them, show Alix the proof that I am a hero. And at the same time I imagine Rhonda at Sanctuary House, right now at this exact moment, curled on a donated couch and watching me here, knowing my secret face beneath the mask.

The cheering dies down some when I pass the mike to Paul. Before he can begin, a Dark Disciple at ringside points a finger and shouts, "Don't trust that two-faced bastard!"

Another joins in: "Sonuvabitch told us he'd—"

Hardy stomps on the canvas and yells, "Y'all be nice!"

But Paul settles a hand on Hardy's thick arm and stops him, then lifts the mike to his black lips. "Don't be angry, Hardy. We can't blame them for their distrust. They speak for many here, no doubt. Many who even now suspect me of some trickery. This face is the face of deceit and betrayal. And the name Snake Handler carries with it lies and bitterness."

"Then you must have a new name," I suggest on cue.

"And a new face," Hardy adds.

The audience is transfixed. I picture Quinn in the boat, grinning as he follows along with the script he concocted. Solemnly, I walk to the corner and pick up the waiting props, a towel and a plastic water bottle. I return to center ring, where Paul now kneels before Hardy like a squire about to be knighted, or a convert about to receive first communion. He folds his hands together around the mike and it looks like he's praying. "Go ahead," Paul says to us. "Do what must be done."

I squirt water into the towel. Hardy steadies Paul's head with one big hand, and with the other he takes the wet cloth from me and gently dabs at Paul's forehead, making small tender circles, revealing the thin pink scars from River Road. The crowd has fallen to unbearable silence. A single female Disciple shouts out "No!" but no one responds or picks up her cry.

Paul's one eye is closed peacefully, and Hardy lifts away the pirate patch, drops it to the canvas. Wine still colors the eye. As Hardy washes the face paint from his nose and his sunken cheeks, the purple bruise becomes clear. Hardy dabs the wet whiteness from his goatee. Even the black lipstick is wiped clean. When Hardy's finished, Paul's upturned face glistens with newborn slickness. Hardy drops the wet towel on the mat and turns his head side to side, looking for something to dry Paul's face. We hadn't considered this. Improvising, Hardy reaches back and gathers up a corner of his own All-American cape, then brings it to Paul's face.

When Paul stands, he unbuttons his long black coat, pulls it off his shoulders and reverses it, exposing a pure white inside. He puts his arms through the sleeves and buttons the coat again. Hardy declares, "Snake Handler is dead. From now on, you'll be Saint Handler."

Saint/Snake nods his head in approval and says, "No longer will I deal with the snakes and devils of this world. Now I will walk with the righteous and the just. With the angels."

Three seconds of absolute silence, then someone in the crowd pumps his fist and chants "Saint-Saint-Saint" and the audience snaps out of its trance, falls in step with the rhythm of the new mantra. Their faces gleam with wonder and joy, as if they're witnessing something essential and meaningful. And because we're what they're looking at, I feel elevated. But then some voices, probably the scattered Disciples, begin countering the Saint chant with "Snake-Snake-Snake." A dozen faces in the crowd look left and I turn to a circle of fans huddled together like a rugby scrum. Because of all the movement it's hard to see exactly what's at the center, but then a ripped piece of black clothing gets tossed into the air. I see an arm, then the flash of a bloodied face. Just then another scrap breaks out closer to the ring. Two men have got a Dark Disciple's arms locked behind his back and a third one is kicking him in the ribs. "Reform your evil ways!" screams the kicker.

Snake, or Saint, or Paul, still has the mike, and he holds up one hand and shouts, "Wait! This was to be a day of great celebration. Everyone is entitled to a second chance!"

A middle-aged man rams his beach umbrella into the gut of that kid with the cobra tattoo.

Hardy's head twitches, such a fast snap that I think he's been stung by a wasp. When I turn to him he's staring and blinking hard, but not looking at me or anything.

Someone with a bullhorn orders, "This violence will stop. Cease and desist the disruptive behavior or be designated hostile."

Saint/Snake, now leaning over a rope into the crowd, begs, "Please. It's never too late to begin again."

Hardy cups a hand over his right ear and closes his eyes. He says, "What? What?" It's like back in the pet church.

The bullhorn blasts, "We have German-made stun guns. They are fully charged."

But the crowd has turned to riot. For fifty feet around the ring every body seems locked into every other body, a mosh pit gone mad. A kid wearing white face paint starts crawling under the bottom rope. In one fist he grips a steak knife. I grab Paul's cane and nine-iron the punk with a one-armed swing. I glance back toward the boat, but the security tunnel has collapsed. "We need to be someplace else!" I yell, but Paul has started to cry, and Hardy's on one knee now, both hands covering his ears.

Just about everyone else is screaming.

Suddenly Hardy stands, yanks the mike from Paul, and leaps up onto the top turnbuckle. He hollers through the speakers, "Would ya'll shut the heck up! I can't hear my Jesus."

Remarkably, the crowd freezes. Two thousand faces stare at Hardy in silence.

"Well, thanks." Hardy shakes his head. "OK," he says, giving God the go ahead to retransmit, I suppose. We all wait as Hardy listens, his face focused intensely. "Oh no," he says. Then, "Well, of course I'll help. Where is she?" He turns to the ocean. After dropping the mike, he jumps down into the crowd.

Hoping this is part of Quinn's action plan, and not a divinely inspired diversion, I turn and say, "Snake, do you know what's going on?"

"Don't call me that," he shouts, and I begin to realize he's not acting. But clearly, he's also surprised by this turn. We're off the script. I picture Quinn in the boat yelling "Cut!" into his headset.

"Sorry," I say to Paul, and slide under the bottom rope. I fall in behind Hardy, and the crowd parts for him like the Red Sea for Moses. It's crazy and creepy, but no one says anything as we cross the sand. Blood streaks a few faces. Hardy has to step over a moaning teenager, but his pace is methodical and deliberate, the stride of a man possessed. We reach the edge of the crowd and step onto the open beach. Finally I move beside Hardy, about to ask him where we're going, but then I see the answer. Not fifteen feet in front of us is Marna, parked in her wheelchair in the wet sand. Her two crooked arms wrapped in on themselves, her wrists locked at sharp angles.

We step up behind her and Hardy says, "Hi."

She looks up at us. Her curly black hair and her freckled cheeks. Her eyes fix on a point above and beyond our faces. Hardy says, "Was you looking at the ocean? I like the ocean."

She grins, nods what could be a response. The waves crash to white foam and ripple up to our feet. Behind us the crowd is afraid to come any closer. Over their heads, I notice the pay-per-view cameras are aimed in our direction. Hardy asks Marna, "How 'bout we go for a dip? Wouldn't you like that?"

Two thick black buckles crisscross her legs, one above and one below her knees. "Hardy," I say. "This girl can't swim. She shouldn't go in the ocean."

Ignoring me, Hardy kneels down next to the wheelchair and whispers to Marna, "Don't fret none. I'm awful strong. Strong enough to carry you. You'll be safe with me."

"Hardy," I say. "This maybe isn't such a good idea."

He looks up at me, smiling. "It's definitely a good idea, Mr. Cooper." He taps the Miracle Ear. "It's my Jesus's idea."

With this he begins to unbuckle Marna's legs. He stands, puts one arm under her knees, the other around her back. Grinning madly, she lays her arm around his neck and he hoists her frail body. He seems huge, and she, somehow, even smaller. He turns to the ocean. "C'mon, Mr. Cooper. Jesus says you can come too."

"Are you talking to him now, Hardy?"

"No sir," he says. "He's just talking to me. But I'm listening."

I look up at Hardy's bright shining face and I envy him. I wish I could believe that Jesus was speaking to him now. That bullets had miraculously passed through him in the ring last week. That Paul's eternal soul had been saved. That Rhonda could see the future. That the Svobodians were coming for Dr. Winston and all believers. That my plan to get my life back is anything but a joke. But I've learned the truth about such things. I've learned the cost of believing things might get better. So as much as I'd like to follow, when Hardy wades into the water, I simply can't go with him.

He steps into the sea strong and sure and confident, no doubt that he is exactly where he's supposed to be in the universe. The waves break against his muscled legs and when the water rises past his hips the ocean ripples his red cape out behind him on the surface of the water. The two of them seem like newlywed lovers, like he's carrying her across the threshold into a new life fresh from the wedding. When the waves get higher he turns to protect her, letting them smash into his broad back. Above the roar I hear Marna giggling, squealing with delight. There is no other sound but the waves and her laughter. I'm afraid Hardy's going to keep going, that he's heading for the horizon and that waterfall tumbling off the edge of the world. But then he stops. He's standing in the deep water just past the breakers, where the waves seem calmer.

Their heads bob with the rolling ocean, and each time they disappear behind a rising wave, I worry they won't reappear. Hardy must be holding her away from him, because her head is no longer settled on his shoulder. A wave comes up, a wave comes down and there's more distance between their faces. I don't want to believe it, but after the next one there's no doubt—she's too far away for Hardy to still be holding her—he's let her go.

A dozen fans appear at my side, leaning out, but no one goes in.

When the next wave crests and falls, Marna's head is gone. A Dark Disciple with a bloody nose next to me says, "Christ!" and starts in. But he stops when her face reappears, closer to shore. She must be floating, about ten feet ahead of Hardy. Just her face is there, nothing else, but we all can see she's smiling, and something holds us all in place. Even when a small wave swallows her from behind and her face vanishes for a moment, no one panics. And sure enough, there is her face and neck, closer to us now. After the wave behind that comes and goes she is closer still and somehow we see her shoulders, draped in the soaked T-shirt. Her body is bobbing in a familiar way that can't be possible, her freckled face is rising out of the water as she comes toward shore, lifting out of the waves like someone walking. We all can sense it, but no one believes it—even when her chest and stomach lift straight and true from the water. Only when the waves give way and reveal her legs—her legs supporting her weight—do people begin to whisper it: *She's walking.*

Appleseed healed her.

It's a miracle.

With that the fans surge, splashing into the water to meet Marna, whose head is still tilted and whose eyes still roll, whose hands are still bent back into her elbows. But who is standing now on her own. A few Disciples plunge into the waves and start throwing seawater onto their faces, rubbing at white face paint and black lipstick. A group of fans lift Marna on their shoulders, begin passing her around on their outstretched arms. And her laughter ignites theirs and suddenly they're all applauding and laughing, security guards and smeary-faced Dark Disciples and bruise-knuckled fans. As for Hardy, I force my way through the crowd and see him well out beyond the breakers, flat on his back, arms lifting from his side and stretching backward toward his head, angling along the beach, executing the backstroke perfectly.

CHAPTER THE FIFTEENTH

A Walk in the Park. Not Bread but Meat.
Bewaring Alligators. The Planning of Ducks.
Otter Orthodontics. Jhondu Achieves Jalcina.

As I'm crossing the arched bridge, two yellow paddleboats putter beneath me, heading toward the cypress forest that sprouts from the center of Greenfield Lake. These Tupperware cheapos are the illegitimate descendants of the elegant wooden crafts Alix and I rented over a decade ago, early in our courtship. A teenage boy and his father pilot the boat in the rear, pursuing a woman and girl with nearly identical ponytails. The mother and daughter's laughter skips across the lake. Below me in the water, turtles float suspended just below the surface, their sharp little heads stretched expectantly toward me. But I have no food to offer. Under them, a murky junkyard of items discarded from this bridge: a beach chair, a tricycle, what looks like a perfectly good baby stroller. I keep moving.

The path winds along a parking lot filling with families who decided against church this fine Sunday morning. A bright-faced boy tumbles from a minivan to help his father heft a blue ice chest. Carrying the crooked cooler between them, they walk through the shade toward a woman drifting a red-and-white checkered cloth over a picnic table. Nearby a white-haired man and a girl loft horseshoes in smooth arcs. Horseshoes! This is a game I thought people simply didn't play anymore.

Joggers bounce around a curve in the path, nod as they pass and trot by, working their way around the five-mile course that circles the lake. From a pine tree overhead, a bluejay cackles, though when I look up I can't find him. A chubby little boy in green overalls stands along the water's edge. In front of him, a congregation of ducks spreads out on the still water. At first I think he's heaving hot dog rolls at them, but as I near I realize it's not bread but meat. A package of Ball Park franks dangles from one hand, and with the other he's reaching in and lobbing the dogs one at a time. But the kid's got no technique, and the hot dogs drop one by one into the city of knobby cypress roots skylining the bank. The ducks seem unsure what to do. None of them appear hungry enough to risk coming ashore, but some of the ones in the back are honking. Ducks, like all of us, have only so much tolerance for inadequacy and failure. I look again to the parking lot, but there's still no sign of Alix.

I turn back to the boy and raise a friendly hand. "Hey, kiddo."

He smiles up at me, shows me the missing tooth just off center on bottom. At his feet sits a bag of Wonder Bread hot dog rolls.

"I'm five," he says, holding up a handful of fat fingers.

"Five's a great age."

He flops another hot dog into the roots and the ducks quack.

In the way-back-when, at this same park, I showed young Brook how to squeeze bread into tiny balls, toss them high so the ducks would pluck them from the air. Helping the boy is what the Better Buddy would do, and that's who I'm supposed to be now. I scan the park, find his parents twenty feet beyond the trail. The father presides over a pyramid of charcoal briquets, squirting lighter fluid from a square, white can. Next to him, mom holds a Budweiser and gives me the hard stare. When I try a smile, she taps her husband's shoulder and points at me. Just stopping here has branded me a pervert. Somehow the rule of the Army has made the leap to the civilian population: Presume all unknowns hostile. So I walk on without saying good-bye, and when I look back I notice the mother is heading for the boy, probably to be sure I didn't scar him for life with foul words or bad intentions.

Every fifty feet or so along the path, faded signs nailed to pine trees warn BEWARE OF ALLIGATORS. The alligators that lurk beneath the surface of Greenfield Lake are hardly worth bewaring. Sure, there's a handful of five-, six-footers, but they're overfed and lazy. Rumors of Grendel, a fifteen-footer with a taste for human blood, have circulated for years. Some field-tripping eighth-graders capsized their canoe a decade back, and every now and then a neighborhood dog goes missing. This is all the evidence a myth needs to maintain credibility.

I'm just considering what those smaller gators might think of the smell of Ball Park franks when a shout rings out from the park. "Poppa-San!" I turn to see Brook charging across the grass and pine needles, weaving through the trees. I raise both arms—the left one against its will—and she slides inside my embrace.

"Baby Bird," I whisper.

Chin on my shoulder, she says, "Mom's right behind me. Don't forget your amnesia."

I open my eyes and sure enough, Alix approaches through the pines, a thin, uncertain smile on her face.

Brook pulls back and I stare at her. "You got so tall," I try awkwardly. "Where are your glasses?" This is a line I had ready.

Brook points to the same blue eyes my mother had and announces, "Contacts."

"Sure," Alix says, now next to our daughter. "Couple years back."

"It's so good to see you," I say, though I make sure not to direct the comment at either one of them. Maybe they'll both think I'm talking to them.

"Where's your sling?" Alix asks.

I rotate my arm in a slow windmill to demonstrate my range of motion and say, "I'm a healing machine. I'll be back to a hundred percent before long." While this is not a complete lie, my real motivation for not wearing the immobilizer has more to do with not wanting to show up looking wounded and weak.

"That's great. You're off the Percocet?"

At AA, they made it clear that any addiction is an addiction. "I'm popping a few a day, Al. Everything's under control."

"How 'bout the rest of you?" Brook asks. "Like, y'know, your memory?"

A conspiratorial spark shines in her eyes. "Coming along," I say. "In my head you're still in junior high and only this tall." I hold my hand at her shoulder and she smiles. "I can't get over how long your hair is, Bird."

"Did Mom tell you I'm going to be an extra?"

"An extra what?"

"In the show you guys are making. At the studio."

I bring my eyes to Alix, who dips her chin and says, "Trevor thought it would be a good experience."

"Trevor," I say. "A good experience."

"I want to be an actress," Brook announces, "but not a stuntperson."

"You can be anything you want to be, Bird. As long as you work hard at it." Fatherly clichés such as this are usually the best I can muster.

"We'll all be, like, working together," Brook says. "It'll be bullet sweet." She steps between us and takes hold of our hands and we start walking, three abreast down the path, back the way I came.

Alix looks over at me. "Quinn's back at the house with Trevor, working over the script."

I try to imagine Quinn in the house on Asgard, sitting on my deck, drinking from my glasses. "It's a reality-based show," I say. "How much can they work it up?"

"They're massaging some of the facts, dramatizing. Plus they've got yesterday to consider now."

Brook says, "The paper said that girl couldn't walk, and then she could."

The article was front page of the local section. "I read the story, Bird."

"Yeah, but you were there too. What happened?"

Together, Alix and Brook wait for an answer. I see a BEWARE OF ALLIGATOR sign rotting in the bushes. "I'm not really sure what I saw."

Neither is pleased by my nonresponse, but since most have got me figured for either crazy or amnesic, I'm not about to go spouting miracle healing. Last night when I got home, I looked up the number for Sanctuary House, hoping Rhonda could supply some reliable information on unexplained phenomenon. But I never called. What do I say, I kept wondering, if she asks what I'm doing tomorrow?

"Nobody's claimed the poor girl yet," Alix says. "Doesn't that seem odd? I'd hate to think somebody could just abandon a sick kid like that."

"The world's full of twisted people," I say. According to the paper, Quinn has petitioned the court for temporary legal guardianship, claiming he feels "a powerful moral obligation to care for the weak in society." But I'm not here to waste time talking business. I go to my list of prepared questions. "So, Bird," I say, "Mom said you had some deal in Raleigh."

"We were righteous, but the *Dance in My Pants* sluts stripped down to thongs so of course they took first."

"She's not exaggerating," Alix says. "Those mothers need to have their heads examined."

"So you switched to dance after you got your black belt or what?"

Alix looks away and my daughter shakes her head. "Nah. You guys sold the dojo. I stalled out at brown but I've been thinking about checking out Dragon Steve's."

"Dragon Steve's a loser," Alix says. "If you want to continue training, I'll train you myself. I thought you liked dance."

"I think I was acting out. You got ticked when I mentioned dance. It began as an attempt to generate negative attention."

"You need to stop reading so much," Alix says.

I smile at Brook. "I'll bet you're a great dancer."

Brook pirouettes in front of us, but when she lands she assumes a fighter's stance. Her hands thin into blades and she bends her knees. "No," Alix says. "Your father's arm."

Playfully Brook flips a kick at my head, which I block with a forearm. I bring the same hand in and tap her on the forehead, my only attack whenever we sparred. Brook spins and leaps, driving an elbow into my ribs. I fold sideways. "Thought you were head-hunting," I explain. "You got faster."

"I got smarter," she answers. "And whether you remember or not, you got older."

"Enough, you two," Alix commands. "We're drawing attention."

I turn to Alix, my hands now loose fists. "What's the matter, Al? The good life soften you up?"

"Not funny," she says, but when Brook and I take up offensive stances on either side of her, like we used to so many times after hours in Tae-Kwon-Do for Tots, fighting instincts take over. Alix halfheartedly snaps a punch in my direction, a fake that Brook bites on, advancing too quickly. Alix's leg blurs as she twirls and sweeps Brook's front foot, knocking it out from under her and spilling her onto the grass. Completing her spin, she faces me again, fists up front, knees flexed and ready to spring. A strange grin on her face.

"You want a shot at the title?" I joke.

"I think I've earned that much."

From the ground, Brook says, "So, Dad. In your head, you're like, still married, right?"

Alix's face jerks sideways as if she were punched. "Brook. You need to remember your father's condition. We talked about being delicate."

"This is delicate."

"Yeah, Bird," I say. "That's about the size of it." Since I know Brook knows the truth, I'm not sure what she's up to.

"Well, how does that feel? I mean, do you like the feeling of being married to her?"

I look to Alix, who's dropped out of her fighting stance. Her arms hang at her sides. I wonder what answer she'd wish for.

"This is making your mom uncomfortable," I say. "Let's just walk."

I start down the path and after a moment of whispered scolding, Alix and Brook catch up to me, though we no longer hold hands. My ribs ache from Brook's elbow. We pass the duck boy, who is now trapped inside a small circle of mallards that have braved the land. He's out of hot dogs, but something keeps him from going to the rolls, still bagged at his feet, for which the ducks clearly have plans. The boy's father, just across the trail, stands over an open flame leaping through the charcoal grill. He shouts to his wife, "OK, Maddy, break out the Ball Parks."

Knowing where that scene is heading, I turn away and find Brook looking into my face. "So, like, do you remember my eighth-grade graduation?"

"No."

"Do you remember promising to buy me a car?"

Alix laughs. I say, "Can't say that I do."

"Do you remember all the times we ate dinner at T.G.I. Friday's and watched movies?"

I don't smile. "No. I remember you as a little kid. That's it. I told you this."

Brook nods her head. "I understand," she says. "So tell me something you do remember about me."

This, I clearly sense, is a request she wants answered, amnesia or no. I'm being tested. My mind scurries for a good response, something warm and happy and family-oriented. Not her in the hospital with those tubes up her nose. Not her pouring my whiskey down the toilet. Not her hiding in the branches of the pine tree out back, afraid I'd be angry at her for skipping school. Just as we reach the bridge, I stumble on the perfect flashback. "I'm thinking of the Asheville Zoo," I say. "This is when you're five, maybe six, but you're still carrying around that purple wubbie blanket."

"I remember wubbie."

"Yeah, your mother and I were desperate to get it away from you. Dr. Spock thought it would impair your ability to interact with others."

"Chapter Seven," Alix says, with all the respect of someone quoting the Bible. "Developing Your Child's Sense of Self-Security."

"Exactly. Anyway we're in the parking lot, fighting with you in the Subaru about it, telling you that big girls don't need wubbies."

Alix says, "The Duster. The Subaru had just died."

"Sure, the Duster. So Brook, you're in the backseat of the Duster screaming bloody murder because we want you to leave the blanket in the car. But just like always, we finally cave in and let you bring it into the zoo. You drag this wubbie around through dirt and grass, through the Reptile House and across the walkways over Monkey Island. Finally the three of us are watching the otters play. They've got this dug-out playground all their own, a little quarry with a green water pool and a molded concrete mountain to frolic on. The whole nine yards."

"I remember this," Brook says, and her smile beams. It is perhaps the first genuine one we've seen all day. She wants me to go on. Alix is trying not to smile, but failing.

"We're leaning against the brick wall around OtterLand and I've got you sitting on it with my arm around you. Your mother's nagging me that this is not safe, so I was distracted."

"Don't pin this on me," Alix says from my side. She has moved next to me, is leaning in and listening intently to a story we all know by heart. This is a tale from our earliest mythology, something from chapter one in the Book of the Better Buddy.

"Like I was saying," I tell Brook, "bottom line is that when I turn back from your mom, I see your wubbie drifting down into Otter-Land. It slips down the smooth concrete side and not three seconds later one of those slick suckers shoots out of the water, snags the blanket in the corner of its mouth, and bolts up Otter Mountain. Well, you unload with a sound like an air raid siren. I mean, the missiles are clearly on their way."

Alix chuckles. "God, Brook, could you scream."

Brook shoots her a half-dirty look, but it's pretend.

I'm almost at the best part. "So what are my options? I pass you to your mother, and I vault the wall. My ass hits the concrete side and down I slide into the pit. Then I'm splashing through the little green pond and scrambling up the side of the concrete mountain. Time is a factor because the otter has taken a real disliking to the wubbie, is shredding the material like it's crucial evidence. But I come up behind him, and surprise is with me. He's never seen a human being come up Otter Mountain. Not from that direction. So before he knows what's what, I get a good grip on one end of what's left of the blanket and try to snap it away.

"By now a crowd has formed. People are staring. Somebody with a walkie-talkie is running along the side of the quarry and yelling at me. You're still screaming. But I try to block all that out. I'm in mortal combat with this water rat. And I'll tell you, he's no wimp. He has blood lust in his eyes. Our tug-of-war is going to rip the wubbie in two, and I realize I've exhausted my nonviolent options. I yank the wubbie up a little to lift his chin and I kind of, well, tap him under his jaw. Gently, with my boot."

"For Christ's sake, Coop," Alix shouts, "you punted the poor thing."

"I think the word *punting* is a gross exaggeration."

Brook laughs. "Why didn't you just let it have the stupid blanket?"

"Because you were six and crying and I didn't think like that. Anyway, I won. He let go."

"Sure," Alix says, "and we got ejected from the park. A lifetime ban."

"But I got the wubbie," I say, remembering how the men above me in the pit cheered my victory. How, while I waited for zoo personnel to open the secret door, the other otters kept their distance.

"That's not all you got. That bill was how much? Seven, eight hundred?"

I shake my head. "Otter orthodontics," I say. A phrase like that you don't forget, especially when it's on an inventory of charges with your name attached.

Alix giggles. "Who would even go into veterinary dentistry?" This was a standing private joke we ran for years after that zoo trip. We used the voice of that elf from the Christmas special, *I want to be an otter dentist.*

"The best part is," I start, but Alix steps in, and her voice is light and young. "The best part is that back at the Duster, you made us put wubbie in the trunk," she says to Brook. "It smelled like a sewer. And no matter how many times I cleaned it, you never wanted anything to do with it again."

Brook starts laughing again, knowing she made trouble for us, and Alix laughs with her, probably thinking of the shreds of purple blanket that we found in the washing machine for months. We've stopped walking on the trail, and even though I'm not laughing with them, the three of us stand in a circle together, and I feel like I've found something I thought was lost forever. I understand this as rare and precious, golden.

From behind us sounds a man's voice. "Beg pardon. But have you seen the painted bunting?"

Alix and Brook stop laughing. I turn to the voice, which belongs to a thin guy about sixty or so, holding a set of binoculars. None of us says anything, and so he smiles and asks again, "Have you seen the painted bunting?"

I shake my head. Brook shrugs. "I don't think so."

"No," Alix says. "We haven't seen any panting bunting."

"*Painted bunting* actually. A bright blue head? Prominent crimson breast? A bit smaller than a finch."

"Doesn't sound familiar," Brook says. "There were some ducks back by the bridge."

I check out the binoculars. They're high-end field glasses. Three, four hundred bucks easy. One of his sneakers, ancient red Keds, is patched with a piece of duct tape. He has a Band-Aid across the back of one hand.

"Yes, some mallards and a pair of green-winged teal. Not uncommon. But the painted bunting would be quite a find. Such a shy bird. There was a sighting reported on the Internet this morning. A member named Mansfield. I drove in from Charlotte. This is Greenfield Lake, is it not?"

"The one and only," Alix says. "Maybe your bird is gone."

"That's quite possibly the case. You see to find the painted bunting here now would be highly unusual. Mansfield suggests it may be the odd weather."

"Could be that asteroid," Alix offers.

The bird-watcher frowns, understands instantly that he's being insulted. "Indeed. My apologies for having intruded on your outing. If you happen to—"

"If we see any panting birds," Alix stabs out, "we'll send up a flare."

He grins awkwardly and walks in the direction we came. Before he's even out of earshot, Brook says, "How come you were so mean to him?"

"Oh please. Painted bunting. There's no such bird. Internet posting. Prominent red breast my ass."

"Mom, he's just, like, looking for a bird."

He's halfway down the path. Siding with Brook, I say, "Those binoculars were high priced. The real thing."

"No doubt," Alix says. "The better for him to look at little girls. Do I have to spell this out for you two?"

Past the bird-watcher, across the bridge, I can just make out the hot dog family. The husband stands on the water's edge with a beer. The wife sits on the picnic table, the boy cradled on her lap. I turn away.

"I believe him," Brook declares. "He wants to see this bird, you know? This bird means a lot to the guy. Can't you see that, Mom? Is that such a crime?"

We're quiet for a moment. Brook folds her arms across her chest. Alix says, "Baby, I'm sorry. But you need to understand that the world's a lot meaner than you think. That's all. I only want you to be safe. I want you to be happy."

"I'm safe," she says. "I'm here with my mom and dad walking through the park on a sunny day. How could I be, like, safer or happier? I may just explode with joy."

"C'mon," I say, reaching out for both their hands as I start walking. Alix and Brook move to either side of me, but neither takes my hand. In this uneasy truce we round the north end of the lake without saying much. We pass a couple more family picnics, and a group of retarded teenagers playing volleyball in red T-shirts. Nobody's keeping score and there isn't a net. The T-shirts say CAMP FRIENDLY.

After a few minutes of silence, I again pull up the script in my mind and remember that I should be more curious about Brook's life. The wording is tricky here—you rarely have to ask your daughter how the last four years have been. Ultimately, I take a deep breath and say, "So Brook, what's been going on with you?"

Brook brightens some, recalls the play we have going on. She slides into a long explanation of many of the things I know. She tells me about high school and dance and the trip she took last summer to California. Alix and she visited Trevor's family—went to Disney and all. Oddly enough, this was a vacation about which I heard remarkably little, so I'm suddenly interested in a genuine way. Unfortunately, her details don't reveal much about Trevor's extended family. She focuses instead on the important things: The highways there have eight lanes, Bruce Willis smiling at her outside a McDonald's.

"We did a lot of fun stuff," Alix says, almost protesting. "Tell him about the opera. Tell him about the museum."

"Right, the wonderful opera," Brook says. "What a blast. Never had such a good time in my whole entire life. They were singing in, like, this other language. I didn't even know what was going on."

"You told Trevor you loved it. He bought you the CD."

"I wanted to stay up late."

I've watched operas on PBS. Like Brook, I have trouble following the plot. I always think the wrong guy is going to die.

"And all the museum had was these creepy bones. Giant skeletons of dinosaurs. *Jurassic Park* was so much more realistic."

Alix sighs. Things are not improving. The mission objective is in serious jeopardy. I need something to turn this around but can't think of any magic words. But then all our heads lift just a little at distant tinkling sounds, and I smile. Deus ex ice cream truck. Not fifty feet ahead of us, right by the main pavilion, the Captain Ice Cream van is mobbed with children, its happy xylophone song chiming out like a church bell. A white-shirted man leans out the service window, pulling money from straining hands, passing out cold treats.

Without even asking, the three of us move toward the chaos and join the mob.

As we work our way in, we scan the pictures posted on the side of the van. This Captain Ice Cream has potential to turn pro-wrestler. He's got a whole arsenal of ready-made moves: a Freezie-Bomb, the Red Rocket, a Choco-Blitz. I tap Alix on the shoulder, point to the picture in the upper corner: Nutty Buddy. "Think that's me?" I whisper. She doesn't laugh.

When we get to the front, Brook orders something called a Fudge Nightmare, Alix gets a small vanilla shake, and, convinced my joke is funny, I go with the Nutty Buddy. After I pay, the three of us walk to a bench on the edge of the playground, a series of wooden jungle gyms anchored in bark chips. I settle between the two of them, and the three of us sit quietly licking and slurping at our treats. Anybody walking by wouldn't guess the truth. We seem the absolute perfect nuclear family.

Despite my warnings of an ice cream headache, Brook plows through her Fudge Nightmare and is left with an empty cup and a spoon. She stands, looks around, and heads for a garbage can by the seesaw. As soon as she's out of earshot, Alix says, "I caught the pay-per-view highlights. Be straight with me—what the hell happened at the beach?"

"That's a good question."

"Trevor got two calls last night. Three more after the news. If the public bites, we may be looking at a movie of the week somewhere down the road. He's half-afraid Quinn will try to renege on the *Under the Gun* contracts."

"No," I say. "Quinn's excited to get started."

Alix looks over her shoulder, and together we see Brook staring up into the sprawl of a cypress. While I scan the branches for color, Alix asks, "Don't bullshit me, you guys planned the whole thing, huh?"

I look at her. "What whole thing?"

"The healing. That girl."

"The miracle wasn't part of any plan I was given. And Quinn looked pretty damned surprised after the fact."

"So who rigged this? Snake? Who set this up?"

I picture Hardy's hearing aid, him covering both ears, and think of a song Brook played for me once with a line about your own personal Jesus.

"I don't know," I say. "Maybe nobody rigged it. Maybe it wasn't rigged at all."

Alix studies my face, trying to figure if I'm serious or not.

"Hey," Brook says, "I think I maybe saw that funky bird. Should I track down Mr. Rogers?"

"No," Alix says.

Sensing that something is up, Brook doesn't argue. She sits next to me again. Twice Alix leans forward to say something, but both time she sits back without speaking. Finally, it is Brook who breaks the silence. She reaches for my chest and says, "You're wearing my vsaji."

I look down at the pendant, hanging off my neck. I'd forgotten I put it on this morning. "Say, what does vsaji mean anyway?"

"Sacred truth from the heart."

"In what language?" I ask.

"The language Jhondu speaks." She stops there, but then remem-

bers my amnesia and goes on for Alix's sake. "He's my dance counselor. He's from someplace way off. Like Malaysia or Kuala Lumpur,
I think."

Alix tenses on my right and I remember her concern about this
Jhondu character. I ask, "What's Jhondu do? I mean, other than
being your dance instructor?"

"Oh he, like, counsels all kinds of people. Coach Hallorahan
had him in at the high school and Eddie Jawolski made five out of
five three-pointers that night. Jhondu helped Jack Lahnstein's dad
increase car sales by thirty-four percent. It all has to do with manip-
ulating your natural energies. Boosting your inner confidence."

Violently, Alix sucks on her straw.

Brook ignores this and continues. "Jhondu says the path to outer
peace is inner purity."

Since I have no idea what this means, I nod and say, "I understand."

"Tell him about the cold showers," Alix prompts.

"Hot water steams the mind," Brook explains. "Cooks the brain.
Cold water clarifies. Back in his homeland he once stood naked
under an icy waterfall for ten hours until he achieved jalcina."

"Naked?" Alix says. "You never said he was *naked* before."

"Well," Brook says. "He was under a waterfall. Duh."

"Don't say *duh* to your mother."

"He could have been wearing a swimsuit," Alix says, still hoping.
"You know, like when people go swimming."

"Back up," I say. "What exactly is involved in achieving jalcina?"

Alix crosses her arms. "Well, apparently you have to be naked."

"Mom thinks Jhondu's a whacko."

"Nobody said *whacko*."

"Just 'cause he doesn't think the same way she does."

"That's not fair," Alix says.

"But it's true."

Our orbit is deteriorating rapidly. I stand up, clap my hands
together. "Who wants to take out a paddleboat?"

They both stare at me, united in their complete and total indifference.

"Come on," I say. "It'll be fun." The Better Buddy will not be denied.

Ten seconds of stillness, then Brook's eyes lift and she suddenly becomes enthusiastic. Looking at her mother, she says, "Don't be a Gloomy-Gus." This is something Alix used to always say to her when she was sad. The nostalgia makes Alix smile and just that quickly we're on track again, heading for the pavilion dock.

Alix and Brook walk over to pick a boat while I take care of business at the snack shop. Grendel T-shirts, which feature him chomping a canoe in half, are ten percent off. It's been a while since he made the news. I hand the woman two bucks, and in return I am given three life jackets. She recites:

"Greenfield Lake is not responsible for any injury which may occur during your rental. Keep your life jacket on at all times. No more than four occupants allowed in one boat. Do not stand up in the boat at any time. Do not leave the boat for any reason in the open water."

From the dock I hear Alix shout, "Wait!" and turn to see Brook alone in a paddleboat, motoring out into the lake. I'm about to bolt after her when the woman says, "That's another two dollars, sir. And please get a jacket on that child. These are Coast Guard regulations, not ours."

Cruising away from the dock, Brook yells over a shoulder, "You'll never catch me, coppers."

I pay up, then join Alix on the dock. I hand her a life jacket. She says, "I guess we're together."

Once we're conforming to Coast Guard regs, we move to a boat tied to the end, a blue one. I hold Alix's hand, steadying her as she steps across to the far plastic seat. I lower myself in. My right hand holds the metal rudder, positioned like an emergency brake between us. Together, we start pedaling.

Since the pedals are connected as one mechanism, there is the illusion that Alix and I are in perfect natural sync, that we've been practicing this for a long time. Whether she's getting flashbacks of the trips we took here years ago or not is hard to tell. I pump with a bit more gusto and Alix's feet basically ride the pedals.

"Slow down," she says. "It's not like she's heading for a waterfall."

Brook's got a good fifty yards on us. She's making a beeline for the cypress forest.

"She's a great kid," I say. "You've done a really great job raising her." This is a line I had ready for Alix, and I hope the fact that nothing has happened to prompt such a comment will go unnoticed.

Alix thanks me. "You raised her too, Coop. Really, all along we've been together when it comes to Brook."

I nod. We are silent. The next line seems inevitable. "But not when it comes to other stuff, huh?"

"I guess not. You need to be clear on something. We both agreed to the divorce. You understand? It was best for both of us. It was a crazy time."

"I understand," I say. "I just hope it wasn't bad."

She shrugs. "Well, it wasn't all peaches and cream, you know?"

Brook has reached the tree line, and slowed, almost like she's waiting for us.

Alix's face is down, but suddenly her shoulders jerk. Though she tries to hold it in, in three seconds she's laughing out loud. On the open lake, the sound echos.

"What?" I finally ask her.

"Know that scar on your butt? Thirteen stitches? That's me."

The Spock plate. I reach back, rub my back pocket, and act like I didn't know that. "So, that's your handiwork. Well thanks, Al."

Still grinning, she says, "Hey, you weren't the only one in the emergency room that night."

My feet freeze in midkick, and for a second Alix's pumping legs have all the weight. We slow, then when she notices I've stopped, her feet fall still. Our paddleboat starts to drift toward the forest, twirling softly. She understands what she just said, but can't pull the words back.

"What do you mean by that?" I ask. "Are you telling me you were in the emergency room?"

"I'm sorry," she says. "I keep forgetting you can't remember."

"Yeah. I can't remember. So why don't you tell me. Tell me what you were doing in the emergency room." The Monday night I got Spocked, Alix did not go to the emergency room. I drove myself. She mopped spaghetti sauce and finished putting away the groceries.

Looking away, Alix says quietly, "I had a sliver of glass . . . in my eye. That's all."

"Sure, sure." I say. "That glass jar of Ragú. But how is that my fault?"

"Nobody said anything was your fault, Coop. Nothing is your fault, OK? Is that what you need to hear?"

"I need to hear Al's version of the truth."

She huffs, turns to confront me. "There's only one version, Coop. You fastballed that Ragú at my head—it smashed into the fridge right next to my face and a piece—"

"No," I say. "No no no. Maybe I was holding it when it dropped. Maybe I even spiked it onto the floor. But no way did I throw it at you. Not even if maybe I did get angry."

We're silent, still drifting toward the dark forest. Other paddle-boats veer, giving us a wide berth. Our voices carry across the water. Along the banks, I see some people staring at us. Ahead of us, Brook's paddleboat is parked behind a tree. She's looking in our direction.

Alix says, "Coop, how'd you know it was a jar of Ragú?"

"I just got a flash," I say. "That's all."

She studies my face before saying, "Well, it's the truth. Whether you remember it or not. That's the way it happened."

But it's not the way it happened. I would never do anything like that. I have no defense against something I don't remember doing. Something I didn't do.

"Coop," she says, "all this is in the past now. And I think we need to leave it there. I think that—"

Alix keeps talking, but my eyes focus past her, on Brook. She's standing up in her boat. Clearly, she's heard us fighting. From behind a clump of cypress, she can't be seen by folks along the bank or the other paddleboaters. I am her only audience. She gives me the A-OK sign, which I don't understand. Then she flashes one finger, then the peace sign, then three fingers, after which she screams the one word guaranteed to draw the most attention in this place: "Gator! Gator! Gator!"

She waits a beat, then with a dancer's precision she rocks her feet sideways, jarring the boat, and drops flailing out from the tree line, into the plain view of everyone. She is forty yards from me.

I know all her thrashing is probably an act, but still I panic. Brook's life jacket is behind me. Alix and I start trying to turn the boat, instantly begin pedaling to the rescue, but a paddleboat at maximum warp is still a paddleboat. Five seconds into the crisis, I make my decision.

I stand and dive into the murky crap. The water is clammy cold and stagnant. I kick hard and move through the water. My wounded shoulder, which should be burning, feels perfect. It takes forever for me to reach Brook, still swinging her arms. She's crying out, "Help! Help!" but it sounds so fake I actually say, "Cut that out," when I get close. I put my feet down and feel the thick muddy bottom. We are in maybe five feet of water.

Using the technique I've studied on *Baywatch,* I get behind her and drag Brook up to one of the cypress trees that has a small landing, enough for me to shove her up and out of the water. At this moment, a kayaker appears from inside the forest. He's young but trying to grow a beard.

"Everything alright?"

"There was an alligator," Brook says, breathing fast and pointing into the water. "He knocked my boat over and tried to get me."

I corral Brook's overturned paddleboat and right it, then crawl up inside, wet and exhausted, my heart pumping like it does halfway into a match. I reach for my shoulder, which has decided in the wake of the adrenaline buzz to thump with jackhammer fury. The infection in my future makes me think of amputation.

Alix arrives on the scene, along with four other paddleboats, including the ponytail family I saw earlier from the bridge. The father asks, "What's going on?"

The punk kayaker answers: "Gator, man. Tried to take her down. This dude chased it away."

The little boy says, "Was it Grendel?"

"Could be," the kayaker says, scanning the water.

"He's not just some dude," Brook says. "He's my father. My father saved me from an alligator attack."

The lie is so transparent, so clearly false, that I fear the whole small crowd will start scoffing. There is thoughtful silence among the group. I'm worried that any second Alix will say, "I'm sorry, everyone. My daughter takes after her father and is prone to severe delusions. When she was young, she faked seizures for six months."

But instead Alix says, "It was an eight-footer, maybe ten. It passed me as I came in."

The ponytail girl's father grins at me. "Well, good job, Dad. Let's get you people someplace dry."

Alix paddles in close. I climb back into my chair and Brook kneels behind us in the rumble seat, facing forward. The kayaker asks if I'll be OK and I reassure him. "Can you tow in the other boat?" I ask, and he agrees, happy to fill the role of the hero's side-kick.

The procession toward shore is a slow one, a parade of paddle-boats cruising in patiently like a fleet of victorious battleships. Word of the rescue reaches land ahead of us, and onlookers line the dock, waiting and staring. Around us, the others in the armada are smiling and excited, unaware they are supporting actors in the year's best melodrama. As the audience along shore begins to applaud, Brook squeezes my hand to her right and Alix's to her left.

Simultaneously we return our daughter's secret signal, and all three of us understand exactly what's going on here. And it feels so damn good, to be here in this bubble with them. Incredibly, unbelievably, a family.

CHAPTER THE SIXTEENTH

The Truest True American. A Presidential Update.
The Things Darwin Had to Say. Goldilocks Syndrome.

O n the drive home even having the windows down doesn't help with the stench. My clothes smell like a combination of wet garbage and duck shit. And I'm worried too about infecting the bullet wound in my shoulder, where the muscles have grown so stiff it's difficult to turn the steering wheel. So as I rumble down the back alley, I'm thinking about a shower, a long hot one like the kind Hardy takes before matches. After that, I'll order out for some pizza and take in a marathon session of ESPN. Later on, if my mind settles like I hope it will, I may call Rhonda, though I have no idea exactly what I'll say. Before, when Alix held my hand, it felt warm and good.

But just after I park, as I'm reaching for the keys, I see Winston coming toward me in the rearview mirror. Despite the afternoon heat, he is wearing a black turtleneck sweater. One hand swipes his bald head, and his stride is uneven and hurried. I slide out of my Ford onto the gravel and turn to meet him. The golden boots adorn his feet.

"Dr. Cooper!" he shouts, throwing up the sweaty hand as he crosses the church lot. Behind him, a few homeless sit atop the rubble wall, backs toward me, facing the TV altar. I wonder what they're watching. Winston steps up to me, bringing his face within a foot of mine, and asks, "Where have you been all day? I've had grave concerns."

"Down at the lake," I say, a statement immediately supported by the state of my clothing.

But Winston ignores my clothes, instead flashing a look left and right before leaning in even closer and cupping his hand to my ear. "We need to talk. But not here. We may be under surveillance."

I jack a thumb toward my apartment, "Come on up. Let me wash."

Winston shakes his head. "Early this a.m. Brother Gladstone reported a strange figure in the tree by the front of your house. I'm not sure your home hasn't been compromised."

I shrug, look around, then open my pickup door and say, "Hop in."

Nodding his approval of my secret agent skills, Winston crawls across the driver side. When he sees the giant cardboard sunglasses folded up on the floor of the cab, he stretches out their accordion shape and props them in the windshield. I slide back behind the wheel and close the door. He says, "Turn the radio on. That should counteract any whisper technology."

I turn the key and bring on my only station, WAOK. This late in the day, I'm surprised to hear a preacher still going at it: "Better to be a foot soldier in Jesus's army," he rants, "than to be a five-star general for Satan."

For a reason I can't fathom, Winston fastens his seat belt.

"OK," I say. "Lay it on me."

"This morning, early, we were being observed. I think they know."

"Slow down," I say. "Who knows what?"

"Two trucks circled the block. Tinted windows. City of Wilmington insignia on the doors, but clearly fraudulent. Dr. Cooper, I've begun to fear the worst—the UN has become aware of my Svobodian connections."

"Maybe the trucks were lost," I offer.

"People with tinted windows don't get lost. No, the truth is that they understand this place is a nexus, perhaps the most powerful one on the planet. Certainly, they'll attempt to secure this location."

On the radio, the voice says, "But Jesus's army never has a draft! It's a volunteer corps. Because Jesus is the truest-true American. He believes in absolute freedom of choice. So you sinners can choose to go straight to hell and that's fine with the rest of us." Laughter follows.

"We have to prepare for an assault," Winston says. "Damn, I wish we had that fourth wall up. *A castle with three walls is difficult to defend.* I think that's Sun Tzu."

I'm tired and dirty. My shoulder pulses and I'm picturing the antibiotic cream in my medicine cabinet. "Winston," I say, "I don't think anybody's going to attack."

"Because we've got squadrons of angels on our side. Whole skies full of flaming swords. We beat Satan before and we can do it again."

Nodding at the radio, Winston says, "Pray for peace, Buddy. But plan for war."

The congregation has begun chanting, "We did it before and we can do it again," like students at a high school pep rally. I picture pom-pom cheerleaders back-flipping for Christ.

Realizing I can't alter the flow of Winston's argument, I ask him, "So you want me to call the cops?" I feel guilty for not taking him seriously, but right now I just need to be upstairs.

Winston looks me straight in the eye and says, "The cops? I fear you misunderstand the enemy's resources."

Something *bang-boom-bangs* my rear quarter panel, and Winston ducks his face into the dashboard, assuming the crash position. "Take cover!" he shouts. "Incoming!"

I spin to find Dr. Gladstone banging on my truck. My WORLD'S #1 DAD baseball cap is on his head. "Alert!" he shouts. "Emergency coming on the TV! Alert! Emergency!"

Winston lifts his face. On the radio, the preacher's voice disappears, then there's a second of silence before, "We interrupt this broadcast for an important message from the president of the United States."

Winston scrambles out his side of the truck and I mine. We run with Gladstone to the top of the rubble wall, where a two dozen–strong congregation stares at the TV. Some faces are familiar from the cleanup, but many are new. Winston's followers are growing. Gladstone points and says, "The president's coming on with an important message for all Americans. Please stand by." And sure enough, the screen fills with the familiar image of the president sitting at the world's most famous desk.

The ruddy-faced man who scrubbed the pews clean shouts, "Hey, put the damn game back on."

Dr. Gladstone shushes him, explains, "We all have to pay attention."

Our leader smiles, hands folded calmly before him, and begins. "My fellow Americans and citizens of the world. It seems oddly appropriate that I come to you on a Sunday with a message of good news and hope. Our global crisis is over. Just half an hour ago, our best scientific minds concluded that due to recent unexplained changes, the asteroid no longer poses any threat to our planet. It will pass by the earth harmlessly sometime Tuesday. I say again, the earth is safe."

Some of the homeless leap up and hug each other. Gladstone shakes my hand and beams. Then he sees Winston frowning next to me, arms crossed, stone-faced. "They've gotten to the president," Winston says. "He's lying. He's afraid of what the truth will do to the stock market. He's trying to prevent widespread panic. He sent those trucks this morning. He's planning to assault my nexus."

The television screen fades to black, and the image that rises from the blackness confuses me. It's a baseball stadium, only the players are standing around, staring at a huge video screen over center field. And the crowd too is staring. There are no commentators' voices, no movement of the camera. When the crowd begins to cheer, I think at first I've missed a home run, but then I see the players clapping too. The shortstop runs to the third-base coach and embraces him. They've seen the same message we just did. On the big screen. The catcher rips off his mask and wraps his arms around the umpire. The ovation in the stadium rises to an unbelievable pitch, and then I realize the applause isn't coming from just the tiny speaker of the Trinitron.

Turning, I see people in every building in my view throwing open their windows and cheering, hands over their heads praising and celebrating. Beneath the blue sky of the summer sun, downtown Wilmington, possibly the whole city, the whole planet, is applauding. The rays of the sun sprinkle light through the shards of stained glass still clinging in the high broken windows of the Salvation Station.

"C'mon," shouts the ruddy-faced pew scrubber. "Play ball."

And looking back to the screen, I see the shifting motion in the stadium that can mean only one thing: They're doing the wave. To celebrate the salvation of life on earth, they're doing the wave.

I feel woozy.

One of the homeless stands up and squats down, stands up and squats down, tossing his hands over his head. But the man next to him grabs his shirt to stop him, then nods in Winston's direction. The sound around us is like the ocean. In addition to the clapping and screaming, car horns are honking. And now church bells clamor away in madness and joy. And strange as Winston's crazed nexus notion sounds, it does indeed feel to me like we're at the center of the universe, like the whole of life is orbiting around us in this moment.

Winston turns in a slow circle, his face filling with red. His hands latch onto the side of his head, covering his ears. But it's not enough. The sound coming from him starts as a moan but forms quickly into a growl. He looks up, his eyes wild, then leaps onto the marble altar. He screams, "Pygmies! All of you! Pygmies!" When he shoves the Trinitron onto the floor, the screen shatters, and as the set cartwheels down the steps, mechanical guts pop and whiz from the exploding box.

The ruddy-faced man walks away shaking his head. "We missed the seventh-inning stretch."

Winston collapses, crying. He spreads out across the top of the altar, waiting for Abraham to come by and end the confusion in his brain. Gladstone pats his head, brushing his hair with his hand as if he were a wounded child or a scolded dog. Without looking at me, Gladstone coaxes Winston off the altar and leads him up into the tower, hoping I'm sure that the power of the Chronicle Wall will somehow restore him.

Once inside my apartment, I lock the door—the deadbolt too—and head straight for the bathroom. I strip off my stinking clothes and clump them in a corner. Naked, I step into the shower, then crank up the hot water and let it blast into my chest. The water stings the bullet hole in my shoulder, but it's a good sting. I reach one hand up and run a finger over the exit wound on my back. Despite all the turmoil of the last week, things feel fine here in this moment, and it's more than the euphoria of knowing planet-wide destruction has been averted. I'm beginning to think maybe Hardy's coach had a point about the benefits of hot showers. Then I think of Jhondu, how clarity found him beneath a waterfall, albeit a freezing one. My mind feels like it's settling again. Back at Greenfield Lake I saw the true path for an instant. My course of action was simple and clean. Swimming toward Brook, my arms pumping and my legs kicking, all my injuries forgotten, this old warhorse body did well. It feels good to rub the soap over the muscles in my shoulders and remember that adrenaline high. There was a second, as I swam hard for my daughter, when I wished that Grendel was real. I'm not saying I wish Brook was actually in genuine danger, but afterward while I was concocting the official incident report for the paddleboat lady, I thrilled as I reimagined my approach to a savage predator. Mano a mano. No doubts or complications or court fees. Just the two of us.

I'm not convinced that killing Trevor would be a completely immoral act. It's just a part of the natural world. I believe in the things Darwin had to say. You see it all the time on the Discovery Channel. Things die. Things get killed. Nobody arrests the lion. Nobody judges the wolf.

I shove my face into the rush of shower water and pretend I'm again approaching Brook, though now I have a Tarzan knife clenched between my teeth. Only suddenly there's no alligator at all. In my mind, Trevor's attacking her, yanking at her hair and trying to pull her under. I come up behind him and pull the knife from my teeth. The next part will be easy. Even just these thoughts set my heart skittering, my veins gorging with the rush. I remember what happened in the frozen-food aisle at Planet Foodville, and Chas on the floor at the dance benefit. The night I took out the Arab Assassin. These are the moments that truly make sense to me. When only the pulse of this blood seems real.

In my fantasy, my mind has skipped to Trevor's funeral, where Al and Brook are dressed in black, upset for sure, but hardly devastated. Devastated would be a gross exaggeration. I deliver the eulogy because somehow nobody knows I killed him. And gathered to hear me speak is everyone, Quinn and Hardy and Paul and Rhonda and Winston and Jhondu and Marna the no-longer-quite-crippled girl. From the pulpit, looking out on them, everything makes sense to me. The pieces fit. The numbers add up. In Trevor's death, all the madness in my life will find meaning. All the signs I've been unable to interpret will suddenly align like stars in a perfect, complex constellation.

I shut off the water.

When I step out of the shower I examine the wound in the mirror. It's a tiny hole really, a purple-blue bull's-eye at the center of a red cloud. I dab antibiotic cream onto it, but it smells just like Ben-

Gay, so I question its effectiveness at preventing infection. Stepping into the living room naked, I feel the cool air of the AC float onto my body and the sensation is fine. My mind feels sharp and my body real. I head for the bedroom and clean clothes, wondering if I should call Al and ask her how Brook is doing, explain how I took care of everything at the lake after she left. She wanted to get back and help Quinn and Trevor with the script.

I round the corner into my bedroom and I'm surprised at how the blankets have crumpled so large on my unmade bed. But then their shape becomes clear and I realize that what I'm seeing is a body. I'm Goldilocks—someone is sleeping in my bed. Beneath the blankets and turned away, the figure is too large to be Alix, though it could be Rhonda. But then it occurs to me, who else would be in my bed but me? My evil twin has returned. I'm actually kind of happy to see Buddy. I can update him and he'll be able to help me.

I lean in, one knee on the mattress, and shove him in the back. "Wake up," I say. "Hear the good news."

The body shrugs and rolls over. Dr. Bacchus, unshaven and with a scab crusted over one eye, says, "What the hell's everybody clapping about?"

The shock stands me up. "Jesus," I shout.

"I thought it was a dream," he says, "but then I heard it for sure. People were clapping, right?"

"What're you doing in my bed?"

Dr. Bacchus blinks at me. "Trying to catch a little shut-eye." He sits up, knuckles his eyes.

His gaze wanders to the corner window, where a breeze is brushing back the curtain. Beneath the fluttering curtain, glass fragments catch the early-evening sunlight. Just outside the window is the large elm tree Bacchus climbed before.

"Do you have some kind of door phobia?"

"I wouldn't have done this if it wasn't important."

In addition to the scab on his forehead, I notice one of his eyes has a yellow bruise beneath it. He looks like a woman from one of those domestic violence public-service announcements. I ask the obvious question: "Who gave you the beat-down?"

"That's part of what we need to talk about."

"So talk," I say.

He's still staring at the window, averting his eyes. "How about if I put on some coffee and you get dressed? Then we'll get down to business."

I look down and return to the fact that I'm stark naked. "Coffee's over the sink," I say, but then I remember that he already knows.

Five minutes later, fully clothed, I'm walking into the kitchen. Bacchus is sitting at my table, sipping coffee from an Elvis mug. "We're almost out of sugar, honey."

I pour myself a cup and Bacchus stands, steps over to the back window. He splits the slats of the miniblinds. Looking out into the world, he gives the Salvation Station the once-over. "I saw you over there the other day. How's Gladstone?"

"Fine," I say. "A bit confused, but that's nothing new."

"Yeah. Confused." Bacchus blows across Elvis's pompadour, cooling his coffee. "Winston's insane. That's clear to you, right?"

I take a sip. "He does seem a bit paranoid."

"His delusions have gone beyond simple paranoia, that was clear from the first second he came back. We'd been keeping vigil, you know. Gladstone had rounded up a lot of support from the gang down by the river and the bridge crew, and I saw no harm in humoring him, playing along until he realized just how wrong he was. Out of the blue Winston sweeps in about three a.m. saying he's been returned to us from outer space. Or inner space. Something about dimensional shifts."

"Yeah, I got that part."

Suddenly something strange, something different about Bacchus occurs to me. "You're sober," I say without thinking.

"Damn straight I'm sober. You think I need to drink with all this going on?"

"No, I guess not."

"Have you seen that flippin' wall? He worked on that till his fingers bled. For two days, he didn't eat anything, just wrote and talked gibberish. Pain-Regret-Bliss–Sacred Tennis. And where the hell were you?"

"Tenets," I correct.

"Fine. Sacred Tenants. Whatever. Some of the guys got spooked and took off, hightailed it for the beach or went over the river, but a lot of the boys liked what they heard, I guess. About a dozen from across the bridge moved their gear in after going up into the tower. Gladstone's pretty much hypnotized, gullible bastard."

Shaking his head, Bacchus moves away from the window and settles into a chair at my kitchen table and brings Elvis to his lips. I sit down and say, "I'm still not sure what happened to you."

He lowers his mug. "When Winston finally finished with that room, I got him by myself and told him he had to come with me. I just wanted him to go to the shelter and have Lori take a quick look. A quick look, I said. He freaks. He yells for everyone to come and points a finger at me and says, *At last, my Judas is revealed,* like we're in some flippin' play. Then it's, *How will you spend your silver?* All the other guys circle around me and Winston tells them that I was out to trick him, get him to the shelter so the UN could lobotomize his brain. Two seconds later a rock, or a brick, something hard, plunks off the top of my nugget."

Bacchus tilts his head forward, and I can see the caked-blood stain flaring on his scalp.

"Everything's fuzzy from there, but I remember getting shoved back and forth, taking a couple shots in the gut. I woke up in a Dumpster down behind the Hilton."

I don't want to believe Bacchus's story, but it rings true. Still, some TV-cop part of me wants to disprove his version of events, so I ask, "So why'd you come back?"

He holds his mug with both hands on the table, turns the King's face this way and that. "Things have gotten too funky around here. I've been thinking about Canada, giving socialism a try. But Winston and Gladstone—screwed up or not—are my friends. I'm not leaving them like this. I've got a bad feeling about where this might be going, Buddy, and your help may be needed."

The Better Buddy in me answers the call. "I'll do whatever I can."

But I'm not sure Bacchus hears me. "Think this through," he says. "Right now everything makes sense to Winston because all his stories make sense. He believes everything he's preaching. The guys who believe are living inside that with him, part of the fantasy. He's harmless for now, they all are, as long as they can maintain the story. But what's going to happen when the appointed hour arrives and Scotty doesn't beam him back to the flippin' mother ship? What happens when everything they're believing in turns out to be a crock?"

Strangely, I picture the splintered wood of the telephone pole that Paul smashed his truck into after Moniqua left. "Bad things happen."

Bacchus nods. "Clearly I'm not welcome over there, but you are. So do something. Ease them off the mountain before they get shot down."

"I'll do whatever I can," I repeat.

"Nobody should ask you to do more."

He takes a final drink and puts down Elvis, then heads into the bedroom. I follow. The curtain blows into him and he sweeps it to one side, looking through the broken window. Outside, the elm branches offer themselves from the darkness.

"You don't have to go," I say. "You can stay here if you want."

"No," he says. "Sleeping on soft surfaces really screws up my spine. My whole lower-lumbar region is shot to hell. I'm better off on the street."

"You won't be safe out there."

"Yeah, I know. By the way, there're some government agents snooping around. Real men-in-black types. I saw their trucks this morning. So keep your head down. I don't know their angle yet. And some redhead stopped by this afternoon, a real tall glass of iced tea. I watched her through the miniblinds—had the strangest feeling she knew I was there."

Bacchus opens the broken window so he won't have to deal with glass, and then, with surprising grace, he snakes out into the elm, and is gone. Once again I consider calling Rhonda at Sanctuary House, and my mind fills with wildflowers. But then I think of Alix on the lake, and I just stand at the broken window and watch the night settle in.

CHAPTER THE SEVENTEENTH

No Way Out. The One True Marna.
Real Professionals. A Snake and a Tree.
World War V.

Like a chariot of the gods our limousine slides up to the curb, sleek and black, and on cue the mob of young fans crushes up against it, hands and faces pressing hard into the tinted-glass window. They want into our world. The limo rocks to one side and from the seat next to me Hardy says "Hey!"—like this surge scared him, like this was somehow unexpected. I put one hand on the door but keep my eyes on Hardy. "Are we ready for action?"

"Roger-dodger, Mr. Cooper."

"I don't have to open this until you're set," I tell him. "But once we're out there, it's go time. We've done this before, pal. You good?"

"Yessir. Go code. Go code."

With a heave on the door, I bulldoze some bodies clear and step out. Two dozen kids, all MTV-beautiful, bounce and cheer, crane their necks to see their heros. A few wave cardboard signs, KEEP THE DREAM ALIVE!, FOREVER ALL-AMERICAN. Some of the fans are no older than Brook, who herself stands dead center in the middle of the crowd. At the moment we share eye contact, I can't keep my smile from growing wide. But then an overeager boy at my side whacks me in the head with a blue foam NUMBER ONE hand. I turn and consider smacking him, but force the smile back to my face instead, and the action keeps rolling.

I step aside so Hardy can emerge, prompting a brunette close by to point and shout, "It's him! It's the Dream!" He barely gets the door closed before the press of the crowd jams us straight-backed into the limo. They shove pens at our faces like knives, and it almost feels like we're about to be mugged.

"Savior!" one girl yells, offering me a blank notebook. "To Betsy with love!"

I scribble, "Love's a big word."

"To our biggest fan," a pretty boy with designer glasses says. I'd be surprised if he's ever been to a wrestling match. I scratch in his autograph book, "Get a job."

Hanging over the glass double doors ahead of us, a banner flaps in the early-evening breeze. SWC TAG-TEAM CHAMPIONSHIP! THE MAD MAESTRO & CRO-MAGNUM MAN VS. THE ALL-AMERICAN DREAM & THE UNKNOWN KENTUCKY SAVIOR. I'm still not accustomed to the new name. Strange as it may sound, I'm more comfortable with Terror. Here's one thing I'm sure of: It takes time to adapt to big changes.

Next to me, Hardy asks a beauty her name. "Samantha," she sighs. "Sign it for Sammy?"

I watch as he actually writes out "To Sammy," then begins signing his name in big loopy third-grade cursive, painstakingly slowly, enough that everyone notices. We're losing our momentum in this lull. He gets through H-A-R before Sammy finally plucks her autograph book back. "That's great! Thanks!" This kid's got class— Sammy's a professional.

Once Hardy no longer has the book, one of the fans in the back shouts, "Kill that caveman!"

I snarl and shout back, "I guarantee his extinction!" A good line.

"Yeah," another fan hollers, "murder him and that fancy-pants British geek!"

Everything stills for a moment and Hardy stiffens, understands that the silence is his to fill. "We will do our best. Cro-Magnum Man and the Mad Maestro are sneaky and clever opponents. But with fans like you all, how can we lose?"

In response, the kids shake their signs and applaud until I begin to speak again. "Hardy Appleseed and I have been through a great deal together. As you all know, once we fought as adversaries. But since we joined forces, our tag-team supreme is undefeated!"

"Twenty and oh! Twenty and oh!" the chorus chants, referring to our record, the culmination of a supposed six-week winning streak.

As we push through the crowd, just like back at the beach, the fans part to let us pass. And just like back at the beach, when we reach the fringe, right there in front of us is the wheelchair girl. We all stop.

She's perfect. A blue bike flag sprouts from the back of the chair, competing for attention against the red balloon tied to one handle. I can't keep my eyes from sliding to her legs, but no straps bind them to the wheelchair. Her cut-off jeans reveal skin glowing with a Coppertone tan. Her black tank top hugs a body you wouldn't be surprised to see, a couple years down the road, spinning around a gold pole somewhere. Thoughts like that, I wish I could stop.

I follow Hardy to her side, where he stops dead on his mark. "Would you like a autograph?"

She nods, pretending to be too shy to look straight at Hardy, but then casts him a look as she hands over her little black book and a pen. Shaking her head to one side, she shifts the dirty blond wave of hair from her face and bats her Maybellined eyelashes. "My name is Marna," she explains. "Today's my birthday."

Hearing her speak startles me, though it shouldn't. My eyes float to the balloon, which predictably announces HAPPY 16TH! I'd like to ask just how old she really is. This is all wrong.

Pen to page, Hardy acts like he's thinking, then remembers. "Have you made a birthday wish?" he asks.

Her hands, tipped by fingernails painted deep purple, settle softly on her thighs, the same way a pianist's fingers fall to a keyboard. She stares sadly at her legs. So it's perfectly clear to all of us what she's supposed to be wishing for. "All I really want," she says, "is for you to win. Can you win for me tonight?"

Hardy nods his head. "We will win tonight for you," he promises. Then to me he says, "We will dedicate our championship victory to Hazel."

I wince.

"Marna!" Trevor shouts. He stands from his director's chair, raises a megaphone to his lips. "Cut!" he says, one hand to forehead. "Cut. Cut. Cut. Just cut." He's coming at us smoothing an eyebrow, leaving behind the crowd of camera and sound men grouped on the sidewalk—about fifteen feet to the side of the wheelchair girl. He yells, "OK, sports fans. Take five."

Our fans drop their fake signs and phony smiles and wander away from me and Hardy like we've contracted the plague. Brook lingers long enough to send a sympathetic look my way. It's been a long day, and she knows Trevor's running out of patience.

"OK," our director says. "That was super, you two. Very exciting. Easily your best work. Top, top-notch. But ah, Hardy, who is this person?" Here he points to the wheelchair girl, who rises up effortlessly on those tanned legs. She pulls a pack of Marlboros from her shorts pocket and shakes one loose as Hardy thinks, then she pops the cigarette into her mouth and holds it with lips that makeup spent fifteen minutes perfecting.

"That's Hazel," Hardy says. Hazel winks and nods as she cups a white lighter to her mouth.

Trevor drums his chin with his fingers. "Well yes, that's her name, but right now she's Marna. Mar-na."

"She ain't Marna," Hardy chuckles. "That's Marna." His finger aims at the wheelchair girl—the real one—who's being pushed by Quinn toward the tables of catered food set up near the Eats All 4U trailer. I'm still not sure why Quinn brought her here.

Hazel kisses smoke at Hardy. "I'm Marna too. Get it?"

"This is all pretend, Hardy," I say. "Just like when we wrestle. From now on, just call Hazel Marna, OK?"

"I understand," Hardy says, shaking his head. He looks at Trevor. "I'm awful sorry. I'll remember this time." We've been through six takes of Act One by my count, though this last one was by far the smoothest, and can probably be saved with some creative editing. All afternoon Hardy's been forgetting his lines. After two takes they tried cue cards, but Hardy kept squinting and shifting his face back and forth. He's much more relaxed in the ring. Part of the problem is Trevor's insistence on this long opening shot. He keeps ranting about *Touch of Evil.*

"I'm not mad," Trevor tells Hardy. "I'm just here to help you do your best. You did a lot better this time. I'm proud of you."

Samantha, the autograph-book fan, walks by holding a Coke, and Hardy asks, "Can I get one of those?"

Unsure of whose permission he's asking, Trevor and I both nod, and Hardy heads toward the food.

"Is there any diet Yoo-hoo?" Hazel asks, trotting to catch up to Hardy, who stares without apology at her breasts, straining against the black tank top.

Once we're alone, Trevor says, "Thanks for the assist, Buddy. I have a hard time getting through to that one." He pats my shoulder, cups the muscle.

I turn my chin, eye that hand.

He removes it.

"Hazel's too old to play Marna," I say. "She's got ten years on her easy."

"Oh, the camera takes off ten years."

"I thought that was add fifteen pounds."

"That too," Trevor says.

"No one's going to believe these kids are wrestling fans," I tell him. "They're too pretty."

"You worry too much," he says. "They'll believe what we want them to."

"You're the director." After I say this, I stand very still and wait for him to go away. But he doesn't. He stands right there next to me.

He kicks at the ground. He turns the megaphone in his hands. It has a hairline fracture along one side.

I ask, "How come you don't use a speaker or something?"

"Sentimental reasons. This was a gift from my mother. Film school graduation."

Standing with Trevor like this, the two of us alone, I understand that I have no genuine animosity toward the man. It's not that I'm planning to murder him or even that I particularly want to see him dead. It's just what I'm sort of expecting to happen next. Like with the way my world is running, his death scene is already out there, waiting on the next page. When the time comes, I'll simply play my part.

Trevor takes this deep breath like a confession's coming, and then he says, "You know, Buddy, everybody's really glad you signed on for this project. I'm sure it's been difficult for you, with your memory issues and everything, but Ally and Brook are thrilled. It's very exciting."

I don't know why he'd say this. I don't know what he wants me to say back to him. "I'm thrilled too. And excited. Very excited."

Whether he knows I'm mocking him or not is unclear.

"You're doing a fine job," he tells me.

"You too," I say. "Top, top-notch."

Again, we stare at each other in silence until we both hear, "How 'bout me?"

Our heads turn to Brook, who bounces up between us. The frown leaves my face. I nod and say, "Hey."

Trevor says to her, "You're the best extra I've ever had." I don't like the sound of this, and mentally I renew my objection to Brook's part in all this. Though to be honest, I was glad to find her waiting for me after I pulled through the ReelWorld gates this morning. She and Alix were outside Al's office—a huge, sharp-angled, multicolored building that looks like it was designed by Mike Brady.

She moves closer to me and says, "Mom wants to talk to you about Mr. Hillwigger. He's kind of like freaking out again. About the snake thing."

"Freaking out how?"

"Just a general freaking out. Trust me. He's on the edge."

Trevor rakes his crown of blond hair. "I'll run over and see what solutions Marty's come up with."

"I'll lend a hand with Snake."

As Trevor steps away from us, he raises Mom's megaphone and booms, "Fifteen minutes, people. Smoke 'em if you got 'em." This is a saying he picked up from war movies. In two years in the Army, I never heard it. Trevor hops into a golf cart and scoots off in the direction of the Brady Building, heading for Marty, I suppose, whoever the hell that is.

I stand next to my daughter, and she pats me on the back. "Mom says you should always expect trouble on the first day of shooting."

"Trouble's what you get when you go making changes," I say, looking again at the banner flapping over the door of Studio B, the words declaring me a savior. This morning when they handed me a copy of the newly revised script, the name change jumped out at me on page numero uno: The Unknown Kentucky *Savior*. I'm still not sure who made that decision, but I have my suspicions.

"Has Mom talked to you at all about the rewrite," I ask Brook. "Or are extras working on a need-to-know basis?"

"I read the whole thing," she says. "Bullet sweet."

Other changes have me more upset. The idea to tag-team me and Hardy makes sense, but adding Marna to the mix seems a bit excessive.

"How come Mr. Hillwigger's so upset?" Brook asks as we head into the crowd of extras and crew grazing on catered food.

"He's just upset, Bird," I say. "He's not so sure about some of the things in the script."

"Like what kind of things?"

"Snake things," I say. "You know."

The read-through took place in a bright, red-walled room inside the Brady Building. Paul twitched whenever anybody used his old name. When he first appears in the script, managing Cro-Mag and the Maestro, he's still Snake Handler. As we read through his entrance, the description of an albino python looped around his neck was too much for Paul. He simply came undone. "I'm not sure I can handle a python right now," he tried to explain. "It's just too soon. It'd just be, well, it'd be hard for me."

I have no idea what kind of "solution" Marty could have for Paul's phobia of his former self.

Brook and I cut through a crowd of folks forking what looks like chicken salad. She says, "You were great yesterday. At the lake."

"I was great?" I say. "How about you?"

"I've learned from the best," she says, and I smile, happy until I realize the lessons I'm teaching.

By the Eats All 4U catering trailer, we come across Hardy kneeling down with Marna. Real Marna. He's helping her maneuver a can of Sprite up to her freckled face. She's grasping it between her claw hands with all the effort and concentration of someone accustomed to physical therapy. Spill stains mark her T-shirt (SWC: NEW RULES FOR THE NEW MILLENNIUM), but she is grinning crookedly, radiant in Hardy's attention. Black straps crisscross her legs. I haven't seen her standing since the beach. I don't know if Hardy's miracle was only temporary, or if Quinn is taking his role as legal guardian seriously and keeping her in the chair as a precaution. Of course, it could just be he's protecting his investment. I've heard rumor that he plans on using her at future SWC events.

Brook lifts a hand, says, "Hey Marna," and Marna grins, jerks her head sideways. Her tongue silent as stone. I wonder if she looks at Hazel, the actress playing her, and comprehends what's going on.

Hardy says, "Hi Brook! We got some sodas."

Brook says, "Hey Hardy," and takes a swig from his Coke can.

Worried about who's watching Marna, I ask Hardy if he's seen Mr. Quinn.

"No sir," he says. "He ain't here."

"I got him," Brook says, tapping me on the shoulder and then pointing. Past the food trailer I can see them now, across the parking lot: Quinn's and Alix's outlines beneath a trio of pine trees. Sitting against the base of one is a figure I assume to be Paul.

"Stay with Marna," I tell Hardy, though I know he would've anyway.

Beyond the parking lot and the three pine trees spreads an open field with a water tower planted in the center, like a lighthouse keeping an eye on the studio grounds. On the other side of the open field, a Wild West town waits. But as Brook and I cross the lot, I can tell the storefronts are one-dimensional facades propped up by two-by-fours.

Brook shakes her head at the fake town and says, "Mom brought me to some stunt-show crap there one time. It heaves chunky style. They totally mistreat those horses."

I can only offer, "Horses are a lot more sturdy than you think."

"I guess," Brook says, now facing the macadam. "So like, what's wrong with Marna?"

I tell her I don't know, the honest truth. No one's ever mentioned a specific diagnosis. I wonder if Quinn brought her to see Dr. Karmichael.

"It's sad that she's sick," Brook says.

I look down at my daughter, her long auburn hair bouncing as we walk along, and I remember Alix brushing it in the hospital, when we didn't know the truth behind her attacks. "It's a real tragedy," I say.

"In the car, Mom and Trev got in a fight about using Marna. Mom says it's a cheap ratings stunt. That some things are sacred and should be left alone."

Brook's referring to the final act of the script, when Hardy and I emerge from the ring victorious over the man-child assassin, just after Paul has been shot but before he's converted to the side of good. Hardy's scripted to lay healing hands on the crippled girl at ringside. He'll raise Hazel up on wobbly legs just like Marna at the beach. Trevor and Quinn must have worked overtime yesterday, because it all weaves together now like this was all part of the script from minute one.

We're almost across the lot, and my daughter's not going to accept my silence. "So what do you think?" Like everybody else, Brook wants answers. Ahead of us, Al turns and lifts a hand. Next to her Quinn looks down on Paul, sitting at their feet.

"It makes a nice ending I guess, but—"

"No," Brook says. "I don't mean about using Marna in the script. I mean have you thought about what really happened at the beach? This kid before said Hardy hears voices through his hearing aid. Some people are calling it a miracle."

"Thank God," Quinn says, looming over Paul. "B. C. Perhaps you can reason with him."

We step into the shade of the three pine trees. I look into the branches, thick with lush pom-poms of green needles. "She walked out of the water," I say to Brook. "I don't know about the rest of that stuff."

"But it's possible?"

"I guess."

"Bullet," Brook says. She stands next to Alix and looks down at Paul, curled up on the pine straw.

Quinn shakes his head. "I've exhausted my therapeutic strategems."

Alix looks at me and shrugs. So I crouch down by Paul, who's sitting with his head bent, holding his own bony knees and rocking quietly. His fingers twist a paper clip that he's studying intently. Without looking up, he says, "I'm sorry, Buddy. I'm sorry. I just can't do this."

"It's OK, Paul. You don't have to do anything you don't want to. Tell me what you're upset about."

He reaches to his side, grabs the black leather jacket that wardrobe gave him back at the Brady Building. "I can't wear this. The Lord doesn't want me to be that person anymore. I have sloughed off that skin." When he looks at me, I see the thick white powder that makeup plastered on his face to cover up the purple bruising. They decided to ditch the patch, so I can see the red clouding one eye.

Thumbs hooked inside gold suspenders, Quinn says, "Claiming God is on your side does not validate your position in legal negotiations. Try again. Dipshit."

"Brook baby, go get a little food," I hear Alix say quietly.

"I want to stay."

"Obey your mother," Quinn snaps.

I turn, but Alix is already stepping into him. "Talk to my daughter like that again," she says, "and we'll get into it."

Quinn's open hands flash up at Alix as he backs away. "There's no call to lose your composure. Keep your panties on."

Gunshots ring out from the Wild West town beyond the water tower. I see horses kicking up dust, a wagon rumbling to a stop. The action is too far off to be certain, but it seems like trouble.

I nod once at Brook, who shrugs her shoulders but understands, heads back for the catering trailer and Hardy and Marna.

"How can you expect me to work with a python?" Paul asks. He's pointing the paper clip at me for emphasis.

Quinn leans into him. "You understand of course the significant resources devoted to the acquisition of this animal?" Trevor scoured the state in search of an albino but couldn't find one, so he had to settle for a normal python, though they're investigating bleaching it.

"Not my fault!" Paul shouts. "Nobody asked me! I'm not sleeping so good, you know. Now I've prayed about this—I've asked for guidance—and I want to fulfill my contract. But does it have to be a python? Maybe I could deal with a rattler. That wouldn't be too traumatic. I could do that. I think."

Quinn smirks and I say, "C'mon, he's trying."

"I won't tolerate this kind of behavior. Not from professionals under contract."

"How about an anaconda?" Paul offers. "Anacondas are scary."

Alix steps in, says to me, "This just isn't going to fly. Help me get him up." We each take an arm, hoist him to his feet. Quinn steps in front of us. "Whoa there, Mother Teresa. Would you care to outline your action plan?"

"We need to get him out of this heat," Alix explains. "Get a little water in his system and lay him down inside. The trailer's got AC. He just needs to calm down."

Paul seems too weak to walk, so we drape his arms over our necks. Though it raises dull pain in my shoulder, I run my arm across his back, and I wish again that I was healed enough to do my own stunts.

Alix puts her arm across Paul's shoulders, and our skin comes into contact. At the touch, Al leans forward and glances my way. All day long I've wanted to be alone with her, to ask her about what happened yesterday at the lake and talk to her about what's going on. But we haven't had a second by ourselves, always there's been Trevor or Quinn or even Brook. Alix wants to be alone with me too—I can tell by the way she looks away quick when our eyes meet, and by the fact that she's left her arm beneath mine on Paul's back. I squeeze her forearm gently and we start forward together, shuffling slowly across the open field. Quinn follows. I'm keeping an eye on Paul's feet, which trip over one another.

"Think about it," Paul pleads. "Why does it even have to be a snake at all? Why couldn't it be some other animal?"

"This is brilliant," Quinn whines from behind us. "First Hardy can't recall five lines of dialogue, now Paul's become feeble-minded. How many contingencies does one executive need?"

"Leave Hardy out of this," I say.

Alix's face tenses. She's angry and nervous about the project, in which she has a lot invested. I squeeze her arm again and she looks over at me, presses out a smile.

"No really," Paul says. "How about a monkey? Or a ferret?"

"A ferret!" Quinn repeats. "You're proposing that we frighten wrestling fans with a ferret?"

We're in the parking lot. The trailer is just ahead of us. "Almost there," I say.

"Well," Paul mumbles. "Naturally we'd have to make it a monster ferret, that's all. A mutant."

"Tell me please he's not saying these things," Quinn moans.

"Shut up," Alix says. "Everybody needs to stop talking."

We round the corner of the Eats All 4U trailer and run smack into Trevor, who's moving so fast he almost knocks us over. Plus he's got some weight behind him, a garbage bag he's carrying like Santa Claus's sack. "Hey gang!" he says excitedly. The urge to strangle him is almost irresistible. Paul droops almost unconscious between Alix and me, his head hanging. He doesn't even look at our director.

Quinn steps around to Trevor. "Snake here has offered some innovative ideas for—"

Al kicks Quinn in the shin. He says, "Yo" and gives her a dirty look.

"Be thankful I didn't break it," she says.

Trevor ignores all this. "Our problems are over. That Marty's pure genius." He plops the bag down, reaches into it. "Our man's got an issue with a live python. Here's the next best thing."

The white snake that Trevor uncurls from the bag is rubber, made in Taiwan. It is not real. But in the heat its rubbery skin glistens. Then Quinn, who's decided to help out, finds the head and aims it at us, and I'd bet for a second every penny I had that this was not a fake python, but simply a dead one.

"Jesus," Alix says, and this makes Paul lift his face, fix his eyes on the sight before us.

His body convulses between me and Alix, bucks once, twice. Then the stream of vomit blasts from his mouth, sprays stomach acid and catered chicken salad across Trevor and Quinn. Alix and I each turn our faces, but we don't drop him. Even when a second wave crashes immediately behind the first, strafing high across the retreating Quinn and Trevor, we hold our friend.

There's a silence as we wait for another attack, but it doesn't come. Paul coughs, spits. One fist opens and his paper clip falls into the grass.

"Nuts nuts nuts," Trevor says, holding his arms up and away from his dripping Dockers.

"Perfect," Quinn says. "I bought this shirt in Vienna." Both men are splotched with vomit from their knees to their chests.

Between us on the ground lies the fake albino python, abandoned midassault. It rests in a puddle of vomit, splatters glistening on its rubbery skin, staring up at us with pink button eyes.

Paul, spent and wasted, hangs between us, dead weight. "I'm so sorry," is all he can manage.

"Let's get him down," Alix suggests, and gingerly, we lower him onto the trailer steps and take a seat on either side. It's good to be sitting. My shoulder aches. I want to ask Alix to massage my muscles the way she used to, but I know I can't. Instead, I pat Paul on the back. "It's always good to get that stuff out. You'll feel better now."

Quinn has yanked a white handkerchief from his pocket and is mopping the vomit from his pants. "This is precisely what I wanted to have happen today."

I see Hardy's massive form coming up behind them. He says, "Hey? Did I hear somebody throw up?"

Too late, I begin to stand, hoping to prevent Hardy from stepping into our circle. But I'm too slow, and as soon as Trevor steps back, Hardy gets a look at what's on the ground. His snake-fearing eyes go wide and he pushes Quinn out of the way as he bolts to the rescue. "Bad!" he shouts as he kicks the slimed snake, splashing vomit into the grass.

"It's fake, Hardy!" I yell. "It's a toy!"

He pauses, chest heaving with breath. "Fake?"

Quinn, offended at being thrown up on and then shoved, says, "Fake! Phony. An imitation. A false duplicate. Comprehend?"

Trevor starts unbuttoning his soaked shirt with the tips of his fingers.

"Who would want a toy snake this big?" Hardy wants to know.

Paul groans next to me, overcome by all this. Thin globs of vomit cling to his goatee. Alix says, "You want to go inside the trailer, Paul? Lie down for a minute?"

"I want to go home," Paul answers, sounding like a tired kindergartner.

Hardy says, "I got my Jeep here."

"Just a moment," Quinn says, one finger in the air. "We have budgetary concerns and time constraints that need to be considered. With that killer kid at large, the buzz on this project has gone through the roof. The minute they catch him—"

I hold up a hand to stop him. "I really think we should be done."

We all turn to Trevor, Mr. Director. His shirt is half unbuttoned, and his undershirt is wet with sticky bile. He considers our faces, then his soaked pants. "I'm declaring this an omen." He checks his watch. "Ally, tell the crew we're calling it a day. Tomorrow I want to try and get through the locker-room scene. Maybe we can even walk through the match itself, so let's say seven a.m. By Wednesday we should be editing."

"They won't be happy about tomorrow," Alix says. "Everybody says the asteroid's passing. Folks were hoping for the day off."

"We're not in the happy business," Quinn says. "We're in the entertainment business."

Trevor nods his approval.

Hardy helps Paul up. "C'mon, sir. I'll take you home. You'll be OK. I can make some soup on my stove." The two of them shuffle off stage.

Trevor looks down at his sopping clothes and at Quinn. "There's a shower back at the office. And wardrobe's got to have something that'll fit."

"Marna will be fine with Brook," Alix tells Quinn, who seems more concerned with his suspenders.

"What about you?" Trevor asks her.

She looks away from me. "I'll run lines with Cooper. The locker-room scene?"

She wants to be alone with me.

Trevor drums his fingers across his chin, calculating.

"I could use the practice," I say.

"Very exciting," Trevor concludes, clapping his hands once. "Tomorrow has to run smoothly. We'll be back in twenty, thirty minutes tops. Until then, you two run lines. Get sharp."

Alix and I say nothing, don't even look at one another as Trevor and Quinn walk together to Trevor's golf cart and climb in. They drive down past Studio B, heading back for wardrobe in the Brady Building. We simply stand there watching the backs of their heads until it's clear neither one plans on looking back.

Ten minutes later, we're standing outside a studio that has no letter, as if this particular location is ultra secret. Alix has led me beyond Studio B, to this farthest edge of the ReelWorld property, away from the crew and the extras, to a place where even outside we already feel isolated. Now, she's flipping keys on a huge ring. Standing behind her, I focus on the peachy fuzz on the back of her neck, displayed these days for everyone to see but once a mystery hidden by her long hair, reserved only for me. Inside this windowless building, we'll reveal ourselves to each other. She'll tell me the truth about how she felt yesterday at the lake, and we'll confess the truth about all our feelings. And when we walk away from here later, Alix will be ready to be my wife once more.

One of the keys clicks and she pushes open the door. It's pitch-black inside, no way to know what's in there, but when Alix steps in I follow her without thinking twice. The door swings shut and we are dropped into total darkness, the kind that only comes in caves and nightmares. "This way," Alix says, and her hand slides into mine. Her fingers feel soft and warm.

Taking tiny steps, I am led around a few obstacles, what could be folding chairs. From outside I could tell this building is much smaller than the gigantic Studio B, but in here, even in the darkness, I feel almost claustrophobic. Our breathing echoes off the corrugated metal walls. "Step up," Alix says, and I follow her onto a rise. She stops.

I picture a bed with pink ruffled pillows, some scene from a soft-core porn that ReelWorld is filming to make ends meet. From just in front of Alix, there's a series of clicking noises, one of which I swear sounds like a deadbolt being secured. A dull red glow rises just above me, and the words RED ALERT pulse from a sign on the wall. Low pipes crisscross the ceiling. Black metal walls curve over us with video monitors and glowing dials, and there's something in the floor that looks like a manhole cover with a crank on it. The ceiling crowds in over us, but only halfway, like the shell of the world's tiniest amphitheater. Empty cameras and director's chairs sit on the edge of the low light, waiting for the action to begin. Alix walks to a swivel chair in the center of the bridge and takes a seat. "Welcome to the future," she explains. "It's the year 2084."

"Standard *Star Trek* setup," I say, "with some bad attitude from *Aliens* or *Blade Runner* thrown in. What planet are we headed for?"

From Kirk's seat, Alix answers. "Actually we're onboard a nuclear submarine. The LOP *Windcatcher*, captained by Patrick Swayze."

I find an empty chair beneath her, where Chekhov would navigate from, and take a load off. "Is he dancing in this one and falling in love, or using that lame karate and falling in love?"

"Fighting World War V and falling in love. His mission is to investigate the mysterious disappearance of another sub. The League of Peace thinks the Russians sank it, or maybe the Alaskans."

I spin my chair, which squeaks. "I'm surprised Swayze would sign on for a low budget sci-fi. *Steel Dawn* was a mess."

Alix explains, "We're letting him direct."

"Right," I say. "So let me guess. He's falling in love with the daughter of the enemy captain?"

Al shakes her head. "Mermaid queen. The missing sub isn't missing. The crew is living the high life in an underwater metropolis with a race of sexy mermaids in need of men."

"Sounds like heaven," I say skeptically. Here's one thing I'm sure of: Beware any scenario that involves utopian cultures.

"It's awfully close, until Swayze shows up on page seventeen. After he and the queen go ga-ga, the Alaskans appear with their own nuclear subs and testosteroned sailors. At that point, things kind of fall apart in paradise."

"That's the way these things go," I say, not really thinking. But we both hear the words and fall silent, aware of the sudden extra weight. I swivel away from her in my squeaky chair, face the navigating console in front of me, a TV screen and the usual sci-fi keyboards and viewscreens. I run my fingers across the topographical map on display, a series of ripple drawings detailing the canyons and valleys, the unexplorable abysses that score the ocean floor.

From behind me, Alix says, "You always liked this stuff in the good old days. I just thought . . ." She doesn't finish, but I can tell she's staring at the back of my head.

"The good old days," I repeat. What I'm wondering is if they built a captain's quarters—with a cot that could hold us both—and if they built it close by.

I swivel back around in my chair to face Alix. Behind her, the RED ALERT glows crimson onto her soft cheeks. When I try to hold eye contact she looks down, fiddles with the arm pad like she's checking in with Scotty about restoring warp drive. I stand up, quick enough to send my chair spinning behind me, and step to the captain—settle my hand on hers—and say, "Al."

She rotates away from my touch and gets to her feet. For a moment she just stands like that with her back to me, then she walks around to Sulu's chair up front and repositions herself. She unrolls some pages from her back pocket. "Maybe we need to look over the script. That would be a good idea, I think. For us to just run some lines."

"Sure, fine," I say, worried that she's about to spook and run for cover. I step back down to Chekhov's chair next to her. She lays the pages out on the console between us, where there's just enough light to read by. We're side by side like two lost travelers in a car late at night, reading from the same map on the dashboard.

Things have taken a turn toward the tense, so I back off. "This is quite a story. You weren't kidding about that whole 'massaging the truth' stuff."

"Quinn and Trevor worked hard on it."

"Did you do any of the writing?"

Alix shakes her head. "Some polishing maybe. Let's look at that locker-room scene."

She flips some pages, smooths out the script when she reaches the right spot. "I'll be Hardy," she says. "You be you."

I look at the top of the page, see again how they've renamed me for *Under the Gun*. "Whose brainstorm was it," I ask, "to change me from the Terror to the Savior?"

She hesitates, half shrugs. "Quinn's, I think. Maybe Trevor's." The truth, crystal clear to me, is that this was Alix's idea.

The scene she's picked takes place right after we meet Marna out front. Here in the locker room, Hardy and I prepare for our match. Alix's finger points at the Savior's opening line and I read it: "It sure is strange to be teamed up with you after our long grudge, Hardy."

Alix reads Hardy's line: "I like the idea of being your partner. I think we work well together."

I stop, take a breath, keep my eyes on the page, and then read, "Me too, pal."

"Because I always have respected you," Alix reads. "I have always admired how you handle yourself. You are a real class act."

I read, "Listen, all that stuff I said in the old days, when we were opponents, you know, about how much I hated your guts. Those were just words."

Alix reads, "Well, you didn't have to always say them with such feeling."

I lift my eyes from the page. "That part's good. Makes us sound like real friends."

"We are friends," Alix says. Her face is inches from mine. "I mean, you and Hardy are real friends. But we're friends too, Coop.

Not that we're not friends. You're reading real fine. How about your next line?"

Our hands are side by side on the console. Alix is wearing shorts, and I can see the bare flesh of her knee. I go on with the script. "You know, even when we were opponents, I never felt like we were enemies. I felt a bond between us. The bond of true warriors."

"I know what you mean. It is something hard to explain to normal people, to folks outside this world."

"Most people do not understand that," I read, "the kind of trust that can develop in these situations."

Alix reads, "Can I trust you with a secret?" And I know what she wants to tell me, that she loves me still and wants me back, that we're going to pick up our happy life right at the scene where our original script took a wrong turn. That secretly, she wants Trevor gone as much as I do.

"Absolutely," I answer, with a word from the script I recognize as genuinely mine.

"I am afraid of something," she reads.

"That's really good," I say. "That's almost exactly what Hardy said."

Alix turns from the script. She studies my face before asking, "Are you starting to remember, Coop?"

"No. It's just." I think. "Hardy was telling me how accurate this part was. He remembers it all."

Her eyes linger on mine.

I point to the script. "Let's get back to your secret, huh?" The stage directions after Hardy tells me he's afraid have him handing me a note, a death threat he supposedly found in his locker. The script calls for me to read it out loud, so I do: "R.I.P. Hardy Appleseed, the American Dream. Death to all Dreamers."

"I just do not understand," Alix reads. "This just don't seem right."

"Some people," I read, "have a hard time believing in dreams."

"That's awful," Alix reads. "Dreams is what makes life worth living. Imagine if that poor girl in the wheelchair couldn't dream of making a birthday wish. Imagine if we were just stuck with life as it is. Imagine what would happen to a person who didn't have nothing good to hope for. He'd be awful sad."

"Worse than that," I read, pretending to hold up the death threat. "He'd be deadly."

In the script, we fade to a commercial, then open midmatch inside the wrestling arena. But here, on the bridge of a futuristic nuclear submarine, Alix and I can only fall silent once again. I'm aware of her breathing—it's uneven and heavy. I lift my eyes and see her, still looking down at the script on the console even though the scene is over.

As if I'm reading my next line, I say, "What would happen, if Trevor were gone?"

Alix raises her face into the glow of the red-alert sign. She says nothing. I see us three minutes in the future, spread across this console, making love on delicate instruments. I reach across the slim space between us and settle my palm on her bare knee, flesh on flesh. "Don't you ever think about me? About what could have been?"

She rests her hand on mine, a warm burn. "Of course I do, Coop. Of course I do." With a gentle squeeze, she lifts my hand away from her leg. "But whatever it could have been, it wasn't. You need to understand that things between us didn't happen the way they were supposed to. Nothing did."

I pull my hand back and crack my elbow on the metal armrest of my chair. "The way they were supposed to? What does that mean exactly? Really, I'd like to know what that means."

"It means what it means, Coop. It means we had dreams and dreams. But that's all they ever were, you know? Maybe we wanted too much. God, I wish you remembered."

"I don't have to remember. I was at the lake yesterday. We were a family. You lied for us."

Her head shakes. "I didn't lie for us. I lied for Brook."

"Yeah right," I say. "Just like the night of the damn dance benefit. You don't care about me at all. I'm just your ex-husband and nothing else."

"Of course I care about you, Coop," Alix starts, but then something registers in her eyes. She tilts her head and repeats, "The dance benefit."

"You bet," I say. "I remember the parking lot security guard. And how you said you were doing that for Brook."

"I was. I did. For Brook. Wait. So you remember all this?"

"Everything," I answer. "I remember Thursdays. You care to explain those away too? You screw me for our daughter's sake?"

Alix's hand is hardly a flash, the pain in my cheek a quick sting of heat. It turns my face, and I focus for a second at the metal hatch in the floor. I hear a sniffle. When I lift my face again, no tears are settled in her eyes. "Goddamn you, Buddy Cooper."

"I'm sorry," I say.

"What do you want to hear, Coop? That I come by Thursdays because I feel sorry for you? *I do.* That I come by because it feels good to me? *It does.*"

She stands up. Sagging and tired, I rest my arms on my knees. The bullet wound throbs. My eyes fall again to that manhole cover, and I wish I could somehow crawl into the bowels of this fake ship. "Don't go," I say.

From above me, Alix huffs. "So you remember everything? That's where we are now?"

"Pretty much," I say.

"You've been faking all along. Even for you, this is amazing."

Her legs disappear from in front of me, and I hear her footsteps clacking back the way we came. I turn to look and when she opens the door to the outside I can see that night's coming on, but before she can step into it, I call out. "Alix. Please. Pretend for a second that I really don't remember. Pretend that I don't know why what happened happened. And tell me. Just tell me why."

She stands in the doorway, a dark silhouette against a dark backdrop. Like a closing curtain the door cuts her off from my view, and I'm left alone. My head hangs, and I'm wondering just how things went so wrong so fast from what I had planned. So I sit in the silent darkness, hoping, waiting for someone to step out from behind a wall and yell, "Cut." To give me another chance at this scene I've rehearsed so many times.

CHAPTER THE EIGHTEENTH

Somebody in Charge. Bullhorns and Bulletproof Vests.
Bacchus Seeks Absolution. Winston Seeks Salvation.
Our Hero Seeks Revelation.

Navigating crosstown traffic, I let everybody pass me. Even the school buses and the student drivers cruise smoothly by in the left-hand lanes. My shoulder is stiff from all the excitement at the lake yesterday, so I'm having a hard time shifting, and over and over I find myself floating in neutral, engine racing but no sign of acceleration. I don't think about Alix and where she is, if she's crying behind Studio B or sitting down with Brook, explaining that Daddy has had another break with reality. I don't imagine her seeking out Trevor in the Brady Building, laughing at my fake amnesia before making love on his executive director's desk. Instead I focus on WAOK, where the talk show host expresses doubt about what NASA and the president have said. He warns listeners that the asteroid's arrival was foretold by Nostradamus. Catholic churches have confessional lines running out the doors. There's a rumor that Pierre Trudeau and a thousand of Canada's elite have locked themselves in an enormous underground vault. Not everyone, it appears, is convinced we'll come through this OK.

Driving down Market, I'm mentally counting the Bud Lights in my fridge, flipping through the *TV Guide* in my head, calculating

how many drinks I'd need before calling Alix. Or Rhonda. But when
I make the left into the alley, I find blue lights flashing from the tops
of emergency vehicles two blocks in, between my home and the Salvation Station. A gang of neighborhood kids jogs down the alley
like they're on their way to the circus or the county fair. So I crank
the Ford to the side and park, approach the scene of the crime on
foot with everybody else.

I join a crowd, about three dozen thick, spilling into the shadow
of my deck. We're fenced back from the Salvation Station by a few
wooden police barriers and two members of Wilmington's finest, a
good-sized guy and a tiny lady. Both cops wear these hip Elvis
Costello glasses, black and square, and I decide they must be a couple. The guy paces with his arms out and says, "Nothing to see here.
You people can move along." On the grounds of the crumbled
church behind him are the following nothings-to-see: an ambu-
lance, a fire truck, a police cruiser, two battered yellow bulldozers, a
crane topped by a wrecking ball, a pickup with City of Wilmington
insignia on the door and a brick in its tinted windshield, and a large
black police van with a snarling boar's head painted on the side.
Beneath the head are the words W.A.R.T. HOGS: WILMINGTON ACTION
RESPONSE TEAM. Three "hogs," men in black uniforms with assault
rifles, have taken up positions around the van. I scan the rooftops
and mark four snipers, including one behind the chimney on my
house. Sitting on the brick above him is a squirrel, tail curled,
watching the show.

At center stage of all this stands Lieutenant Tyrelli, the bronze-
skinned cop who asked me questions back in the hospital. Staring
at the Salvation Station before him, he's wearing a bulletproof vest
and holding a black bullhorn.

A man in the back of the crowd has a little boy, maybe three,
perched on his shoulders. "Hey," I say. "What's the deal?"

"Don't know exactly," the father says. "We were heading downtown and heard there was trouble so we thought we'd check it out.
Seems that—"

The little boy's eyes focus on something behind me, and his hand raises as he points. "That man naked."

I spin to the church, and there in the open window of the steeple stands Dr. Winston—nude except for the golden boots of Bull Invinso. One thin arm leans against the brick wall at his side. He's not looking down at us, but up into the heavens. In my heart I know instantly what he's waiting for, the charge of the Svobodian cavalry.

"There's your trouble right there," the father explains. "Basically. Somebody said something about hostages too."

"Jump!" a rough female voice from the front of the crowd shouts. "Do it!" At first I think it's the lady cop, but when I spot the woman who actually spoke, I'm surprised to find a yellow hard hat capped over her brown hair. An orange safety vest spreads across a muscular back. Next to her is a second construction worker, this one a guy who's country-singer lanky—Lyle Lovett or Dwight Yoakam.

Up front, the female police officer aims her nightstick at her fellow sister-in-arms. "You. Shut up."

"Let us back in there," Yoakam demands. "We'll finish what we started." The lady hard hat punches her pal in the arm and is about to say something when she's drowned out by Tyrelli, booming through the bullhorn. "Please, Mr. Windstorm. Just talk to me. We're here to help you."

"Liar!" Winston shouts, eyes still fixed on the heavens. "Deceiver!"

Weaving my way into the crowd, I keep looking up, waiting for Winston to peer down and see me, though I have no idea what I'll say. I'm trying not to shove, but my elbows edge in where they have to. I'm not out to bully anybody, but I'm also not about to tiptoe around this: I need to talk to somebody in charge, clearly Tyrelli. Close to the front of the crowd, I bump into an older woman cradling a Pekinese, one of those dogs with a kicked-in face. The dog lover says, "Quit butting, jerkweed. I got here first."

Stalled next to her, I smile and nod. The two construction workers are just in front of me, and smoke from the cigarettes they're both working floats back into my face. I cough. But I can see better from my new vantage point. I note the 9mm on Tyrelli's hip is unhooked, ready for quick action, a laser scope mounted on the barrel. He brings the bullhorn to his mouth, and his voice comes God-like from the speakers atop the black van. "Would you like something to eat, Mr. Windstorm? Some pizza or McDonald's? Maybe some clothing? Don't you think some clothing might be nice? I'd just like you to be comfortable so we can negotiate."

"You think I don't know who sent you?" Winston wails. "Only the truth can set me free. The sweet Svobodian joy of absolute truth. Nothing I'd expect people who work for NASA to understand."

Tyrelli says, "We don't want anyone else to get hurt here today."

"Who got hurt?" I ask, looking left and right for some answer. The Pekinese barks once.

"I studied at Harvard," Winston says. "I solved complex equations on green chalkboards. I know how things work. I understand."

"What do you understand, you loony?" the lady hard hat screams, hands cupped.

Half the crowd chuckles, but Winston answers. "Everything. All of it. Those foul-smelling trespassers came to occupy my nexus."

"Nobody wants to occupy your nexus, sir," Tyrelli explains.

"Foul-smelling?" Yoakam repeats. "I don't need two minutes. Give me thirty seconds."

"Calm down," the lady cop tells him, again using her nightstick for emphasis. Her name badge reads HARRELSON.

"Listen, Cupcake," the lady hard hat says, "watch where you point that thing."

"I'll point it," Harrelson declares, "anywhere I need to."

Officer Harrelson faces off against the female construction worker, and though the cop is smaller, she has the advantage. From her stance, I can tell she's had training, and not just the standard academy stuff. Brazilian jujitsu is not something to be trifled with.

I take advantage of the crowd's distraction with the potential catfight and edge my way up to the front. I squeeze in next to the lady hard hat, settle my hands on the wooden horse before me. The thick male cop studies my face. His name badge reads MARSHALL.

Still staring into the empty sky, Winston explains, "This is clearly a violation of the separation of church and state. I am on holy ground. Obvious to anyone."

"You're on city property, you dingleberry!" Yoakam yells.

"Go for it!" the lady hard hat yells over Harrelson's head. "Let's see your Greg Louganis impersonation."

I reach over and steady a hand on her shoulder. "Enough," I say. She turns to me, one eyebrow cocked.

"Mr. Windstorm, are you sure you don't want a soda or some chicken nuggets? Maybe a blanket or a sheet? Is anyone else up there hungry?"

"Tempt me as you will!" Winston shouts. "I have no need for what you offer."

The lady hard hat sizes me up. Her biceps are half the size of mine, but her skin has the dirty tan of someone who's never worked indoors, and her nose tells the story of a few brawls. "And just who the hell are you?" she asks.

Cupping my hands to my mouth, I turn to the steeple. "Winston," I shout. "Dr. Winston?"

"Please, sir," Harrelson says. "Let us handle this."

The lady hard hat says, "Big Boy knows the whackjob."

Winston's face turns from the sky, and his eyes find mine. He smiles, calmly, like he expected me to be here all along. "Buddy," he says. "I'm so gratified you're here at last. They took away the others—I tried to stop them—I was afraid I'd be alone. But you'll be here now. You will be my witness."

"Hold everything," Tyrelli booms. "Nobody's witnessing anything here today. Let's all just calm down." He looks back at me, recognition clear in his eyes, and lowers the bullhorn. "Cooper," he says.

"It's too early, Winston," I shout. "You have to wait until the time is right."

"Right for what?" Tyrelli demands, walking my way now, bull-horn at his side.

Looking down on us from the steeple like the Pope over a Sunday crowd, Winston explains. "Time and space flow freely, Buddy. That's what I'm coming to understand. So there's no such thing as too early. And there's no such thing as too late. Everything is perfect. Now that I have a witness who'll understand, I must prepare. I must purify my heart and soul."

Winston kneels on the edge of open space. He's fifty feet up. He spreads his arms and opens his mouth—a low, grinding moan comes out of him, like the chanting those monks in Tibet do. Behind me, the Pekingese yips. The little boy in the back starts to cry.

Tyrelli steps up to the other side of the wooden police horse. With his eyes on me, he speaks into a walkie-talkie attached to his vest. "Hog Pen Alpha: Maintain surveillance. No dessert unless you finish your meat." Then he turns to me. "Small world, Mr. Cooper."

"Life's full of coincidences," I say back.

"Coincidences are only patterns we don't understand yet," Tyrelli says. "I was looking for you when this situation developed."

"Looking for me why?"

"We've decided to bring in a special consultant and hoped you might make yourself available to her tomorrow. But all that can wait. Does any of what this guy is saying make sense to you?"

"Absolutely," I say. "Every word."

"I knew it," the lady hard hat says. "He's a whackjob too. I can always tell a whackjob."

Tyrelli tilts his head back toward Winston. "So how about a translation?"

"My friend's obviously not well," I tell him. "Let me go up there and talk with him."

"Are you part of their little gang?" Officer Harrelson wants to know.

"It's not a gang," I say. "They live together in the church."

"So it's more of a cult thing?" Officer Marshall asks.

Tyrelli nods. "Either way, it falls under my jurisdiction."

"Freaks," the lady hard hat says. "Nothing more dangerous than true believers."

"So, Mr. Cooper," Tyrelli says. "You remember all this? Your relationship with Windstorm and these other homeless folks?"

I don't have time for memory games. "My amnesia is spotty. The doctors told you that. I spoke to these gentlemen just yesterday and we renewed our friendship. Is Winston alone in there?"

"We believe he may have hostages."

"Your sonuvabitch friend tried to stone us," Yoakam whines. "Sent Tony and Lex to the hospital."

"He's confused," I say. "He just needs to calm down. Let me go up there."

"Out of the question. I'm not risking more hostages."

"But I can end this," I say.

Above us, Winston stops chanting and begins to sing a song. The language is unrecognizable, pure gibberish, but I know the tune: "Lucy in the Sky with Diamonds."

"Please," I say to Tyrelli. "Just leave. Clear out and I'll drive him down to the police station in half an hour. I swear."

"Let him go up there," the lady hard hat says. "Maybe he'll get a brick fastball like Lex did."

"If Lex is who I think he is, he had it coming."

This new voice turns all our heads, and I'm amazed to see the pudgy form of Dr. Bacchus coming through the parting crowd. Not only is he cleaned up from the last time I saw him, but he's wearing one of my ancient T-shirts. Beneath the drawing of the elephants, giraffes, and tigers, it reads: ASHEVILLE ZOO. ZOOPER FAMILY FUN.

"Now who the hell is this?" Tyrelli demands.

"He's with us," I say. "Bacchus, talk to me."

He points to the hard hats. "These flippin' yahoos were trying to evict Winston's crew before trashing the church. Things were at a standoff until he showed up." He points at Tyrelli. "From what I could tell, Winston got spooked by the sight of someone with sunglasses. He probably figures him for the leader of the invasion force, if you follow me. Things got messy fast, and this Lex guy got a baseball bat from his truck."

"I don't care who you are," the lady hard hat says. "Nobody in my crew had any baseball bat. My men aren't violent, and if you don't take that back I'll smash your face in."

Tyrelli puts a hand on the lady hard hat's chest. "Nobody's smashing anybody. Just like nobody's witnessing anything. I am in charge here and no one's getting beat up or dying without my consent."

The lady hard hat says to Tyrelli, "You know, we're on the same team. You'd expect some courtesy from a fellow city employee."

Suddenly, Winston's singing stops. We turn and he's looking down on us. "I forgive you, brother," Winston says, making the sign of the cross toward Bacchus. "I know now that you presented me to mine enemies. But you had no choice. We all must play our parts. We all have destinies which must be fulfilled. I forgive you."

"Winston," Bacchus shouts. "Nobody gave you up. They came from the city. This is all a mistake."

"I understand," Winston says. "NASA has advanced brainwashing techniques. In the years to come, don't blame yourself." Winston flips his wrist, checks a watch that isn't there. "The appointed hour is upon us and I am cleansed. Do you hear them coming, Dr. Cooper? Do you hear the sweet sounds of their perfect propulsion engines?"

I shove into the barricade to squeeze by, but Marshall, just across the wooden horse from me, puts his hand up. "Hold it, hero."

"You don't understand," I plead. "He's gonna go."

"One less whackjob," the lady hard hat says. "I'll notify the census bureau."

"Lady, you are some kind of flippin' bitch," Bacchus says.

Tyrelli says, "Stay calm. I'm in control." He turns and takes a few steps toward Winston, raising the bullhorn to his mouth. "Mr. Windstorm," he says. "How about some pepperoni on that pizza?"

Winston stands up, his chin lifted to the sky. I'm out of time. With my hands gripping the top plank of the wooden horse, I lift it straight out of the legs and drive the plank up into Officer Marshall's jaw. This results in a satisfying *pop* and his face rises skyward as he stumbles back. He drops on his ass. I ram one blunt end sideways into the lady hard hat's stomach and she doubles over nicely. Then pain rings from my hand as Harrelson's nightstick careens off my knuckles. The wooden plank clatters to the ground. Tyrelli ditches the bullhorn and is reaching calmly for that 9mm when Bacchus blindsides the lanky construction worker, drawing the lieutenant's attention.

Without the board, I face off against Harrelson and her nightstick. "Let me help my friend," I say, afraid to look up.

She comes in high overhead, like a knife attack, and I step into it so she can't get a full swing. I catch her wrist in my left hand and reach for her head with my right. When I get a handful of hair, I tug it—and her face twists sideways just as she makes the distinctive tough grunt of a true warrior woman. With that sound, time stops.

I remember my fingers wrapped in Alix's hair this way, the same grunt coming from her throat. In the kitchen on Asgard Lane. The Monday Night Football night. I held her by the hair and punched her dead square in the face. This vision comes to me not like a forgotten memory or a dream that had slipped away, but like a remembered scene from a movie. Like something I'd simply edited out.

My hands release the lady cop, my arms droop at my side. Her nightstick catches me flush on the side of my head, and my vision sweeps across the steeple, across Tyrelli with his 9mm, and then the world tumbles as I drop. Next to me Bacchus gets tackled. A yellow hard hat bounces on the ground. Something explodes in my ribs. Faces cover the sky. A boot drops over my eyes. My head crushes into gravel. Somebody kicks my shoulder, waking the bullet wound. There's a gunshot. Everything stops.

Bacchus is tucked into my ribs, shaking. The hard hats step away, and with blurry vision I see Tyrelli standing over us, gun drawn.

Officer Harrelson is helping Officer Marshall get to his feet. Tyrelli says, "Officers, arrest all four. I will shoot anyone who resists. We will all stay calm. I am in charge."

The edge of my vision pulses, like a tunnel growing smaller with every breath. I'm passing out, a sensation I know too well. The figures around me sway and melt. The ground goes soggy. When I blink, I see the still frame of my fist falling onto my wife's face, her eyes blank and wide open. I don't want Tyrelli to stop them. I want these people to beat me into oblivion so I'll never see this again.

My eyes search for Tyrelli's, hoping I can somehow transmit this message to him. But my focus rolls on its own, from Marshall and Harrelson cuffing the construction workers to Bacchus's bloodied scalp tucked into my chest. Tyrelli's barking orders but it sounds like he's talking to me down a well. His voice draws my eyes though, and I find his face. It is calm. He is in charge. Behind him, in the patch of vision just over his right shoulder, I see Winston in the steeple window. No one else seems to be looking. I am his only witness. Without the slightest fear or doubt, he raises his arms and faces the empty sky, then raises one golden boot and steps out into the nothing.

CHAPTER THE NINETEENTH

Prophecy of Death. Cutting off Hearses.
A Bigfoot Sighting. Hearing the Awful, Horrible Truth.
The Imitation of Life.

The floor is real. The unclean concrete is the first thing I see when I hear my name—distant and dreamy—barely loud enough to make me ease open my left eye. The right one stays shut, swelled inside a tight and pulsing bruise. I imagine it's the same shade of eggplant as my ballooned hand, the one Officer Harrelson clipped with the nightstick. The bench is real. My tender face rests on its wood. So I sit up on the real bench and plant my feet on the real floor. Real blood stains my jeans, though I'm not clear on the donor. I don't recognize the shirt I have on. It's gray and a size too small. Beneath a black cowboy hat, words are pulled taut against my chest: NEW HANOVER REGIONAL MEDICAL CENTER'S HOE-DOWN FOR THE HEART CHARITY AUCTION. For a moment, I think I'm being sold. But then I hear my name again—close by and more clearly—and I lift my good eye to find red hair on the free side of the prison bars. *Rhonda*, I'm about to ask, *can it really be you?* But her green eyes stop me from speaking and she says, "You never called."

I look around the empty cell, as if an excuse might be written in the graffiti.

"It's been three days, Seamus. A phone call takes five minutes. I left a dozen messages on your machine yesterday."

My fingertips run over the prickly caterpillar that a nervous intern stitched into my forehead last night, and I consider the events that have taken place in the three days since the wildflower weeds. Winston's return. Hardy's miracle healing. Brook's encounter with Grendel. My heart-to-heart with Alix on the nuclear sub. "Listen," I say, "I should have called you. I'm sorry. A lot's happened. And last night, my friend was kind of in an accident. Do you know if he's alive?"

Rhonda shrugs. "What kind of accident?"

I take a deep breath and debrief her on Winston's situation, beginning with his abduction, through the Sacred Tenets of the Svobodians, up to his breakdown and yesterday's mess.

When I'm finished, Rhonda nods and says, "Sorry. I hope your friend is alright."

"Me too," I say. We're awkwardly quiet then, neither of us sure how to interpret what happened in that field and its implications. Finally I wonder how she came to be standing before me, and I ask, "So your psychic powers brought you here?"

She shakes her head. "Manner of speaking. I came down to help out on the case."

"My case?"

"Is there any other? A lieutenant got my number from his brother-in-law, Hal Caruso. He's in the business, a hypnotist friend of mine."

"Sure," I say. "Hal's been on *Montel*." I try not to look surprised. After all, how big can the paranormal community be in North Carolina?

Rhonda explains, "This lieutenant's going to bring me to the hospital room the kid disappeared from, see if I can pick up his psychic trail. But it's all got to be on the q.t. Even if I help break the case, I can't make any public statements. This kind of thing, it goes on more than you'd guess."

I can't think of much to say, so I offer, "Good hunting."

Rhonda says thanks and glances at the door. "So your friend, the jumper, do you figure he's nutso?"

It takes effort to stand, concentration to keep my balance. Every step drives a small nail into my left kneecap. I stumble over and lean into the bars. The cool metal feels good on my swollen hand. I look at Rhonda through the gate and shake my head. "I figure Winston just believed too much."

"That's dangerous," she says. "But so is not believing enough."

From the way she's fixing me with that green stare, I know this statement is supposed to be some grand revelation for me. I roll it over in my head for a few seconds, then shrug and look back at her. "What's that supposed to mean?"

Now she grips the bars, brings her face in so we're in kissing range. "It means your life is in danger. I had a vision yesterday morning. A not-good vision. There is a confrontation. A gun is aimed at you. Blood is shed. I see you falling from a great height."

I picture the Salvation Station. Snipers with laser scopes and cops with billy clubs. "Yeah, I think I got through that OK. But thanks."

Rhonda frowns. "I'm not talking about a beating. I'm talking about death. The vision is foggy so it's not a certainty, but understand this, your life is in danger. That's why I kept calling you."

The prospect of my looming death fails to unsettle me. I'm a long way from where Paul was on River Road. "And you're telling me this happens—that I might die—because I don't believe enough. In what? Space aliens? Healing crystals? The American dream?"

She pulls her face back, lets go of the bars, and turns away. "I'm not here to tell you you've got to believe in anything. But it's like you told me in the rain—why can't you see it?"

With her back to me, she sniffles. I feel weak with the need to tell her I believe in everything, that doubt has fled my heart forever and I'll live the rest of my life sustained only by perfect faith. But I can't. I take a deep breath and say, "Tell me what to believe."

She turns suddenly and reaches one hand through the bars, slender fingers stretching. Her hand cradles the curve of my bruised jaw, and her palm is warm. "Seamus. Believe that I care about you. Believe that you are in jeopardy. Believe that sometimes things can change. Sometimes life gets better."

I nod my head into her hand and lean my cheek into the cool of the bars.

Looking down the hallway, Rhonda says, "I should go. Right now, Alix is posting bail for you. You'll be out of this cell in fifteen minutes."

Instantly, I believe her prediction. I say, "That's quite a gift you have." But Rhonda shakes her head. "I saw Alix filling out paperwork when I walked in. She looks not so happy."

Rhonda grants me a thin smile, then heads down the hallway. When she mentioned Alix, she didn't seem angry. I want to try and explain to Rhonda that though I still love my wife, something in her green eyes stirs me. To the red curtain of her hair, I ask, "Will I see you again?"

She stops at the open door. Without turning, she shrugs. "The tree of tomorrow is ripe with possibilities," she says. And then I'm alone again.

I don't have a watch and there's no clock, but it feels like fifteen minutes has just passed when the guard arrives to lead me out. I follow him through the door and Alix crosses her arms and looks at the high ceiling. She is silent as I struggle left-handed to sign a form I don't read. She is silent as the guard empties a manila envelope onto the table. Out pours my wallet and Brook's vsaji. I push them into the pockets of my stained jeans. The guard explains that if I leave the city limits without notifying the department in writing or if I fail to make my appointed court appearance, I will be subject to immediate incarceration. He also reads a note from the ER doctor stating that because of blunt force trauma and pain medication, I shouldn't operate heavy machinery for twenty-four hours. When he's finished, I glance at Alix. She turns and strides across the tile floor, shoves the big doors open, and steps into the sunlight. The guard says, "You want me to call you a taxi, Bub? Looks pretty bad."

"I know," I say. "And it's worse than it looks." Still, I decline the taxi.

The brightness of the day closes my good eye. My left knee aches, my wounded shoulder feels frozen stiff, my face is a living bruise, and the purple-black skin of my right hand is swelled so tight I fear it may burst. If I had a bell tower I could easily pass for Quasimodo. From the position of the sun, I'd figure it for late morning, almost noon. I stumble down the steps and into the parking lot. The Lincoln's engine roars and then I see it rounding a bend. As Alix approaches, the big front grille seems to me very much like an open mouth. At this moment I would be completely unsurprised if she ran me down. Instead she pulls alongside me, and the electronic lock on the passenger door hops up. I open the door with my left hand and slide in without looking at her. Without speaking, Alix guides us onto 3rd Street.

All this time I've tried to keep from looking directly at Alix's face because it makes me think of hitting her. Not hitting her now—here in this car—but hitting her then, there in the kitchen on Asgard. This thing that I did and that I always will have done and that I can't undo. This plot twist that permanently screwed up my life.

The stitches on my forehead itch like crazy, but I remain still.

Through the passenger's side window I see people crowd the sidewalk outside the library, normal everyday people taking an early lunch from their jobs at the bank or city hall. People who will go home at five o'clock and have dinner with Tom Brokaw, then take their coffee while guessing the answers on *Jeopardy.* These people who have some understanding of who they are and how they've come to this place in their lives and maybe even some idea of where they are heading. These people.

Alix just beats the red light as she cranks us left up Market Street, narrowly missing the center island statue of George Davis: Soldier, Patriot, Statesman, Christian.

Making the atmosphere in the car even more tense, Alix isn't playing any music, so I'm horribly aware of the gears rising and whining. The AC's cool blast brushes my bruised right eye just as we pass the squirting stone turtles of Keenan Plaza. The air feels nice, and I lean my face forward, into the fan stream. I'm figuring she'll make this right coming up, pull down my alley and drop me off. But when we get to my turn she plows past it, not even sparing a glance in the direction of my home, where there are ice packs and Vicodin and cold Bud Light. Down the alley I see empty sky where the Salvation Station spire should be. In the snapshot flash, a yellow crane's mouth drops rubble into a dump truck. The church is history. I worry about the boys. I worry about Winston.

For the first time I look directly at Alix, at the soft roll of this cheek I once blackened. One hand edges into her purse and comes out with the green cell phone Bacchus liberated weeks ago. Her thumb runs the numbers and she cups it to her face. "Hey. I got him. We're en route. Ten minutes. Yeah, he's bad. How's the shoot?"

She listens, nods, and folds the cell shut. Staring straight ahead, she explains, "Trevor wants to see you for himself. He needs to decide what we'll do."

When she says *what we'll do*, I think for a second she's talking about us, not the project, and I picture Trevor studying me from his director's chair on a stage, judging my worth regarding his wife. "Frankly, Allie, I think you should ditch this loser once and for all," he says in my mind. "Clearly a restraining order might be called for."

I swallow and taste blood. "Do you know what happened to my friend?"

"They did all that they could," she says flatly. "It wasn't enough."

This line strikes me as remarkably true, about a great many things. I figured Winston wouldn't survive that fall, but I was hoping to be wrong once again. "He was a fine, good man," I say. "He just had a hard time coming to terms with the real world."

The Lincoln veers dangerously close to some students in front of New Hanover High School. The girls sport the same style bell-bottoms that Alix wore twenty years ago, when we first met. "I'm over here trying to generate sympathy, Cooper. I really really am. I'm sorry this guy is dead and all. But you've been lying to us. Your actions have consequences."

"What are they shooting?" I ask.

Half a block ahead, the light at 17th switches to red. To our left, a procession of solemn black cars begins its slow roll from Gunderto's Funeral Home. Though it's impossible, I imagine for a moment that the vehicle just entering the intersection is Winston's hearse. "No fucking way," Alix says, and she guns the Lincoln's engine, sends us lurching in front of the huge black hood. Only Alix's juke into the empty right lane prevents a collision. The swift motion bounces my face against the window.

"The big match, Coop," Alix laughs. "They're shooting the grand finale. After you made this executive decision to get the shit beat out of you and not call anybody, Trevor wanted to push things back. But Quinn raised the mother of all stinks. Investors demand results. Hot time window. Expedite. He insisted we press on, even shoot out of sequence. When I left to find you, Hardy was throwing your stunt double around something fierce inside the ring. Just now, they're working through the assassin's attack. Trevor's hoping we might still salvage this nightmare." She studies me for a moment, examines my battered face at close range. I try a smile but my split lip stings. My good eye blinks once, but she's looking at the other, squeezed mostly shut by a plum above and below it.

"Jesus," she says. "I hope this was worth it."

If I had saved Winston, I think, it would have been worth it. I add his name to the list of those I've failed. We fly past the strip mall parking lot where the Subaru died six years ago. And there's the pay phone Alix called me from, needing my help.

"Maybe the folks in makeup could do something with the swelling," I say. She doesn't even waste a sigh.

At 23rd, where a green sign with a white plane shows the way to the airport, we have to wait for the light to let us turn. To our left the Baptist church at the edge of the city announces on its messenger board that GOD IS LIKE TIDE: HE GETS OUT TOUGH STAINS OTHERS LEAVE BEHIND. I study the blood on my jeans. In the church parking lot, a group of believers must be reenacting some biblical event. A dozen of them wearing tattered robes are walking along looking somber. One carries a cardboard sign I can't read.

"I'm sorry you're so pissed," I say. "But thanks for bailing me out."

"Thank Trevor." Alix taps her fingers on the steering wheel. "All morning he was worried you were in a morgue somewhere." She looks up at the light, still red.

"How many times can I say it?" I ask. "I'm sorry."

Those thrumming fingers suddenly grip the wheel, and she turns to me. "And what are you sorry for, Coop? For screwing up the project? For lying to me and everybody else about having amnesia? For whatever the hell kind of stupid fight you got involved in last night? I mean it. I'm curious to know exactly what you're apologizing for."

The muscles in her face tighten. Wrinkles crowd in from her forehead over narrow eyes.

I take a long, full breath, like I'm about to plunge into a cold river, and my lungs fill with air until my sore ribs flash with pain. I say the words: "I'm sorry I hit you."

The wrinkles smooth as her face goes blank. "Hit me?" she finally says. "Hit me when?"

"Black Monday, Al. I'm talking now about Black Monday."

A car horn blasts behind us. We both look up to see the green arrow, and she accelerates through the turn, pressing me back into my seat. A block beyond the Baptist church, we pass the group of believers, shuffling along the sidewalk. I recognize the ruddy-faced pew scrubber from the Salvation Station. The cardboard sign he holds reads THE END IS OVER. CANADA OR BUST. Dr. Bacchus, head high, leads the homeless tribe. His forehead is bandaged. Just behind Bacchus walks Dr. Gladstone. Somehow, he's wearing the golden boots and carrying Trevor's satellite dish. Alix doesn't seem to notice.

Part of me wishes I belonged with them, that I too had a clear destination.

We drive beneath a canopy of trees, slide in silence now through the shade of the suburban neighborhood that gives way to the industrial park dominated by the airport and the movie studio. Alix says nothing. She just drives. A collarless dog trots across the street. I swear I see a cigarette in its mouth. I wonder what they shot me up with in the ER last night.

Alix turns us off 23rd into the studio complex, and we roll slowly under the Technicolor rainbow. On the side of the guard shack, a sign reads WELCOME TO REELWORLD STUDIOS. WHAT YOU DREAM WE MAKE REEL. NO ADMITTANCE WITHOUT PROPER ID.

The guard recognizes the Lincoln and waves us past. We cruise through the outer parking lot, cut between two buildings. Alix swings wide around a gleaming Roman chariot being pulled by a white horse, and I nod at the charioteer, a short guy wearing a Yankees baseball cap. A right turn puts the familiar art deco shades of the Brady Building dead center in front of us. On the roof, a huge blue triangle knifes into the sky, jutting from an orange wall. I stare up at the shadow and think *shark fin*.

Alix parks the Lincoln in the reserved space, right next to a silver Lexus. She keeps the engine running for the AC and her hands remain on the steering wheel, as if she were still driving. The scabbing around the stitches in my forehead begs me to scratch, but I'm afraid to move.

"Cooper," Alix finally says, eyes fixed straight ahead, "this Monday you're talking about. It's four, five years ago. What exactly do you think—"

"I understand what happened now," I explain to her profile.

"I'm admitting it. This is a confession. It's out in the open so we can deal with this."

Still stiff-arming the wheel, she faces me. "There's no *this* to deal with, Coop. It's not like that was the only time we ever fought, you know? It was just the last time."

"But I hit you." I hold her eyes in mine. "Everything else is clear now because I hit you."

Her expression softens and she releases the wheel, leans back into the seat and sighs. "You've got it in your head that one punch killed our marriage?"

"Don't pretend it was nothing, Al. I know better now."

"Don't you pretend it was everything." She shakes her head and looks out her window, where a Bigfoot lopes by looking our way. He's wearing white Air Jordans.

I wait until he's around the corner of the building before I say, "Dr. Collins always tells me I need to face the consequences of my actions. You just said it yourself."

Alix's eyes snap back to me. "Face whatever you need to, Coop, but here's the truth: That night Brook and I came in with the groceries and I was angry because you didn't help carry any in. When you finally pulled yourself away from the NFL, I told you to screw off. Brook cried and locked herself in the bathroom. You attacked me with our agreement about not fighting in front of her. Then I said something about her getting used to the real world. You spiked the Ragú into the wall and glass shot into my eye but you turned away, like you were just going back to the TV, walk away like you always did. And that pissed me off. The Sulu plate was right there on the shelf and I—"

"Stop," I shout. "This is wrong. This is all wrong. You don't even have the plate right—it was Spock. And you were—"

"Sulu, Spock, fucking Peter Pan. I broke the damn thing over your head and stabbed you in the ass. You turned and smacked me pretty good."

"Al, you've got it all screwed up. I grabbed your hair and hit you and then you stabbed me. *In self-defense.* I remember it all now. Everything, it was all my fault. Your version, it doesn't make any sense."

"My version makes all the sense I need it to. Just like yours does for you."

Behind Alix, three silver aliens pass by, complete with whirling antennae. I'm certain they are Svobodians, lost and looking for Winston and their Salvation Station nexus, the place of harmonic convergence where all mysteries become clear.

"OK," I try. "Great. You didn't leave me because I hit you. So what then?"

Now Alix settles one palm on my leg, so softly I only know it's there because I see it. "Coop. After all this time, there's just no reason anymore. You want me to say we had an unhealthy dynamic? You want me to discuss communication patterns? Look, while you were in the hospital, it's true, I thought a lot about why we didn't work. And the awful, horrible truth I came up with is simple: I don't know."

Every wound in my body flares at once and I see white, like a flash grenade exploded at point-blank range. When the brightness fades, Alix is looking at me and I hear myself say, "That's no answer at all."

Alix kills the engine, and the cool air blowing from the vent dies instantly. The silence feels strange. "Look, Coop, I need for you to understand that I'm glad that what happened happened. I'm sorry things haven't turned out so great for you, and I've tried to help out as much as I can. With Trevor, my life just feels more . . . even. I can't keep regretting the choices that got made in the past. I've let go of it, Buddy, and I think you need to too. Let it go."

I consider the weight of her words, and it feels like I'm leaning over the edge of the Grand Canyon, holding her hand, and she's asking me to just release it and tumble free.

"But if I let go," I want to tell her, *"I don't know what will happen next."*

The car keeps getting hotter. "You make it sound so easy, Al."

"It's not easy, Coop," she says. "It's life."

We occupy the silence. Sweat forms on my face, stings my bruises. I taste it in the corner of my mouth. The stitches itch. It seems there's nothing left to say now, but neither of us wants to be the one to open a door or roll down a window, trigger that action that will end our final scene.

When Trevor skids to a halt in a golf cart next to us, part of me is almost relieved. But only part of me.

I'm looking straight ahead when he opens my door. "Very exciting! Our Savior has been returned unto us. Let me see your face."

"Go fuck yourself."

Al climbs out her side of the Lincoln and speaks over its top. "Trev, he's had a long night and a rough morning."

"I understand," Trevor says. "But this is no time for open hostility. Let's be professional about this. What do you say, Buddy? How about working together toward the common good?"

I aim my hamburger face at him and he can't help but wince. "Lord, is that as painful as it looks?"

"It would be easier if I showed you," I say. What I have in mind involves the grille of the Lincoln. Trevor laughs, a bit uneasily, but then his eyes sparkle.

"Actually, this could work. Those wounds, they're pure gold."

Over my head, Al says, "You need to think this through."

"Consider where we are in the story. The big fight's over. All that's left now is the healing and Snake's conversion. We're way beyond verisimilitude. This is what Coppola would do. Remember Brando and that cat? Trust me, this is a masterstroke. Great art imitates life."

Alix circles around the front of the Lincoln and joins her husband. When she hands him the keys, he grips her fingers for a second and squeezes. She squeezes back, a secret signal between lovers. If I weren't here, they would kiss now, briefly. Alix steps inside the open door and hunches down. "Coop, this isn't at all something you have to do."

For a second I think that she's read my mind and seen the image of Trevor's bloody face, that my wife knows that if provided with opportunity, I would gladly bludgeon her husband like a baby seal. Assault and battery would not bring Alix back to me, so beating Trevor would make no sense at all. But these days things making sense doesn't seem to be part of the criteria for making choices.

"Point me toward wardrobe," I say. "And we can all get back to imitating life."

CHAPTER THE LAST

Life After Cancellation. The Known Laws of Physics.
The Official Contract. Some Serious Pathos.
Milking the Miracle. The Way Things Were Going to Be.
Imminent Extinction.

S ince my big story with Alix has apparently reached its ulti-
mate end, it feels strange to still even be breathing and walking around, though of course now I'm just acting. It's like a
part of me assumed that without that ongoing narrative, Buddy
Cooper simply couldn't exist. This odd sensation reminds me of the
way I've always worried about the lives of TV characters after their
series get canceled. Sure, some have reunion specials, so we know
that Gilligan and his gang eventually escaped that wacky island, and
then there are phenomenons like *Star Trek*, so fans are well
acquainted with the final fate of Captain Kirk. But mostly, series go
off the air in between seasons, and the stories just stop. Not much
gets resolved, no one grows old, and reruns loop the characters into
stale but perpetual orbits. In my mind, Fonzie is forever young in
his leather jacket, Hogan and the other prisoners are still fighting
WWII from behind the barbed wire of Stalag 13, and Mr. Rourke
and Tattoo are still granting fantasies.

Standing just inside the door of Studio B, wearing once more the
blue bodysuit of the Terror, I can't help but wonder if I've been

assigned the same fate as these TV people, if my life isn't locked in a cycle of endless repetition. Fifty feet ahead of me in the hangar, a crowd mills around a perfect replica of the inside of the Civic Center arena the night I got shot. At the sight of the wrestling ring, surrounded by stadium seating on three sides, my shoulder wound pulses a Morse code of pain, like maybe it's afraid we're about to be shot again. Among the crowd of people waiting for my appearance, my one good eye can make out Trevor and Alix, Quinn. Closer to the ring, Cro-Magnum Man chats with an actor in a black-and-white-striped shirt. The resurrected Barney looks identical to the referee who died that night, and of course this bothers me deeply. For some reason I'm equally disturbed by the fans, many of whom seem to be dead ringers for the actual people who witnessed the shooting. There are the drunken frat boys drinking from plastic cups that I'm sure contain real alcohol. There is the old man with his green oxygen tank and mask. Hazel, the make-believe crippled girl, stands behind her wheelchair, flirting with the Mad Maestro.

Given such meticulous attention to detail, the way my brain's been lately, and recent events, it wouldn't be at all hard for me to become convinced that in fact I have somehow stumbled into the literal past, that such temporal journeys are not in conflict with the known laws of physics. This notion triggers a dreamy and troubling image: Somewhere on the vast grounds of ReelWorld, right now—at this very instant—I picture stagehands dismantling our home on Asgard Lane. They hoist the La-Z-Boy and carry out the giant Trinitron. Somebody's sweeping up the shattered fragments of that Spock plate. After the parking lot scene I had with Alix, this is a set no one has much use for, so it's time to shut it down.

"And this would be such a terrible thing?" These words turn my head to a large figure suddenly beside me in the shadows, shoulder to shoulder. I'm barely surprised to see Buddy, wearing the full costume of the Unknown Kentucky Savior, complete with blue latex mask. "Why is it," he asks, eyeing up my battered face, "that every time I see you, you look worse?"

I shrug. "Maybe every time I am worse."

"That sounds pretty defeatist. Making the effort to be more hopeful will produce positive results."

"More fortune cookie wisdom. You know, I think that's exactly what I need right now. Thanks."

"Hey. You might want to check the attitude. I'm the one who's been filling in for your sorry ass. No offense, but the show had to go on. Besides, the costume fits me pretty good." He pats his belly, which doesn't strain against the fabric nearly as much as mine does. In those days, I did 250 sit-ups before breakfast.

"Well," I say, "I'm here now."

"Yeah, we all can see that. I'm superfluous. That's the life of an extra—standing in for somebody else. Honestly, there's no real reason for me to be here anymore. Look, you want the mask?"

He reaches up to peel it away, but I hold up a hand to stop him. "I'm done with all that now." This declaration sounds powerful and weighty, though I really don't know what I mean by it.

Buddy lowers his hand. "Suit yourself. Hey listen. Pick your chin up, huh? You navigated some pretty tricky rapids here. Take a little credit."

I take a long breath and consider the events of the last two weeks, looking for evidence of accomplishment or hope. "Winston is dead. Alix and I are living off different versions of the same past. My daughter still thinks I'm an absolute loser. I have a court appearance next Thursday. On top of this, I totally screwed up a relationship with a kind and gifted psychic."

Buddy's eyes tighten and he brings his face in close to mine. "You're off the fucking brown couch. That's a start."

I look down to the loose laces of my knee-high boots. With only one working hand, I couldn't even tie them. "There's just so much I don't really understand."

"And who promised this understanding? When was total enlightenment part of the official contract?"

I hear something in his tone and realize that the two of us, like me and Alix, have come to the end of things. Looking into his masked face, I say, "I figure this is the last time we'll talk."

He nods. "Pretty much."

This notion, that I'll never again see my younger self, strikes a chord of genuine regret in me. Whether he's a delusion brought on by trauma and pain medicine or a phantom from beyond seems terribly irrelevant. I know that I will miss him. After all, he's basically a good-hearted guy. "Where will you go?" I ask.

"I'll stick around and watch for a while yet, but then I'm off to the same place as you. Same as everybody. On to the next scene."

Trevor's voice booms in the hangar, amplified by that Cecil B. DeMille–style megaphone his mother gave him. "Let's pull this together, sports fans. Has anyone seen Buddy? Will one of you interns get the assassin out of the john?"

As I start forward, my twin says, "You watch your back, Buddy Cooper."

"Same to you," I say. I feel the urge to shake as a sign of manly appreciation, but the right hand's out of commission, so I have to settle for the combination solemn eye contact/earnest head nod. He returns the gesture, and I walk away.

I wander through the crowd of technicians, careful not to trip on the cables snaking across the dark concrete floor. Between the curved line of cameras and the ring itself is a large open space. Once I cross the border into illumination, people start recognizing me. Heads begin to turn. I move toward Brook at ringside. She's talking with Hardy and the real Marna, seated in, but not strapped into, her real wheelchair.

My daughter's eyes dim when she sees my face, and in a moment of deliberate optimism, I decide it's because of the bruises, not just because I disappoint her as a human being. "It's not as bad as it looks, Bird," I say.

Gently, my daughter hugs me. "That's good," she says. " 'Cause it looks really bad."

We pull back from our embrace and I reach inside the neckline of my costume, tug out the vsaji, and show Brook, who seems happy I'm wearing her good-luck charm.

Quinn walks behind Hardy and stops. "Christ. You're sending my insurance premiums through the roof. Try to save the bleeding for the ring, will you?"

Hardy smiles broadly. "I told you he'd be here, Marna. Mr. Cooper never does let nobody down."

If only I could be half the man Hardy Appleseed thinks I am. He leans in close and inspects my bruises. "Sir, they done your makeup awful good."

Paul, who's been sitting by himself along the side, limps toward us in the long black coat of Snake Handler, leaning on the skull-capped cane. White powder dusts his face, and around his neck hangs not a python but a Slinky toy, the dachshund you could take for wobbly walks. I think this is some kind of hallucination until Mad Maestro notices me staring and says, "Emergent technologies offer amazing possibilities."

Quinn raises his eyebrows. "CGI. Marty's idea. We'll edit the damn snake in."

Paul nods his understanding and approval, then says to me, "I don't think it's too disrespectful, do you? To Lucy?"

I tell my friend that I'm sure it's fine. My eyes fall to a bloodstain on his white shirt. Paul explains, "I just got shot."

"Yeah," I say. "I remember."

Brook kneels in front of me and begins tying the laces of my boots.

Alix is avoiding the huddle around me, lingering by Trevor. I'd like to think they're talking about me, but I realize that other concerns likely occupy their minds. The director raises the megaphone once more and his words echo off the high metal dome. "Take your marks. This is not a drill."

As if in response, Brook finishes my laces and stands. "Good luck," she says, though her tone makes it clear that this is more prayer than advice. She pushes Marna and her wheelchair out of camera range, then joins Hazel at ringside. Atop the stairs, Hardy spreads the ropes for me as I stoop and step, enter once more the squared circle where so much of my life has been decided. Paul and the Mad Maestro follow. Cro-Magnum, waiting in the corner with the resurrected Barney, lifts his caveman club in greeting. "Cro-Mag heart leap to see friend Cooper no longer in pokey."

I thank him for the sentiment.

Trevor climbs up onto the ring apron and slowly the room falls quiet. Through the megaphone, which I would very much like to shove briskly up his ass, he begins explaining the final scene. "OK, the big fight is over and evil has been defeated, but at a heavy price." Here, he looks at Barney the ref, playing possum on the canvas next to the wounded Paul, slumped against the turnbuckle, and then at my face. "The audience thinks the story is over. We've got them right where we want them. Now we nail them with some serious pathos."

His gaze falls to the fake Marna, planted in her wheelchair alongside the ring to the right with Brook and the other fans who didn't flee. Hazel bats false eyelashes and puckers thick lips at Hardy, standing proudly next to me, beaming like always. Maybe it's just his energy, but I suddenly recall that in the reality of this scenario, he and I are tag-team partners, that I am not the Terror but the Savior. In this make-believe world, falsely re-creating a fake fight that went terribly wrong, I am something more than myself. Something better. And as I have so many times in my life, I find myself wishing I could replay these actual events, revise the past now that I've had a rehearsal.

Soft static crackles from Hardy's Miracle Ear, so quiet I'm the only other one who can hear it. His lips ease into a thin and knowing smile. I'd swear the music is easy listening, though it could well be choirs of angels. Still, it sure sounds a lot like ABBA.

Trevor turns to us and reviews the script. "Buddy, you'll notice her crying, but Hardy, you move first. Come on down, then wheel her around front here, out into this good light. Then kneel like you're praying. Take it slow and steady. Don't heal her too fast. We've got to milk the miracle."

The director climbs down and disappears behind the blinding lights posted along the camera line. All the actors settle into quiet preparation. Hazel's face turns sad and grim and, remarkably, actual tears begin to slip from her eyes.

But another set of eyes steals my attention. Over Hazel's shoulder, in the shadows of the stadium seating, clearly off camera, Marna watches from her wheelchair. Her hands are claws and her arms fold in on themselves, but her freckled face is radiant with joy, and her chest is rising and falling excitedly as she draws breath. And there is something magnetic in her expression, something about the way she looks at Hardy that makes it impossible for me to turn away. She believes in him. Though her body is crippled and crooked, she believes that she is about to witness the reenactment of a genuine miracle. I recall Hardy's invitation from the D-day invasion at Wrightsville Beach, how he wanted me to join him in the waves and how I refused. Absurd as it sounds, I even wish I could return there. I wish that right now, here in Studio B, I had faith that Hardy's healing hands could cure me, though I cannot name my affliction.

Through the ropes, I see Brook looking at me, sensing my discomfort and hoping to provide encouragement. At her feet, a sign has been trampled by the fleeing mob: YOU'RE #1!! I read this and see her eyes and feel the heat of the bright lights on my bruised face. The stitches burn. In a place that looked exactly like this, on the night that we're all pretending it is, I was supposed to win. It had been decided, predestined, ordained, that at last Buddy Cooper was going to be champion. That was the plan. That was the way things were going to be.

"Just a second," Trevor megaphones, snapping my reverie. He steps out from behind the cameras and enters the empty space in front of the ring. His eyes scan the mat. "This is all wrong. We're absent one subdued assassin."

From behind the glare of lights comes Quinn's voice. "Don't tell me that kid's still on the crapper."

"Here he comes," someone shouts, and the whole room looks right.

The moment I see the man-child assassin—emerging from beneath the stadium seating—I know the truth. While wardrobe could find a perfect match for the preacher suit and makeup might re-create that long gray hair, no cosmetic could reproduce the vacant look of his young eyes. As he approaches Trevor, he holds a gun at his side, and though everyone here thinks it's a prop, I know differently. All this registers in an instant, and ridiculously I shout, "That's him!"

Trevor turns to the kid as he lifts the gun to the director's face. "You're supposed to be subdued," Trevor says, just before the boy cracks his skull with the butt of the gun. He catches Trevor's body with an arm around his neck and turns to the ring, then finds my face. "At last all transgressors are gathered," he says. "Ripe is the time for retribution."

With this, everyone in Studio B realizes that we've once again left behind the original script, drawing screams, shouts, and a curse from the darkness beyond the cameras. The door I came in opens and closes, and shadow figures scurry through. With my arm at my side, I strain to open the fingers of my hand, hoping Brook will see my signal and stay low. The man-child drags Trevor a few steps closer to the ring and waves the gun in our direction. Most of us, including the dead Barney, have retreated into the far turnbuckle. Paul cradles the head of the Slinky dog and huddles against the Mad Maestro. "It wasn't supposed to be this way."

Silently, I agree, recognizing this as a central truth in the life of Buddy Cooper.

The rectangle of light from the door suggests more escapees, and I hope Alix had the sense to flee, though I know she wouldn't leave Brook. Or Trevor.

In the ring, only Hardy has stood his ground, on his mark at the center of the canvas, apparently still convinced he's bulletproof. He points a finger at the gray-haired man-child. "I ain't afraid of you. You're just a plain bad apple."

I glance to the side and thankfully find Brook beside Hazel, both crouching behind the wheelchair.

Dazed and groggy, Trevor mumbles, "Cut. Cut."

The assassin squeezes him in the crook of his neck. "Speak no more or be the first to feel my wrath." He presses the barrel against Trevor's temple.

Shoot him, I think, may God forgive me. *Pull that trigger.*

"No!" Alix yells, appearing at the edge of the camera line with both hands raised. Her eyes are wide with rage and terror.

"Al," I say, though she makes no sign that she hears me. I concentrate, willing her to stop, to go back, but she takes a tentative step forward, leaving the safety of darkness for love. The man-child turns the gun toward her.

"Mom!" Brook yells from ringside. "Don't!"

"Pay heed to the girl," the assassin says. "Stay back."

"Al," I say again.

But she takes another step. "We can talk this through. No one needs to get hurt." Though she holds her empty hands up and in the open, and she's offering good-faith negotiations, my wife is far from harmless. As part of Parents' Night at Tae-Kwon-Do for Tots, she drove her elbow through concrete blocks, flip-kicked target boards against the grain. Sensing the very real threat Alix poses, the assassin taps the barrel against Trevor's jaw. "Hold your ground, woman."

"Cut," Trevor insists, incoherent.

"Silence!" the assassin screams. Alix freezes, still too far away for action, and far from cover. Beside me, my daughter sniffles and whispers, "Daddy," a word I haven't heard in a decade. It seems to fill the hangar. Over the man-child assassin's shoulder, Alix's eyes rise to mine.

It's nothing I'm proud of, but I understand the assassin. I know what it means to be fueled by delusion. And what is about to happen is clear to me. If I do nothing, then Trevor—this man who stole my life and my joy, this man I've murdered in my dreams—will die. But I also know the terror that awaits Brook and Alix, the horrible unknown future of a life completely different than the one they had planned. My daughter's stepfather, a good man, is in danger. My wife's husband is in danger. And despite all my many failings, they look to me for action. Incredibly, miraculously, I've been given yet another shot.

The man-child and Trevor are almost ten feet from the edge of the ring. Even in my champion days, when I was Bull Invinso and my signature move was the Bull from Heaven, I couldn't fly that far. But I suddenly find myself in a place beyond logic, and between breaths my body becomes a blur. My legs drive me forward, huge strides that stomp the canvas, and just as I pass Hardy I launch myself up, eyes focused on the top rope, boots landing and balancing, bruised body riding the elastic bounce down and then up, and I am launched skyward, rising righteous and light. My arms extend like wings as I float in a perfect arc, and my eyes fix on the gun in the assassin's hand, and for an instant I fear that I may actually drift away completely, but then gravity takes hold and in a fast-forward flash I crash, collide with flesh and bone and concrete.

The assassin struggles beneath me, but weakly, and I pin him down as I scan the concrete, check his hands for the gun. I find instead a megaphone, loosely gripped. My eyes turn to his face, and Trevor, stunned and blinking, stares back at me. A pair of legs stands beside us, and when I look up, the man-child leers down at me, sighting my face along the barrel of the gun. His eyes are wild, the purest chaos. I search for something to say, last words that will resonate with significance. But all that occurs to me is what Hardy said, so my final utterance is an act of plagiarism: "I ain't afraid of you."

The assassin nods and a bright red dot shines on the side of his gun. A backfire pop makes me twitch and close my eyes, but in the next instant I find myself still alive. The assassin still stands exactly where he was, his arm is still aimed at me, but the gun has vanished, along with two of his fingers. He yanks his bleeding hand up to his chest, where the red dot now hovers above his heart. I follow the clear beam of red that extends from the dot on his chest to the laser scope on Lieutenant Tyrelli's 9mm, firmly grasped in his out-stretched hands. He stands on the edge of the camera line, partly hidden in shadow. "Police," he says. "Get on the ground."

The gray-haired boy stares down at the floor and me, as if this is an impossible place for him to descend to. He looks back at Tyrelli. "You shot me."

"I de-gunned you," Tyrelli corrects. He steps into the open, keep-ing his gun trained on the boy. "Standard operating procedure."

In the space he leaves behind, I see strong, long legs, red hair, and remarkable green eyes in the half light.

The man-child assassin faints to the floor next to me, or maybe it's more of a collapse from shock and pain. Regardless, Tyrelli plants a knee in his back and handcuffs him roughly. Then he gives me a look. "Small world," he says, in the same tone he used just yes-terday.

"You bet," I say. "Smaller every day."

Alix rushes in and I roll off her husband. Trevor moans when she props him up. Brook charges over, kneels down, and wraps her arms around both. It's good to see her embrace her mother. I'm try-ing to decide if I'm jealous that their group hug includes Trevor and not me when Hardy, still in the ring, says, "Uh-oh."

We all turn. He's got one hand over his bad ear and has the look of a dog tuning in a distant and high frequency. "Mr. Cooper, sir, I think we're in awful trouble."

My teeth begin to rattle and my bones feel as if they are shiver-ing. The rumble comes from nowhere and everywhere all at once. All the citizens of Studio B look around for some explanation. As the trembling intensifies, those standing have to put their hands out for balance. Somebody shouts, "Earthquake!" but Rhonda shakes her head. "No," she says. "It's the asteroid."

Perhaps because her statement is so factual, so calm and free of emotion, no one panics. Tyrelli hoists the man-child up by an elbow and the Mad Maestro escorts Hazel. Alix and Brook duck beneath Trevor's limp arms and Hardy simply picks up Marna—wheelchair and all. Paul, crying inconsolably, hobbles along with his cane and drags his Slinky dachshund over the cables. Rhonda ends up by my side at the back of the pack. Her eyes tell me she witnessed my act of heroism. "Quite a leap," she says. "Brave and stupid."

"Yeah," I say. "I'm in the business."

With the ground quaking beneath us, we all stumble toward the gray daylight of the door like refugees.

Outside, everyone has spilled from the other buildings to bear witness to the cataclysm. A couple hundred people are scattered across the parking lot and the field with the pine trees and the water tower. In the dusky twilight, cowboys from the Wild West show steady their reeling horses. The Creature from Beyond Tomorrow is on his knees, casting two of his lobster arms over his antennaed head, a clearly penitent pose. Fifteen feet from me, Patrick Swayze holds a mermaid in his arms like a bride and gazes heavenward. Cro-Magnum points his caveman club in the same direction and says, "Holy shit."

The monstrous rock is the size of Texas, a dark glacier slow tumbling across the dome of the sky, closing in on the hazy sun. This impossible sight makes me think for a moment that perhaps this is some special effect for a movie with a billion-dollar budget. By the catering truck, a huddle of believers—aliens, gladiators, wrestling fans—recites the Our Father. Hazel and the Mad Maestro begin to kiss passionately. At my side, Rhonda asks, "Is that thing falling or just passing by?"

I'm about to tell her that I have no idea, when the asteroid's rotation swallows up the little sunlight remaining. Its shadow casts us into eclipse. With the darkness, a remarkable silence descends over those congregated, the superstars and the extras and the has-beens and the wannabes. All are perfectly quiet. Even the prayers cease. Around the cragged edges of the asteroid, sunlight warps and flickers like the aurora borealis, wispy wings of flowing orange and red and yellow. In the artificial night, the stars reignite, and Hardy points for Marna, probably explaining constellations. Meteors spark and flare across the sky like huge match heads being struck. One explodes, silently, harmlessly, in the upper atmosphere, and the crowd lets loose a collective "ooh" as if we were watching a Fourth of July fireworks display. Maybe it's just the intoxication brought on by the threat of imminent extinction, but when the next meteor pops, people greet it with applause and even laughter.

"This is totally nuts," I say to Rhonda.

She keeps her face aimed upward. "Sure. But it's beautiful."

On the far side of Rhonda stand my ex-wife and daughter, looking skyward and still supporting Trevor. Neither one notices me watching them, and I'm bothered briefly by the faint desire to occupy Trevor's position. Even if this is the end, I see little point in having some last connection with Alix. After all, we said good-bye so long ago.

No, I figure I'm pretty much where I should be. If I'm to meet my doom I'll do it here with Rhonda. She rests one hand on my shoulder, though I can't tell if it's a sign of affection or simply to help hold up my wounded body. I look again into her upturned face, bathed in the kaleidoscope spectrum of the asteroid's aura, so bright with wonder and delight, and I see that she's not fearful of what may come. And for the first time in a long while, I find myself feeling the same way.

The colors shift on her face and I turn to the sky. Splinters of light pierce through on the far side of the asteroid, a sideways sunrise in the heavens, and the crowd erupts with thunderous applause.

Rhonda and I smile at each other, but we don't embrace. Her lips move, but the deafening roar—wailing and laughing and clapping—is too loud. I shake my head and cup a hand behind my ear. She repeats herself, shouting now, but I still can't make out her words. Then Hardy steps in, offering his hand. In his palm rests the Miracle Ear, and he nods at me and grins strangely. Beside him on shaky legs, Marna watches. Without really thinking it over, I accept. I pick it up and work it into my ear and find that it fits just fine. And then slowly I turn back to Rhonda and wait to see just what I might hear, now that this apocalypse has passed.